THE GOLDEN TOWER

The Golden Tower

by

Edward Hurst

DIADEM BOOKS

Published by Diadem Books

For information, please contact:

Diadem Books
16 Lethen View
Tullibody
Alloa
FK10 2GE UK

www.diadembooks.com

ISBN: 978-1-291-91463-4

Prologue – The Turning Point

The young man's strong tanned muscles rippled as he raised his arm and struck down hard on the red hot iron. Quickly turning the end on the anvil, he struck again and again, until the metal tapered to a fine point. With each strike he resolved to forgive and forge a new life. He would not forget. Could not forget. Bright tears fell from his eyes, each carrying a memory that shattered on the floor and dispersed amongst the grey dust. He stared at the tip, waiting for the colour to waft from yellow to blue, then plunged the point in the old pail beside him and with a violent crackle and hiss of steam it was ready.

Like a Viking God he raised the crook from the water and struck it upon the ancient stone flags. Chips of golden sandstone flew up from the impact and echoed amongst the workshop clutter. Satisfied with his work, the man stepped out from the gloom into a bright May morning. Still with tears in his large brown eyes, he held his crook tightly and examined the neat scrolled end with its strange engravings and the new spike at its lower end. He paused for a moment, as if in prayer, his long hooked nose bowing before Mother Nature. Then, raising his head, he looked up across the bare rolling hills and declared to the world, "We've got a job to do."

Part 1 - Finding Eden

The Freedom of Youth

I had no job. Despite a first in Ecology and great effort trying to find the right position, I had not succeeded in obtaining gainful employment. But then, sometimes, lady luck sits at her table dealing out cards in an unexpected way.

I was in need of a break and was keen to explore, so decided a walking adventure was what I needed to refresh and revitalise my soul. I chose the Pennine Way and equipped myself with a new rucksack, waterproofs, boots and all the paraphernalia the outdoor salesman persuaded me to buy. I abandoned my electronic devices and the urban noise, relishing the thought of a month of peace. I hugged my parents at the door of our suburban villa and departed to catch the train to Derby.

I rose into the glorious Cheviot Hills on a roasting afternoon in early June. The sweltering heat slowed my progress and, not being in any hurry, I was struck with the idea of wandering off the path, creating my own route and sleeping beneath the stars. I took out my compass and unfolded my map on the cope of a grey stone dyke and gazed across the hills before me. I chose a summit with a distinctive peak. I folded up my map, had a drink of water and struck out in my chosen direction.

It did not take me long to realise why one is often told *not* to stray from the path, for very soon I found myself struggling through marshland or fighting through high bracken. In truth distracted by these endeavours I had lost my way and emerged onto a drier ridge where I found I could no longer see the summit I had chosen. A sheep trail led me away from the jungle and the slope rose steeply with patches of scree and rocky outcrops to either side. The soil was thin and dry and parched in the summer sun. A constant wind tore away any remaining moisture, lifting swirls of dust into the air. Nothing seemed to grow here other than dry white grass. Off the beaten track I found the terrain bleak and devoid of hope. Here and there a stunted thorn or ash tree grew, angled before the prevailing wind to provide meagre respite from the overhead sun. Rising higher still I wondered how people had ever populated these hills to the extent they apparently had. It seemed an endless windswept place. Its beauty lay in its hidden valleys and rolling horizons rather than its climate. It seemed too dry on the hillsides and too wet in the valleys.

On reaching a summit, but by no means a high one, I took the opportunity to rest in the lengthening shadows of a lichen-covered outcrop of sharp broken rock. Like the stumps of teeth in the broken jaw of a once majestic beast, the stones cast sad shadows across the empty land. The pale green grey branches of the lichen bent from the wind as if trying to claw back something long gone, like the traces of a cherished memory just beyond recall. Realising that quite a few hours had passed since my last stop, I pulled off my rucksack, extracted some food and took a few minutes to take in the scenery before me. I was on a raised part of a long saddle that stretched between two high rounded hills and I could see the snaking sheep trail coming up the narrow valley of my ascent and knew I had made the right decision to avoid the bracken and marshland that filled extensive tracts below.

I turned to look down the valley that fell away in the other direction and saw a more promising sight. This valley was larger, drier and more sheltered. Feeling a slight unease with the gathering of dark clouds above the distant horizon, my heart was lifted by the sight of a cluster of farm buildings and a farmhouse framed by two ancient sycamores. I was encouraged by imaginings of a barn with dry straw to rest my weary limbs on and perhaps a friendly farmwife with an ample stew, ready on an old black range. Out of curiosity and a good walker's sense I looked to extract my map and compass to pinpoint my location. A known farm should give me a good starting point for the morning. To my dismay and rising panic I could not find either. I rapidly emptied the contents of my rucksack across the dry grass and it slowly dawned upon me that I had left them on top of the wall some hours ago when I left the path. Not giving in to my predicament I knew the good folks at the farm would help me. I repacked and hoisted the rucksack onto my shoulders and headed down the hill.

As I descended into the evening shadows, the golden tipped Cheviots caught the light of the sinking sun, it gave the impression of lowering into Hades away from the life giving rays. My destination in view, I felt that despite minor mishaps it had been a good day. The people at the farm would lend me a map. But as I traversed the hard ground a cool mist rose to meet me, gloaming tendrils snaking up the undulating slope, creeping around my legs and curving back over my head. It was surprisingly dense and moved as if to draw me into some waiting trap, to devour me, perhaps to nourish some evil purpose. I stumbled on over stones and tussocks of tough grass, seeking the welcoming glow of a kitchen window. I walked faster through the dimming fog but tripped and fell, catching my arm badly on a rock. Recovering, somewhat cautioned, I battled on. My arm was bleeding and bruised. The farm couldn't be far now and sure enough the grey silhouette of the high sycamores appeared beside me, like two sentinels guarding some ancient temple. My relief was soon dashed as the walls standing behind were not the well-kept stone of a loved home, but the crumbling remnants of the past. I followed the wall in the dim light and walked on slates slipped from the roof and I came upon the sightless sockets of the windows, dark and foreboding. Fine carpentry and broken glass had fallen like the sagging skin of a sad old woman, blinded by the sorrow of her struggles. Beyond the farmhouse I found a cobbled yard with rusting bath and broken toilet bowl, boldly holding aloft on leaden stalk its rusting cistern. It looked ready to collapse with its enclosing and dangerously leaning brick walls. This place was so derelict, so eerie I felt sad, and to be honest not a little scared. But being of strong heart I was determined to find some degree of shelter from the unknown noises of the night. The fluttering within the walls of the old house had disturbed me and I was beginning to feel very alone.

I came to a small huddle of outbuildings and found at least something with a roof. I ducked low under a thick stone lintel and took refuge in an old pigsty. It was dry and surprisingly clear of debris with only a layer of dusty earth hinting at earlier occupants. I was so tired I unpacked my clothes, laid them out as a thin mattress and unfolded my emergency foil blanket to make a simple bed. My exhaustion made sleep come easily and I slept well, though I was woken sometime in the night, but soon settled as I felt something warm and comforting pushing up against me.

Lost Hope

I awoke slowly, drifting in and out of a dream filled sleep. There were sheep, shepherds, pails of water, the cry of a new born child, the bleating of lambs and the comfort of an old man's voice telling stories. Later I would put this delirious state down to becoming too hot beneath the foil blanket. My extended drowsiness held me within the grasps of past human experience, flitting like flirtatious youth, dancing between stooks of barley. Song and laughter echoed within the walls of the farmyard, as if the hard volcanic rock was protecting them from the future. But the future is like a rising tide—it creeps up with unstoppable power, lapping at your ankles and holding you in the inevitability of your fate. Trying to rouse myself, I became aware of a constant soft breathing at my side, a point of comfort buffering me from the pain of the passing memories. Memories that led to the sounds of marching feet, the falling of shells and cries of pain. A sad man holding the hands of a sobbing wife on the opposite side of a scrubbed pine table. Earth to earth, ashes to ashes, the rattle of the first spade of soil against elm.

I finally awoke with a start, hauled back to reality by the rattling of a large black crow disembowelling a carcass of a dove on the corrugated iron above me. Disturbed, it flew up to a high sycamore branch to wait a second chance. The soft breathing stopped and warmth beside me dissipated and I became acutely aware of my night of dreams. Leaving the sty and stretching in the early morning warmth I tried to shed the tangled imaginings, but for the remainder of that day and indeed ever since, they have never been far beneath the surface.

I had a good look around in the safety of daylight, scraps of gingham curtains hanging on faithful to the end. There was a collapsed floor that had stranded an ornate cast iron fireplace, to serve again as a jackdaw's nest. Broken china and rusting pails leaked sadness upon grey linoleum. The old range I had imagined the night before was indeed there, a cast iron pot still in place, rusted and forlorn, waiting in vain for the return of the bustle and clatter of a busy farmhouse kitchen.

I returned to the sty, packed my things and eating an orange, gladly left. I stared at the dead dove on the roof for a moment. The old crow in the tree cawed its harsh cry. It was time to leave, I had caused enough disturbance. "Rest in peace," I whispered and left.

Using the sun as a rough guide I took an old track that led further down the valley. It soon twisted and headed up the slopes of the largest nearby hill. It was clearly now seldom used, though the track cut deeply into the hillside, showing many alternative ruts where mud and erosion in earlier times had forced a rerouting of ox and cart. A few sheep were scattered across the hillsides and I wondered who tended to their needs, as I had seen no shepherd or indeed another human being since leaving the path the previous day. My aim was to reach a high enough point to plan a route in a direction that would lead to civilisation, food and a bath to soak in. The day was hot like the one before and I replenished my bottles from a trickle of water running between grey stones. It was increasingly humid and I was finding the climb quite difficult and rested frequently to recover. It seemed there was no escape from the heat of the sun, but I could sense a building storm.

Far Away

Not so far from the home of the tall lone walker, a bolshie young man climbed into his Ford Capri, yanked his tie off and breathed out a long sigh of relief. Casey L. Pritchard had successfully blagged his way through the interview and got the job. Admittedly he had lied once or twice, but had managed to remain believable by retaining eye contact and keeping them wide and innocent. It's a trick he had perfected as a young boy to survive in a difficult family.

Casey had indeed clinched a cool job. He was to become a trainee investment manager within a well-established financial organisation. He was good at deceit so knew he was going to be successful and to be fair, in that world, he became very capable and was to rise through the ranks with honour.

Falling into Eden

It took me two hours to reach the summit and I found myself crossing the ditches and banks of an Iron Age fort. Great stone gate posts still held the way open to the plateau above. I collapsed on the dry grass at the highest point and gazed into the deep blue sky. Closing my eyes, the night of dreams started to creep back and not having the energy to engage I sat up and retrieved the remainder of my rations. Looking out from that spot across the stunning expanses of those hills, I realised I did not recognise any landmark or hilltop. In reality, without the map I was truly lost. Recalling what I could of the lay of the land from the Pennine Way, I decided the best choice was to stay on the high ground and follow it round to the north east, where I knew I could pick up the trail again and head for the comforts of Kirk Yetholm. The ridge took me into wilder territory than I expected, up onto heather that rustled in the hot wind. This was tough in the heat, but I dreaded what it would be like in the depths of winter or the lashing rain of a heavy summer storm.

I looked nervously at the dark clouds approaching from the south west. I had eaten all my food and had only half a bottle of water. I needed to focus on sustenance and with renewed vigour headed down a long dip between two hilltops. I proceeded in this manner and kept to the high land and must have walked four miles, but seemed to make no gain on the distant horizon. By this time I was becoming seriously hungry, was shaking slightly and feeling a bit worse for wear. I was genuinely concerned and reaching a prominent cairn along the rocky ridge, I thought it best to seek habitation. A valley stretched south towards fields surrounded with neat stone walls. The white blobs of sheep lay scattered across the slopes. To the north there was narrow gap in the grey outcrop that intrigued me, through which, when I had a closer look, I could see a deep, rugged and long ravine cut into the hills opening up to a broad vale in the distance. The sight revived me; somehow it seemed more alive than the southern option or the wind-torn tops. The fresh growth of young trees beckoned my weary spirit. Something about the view held my eye; perhaps the sun was catching distant objects and a scattering of unusual brown horned sheep grazed on the slopes nearby. It was a narrow opening to the valley that could easily be missed if you weren't in the right spot, like looking through an open door and seeing into a room further inside an ancient house. It felt much older, somehow linking to a deep and fascinating past. In hope I had no hesitation clambering over the rocks, negotiating the precarious ledges to enter this unexpected upland scene and I started to scramble down a long steep scree. As soon as I dipped into the valley I knew the place was special—it just felt different. I heard a rattle of stones behind me and thought I saw an animal of some sort move quickly out of sight, but before I could investigate further there was a shifting beneath my feet. Stones rushed ahead of me like waves hitting the pebbles upon a distant beach; they drifted noisily up against huge boulders below, abandoned long ago by a glacier singed by advancing warmth. As I stepped sideways down this sliding hillside a movement below caught my eye; having to watch my feet, when I looked up again, there was nothing. I came among the boulders on my back on a cascade of noisy stones, the scree having scooped my feet out from beneath me in its haste to deliver its unexpected guest. I was greeted by the inquisitive nose of a sleek black and white collie dog that sniffed my face and wagged his tail. I patted his head and raised my eyes to meet those of his master.

The Shepherd

The Shepherd's eyes were unusually large and brown. He half smiled beneath his flat cap and seeing my predicament, he stretched out a strong brown hand that took hold of my wrist; grasping his in turn, I was returned to an upright position. Somehow in that moment a bond was made: this man exuded great wisdom without the weariness that often accompanies age and I could not help but feel absolute trust in him. He took a flask from his tweed waistcoat pocket and handed it to me. Expecting some fiery liquor I was grateful for the best fresh water I had ever had! Not realising my thirst was so great I finished the offering. He walked away down a dusty path and I followed, intrigued. A mountain goat skipped along behind me. The Shepherd led me to a small circle of stones, a dry stone dyke some eight foot across, upon which a simple ash branch rested; a rope bound around it allowed him to lower a metal bucket down a rocky crevice. He said very little—he didn't need to as he seemed to have a natural intuition and deep understanding of everything around him. He refilled the flask for me and I began to feel a little stronger. He gave his dog, who he said was Pip, a drink in a small bowl that looked like an ancient quern stone; he told me there was a lot of that sort of thing in the valley. He tilted his head at Pip, moved his hand just the tiniest bit and the dog was off like a rocket. The Shepherd returned the pail to his well and, picking up his crook, continued down the path. His beckoning gave me hope of food and rest and I followed, tired but eager. This shepherd was my master and I had become the lost sheep.

A distant rumble of thunder and the need of food kept my aching legs moving. The Shepherd said not to expect much but I was past caring about quality. But what I encountered was astounding. The further we walked, as it must have been a couple of miles, the more I was impressed. Pip appeared to our right with a small flock of thirty or so of the dark sheep following a well-worn path, after which we walked between tall willows whose exquisite silhouette against the bright blue sky was magical; it was like a path leading to fairyland with the thin delicate leaves weaving their spell above us in the breeze. We came to a clearing and central to this a neat circular stell of grey drystone sat, simply fulfilling its function, the sinking sun casting strong shadows. Passing its narrow entrance we found Pip stretched across the narrow gap. The sheep were already settling within. Pip was panting and his tail started thumping the ground, his eyebrows twitching as he looked hopefully at the Shepherd. A meal was taken from between two nearby stones and placed before the hound and the slightest of touches to the top of the dog's head, like a communion blessing, and Pip was left to his vigil.

So impressed by this, I was not quite ready for the Shepherd's home. I had expected a small bothy of sorts, but when we passed through another whispering tunnel of high willows, what rose before me was impressive to say the least. Having seen many pictures and a few on my travels I was transfixed by the most picturesque and enchanting peel tower; it was definitely not the stark edifices or tourist traps so keenly promoted. This was almost, for it was roofless, an intact home that reflected much more than just a place of refuge. With the rich evening sun glancing across its flanks it stood at least three stories and a garret high, glowing almost translucent as if built of blocks of golden amber. There were small moulded window openings scattered upon its walls, slits at ground level, the zig-zag of crowsteps high above and a corner turret, still slated, pointed to the depths of the unknown, reaching out trusting in a heaven. My jaw must have been hanging as the Shepherd chuckled then simply said "Food" and we continued through a door hidden within the shaded angle of the building, passed below a carved crest and he led the way up dim curving stairs to a vast vaulted hall above, where an ancient oak table stretched along its length with chairs pulled out as if many guests had only just departed. However, I could tell we were alone in the tower; somehow I knew already that this man lived in happy solitude, confident and able. He seated me in a carved oak chair at the head of the table, disappeared into an anteroom and returned after a few minutes with a silver tray which he placed before me. A feast to a starving man, for here was the sought after stew, a glass, a jug of water and half a loaf of bread. How he procured this fantasy meal with such ease I did not know.

He sat some twelve feet away at the other end of the oak table after fetching a similar tray; we both ate and said nothing. He finished his meal quickly, took his tray to the kitchen and returned after a few minutes, picked up a wooden box from a stone windowsill and placed it on the table. I ate on, savouring the incredible stew and watched with fascination. Using both hands, he scooped out some of its contents and rolled them carefully onto the table. They were hazel nuts, dry and golden brown from the previous autumn. He proceeded to inspect each nut with meticulous care and placed them in two heaps upon the planks before him. Once his division was complete he took one of the heaps and took the nuts over to a large stone fireplace along one wall; clearly this was a regular activity as the ornate basket grate was almost hidden by a growing pile. The remaining nuts he placed in a broad glass bowl and taking his own jug of water filled it to the brim. Some nuts sank and some floated. I assumed this was preparation for the next meal, perhaps breakfast muesli like one I had had in Switzerland a year back. By the time I had finished I think he saw my sagging eyes. He collected another tray from his hidden kitchen and led me up a narrow turnpike stair to a vaulted room above. It was small and dry with a broad carved oak bed, a large studded chest at its foot, a bedside table and a Windsor chair. The bed was freshly made as if he were expecting guests. He pointed to a galvanised pail in a far corner, lifted his hands as if to apologise and departed closing the elm planked door behind him. The tray he had left on the table held more water and a plate of dull grey biscuits. I nibbled an edge and found them irresistibly delicious, oats, honey and some herb I could not identify. I ate six before rather shyly using the corner pail. It made such a noise I had to stop and start several times. At last retreating to the bed I collapsed beneath a rich red blanket and as I succumbed to my total exhaustion, I glimpsed through the open window and saw Venus held within the cusp of the rising crescent moon.

I woke slowly beneath the red blanket, my blurred eyes gradually taking in the ceiling above me. It was of neat construction with four chamfered ribs meeting at a central octagonal boss. The stones between the ribs were a mix of pale pinks and rusty golds; long and narrow, they seemed to swim like a shoal of fish towards the highest point. The focus was a carved head adorned with a long moustache, formed from two twisted oak leaves, his hair and beard in a similar fashion adorned with interwoven hawthorn and ash leaves with the patterns meshing together confusing to the eye. The deep hooded eyes and long nose struck a bold countenance, an image of the lasting endurance of nature. Near the window delicate stalactites of translucent calcite hung down some four or five inches from the mortar between the stones. Board shutters painted on the inside with deep cobalt blues with fading gold swirls were partly folded back from the window. I wondered about the age of this place, the quiet shepherd and the sheer contrast from my modern world. I rose from the bed and stood before the view. Outside the sun was at its zenith, the heat intense and the humidity was building. The storm was yet to break. I looked down on a cobbled courtyard—a jumble of old tools rested in one corner. I could make out a garden rake, a fork and some strange device with a rusting wheel. On the far wall, bathed in hazy sunshine, were three espalier pears with thick ridged trunks and neatly trained branches; small developing pears stuck out amongst the leaves. Beyond the wall a vegetable patch was well fenced off from the sheep. The hillside rose gradually, then banked steeply up to high summits, a haze of pale greens and blues. I could see the brown sheep lying beneath a broad oak and the Shepherd working within a paddock fenced off with wooden rails. He was carrying a bucket and his crook; every few yards he placed his bucket on the ground, raised his crook and plunged it into the soil, twisted it around, withdrew it, then picking something from the bucket knelt down at the hole and placed the something within it, stood and firmed the soil. He was planting seeds. A similar paddock further up the hillside showed the result, fresh young growth. But not just one, for there was another, then another paddock, each lush with trees at different stages of growth. Now I understood what he was doing with the hazelnuts the evening before.

I found a bathroom on the floor above occupying one of the corner turrets, a rusty bath with a copper cylinder mounted on brackets at one end; a single tap extended far enough to allow flow to fall several feet into the bath. I stretched out with care to try the tap; surprisingly and somewhat alarmingly the simple lever started a series of coughing and spluttering noises from within the bowels of the building, until just acceptably warm water poured rapidly into the bath. I bathed glad to wash off the mud and blood from my sore limbs and used some seriously old-fashioned coal tar soap. It reminded me of an

16

ancient aunt from my childhood. A large towel from a shelf provided coarse but adequate drying.

By the time I made it down to the hall the Shepherd had returned from his morning's work. He waved to the chair that I had occupied the previous evening and I willingly sat again and helped myself to a glass of water. A few minutes later he brought a plate with three fried brown trout with cold potatoes and some simple salad. I was impressed with his ability to look after his guests, as I suspected he did not have many. He said he had had his trout for breakfast, smiling his half smile. I thanked him profusely for his hospitality and ate enthusiastically. They were not large trout but delicious. While I ate he returned to sorting more nuts. I asked him about his home and land, how long he had been there and how many acres he owned. He admitted he was unsure as to ownership, but he had never been approached by anyone about it. He believed that some of the hills had never been seen by their owners, who probably saw it as an investment from a distant office and perhaps thought that there was nothing here but wind and rain. His home, he said, with a wry smile, must be his, as it had his initials carved above the door. For one who spoke very little I managed to extract details of a former life on an arable farm near Kelso, which he worked with his younger brother, but after losing his young wife Mary and delightful daughter Heather in a motor accident, had remained in the hills to seek peace and solitude. He had no need for wealth and no appetite for a new partner and subsistence in his patch of upland was enough. He sold his livestock to a neighbour and had no need to travel far. He produced most of what he needed in the hills and when he did need other provisions he rode out of the valley on an ancient grey tractor using an old drove road, but it was fifteen miles or so and a long hard journey as there was no metalled road for most of the way. As regards post, bureaucracy and the entrapment of the state, he said no official had ever been to see him. I enquired about the tree planting and he said he felt the hills needed their trees back and I asked if I could accompany him to see them. I had no idea of what I was asking for; there were more than a small handful of paddocks.

We left after lunch. First of all he gathered up his soaked nuts in a pail, then took me down to a wonderful vaulted cellar below the Tower. He said there were three vaults and this one was his workshop and tool shed, another being his wood store; he did not tell me what the third vault held. It was amazing and I could have spent a month down there looking through the array of ancient things.

Hanging horizontally on pegs above a workbench was a selection of old shepherds' crooks. Carefully he selected one and passed it to me. It was long, about the same height as me, with a beautifully forged hook at one end and a well-worn spike at the other. It was nicely balanced and was a pleasure to hold. As we left we passed a heavy portcullis gate and studded oak door and he picked up his own crook—his was heavier and the tip was shiny with frequent use. We walked back through the tunnel of willows which he said were only eighteen years old and he had grown them from cuttings. It was astonishing— these trees were well over fifty foot high and I could only just get my arms around the trunk of the nearest one. He led me up a track to a small area of level ground that showed the outline ridges of a former farmstead, and he explained that this had once been a very hospitable and fertile place to live, and that he had found a way of returning it to that state by creating a balance between nature and human need. By planting trees he said shelter from the strong winds was established; shade protected animals and allowed the grass to grow better, which in turn supported more livestock. Quite simply the valley was more productive and I had to admit, stunningly beautiful too.

This particular part of the hills was no different from any other. He pointed out his paddocks scattered across the slopes. Each he explained was around two acres and he generally used only one or two species in each. There were paddocks at different elevations and from what I could see they were all growing well. The one nearest was rowan and birch, others were oak and hazel, ash and elm or other simple mixes. The Shepherd told me these were just trial plots. I was so impressed by what I saw and the difference one man had made for no particular personal gain that I asked if I could help. He took me to the paddock I had seen him working in that morning and together we planted at least one hundred nuts. He said only a proportion would survive and actually become trees, so continual planting was essential.

Later we returned to the Tower. The golden stone made the surroundings glow. A combination of dark shadows and warm stone was a pleasure to behold. While he put together some food I was encouraged to explore, what he described as the public part of the building. Although I only saw a few, I discovered that the rooms were relatively dry because the three main floors had vaults of stone with the highest supporting a thick turf of fine grasses and rare wildflowers. I carefully climbed up as far as I could through this unexpected alpine meadow and sat viewing this man's amazing achievement. I was already excited by the thought of seeing my hazel planting grow and vowed to return someday. The crowsteps showed recent repairs and I saw generally on my tour that rotting stones were being replaced and new turves lay over parts of the vault. It was a stunning building in a most beautiful valley and I really did not want to leave. At supper I asked if I could help him plant more. He seemed content with this and he explained that he would be planting in a higher valley the following day, so it would be an early start.

19

Later that night as I stared at the stone green man looking over me in my simple bedroom, I wondered why the Shepherd did so much when, clearly at his advanced age, he was not going to benefit from his planting, for he had to be over seventy and had no heir. His generosity of spirit and ability to do so much was so uplifting I felt a greater hope for my own future. Having specialised in marine ecology, I was beginning to think about woodland ecology as an alternative career to pursue.

The Effect of Gold and Seed

Early, far too early, the Shepherd shook my shoulder and twenty minutes later we were on our way, rucksack on my back and cloth bags adorning the Shepherd. We both had our planting crooks as we marched off, I in jeans and tee shirt, the Shepherd, as ever, dressed in a clean linen long sleeved shirt, tweed waistcoat, plain cotton trousers and strong leather boots. Across his shoulder a larger canvas bag contained provisions and waterproofs.

We must have climbed some thousand feet up through his home valley to gain entry to the next. We came over the brow and a howling wind met us head on. This was tough upland territory. We sat in a sheltered dip and he pointed out his plans for the area. It took me several minutes to soak up the aspect before us. This valley was a huge shallow scoop in the landscape gently sloping to the north east. The wind tore across this exposed place and despite the strong sun it felt cold. The land was poor with tall tussocks of tough white grass and patches of heather. It was not immediately appealing to the eye. Dominating the lower end was a grey loch surrounded by bog, its surface a constant turmoil of chopping waves as if being thrashed by a witch's broom. I said I could not imagine trees growing here as it seemed just too inhospitable. He shrugged and said "Providence would provide if it chose."

This Shepherd's constant faith and calm determination, even when faced with such obstacles, made me feel I was in the presence of a God. I looked into his large brown eyes and saw a deep sadness; somehow I knew this single act of unselfish endeavour was to return to the world the great joy he had once had with his young family so many years ago. With every seed he cast upon the seemingly barren soil he sowed the hope of future happiness; even upon the worst of ground he was prepared to offer the chance and not turn away from desolation.

We walked across this harsh moor to the western edge of the loch, treading carefully and climbing from dry bank to bank avoiding the deep threatening pools between. Every so often he would stop and show me huge roots or broken stumps within the layers of peat, or jutting up between the tussocks in twisted tortured desperation, as if screaming to be set free, to be reborn. He had found the remains of oak, pine, birch, alder and hazel here and saw no reason why they should not return. With the wind to our backs facing the water he took off his shoulder one of his cloth bags, almost the size of a pillow; it was light and seemed to be filled with some sort of soft material. He loosened the cord at its top and exposed a white down like mass containing small brown flecks. This was seed from a variety of willows from his home valley. He grasped a handful and showed me how to tease it apart and quite simply throw it up into the air over the water; caught in the howling teeth of the wind it was whipped away across the cold waves, catching the sun in its moment of freedom before landing within the tossing waves. We walked along the shore for half an hour performing this enjoyable task. There was something satisfying about feeding the seed into the hands of chance.

"Nature will do the rest," the Shepherd said quietly when we met up and we turned into the wind and walked back some hundred yards or so from the water's edge. Finding a sheltered hollow out of the persistent wind, we enjoyed the warmth of the sun and a welcome snack of thin slices of meat and coarse brown bread.

Opening up another smaller bag he showed me golden brown alder seed. He explained how alder trees thrived in damp places. Another sack contained hazel nuts plump and tactile. He laid both on the ground and proceeded to mix the contents equally between the two bags. He then showed me where best to scatter the alder seed and where to spike holes to plant the hazel nuts. He pointed out a zone to the west and he headed south.

I followed his instructions and clambered down hollows and over heath and tussocks between, choosing the damper muddy places for the alder seed and drier places for the nuts. Some of the hollows were seven or eight feet deep and it was hard work clambering up and down. I used the crook to steady my descent or haul myself up using the many remnant stumps exposed along the eroding banks. As I hauled myself up by this method from one of the peaty holes and having my face close to the ancient roots, something odd caught my eye. Seemingly wedged between thick roots some three feet down from the surface, was the sharp angular corner of a grey man-made object. Finding it unlikely I reached in past the tree remains to see if I could pull it out, but found it firmly wedged in place as if the roots had grown around it holding it in an earthy tomb. Intrigued I stepped down and using my crook like a spear poked at the object; it made a hollow thudding noise. Excited by the prospect of contents I struck harder. The metal seemed soft and the point of the crook made a dent easily. I struck again and it began to tear. I was now so sure of finding bones or an ancient relic of some sort I gave a much stronger thrust and penetrated the lead box, then pulled back but found the crook firmly stuck. Finding a better foothold on the ground and placing the other against the soil beneath the roots I yanked hard and with a sudden release fell over backwards onto the damp soil. As I fell still clutching the crook an odd image flashed into my mind, of a mass of roman helmeted soldiers jabbing at me from above. The odd image disappeared and I was left gripping the crook pointing upwards. I stared in disbelief as there, stuck to the point was a bright gold disc catching the sun just above the lip of the hollow. I lowered my spear and pulled off the object. I brushed away the dirt and to my amazement a large gold coin was revealed. One side in raised relief depicted a chariot pulled by two horses; the other, neatly pierced by a simple shepherd's crook, was the head of an emperor.

Above, hidden in the summer sky, something watched waiting to strike. It circled tempting me, teasing my young mind with thoughts of great wealth. It infiltrated my soul showing me a conveyor of my desires. My inexperience and raw innocence was obvious to the dark creature and it fluttered to a silent perch on a peaty ledge, invisible to all as it spoke its evil. And I admit I succumbed. The beast tilted its ugly eye to the heavens above and flew off cawing its defiant triumph.

With wide-eyed excitement I looked over the edge to see where the Shepherd was to find him working some hundred yards or so away, so I returned to the lead box and finding the hole too narrow for my hand, found a stone to bash it open. In all I found twenty-two very large gold roman coins as bright and heavy as the day they were made. I opened up my rucksack and carefully wrapped them up individually by folding my spare clothes over and over. I felt guilty with the concealment, but at the time justified it with the thought that the Shepherd didn't need money and the possible owners of the land miles away firstly didn't deserve more wealth and secondly would never know about them.

We used up the seeds in our bags and the Shepherd said he would take me back down a different way. We walked about a third of the way around the north side of the loch, up over a windswept ridge to where a long deep valley fell away from us.

The gold began to weigh on my back and my soul, but the problems they could solve were inducement enough to say nothing.

Bleakhope

"This is Bleakhope," announced the Shepherd. "So named after the land was stripped bare, but a false name as you will see."

As soon as I saw the vale before me I was stunned. I forgot about the gold and I had to stop and gaze at the view stretching before me. In all my days walking I had not seen such an amazing place, the particular layering of the hills, the ruggedness of the upper slopes leading to gentler terrain below was as if laid out by a grand master, all framed by the higher Cheviots beyond. It was a composition of perfection leading the eye to fascinating focal points. There was a neat hill fort perched upon the top of a smooth conical hill, the late afternoon sun defining its ridges, a slope horizontally terraced by former farmers in a different climate, high cliffs with flows of scree below, a meandering river, its convoluted bows sparkling in the light, with fields of ridge and furrow to either side enclosed by neat well cared for stone dykes. A track could be seen here and there leading down to a small grey slated farmyard in the distance. But the most striking and wonderful thing was the abundance of trees and woodland that frothed and flowed in multiple shades filling between the features giving the impression of a verdant garden of Eden.

"Wow, this place is truly incredible!" I exclaimed. The Shepherd simply smiled and led me down to the head of the track to lead us back to the Tower.

I must have looked ridiculous, mouth gaping and pausing frequently to take in another unexpected vista or to try to identify the sight or sound of a bird or animal. The woodland, though clearly not ancient, was alive with wildlife. It was like a Scottish safari with sudden bursts in the branches above from erupting flocks of birds, the undergrowth rustling as unidentified creatures avoided us or a distant cry of a raptor attracted to such bounty could be heard. Numerous secondary tracks struck off in all directions leaving the imagination to deliver mysterious destinations.

"This is your planting, isn't it?" I asked, already knowing the answer. The Shepherd paused at a gnarled hawthorn angled at forty-five degrees away from the prevailing wind, rubbed his hand up and down a polished part of the trunk and replied: "Almost. There were around thirty trees left here, all tortured by weather, man or beast."

"But why do the trees around these remnants grow so straight by comparison?"

"Shelter," came the simple response.

We were walking through a sizeable grove of ash trees all about forty years old with trunks almost a foot across. To me they were things of great beauty rising tall to fan their olive-like leaves in a mesmerising mesh against the sky above. A noisy flock of finches fluttered from branch to branch in a clamour of excitement. A forester would have eyed the trees up thinking 'Great timber in fifty years, keep up the good work!'

"But how, with the strength of the wind, surely these would bend too?"

"By applying patience, see what grows beneath the ash? Those were sown first as a dense mass to slow the wind, especially hazel and thorns. I then manage the growth of the secondary trees through light and ground space and perhaps some simple early pruning. But once they are away, so long as there are enough of them they will grow straight and true. I will show you different planting with different aims further on."

We continued down the dusty track listening to the lively woodland around us. The most noticeable thing was that, despite the howling wind by the loch, there was only the faintest movement of the highest leaves. The scale of the woodland filtered the wind and not only that, it also held moisture beneath the canopy, allowing lichens, mosses and lush herbs and grasses to grow where the light allowed. We stopped by a simple plank bridge that crossed a bright babbling burn. Its spirit bounced and gushed and gurgled between dark rounded stones as if in excitement, proclaiming the joy of life. We knelt by the water and scooping up handfuls quenched our thirst with the clearest and most refreshing water I had ever experienced.

"That's amazing water," I said. We refilled our water bottles. Ironically mine was a plastic water bottle from a supermarket; his was the leather clad traditional flask.

"It's how water should be," he replied. "Not tainted by man's hand. It is completely natural and is the fundamental balance within the valley. How it moves and what it does on the way has changed; it is no longer a headlong dash for the North Sea, it has a function to fulfil."

I nodded, understanding, and having experienced the quality couldn't agree more.

As we approached the in-bye fields we came upon areas of woodland that had been felled. It seemed a harsh thing to do considering the effort and result of the maturing woodland further up the valley. The first had stacks of poles laid next to the track. The stumps adjacent were all cut at the same angle facing south. The trees looked about twenty years old. The Shepherd, seeing my concern, explained the principles of coppicing and told me that after the cows were sold and sheep removed from this valley his income had actually increased through the active management of carefully chosen areas of trees to provide firewood which he sold to the nearest villages.

Although the light was dimming rapidly the Shepherd showed me the Bleakhope Steading and his set up for processing his timber and firewood. The steading was a complete square of welsh slated whinstone buildings, very typical of the Cheviot Hills. The entrance was narrow, designed for horse and cart, under a tall arch top with a loft some twelve feet higher than the adjacent roofs. It was very picturesque and held within it a sheltered cobbled yard with a series of low arches on one side and enclosed sheds to the others. I loved places like that and just wanted to explore. The arches housed his two ancient little grey Massey Ferguson tractors, both in immaculate condition. One had rigged on its linkage a simple bench saw for cutting the logs and a fore end loader. A small wooden trailer and other odd implements filled the other arched bays. A long barn housed a Yankie sawmill that he used for cutting posts and planks. He explained that was all he needed. The small tractors didn't use much fuel and he knew how to look after them. He pointed out that the trailer had been completely re-floored using oak planks he had grown and cut up himself. As it was getting dark I didn't get the chance to explore the mysterious doors and stone steps leading to lofts above and we continued along the track to the Tower.

The next morning I had to leave and the Shepherd gave me directions to follow the river as it would eventually lead to civilisation, as I called it. There were shorter routes but it was all too easy to lose your way. I took his advice and we shook hands.

"Come again when you can," he smiled.

"I will," I replied and was on my way back to a very different reality.

By the time I reached the tarmac road I was thinking more about my hoard of gold than the Shepherd or Bleakhope.

Casey on a High

Casey L. Pritchard was doing rather well. After a few false starts he had a cute girlfriend who had entrepreneurial skills and a spirit he could admire. They worked quite near each other and eventually he persuaded her to move in with him. But really this was because he couldn't be bothered going to her place. He also rather liked the thought of someone tidying up behind him. As it turned out the spirited Rosie was not a natural servant and was indeed as equally messy as he.

At work he was riding high. He had achieved some seriously good results from his investment choices and was a dab hand at playing the market. His work colleagues admired and envied his success. He was confident and determined. Everything the company wanted. Even Grimms the managing director smiled at his progress. It was unusual for Grimms to smile, for his attributes lay elsewhere and it tended to result in what appeared to be a forced grimace. But, riding on this glory

Casey became over confident, a bit cheeky and began to take his eye off the ball. True, his fiery romance with the sparky Rosie could be distracting, but his real failing was bloated arrogance.

Gilt Guilt

It was after two and a half years of marriage that I started to have odd nagging dreams about my Cheviot experiences. The guilt of the coins grew and my neglect of the Shepherd slowly hauled itself into my conscious brain like the whitened stumps just poking through the eroding moorland peat that I had seen beside that windswept loch. The guilt stuck up enough to stimulate ideas of taking Penny to see where my changed life had begun. I had only vaguely told her about the great time I had when walking the Pennine Way and she knew nothing of my growing wealth generated by the sale of the coins. She married me for love, not money. The remaining proceeds had been carefully invested and a substantial fund was quietly growing. She knew about the last gold coin as I kept it in the flat; when asked I just said that it had been around forever and she must have assumed it was a family thing as she never asked more about it. I would often hold its weight in my palm looking at the way the Emperor's head had been pierced by the simple shepherd's crook.

On one particular evening I was studying late. Penny was asleep and I was becoming bored reading about the attributes of Sitka Spruce. I sat back in my desk chair and looked around the room. My eyes fell upon a charming watercolour that Penny had just completed. She had been particularly pleased with it but I have to admit when she was trying to show it to me earlier in the evening I hadn't paid a huge amount of attention. Now that it was quiet and I was more relaxed I looked at what she had painted. It was a classic cottage scene with a neat thatched roof and rose-covered porch. She was really good at depicting flowers and had painted in flower beds overflowing with beautiful plants. The focal point of the picture was a garden bench on the far side of the garden. Seated on the bench was a young couple that I instantly recognised as Penny and I. Between us and central to the composition, a small girl sat swinging her legs and staring back at me. She had gorgeous big blue eyes, a splattering of freckles and golden locks that framed her pretty face and spilled onto her delicate laced white summer dress. I stood slowly, staring at the little girl, walked over to a small mahogany tea caddy that sat at the back of a bookshelf, opened it and removed its contents, returning to sit in my chair. I felt the sheer quality of the gold coin in my hand and looking back up at the girl, whispered, "I think it's time I took Penny to see the Shepherd."

Part 2 - The Brewing Storm

I take Penny to meet the Shepherd

So it was in a convenient gap in both our careers between my PhD in Woodland Ecology, Penny's MA in Art and Design and getting really serious jobs that we opted to take six weeks off in summer to go north and our first port of call was to see if the Shepherd was still in his valley, indeed still alive at all and what had happened to the trees. To someone in their twenties a man of over seventy is as good as dead. All Penny knew was that I had spent a couple of days helping with his trees and that it was the Shepherd's passion.

We drove up to Jedburgh in late and typically damp summer and spent our first night in a hotel where we focused on enjoying the luxury of a solid roof, modern plumbing and a rich variety of food, for we were to go on into the hills with our camping gear and our comforts were going to be diminished. Setting off the next day at nine in the morning we took a fascinating varied route into the Cheviots taking in a number of interesting gullies and cleughs that held remnants of the former woodland cover and indeed discovered some very old ash and alders on the way. I could not quite pinpoint where on the map the Shepherd's valley lay, but I had worked out the most likely spots.

We clambered out of a thorny ravine some four miles in and were accosted by a young farm worker on a noisy quad bike who I found quite aggressive and rude; he implied that we had no right to be on their land and were disturbing the sheep, which of course was complete nonsense and compared to the roaring device that he rode on our presence was unobtrusive, especially as we crept around so carefully trying to sneak up on birds and other wildlife. Penny did her eye fluttering magic and the plump boy calmed down and became slightly less guarded. He explained that he was being careful because some people did not like the turbines they were planning to put up. I winced at this but said nothing. I asked if the old shepherd was still planting trees up on top. The unlikeable boy said he had never heard of him and drove off, tyres spinning noisily in the gravel as he left. I got the feeling that some of the people living there really did not appreciate what they had. I was shocked and disappointed that they were trying to put wind turbines up in such a stunningly beautiful area. Especially, when looking at the farmhouses, fancy four-wheel drives and huge shiny equipment, there seemed no lack of wealth or comfort. What, I wondered, did they really want and what was it that drove them to destroy the very thing the rest of us would have given an eye to own. The turbines had spread and from Carter Bar, where we stopped and Penny saw Scotland for the first time ever. I was horrified at the mess of these ridiculous telly-tubby machines that most now knew to be useless in the face of a climate that was always changing anyway. Penny wondered why anybody bothered visiting Scotland if this is what they had done to it. The postcards and tourist brochures did not show these monsters. I really hoped that the Shepherd's Valley had not been affected.

Having spent a fascinating day exploring many hidden ravines and woodland on our way, and avoiding wind turbines and the slavering greed that seemed to adhere to those associated with them, we had not got very far along our proposed route, so as the light fell on that grey day we found a hollow within a large mature pine wood where our tent was out of sight and eating within, protected from the drizzle, we enjoyed an evening listening to the unfamiliar noises.

I told Penny about the God-Shepherd, as tall as a giant, striding across the land, plunging in great oaks complete with squirrels and acorns into the soft hillsides, how huge tracts of hills were empty of people because of the tree hugging nutter who ate walkers or neighbours who strayed upon his land. Penny became quite nervous of the Shepherd. I was too but struggled to understand why. After all, he was just a sad old man lost in his own world of solitude.

That night I awoke. I was positive there was an extra person lying with us in that tiny tent. I did not dare move for fear of disturbing Penny and lay for a while listening to the drip-drip on the fabric above us and the additional soft breathing. I must have slept again as I awoke to Penny clambering all over me to get out into the sunshine, for the sun was at its best, bright and hot, the ground dry already.

Penny's enthusiasm, as ever, swept my spirits high and we packed up quickly and ate our breakfast as we walked. We dipped down into a valley where there was a loch brightly rippling in the morning sun and with the thought of the wildlife attracted to such places we decided to have a closer look. From where we were we could see a lovely pine and willow woodland with a flock of gulls circling overhead; but as we came down the track the woodland to our right ended opening up the vista. Expecting a pastoral scene, we were shocked to see a sprawling mess of farm buildings against the water's edge, black silage bags stacked high and rusting machinery lying along the bank, some having been pushed into the water and worse, the thing that stopped us in our tracks was a pall of black noxious smoke rising into the bright cloudless sky, behind which two huge wind turbines chopped relentlessly away at the landscape. It was an awful sight and we couldn't understand why it was allowed to happen anywhere but especially at a rare loch.

As we watched, a tractor and trailer trundled along from the farm buildings and quite simply reversed up to the burning waste and tipped out more plastic, bits of wood and straw and a blaze of sparks and plume of dark smoke spiralled up to be caught in the vortex of the turbines on the ridge behind. It was a deeply disturbing and conflicting image so we took a whole series of photographs. Clearly the turbines had not been erected to reduce emissions or to prevent climate change. The seagulls swooped down to scream and pick at the waste that had fallen off the trailer on its way to the fire.

At the farm buildings an orange muck spreader was being reversed into the water; once partly submerged it was thrown into life by the large tractor and with a loud clunking and grinding its mechanisms thrashing within its dark chamber, brown churning muck came spinning out across the water, a scum meandering away across the surface. We took some more photographs and retreated.

I studied the map and chose another route rising above the farm so we could penetrate the higher hills. We took a stony track and climbed past old mature oaks and hawthorn hedges that looked like a boundary line between farms. We passed a faded sign declaring the loch to be a Site of Special Scientific Interest. The last six oaks had been felled recently with the twisted trunks still scattered beside the track, as if frozen in their final contortions of death; there could not have been much value in the timber so we found it odd that they had been chopped down. The brash still just green was lying in the ditch. We came across an adder sunning itself on a flat rock at the base of one of the tree stumps. It was lying s-shaped, stared at us for a moment with hard cold eyes then slithered off through the dust into a layer of ivy. I felt it was a kind of warning, like a guardian trying to ward us off. The tree stump was bleeding dark tannic fluids that collected in the harsh chainsaw gouges, the great pumping heart rooted within the ground below with its flow nowhere to go. We were very pleased to have seen the adder but did find it a bit sinister.

We moved on glad to be leaving the vandalism behind and looked forward to seeing better things in the Shepherd's land. Just when we thought we had escaped and aiming to take a break at a small roman fort on the first hill top, we found it was also damaged, for there was a large heap of gravelly soil beside which a pit some eight foot deep and fifteen long had been excavated, the flies buzzing around it; the foulest reek forewarned us of its contents—dead things. Penny did not want to look but I found the rotting carcasses of cattle, calves and pheasants thrown in amongst old pallets and bits of fencing wire and corrugated sheets. It was repugnant and my impression of Scotland and the Borders farmers was rapidly changing. Surely this was just a one off and it could not be common practice? I was distressed at having brought Penny to Scotland, having spent time creating wonderful images in her mind. But what we had seen in the last hour was like a scene from a Brueghel painting.

We rose into the higher Cheviots, turbines encroached the hills from several sides like some sort of fungal disease. Tall white and severely out of place, to me they seemed to have spread their spores within the minds of susceptible land owners, their hidden white mycelium penetrating the most unlikely Border families. 'Shame on them,' I thought, 'they have shown themselves as mere wisps of what they pretend to be. They have become pedlars of the greatest of scams—wind power, and should know better not to damage the best of landscapes for their own selfish gain. There may be a place for the intrusive industrial machines but the stunning Borderline hills are just too special.'

We climbed the final ridge to get to the part of the Pennine Way where I had left my map and compass five years previously. I led Penny, retracing my tracks through the marsh and bracken, up the sheep trails to the higher ground—nothing had really changed. We came down upon the ruined farm where I had slept that spooky night of dreams; it was nothing like as scary as that first night when I took refuge in a pigsty. Penny thought it very funny and somewhat appropriate when I showed her where I had slept. The toilet outhouse with its lead pipe holding up the cistern had collapsed, an embarrassed pan now exposed, flaccid lead buckled over broken bricks. More slates had slipped off the roof and a fox or badger had made a den in a heap of loose soil behind the house. We saw no crows or doves but we did find two small decaying wooden crosses in what looked like the old vegetable garden. Simply carved names remembered Archie and Archimedes. We assumed they were pets of some sort, probably sheepdogs. It seemed a waste to have a home not lived in and Penny suggested that maybe we could do it up and live there. I really liked the concept but was not entirely sure this was the right time to be considering it. Although it would have been amazing to plant up this valley like the Shepherd had nearby, the thought of having my own planting project and the well-known fact that the best time to plant a tree was twenty years ago. I had to drag Penny away as I was desperate to see the Shepherd, his Tower and just how much more planting he had done.

The Fifth Gnomon

When we finally reached the high ridge and cairn, it took me quite a while to find the gap in the sharp rocks that led to the Shepherd's land and after some nerve-racking negotiation of the initial cliff, which I had forgotten about, we skidded down the scree at the head of his home valley in hoots of laughter and landed up in a tangle amongst the tall boulders. I hadn't noticed before but the largest of them could almost have been a line of four majestic gnomon from Easter Island, giant guardians watching who came in this unusual way. When I came before, the Shepherd had been standing in a gap between the middle stones as if he were a fifth one, that had only come to life when I arrived and led me to safety. I remembered first looking into his large brown eyes and just how tall and still he was before he helped me up. The fifth gnomon had been my saviour and host for two days. This time no dog or shepherd could be seen and a slight anxiety filled the back recesses of my mind. Straightening ourselves up and dusting our clothes down, we smiled at each other and holding hands we stepped forth so I could show Penny the Shepherd's valley.

We both looked up and gasped—it was amazing. Clearly the Shepherd had continued as there were now dozens of small woods scattered across the slopes. But they weren't ugly angular blocks, they were subtly designed with different spacing between and some linked to the next in graceful ways. It looked almost like woodland had been cleared rather than planted, because the clear parts were obviously the best grazing land. He had used different mixes in each as he said they were trial areas. It looked like he had given up on the fencing on the more recent woods. Penny was overwhelmed by the beauty unparalleled in all her travels; she instantly loved the place and we took off our rucksacks and rested a while to take in the detail. I pointed out where the peel tower was but we couldn't see it as the willows were too tall. The varying ages, density and colours of the foliage created a green paradise.

Penny particularly liked those that had been sparsely planted that allowed each tree to develop its natural crown with some twenty yards between, so it looked like a small area of parkland and the shadows cast beneath on the turf were entrancing. I was surprised at the volume of planting considering the likely failure rate when sowing seed, followed by herbivore damage and climatic hazards. Regardless of all these obstacles the Shepherd just planted on tending his flock of trees as best he could, not put off by failure, as some seed always fell upon fertile soil and growing vigorously would in time produce its own seed to help the Shepherd with his mission.

We found the well above its gurgling mysterious depths and I drew some water up for Penny. The winding mechanism had been replaced and now had iron bearings crudely fixed at the end of the ash pole, which made the extraction of the clear water much easier. It was perfect, so chemical free. It now lay within a sunny glade between fresh young birch and rowan trees rustling in the breeze. Further down the track there were stone troughs every few hundred yards flowing with bright cool water and we saw a roebuck drinking from one, its hue dappled gold and brown in the filtered light, but it was off into alder depth before we were close, a farewell from its bright bobbing tail. I dreaded the damage it and others would be doing and how frustrating it must be for the man who planted and cared for these young trees. At one point we saw quite a bit of wind damage in amongst some pines and noticed that he had changed to using oak and ash as replacements.

A knoll with a remnant homestead was tonsure like, a monk with a soft green scalp and shaggy oak hair; it made me chuckle and wondered if the Shepherd was also aware of the resemblance. Although there had been a bold wind when we started down from the scree top it was now calm within this wooded valley with little movement of branches. It was warm and you could smell the soil and fresh growth around us. It felt so good to feel the vibrancy of the place; birds sang and flitted around in the treetops and unknown creatures rustled in the undergrowth. I would not have been surprised to come across beavers, bears or wild boar in these woods, as they were comparable with anything I had seen on my travels, though lacked the scale of the old growth forest where the range of habitats had diversified and flourished. Penny was not sure she liked the bear idea, but was enchanted by butterflies that fluttered all around and sunny gaps buzzed with golden hoverflies performing their staccato dance in hot rays of sunlight.

As we came amongst the willows I was truly amazed that five years had added such bulk. I would not be able to get my arms around any of them now; some had fallen and strong young shoots some six inches across at the base were heading boldly towards the light. To the south of the stell a patch had been coppiced fairly recently, as the re-growth was still very spindly although a good six foot already.

On the way down the path I prepared Penny for primitive but picturesque accommodation if we were able to stay. Now that I was more mature and aware of fine vernacular architecture I had seen in many parts of the world, I was pleased to see the Golden Tower still in place as it came into view beyond the trees. Penny hung on to my arm with nervous anticipation of meeting the giant Shepherd-God, especially as he seemed to live in a castle, her mind full of fairy-tale stuff at the best of times—so this emerging sight fired off every associated neuron. Perhaps I had exaggerated my description, but she was already overwhelmed by the quality of the valley.

"Wow, I cannot believe that such a beautiful place exists!" she gasped as she took in the tall edifice with its tumbling barmkin wall, cobbled yard and intriguing architecture. The arched entrance through the wall was half concealed with a giant rambling rose that dripped ruby blossoms; Penny paused to breath in the delightful aroma before passing through to encounter the Tower at close quarters.

Pip's End

It was very quiet, almost too quiet. I stepped in past the iron yet and inner oak door enough to yell a greeting, but only the echo of my voice came bouncing back down the stone spiral stairs. The Shepherd's planting crook was at the door with muddy boots, so I knew he was still living here. We walked around the soft glowing sandstone walls but did not find any sign of life.

In the vegetable patch a hoe stood against a fence post and a small heap of fresh weeds lay nearby. We were close. Continuing around to a ramble of outhouses to the rear that I had not discovered on my previous visit, I heard movement within the first. Approaching I announced my presence and a response came out. We went in; Penny somewhat nervous was clinging onto my arm like a small child hanging onto its mother's apron strings. We found the Shepherd kneeling on the floor amongst old sacks and blankets. He looked up with his large brown eyes, gave an acknowledging nod and turned back. In the middle of a raised area of blankets lay Pip looking grey and ancient, clearly on his last legs. He stroked the poor dog's head and moved to the side so we could too. He was just skin and bone and it seemed like yesterday when I met that dog at his own level, having been taken for a ride on the scree, when I first came. I liked to think that Pip recognised me after all that time, but that was unlikely. He made a feeble whimper and his eyebrows rocked from side to side above his faithful eyes. I could only imagine how deeply this must be hurting the Shepherd after so many years of working together, so many planting adventures and his time with the sheep that satisfied his instincts.

The Shepherd led us out of the kennel and into the Tower where he sat us at the hall table and went to the kitchen. I could swear that the other chairs were still in exactly the same position as they had been five years ago and I whispered to Penny not to touch the others. Penny, feeling she should help, followed the Shepherd and I could hear her chatting to him. An achievement I thought considering how quiet he was. They returned with trays upon which bowls of vegetable soup steamed. Penny made big eye expressions to me when the Shepherd was not looking but I could not interpret the message. Penny, unusually confident, led the conversation, asking if I had behaved myself last time I was here and had I really planted hundreds of seeds. The Shepherd looked at me and confirmed this. I gulped nervously and eyes down concentrated on my soup. An image of gold coins falling out of a peaty bank chinked into my head.

The Shepherd said we were most welcome to stay for as long as it took. I did not know what he meant and did not ask. We spoke briefly about Pip and he said we had to do something for him that afternoon. As regards the trees that I was so excited about he said I would see for myself soon. Penny tidied up the trays and I took our rucksacks to the same room as before. Nothing had changed in the bedroom. But two fresh towels lay on the bed. How did he know we were coming? Or was it just his routine? I looked in the turret bathroom and found the Shepherd had installed, although slightly squint, an old-fashioned toilet with one of those alarming high level cisterns, with a long brass chain and ball dangling at its lower end.

When I went back down I found the hall empty and heard them going down the stairs, Penny full of laughter with the Shepherd's quiet words. We all returned to Pip and the Shepherd made a big fuss of the ailing hound, gave him a final pat and doing the same we then quietly left. At the Tower door he collected his planting crook and from the vegetable patch a garden spade which he passed to me. I put it on my shoulder and followed.

We passed through the screening willows till the valley opened up before us. With mounting doom I understood what this mission was and the Shepherd turned to Penny and using her first name asked her to choose the spot. She knew without hesitation and we both followed her and after a few false starts she led us to a clear grassy ridge that we had seen from the track of our descent down the other side of the valley. Central to the ridge there were three hawthorns in a triangle some fifteen feet apart. Penny stopped between them and checking with the Shepherd first, smiled at me and said "Get to work" in her cheeky way. I laughed which lightened the mood and while I dug the Shepherd pointed out what he had been planting and why he had chosen certain species. Penny pointed to crags, odd mounds and hill forts full of excitement and admiration. The Shepherd enthusiastically related what he knew and it was a real pleasure to listen to them while I toiled in the heat.

I had known Pip for less than three days, but it felt longer. By the time I was done I was sweating profusely and I hate to admit it but I had a lump in my throat. It was such a sad event that we had walked into by chance that it really moved me to the core.

By the time we had walked the mile back Pip was dead. The Shepherd let us say a farewell, then scooping the lifeless body up in his arms, walked with him up the hill. We knew not to follow and both of us had tears in our eyes as the image of the Shepherd with his beloved companion receded into the distance.

Guddling Trout

To recover we walked down the stream which at this point was about ten feet across and running quite fast but clear from the recent rains. We came across all sorts of interesting orchids and meadow plants which must have been flourishing since the sheep had been reduced in numbers; indeed I had seen no sheep at all. Penny could see lots of fish, but it took me a while to get my eye in. We both lay on our bellies on a bit of eroded bank and dipping our hands in the cold water delved in amongst the fresh green water weed, sprinkled with delicate white flowers and beneath exposed roots to try to catch one. I could feel one and had it caught up against the edge but just could not quite get my fingers around it to try to scoop it out. It was great fun trying and Penny was so funny when she almost caught one, her blue eyes so pretty and her twisted expressions making me laugh. Having failed on that task we moved on to explore one of the many tracks that led into the new woodland. We passed through a great thicket of blackthorn and crab apple that had a number of long tailed tits in residence. The thicket was impenetrable as I found out when trying to find one of their nests. I got scratched and spiked on the head. Giving up we continued exploring and found the rusting remains of some sort of ancient agricultural cultivator. It was excessively robust with heavy cast iron wheels; I doubted one of the Shepherd's little grey Fergusons would have been able to lift it. I thought it was a relic from before the Shepherd's time, perhaps. There were so many layers to the history of the Cheviots.

Rosie's Frustrations

Rosie had been going out with Casey for several years but suspected he was not entirely faithful. She was feeling that her life wasn't moving on quickly enough. Her boutique was fine but not as lucrative as she hoped. She needed more, deserved more, so she started to harass Casey. She wanted security and money, lots of it. She manipulated Casey and put pressure on him to make serious money. He replied, "Not a problem babe, not a problem." His pride then took over and he started to play the markets recklessly and take some investment risks well beyond his remit. Such careless actions come back and bite you sooner or later.

The Enchantment of the Golden Tower

When we got back to the Tower the Shepherd was busy in the kitchen. Penny went to help and I looked around the hall. The fire grate was clean of ashes and reject nuts and I managed to duck under the lintel and stood looking up the long tapering flue to a small square of blue sky above. The cooing of a wood pigeon filtered down to me. Retrieving myself from the sooty tunnel I looked at the two pictures hanging in the vaulted room. They hung against the original plastered walls. One was of a bearded man with a frothy white ruff around his neck, who looked proud and serious. The other hanging opposite at the far end of the hall was of a young child blowing a bubble with a piece of real straw. Beneath the bubble was a cream coloured bowl decorated with red and ochre swirls. The child's happy eyes looked at me sharing the enjoyment of the moment. There was the impression that these two pictures were chosen to show simply that regardless of how serious one had to be, it was also important never to lose touch with your inner child. As my eyes became accustomed to the light I began to notice very faded colouration on the plasterwork and could decipher paintings of hunting scenes. There was a large red stag and in another place a dangerous looking ginger boar with long yellow tusks curling up from its jaw. There were hunters, both male and female, dressed in fine garments who smiled and laughed with the excitement of their chase. The walls seemed to be an echo of former times, a snapshot of some distant event, but also perhaps, a vision of the future.

The two windows opposite the fireplace cut through six feet of masonry. Some of the plaster had come away with the rain coming in. There were no windows left but heavy grey oak shutters that could keep the worst of a gale at bay. The floor was a chequer of pale pink and buff stones about eighteen inches square. They were well worn especially by the doorways. The pink were more worn than the buff. Other than the long table and its chairs the only other bit of furniture was a large heavily carved oak dresser. The top shelves contained ancient wine glasses with bubbles twisted in their stems, the bottom shelves silver dishes. Obviously security was not an issue this deep in the hills as the main door always seemed to be open.

Penny came out from the mysterious kitchen, which I had not yet seen, carrying a tray with water, glasses and cutlery. She looked demurely at me, winked and returned to collect another tray with steaming plates of casserole. The Shepherd carried two bottles of what looked like ginger beer. They fizzed when he opened them and the table was splashed with rich smelling froth. That evening we talked about our lives and experiences, how we met and the awful wedding which made the Shepherd laugh. We told him of our plans for the future and he nodded politely. Well made plans that were about to change.

After bathing and retiring to bed we both lay together staring up at the green guardian above us who stared back without blinking, unperturbed by our brief existence. I wondered why I had really come back and then remembered that I had intended to confess about the coins and offer to hand over the funds. I thought that his need was now greater than mine. It felt strange, as if I had always lived here and my outside life was just an odd dream. Penny said she adored the Shepherd and all his woodland and the hills and wanted to stay for as long as possible to help him and explore the area. We soon succumbed to our exhaustion and drifted into a long comfortable sleep.

A Grand Tour, The Shepherd's Passion and Small Dark Cherries

I woke first. Penny's smooth pale arm lay across me, her eyes closed and her long dark lashes making her the picture of innocence. I loved the sound of her soft breathing. I was deeply in love with this girl, fun, bright and totally accepting of my eccentricities. We had met in a public toilet in a garden centre in Salisbury when I had accidently walked into the ladies' toilets. Not understanding why an attractive young lady should be in the gents I politely held the door open so she could leave—quickly. She gave me such a wonderful smile as she stepped through the doorway and I was so struck by her beauty that it took me several moments to discover there were no urinals and it was a bit pink in there. Realising my mistake, but in need of urgent relief, I dived into a scented cubicle and just when I thought I had got away with it I found myself yet again politely holding open the door, only this time for the extremely disapproving looks of two purple haired ladies. I found Penny outside in the lobby doubled over with laughter, tears streaming down her delicately freckled cheeks. I was deeply embarrassed, but she said it had made her day. I said it was her fault and declared that I was going to buy her some petunias. I didn't (they were begonias) but we clicked and pretty much laughed ever since.

That morning we carefully did not sit at the table's 'frozen' chairs, and instead used the ones we had the night before. I had explained to Penny that I thought they had been deliberately left as if preserving some important event. We ate a fabulous breakfast of cold ham and bread. The Shepherd said that if we cared to accompany him he would show us some of his work in the hills. He said we should both go to the loch and high woods another day if we cared to stay longer. We were in no hurry.

I packed a rucksack and we followed the Shepherd to visit his sheep first. He liked to check them before heading out for the day's work. His sheep were small, wild, self-maintaining animals that preferred to roam free; he had sold all but his home flock that he had always had in this valley. However, with Pip's decline and their tree nibbling habits they were now confined to a few acres of grass and some of the mature woodland that lay to the north of the Tower. The sheep were quiet gentle creatures. They all had horns with the rams' thicker and longer, coiled on each side of their heads. We watched them in the shade of an old sycamore; two lambs gambolled around the buttressed trunk. He said that it was unlikely that he would replace Pip and his days of being a shepherd were over. It was said in such a quiet way, with his huge eyes blinking, it was hard to really tell how he was feeling; but I guessed that it was tearing at his soul. For a man who had tended his flock for so many years to strip away that part of his life must be difficult. To accept that he was ageing and had to slow down was I suppose a human reality. I thought that with advancing years this was probably a wise choice.

How old was this, man I wondered—it was hard to tell. He spoke of how long he had been there but gave no clue of how old he was when he came. But the world was a changing place too and perhaps it was a time for the sheep to move over anyway and allow the hills to be productive in other ways. To break that sad moment and with a deep sigh the Shepherd, finding his inner strength still fully intact, pulled himself together and straightened up, grasped his planting crook firmly and led us away. It was as if there had been a flow of energy gradually passing over time from the top of his crook, with its beautifully wrought leg hook, down the hazel of the shaft to the planting point, which gave the opportunity for the Shepherd's work to continue in gifting the land with his selfless toil. He was still a shepherd, just of a different sort.

Walking down towards the burn the Shepherd showed us some odd ridges and ditches and explained that he thought it was part of an ancient mill. Despite having lived there for so long he still found interesting things. The water had recently eroded the ground on that side exposing large neatly squared blocks of sandstone, some of which were being washed by the fast flow. The stones were the same golden stone as the Tower and had to be from outside the area as the rock beneath their feet was dark volcanic lava. The Shepherd thought that perhaps the mill and other buildings had been re-used for building the Tower. It made us realise just how many generations of people must have lived there over the centuries. Penny was having ideas about the ruined cottage in the Ashburn valley and thinking in her youthful way how brilliant it would be to plant up that valley.

Then taking us further up the burn he showed us a new plantation of alders. He said they were easy enough to germinate but could not survive even a short dry spell as seedlings, so to be effective he scattered seed in marshy areas during heavy rain so they would be washed down into damp places. It seemed to be working as every ditch and hollow was showing fresh growth of more than a foot. The most vigorous had already grown almost three feet. Where the burn had meandered along the valley floor he poked in willow cuttings in late winter on the bank side that was not being eroded, giving them more time to root and grow before the snaking burn returned to bite again at the soil. Tight clumps of soft green willow foliage could be seen along the marshy stretches. Some of the steep banks had young beech trees slowly appearing above the grass. He had always found beech tricky so had taken to growing them in a nursery first to have any chance at all. Where old beech trees grew near the Tower, a dozen or so ten foot square enclosures were packed full of three-foot high trees. He said he would transplant them to the hills in winter. We spent several hours working our way up the woodland patches being shown the problems he had had and in most cases a practical way to overcome them.

Penny was enchanted that something as simple as a small seed could transform a space into something so full of the buzz of life. Her positivity was to be admired but was no match to the constant certainty of the Shepherd, who knew that whatever was thrown at him, he would get through. He had a resilience that I had to admire and hoped I would be able to emulate even to a small degree.

As we wound up through the trial paddocks he showed us how his ideas had evolved from simple attempts decades ago to become an effective way to establish woodland in difficult conditions.

Penny and I were so impressed by his constant push to return these hills to a state of balance where both humanity and wildlife benefited. The Shepherd had little need for great riches and no need to seek praise for what he had achieved—it was his way of giving something back for the few years of complete happiness with his wife and child so many years ago. He thought of them every day and each seed or tree planted he did for them. Rather than fighting his sorrow he had found a comfortable way to work with it, as he had learned to work with the natural world. Quiet and careful contemplation had taught him that.

I had become a qualified woodland ecologist but was fascinated at how he had, through trial and error, established different techniques to achieve what he wanted.

Penny was concerned about the loss of habitat where we encountered areas of coppiced woodland and in response the Shepherd chuckled and said because there was a cycle spread over different areas and years it actually increased the variety of wildlife that he came across; for example, in this particular area he noticed the first few years after cutting and letting the light in the quantity of giant dragons increased and there were more birds like woodcock nesting. Penny's eyes grew large at this and patiently I said I would explain later. It was the dynamic nature of woodland and how he managed it that added greatly to the value for wildlife.

As we followed the Shepherd from wood to wood we discussed what we had seen with growing enthusiasm, because without realising it the Shepherd was helping contribute to the demands of the modern world and the more we saw and understood of his work the more we felt that every landowner could be doing their bit towards energy production while enhancing the landscape and habitats too. There really was no need to put up nasty industrial wind turbines across the most beautiful hills. There was genuinely a different approach. A calm steady realistic alternative was growing before our eyes that would benefit everybody. As regards the energy provided by the firewood being grown in these valleys it was worth a thousand wind turbines. Not only would the firewood be used instead of oil or gas, it would look amazing as it grew, provide genuine employment for people and provide extensive habitats for all kinds of animals, birds, insects and wild plants. Growing trees would directly help prevent climate change by absorbing carbon dioxide like the disappearing rain forests of the world.

The Shepherd noticed that his companions had fallen behind, but he did not mind as he was deep in his own quiet contemplation. He had never really latched onto what would happen to all his work once he was gone. But now seeing their vigour and youth he became acutely aware that his life was ticking away. The thought that perhaps after all he did care about the future, clarified his deep troubled hope. Some sort of continuum that made sense of his years of toil. If this wonderful couple could pick up the reins then he would die a happy man. They were not blood relatives or even Scottish as far as he could tell, but he knew they, if anyone, would have the spirit to carry on and hopefully all being well have their own children that would in turn perpetuate. Somehow some of the weight on his shoulders began to lift and dissolve above him in the warm summer light. Unknown to him a young girl's hand was hanging on to his, willing him on.

As we tried to catch up with the Shepherd we were getting very excited about our expanding ideas. Slightly out of breath, Penny stopped on a small knoll where the views opened up between gean trees dripping with thousands of dark cherries catching the warm sun. There were the remains of a wooden rail fence that looked like it had enclosed the area and I suggested to Penny that it must have been some of his earliest planting. The Shepherd, seeing that we had stopped at one of his favourite viewing spots, came and stood beside me. He suggested Penny tried a cherry. There was then a moment that I wished I had photographed: it is as clear in my mind now as it was then. There was a combination of light and shadow, the dappled patterns on the ground, the purple brown of the glossy cherry bark. Behind Penny the backdrop was a rolling landscape of infinite shades of green. It was as if the gentle warm breeze lifted Penny from the ground as she reached up into the branches to pluck a cherry, delivering her upon an invisible zephyr, her slim figure curved as one hand gracefully grasped a branch; the other followed, fingertips apart, her eyes focused on the chosen fruit. Her profile reflected the shapes of the neighbouring trees, her movement like a willow swaying in the wind. The really striking thing was the way the sunlight caught the pale inside of her wrists. For a fleeting moment she became a wood nymph, her body a curving trunk, her arms the branches, wrists and fingers bright fresh growth reaching up to the sun, energy gratefully absorbed feeding the great cycle of life. She placed the cherry between her lips and for the first time tasted the sweet nutty flavour of the wild fruit. Awe struck the Shepherd and I glanced at each other and instantly knew the other had seen it too. We looked back at Penny and she was, not so gracefully this time, reaching up for more cherries and was devouring them with enthusiasm. Becoming aware of being stared at, she turned to us asking, "What are you two gawping at?" Face beaming with purple juice running down her chin, we couldn't help but laugh. "Aw, come on, they are just fantastic!" she declared, wiping off the juice with the pale wrist that moments before had been as white as birch bark. We joined her and with the Shepherd helping by holding down branches with his crook we all ate handfuls.

Caught up in our enjoyment of the harvest we did not notice the flickering ghost of a younger shepherd lying on his side in the sun, elbow on the grass, head propped in his hand, his big brown sparkling eyes gazing into those of a beautiful girl sitting next to him. Her long white dress caught the summer breeze with golden locks trailing down her back. They were sitting on a red tartan travel rug, a wicker hamper between them. On the rug a round bowl decorated with red and ochre swirls held small dark wild cherries. They were chatting, gazing across the naked hills admiring the empty wilderness with a heap of cherry stones accumulating on the rug. "What shall I do with these?" she asked. "Sow them," he replied, "Let's give this valley its trees back"—and in a swirl of merriment and laughter they ran around the naked knoll pushing the stones into the soft warm turf. "I will ask Father to fence this place off so they can grow properly," he said.

The vision faded and the old Shepherd was laughing with Penny and I holding the cherries up to the sun to see how their translucence made them glow, before eagerly eating them. I had never seen the Shepherd so animated and chatty. It was if he had been relieved of a great burden. The Shepherd had placed a square white handkerchief on the ground and we were putting all the cherry stones on it, a purple stain spreading through the fabric. When we had had enough Penny asked, "What shall I do with these?"

"Sow them," the Shepherd and I responded in unison.

She gathered them up and the Shepherd passed her his planting crook. She held its weight in her hand, admired its fine wrought iron hook and looking up at the Shepherd, asked, "What do all these markings mean?" He smiled and replied, "You know, I've never worked it out, but they must be important because the same markings appear in odd places."

The Shepherd led us to a small dell some one hundred and fifty yards long by fifty wide with hazel banks leading down to a stream dancing noisily between grey boulders. "The next issue," he explained, "was to give germinating acorns enough light to grow up fast. Initially I simply coppiced the hazel, but the new growth swamped the oaks within the first season." Only one oak had survived, a broad specimen on the opposite bank.

Less interested in the ecological detail, Penny decided it looked like a good climbing tree, so giving me the crook she hopped across the burn and proceeded to scramble around trying to get some grip on the trunk with her boots while she hung from a rather narrow branch. The Shepherd and I watched with amusement to see, somewhat surprisingly, how she managed to get up and climbed nimbly to sit on a limb with her back against the tree trunk. She listened quietly to the Shepherd as he explained his woodland trials. The sun filtered through the mesh of wavy edged foliage and she half closed her eyes. She thought about her husband, the future and hoped that he would be as always kind and dedicated as the lone shepherd. Like everybody she desired security and peace of mind. She had loved her tall guy ever since she laid eyes on him and though she had missed him desperately while he was away on his woodland field trips, his absence had made her heart grow fonder. She felt the sun caressing her face and the furrowed bark supporting her back. She knew that wherever fate would lead it would not always be as comfortable as she felt then. She found the Cheviots amazing and certainly felt no need to travel further north. She was happy there, content. She felt that if only they could find the right occupations then perhaps they could stay. She had simple needs, a loving man and the opportunity to draw and paint. But most of all she really, really, wanted a baby. An unexpected rustle in the leaves above her plucked her from her daydream. A squirrel, she mistakenly thought and descended to the ground to join the others. She was unaware that she was being followed and watched very closely.

Penny asked the Shepherd to show her how to sow the cherry stones that she had wrapped up in the hanky in her pocket. He took the crook and selecting an earthy spot next to the path poked a hole only an inch deep. Penny dropped in a seed and the Shepherd pushed soil over the hole and firmed it down. He handed back the crook and she repeated this at frequent intervals on our walk till the stones were all used up. She loved the thought that maybe some of these in turn would survive to produce those fabulous cherries. The Shepherd pointed out that each tree had its own flavour with some quite bitter and others sweet. The size of the fruits could vary too. It was a wonderful experiment and he said she must return to see the results. "I am not sure I ever want to leave," she said. There was so much to see and explore and do; she was becoming absorbed by the potential and beauty of everything around her. She was really intrigued by the engravings on the crook and asked, "Where else do you encounter these markings?" The Shepherd had seen them frequently over the years. "They are quite common and sometimes in odd places. For example, on the underside of the oak table in the hall the fish shape with the arrow is carved quite neatly. In other places like down by the old mill there are stone gateposts that have those odd swirls. You would need a lot of time to work out the mystery." Penny was pleased, she liked mysteries.

I was determined to crack the other code, that of how the Shepherd was so successful in growing some trees without the help of weed killers or plastic tubes.

He showed us his most successful trial that was the same but rather than pleaching he simply bent the hazel rods over hard and twisted the tips into the neighbouring trees' bent branches, pinning them with angled stakes driven into the ground and if necessary tying the branches to the stakes to prevent the wind untangling them and letting them spring back into an upright position. The result was cages of bent rods radiating out from every stump with foliage-free stems near the stumps where he planted acorns and a mass of leaf further out overlapping with the neighbours. I said they looked like a gathering of giant spiders across the field. Penny found them a bit creepy. Some kind of surreal mating ritual that was probably best avoided. Or perhaps a network of neurons connecting in mysterious and magical ways. I could see how the oaks shot up through the protective cage of rods and although there was a degree of new stump growth and shoots coming up from the bent stems it was enough to draw the oaks up tall and straight rather than swamping them and helped keep the deer off. After a few years the oaks topped the hazels and were well on their way to forming excellent trees. The Shepherd would then coppice the hazels and all but the best oak at each hazel. The oaks then had a clean straight stem of around eighteen feet and being fifteen foot from the next oak had space for its crown to spread out and upwards maximising growth while maintaining its shape. Beneath the oaks the hazel grew on forming an understory full of birds and where the hazel was thinner a woodland floor carpeted with fine grasses, ferns, harebells and many other species of wild flower developed. I loved how the simple constant work of the Shepherd's hands could create such amazing natural environments. It was like he released a dove from his aged worn palms. A sole human giving nature a chance.

Penny held my hand as we followed the Shepherd and I could feel her gazing up at me. I hoped I was worthy, whatever she was dreaming about.

A long way away

On the seventeenth floor in a warm plush office in Canary Wharf, a young executive straightened his brash tie, twisted his face at his reflection and brushed dust off his expensive jacket. He had cocked up big time and the company had lost a lot of money in bad investments. His investments. He was meant to manage his portfolio at a low risk level but got caught up with the get rich quick mania and had pushed his luck and lost the gamble, actually several really big gambles. He had had a long and painful rollicking from Colonel Brighstone himself, closely followed by evil Grimms, so aptly named. Shaking and concerned for more than just his job, flat and Ferrari, he had been given a month to come up with a very, very lucrative and very safe investment to compensate for his inadequacies and to stay alive. He sweated at the best of times, but he was so nervous even the air con wasn't helping. He hoped the board would accept his proposals. It had taken three weeks of digging through archives and banging his head against the wall to find anything worth looking at. Hell, he had split with Rosie over this. He was seriously disappointed with the state of things and kicked the toilet door hard as he headed out to face the music. But Casey L. Pritchard was a determined bastard and he was going to get through this.

The board room was a tense place at the best of times, this time doubly so. The brilliant Jenny had helped him prepare the PowerPoint presentation and was waiting to help him through it. It was good, he was good and God damn it, his idea was brilliant! He knew how to jazz up his audience and strode in bold and confident. He was a slick operator and within a minute had them wound up with anticipation. The screen came to life with a Google image of planet Earth; it started to spin and zoom in and finally stopped showing a crisp satellite image of the Cheviot Mountains. A red line slowly drew itself around a dozen hills in the heart of the range. The image slipped forwards into 3D and flew in over the hills, circled slowly approaching the red lined area; white lumps appeared on the ground and grew like mushrooms blossoming into spinning turbine blades with green pound signs floating up into the atmosphere, changing the climate in so many ways. Twenty-four of them, the agent had said, one hundred and twenty-five metres high, start with lots then cut back later to pacify the natives… worth millions, guaranteed, and one-hundred percent safe, backed by the government.

Twenty minutes later Grimms stood up and stopped Casey mid-flow. "We have heard enough Pritchard, are we all for it?" he asked looking around the smoked glass table.

Casey paled visibly as if his skin was trying to blend in with the table, chameleon like.

"Yes!" they said one after the other till it was old Elliot's turn.

"What about the people?" Old Elliot asked.

"Stuff them," said Grimms. "The peasants are stupid, put Leonard on PR, he could talk a goat around." They were all scared of Grimms and his bulldozing style. "You are outvoted anyway, Elliot. Pritchard, when can you kick things off?"

Casey, relieved but twitchy, replied, "Agent is already on the case Sir."

"Like your style Pritchard, like your style. Do it and do it quick."

Old Elliot's bushy white brows were knitted. The water glass in his hand trembled.

Flight of the owls

Penny and I spent several days learning a massive amount from the Shepherd. He described germinating techniques, pruning, coppicing, site selection, bracken control and a multitude of other things including in-depth knowledge of the wildlife within the Cheviots. He had shown us how the naked hills, windswept and overgrazed, could become more productive by careful planning and thought. His knowledge of the climate and soils enabled him to plant the right trees in the right place allowing shelter to develop, naturally filtering the harshest of winds. He then found that as a wood developed the protected part of the hillside became greener and was often favoured by the sheep. The vegetation became less rank and a wider range of grassland species grew, the sheep did better enabling him to try different crosses that were more profitable and that allowed him to keep less of them which in turn allowed more space for trees. One aspect of his management came into balance with the other and around one third of the Shepherd's home valley was wooded. It was an attractive and bountiful place to live.

We stayed for another day, then another, then more. Penny and I were fascinated by the whole process of change from bleak and barren to beauty and bounty. This, to us in our twenties, seemed so long and slow, but the Shepherd, who found the passing years had accelerated alarmingly, couldn't stress enough about how crucial it was to get started soon and enjoy the transition from an empty land to one full of life and hope. He felt he had not done enough which resulted in great protest from us.

It was Midsummer's Eve. We sat at the long oak table with its well-worn planks and unusual turned legs and we ate venison with new potatoes and some salad that I had been sent out to select from the vegetable patch. I still hadn't seen the kitchen and Penny said I was not allowed to. Never mind, I didn't have to do the dishes. Actually I was an enthusiastic and able cook but did not dare intrude. To accompany this meal a bottle of red wine was procured from some hidden depths of his Tower and we chatted about his amazing achievement with the lowering sun casting warm rays into the depths of the room. A day didn't pass without some new discovery. Something we hadn't noticed before.

That evening the angle of the sunlight or the way it bounced around the room casting more shadows picked out the slightest detail. I was enjoying the excellent wine, leaning back and wondering how old the lableless bottle might be, when I noticed that the protruding corbels running along the bottom edges of the ceiling vault, which I had always assumed were just heavily eroded, were in fact all subtly carved. Each was an owl looking out over the hall. I could now see the round faces and big eyes, wings to either side raised slightly at the shoulders. As we talked and enjoyed the meal I looked up at the owls every few minutes and noticed an amazing thing. Gradually, as the sun moved, the shadows deepened and changed in size and shape. Those of the wings became broader and higher and looked remarkably like they were slowly extending up and out to each side, stretching as if ready to fly. The more I became aware of them the more I had to look to confirm what I was seeing. So much so, as the wings became fully raised, the owls heads seemed to rock forward and my participation in the conversation must have stopped abruptly, my glass almost at my lips, frozen, my eyes big and round waiting for the owls' next move. Penny and the Shepherd were now watching me and at the last moment Penny saw what I saw. "Owls!" she exclaimed. The Shepherd stood up slowly, glanced through the window and watching carefully suddenly brought his strong brown hands together in an almighty clap.

The light in the room instantly changed. The strong shadows and warm glow vanished leaving us in a colder grey light. I jumped, dropping the glass where it broke upon the oak, red wine seeping into the grain adding to its deep colour and history.

"They all flew away!" I exclaimed, mesmerised by what I had just witnessed.

The rows of barely perceptible owls were back to badly eroded lumps of stone. Their magic complete, their winged shadows had departed for the night, silently rushing through the windows as their darkened domain called. The Shepherd laughed and sat down and lit the candelabra in front of us. I apologised as I stared at the reflecting patterns of the new-born candle flames in the tear shaped bubble caught in the stem of the broken glass. Penny gingerly picked it up and hauled it from my vision. She wiped up the broken pieces and wine and by the time she returned from the kitchen I had regained my composure and was asking the Shepherd about the ruined house we had seen in the neighbouring valley.

He told us that it had been Scott the Steward's house and hadn't been lived in for decades. After he had died of pneumonia his wife and family had left for Australia where her brother lived. He hadn't heard from them since. Billy Tolk, a neighbouring farmer who bought the Shepherd's livestock from him each year, asked if he could keep some sheep in that valley. I recalled a scattering of white woolly muttons from our walk down into that desolate place. The Shepherd had said he couldn't see why not and the sheep came and went. Billy had assured the Shepherd that he would always get the best price for the beasts he bought from him and a fair grazing rent for his sheep, so a long-term relationship was established. Billy knew that the trees were going to be started sooner or later and was making the best of things while he could. Billy assumed the Shepherd must own the land. The Shepherd thought the investment company down south owned the land, but did not mention that to Billy for fear of outside interference. Penny and I doubted the Shepherd was getting top dollar for his livestock but assumed Billy handled all the tagging and paperwork which must have been time consuming. But then again they thought of the Tower with few glazed windows and the four-wheel drives outside well maintained farmhouses they had seen elsewhere.

We agreed to visit the valley the following day and look at its potential and maybe get some seeds sown. Very excited by this prospect, we retired to bed and slept like logs.

Casey and the Agent

They met at two. The agent's office was near Doncaster. Casey had used the rail service and a taxi. He would have preferred to have taken the Ferrari as sitting next to an odorous Scotsman all the way from King's Cross was unpleasant. He could hardly understand a word he said. The conversation seemed rhetorical, lubricated by Newcastle Brown and indeed as largely directed to the can as it was to Casey. He found alternating between 'yep' and 'nope' satisfied the beady eyes. Perhaps he had helped with the wee man's difficulties. Not that he cared. He had a distaste for anybody north of the Watford gap.

The agent was scrawny and creepy but apparently good at what he did. He had seven big wind farms up and running and over two hundred single or pairs of turbines. He was sly, clever and crafty as a fox. He knew every trick in the book.

A very leggy blonde secretary brought in the coffee. Distracted Casey watched the short skirt wiggle out of the door. God, he missed Rosie. She hadn't been responding to his messages or pleading texts. The bitch. The agent cleared his throat. Casey refocused thinking how useful that girl would be at a village hall meeting and took a mental note.

He chatted with the agent who quietly suggested a quick checklist for Casey to focus on...

1. Eliminate all rare species, birds, bats, newts and pretty flowers, whatever.
2. Send a spy amongst the locals to sense the mood, plant seeds for support.
3. Identify and check out neighbours and residents.
4. Suss out local council people, find their weaknesses, likes and dislikes,
5. Check site for peat depth.

6. Check out historic stuff and get rid of anything likely to attract attention.

The agent said he would start work on other background matters. How Casey handled his list was up to him but the more he could do discretely himself the better. The agent would email his invoice and terms to HQ. Casey left, smiling. This could be fun.

For the rest of that week Casey got busy. Utilising the budget allocated, he arranged a helicopter so he could take up a team to have a quick look over the site. His excuse was the speed at which they had to move. In truth he couldn't be bothered with any other forms of transport. He put together his team. Jenny for general administration and information gathering, a post-grad archaeologist from the nearest university, an all-round handy naturalist to look at the wildlife stuff, soils and peat, Martin from the offshore investments department as he was known to be a keen hiker and had the gift of the gab and he quite liked the idea of an all-expenses paid walk in the hills. Sarah, a small dark eyed, attractive girl from the IT department was to be chief photographer. Finally he included Old Elliot, not because he wanted him, but as head of new ventures and a member of the board he was obliged to go along. Two days later they were up and away. Armed with maps and desktop survey data, they set off. The roar of the helicopter was like the coming of some fearsome storm.

Ashburn

The Shepherd took us to the Ashburn valley via part of an old drove road. We didn't have to climb up the scree. The valley was relatively sheltered and we had a pleasant walk to the remains of Scott the Steward's house; it was in a really good spot, facing south and in the lee of a steep slope. Next to the house were the two old sycamores. Apart from one cracked door lintel and a crumbling chimney stack the fabric of the building was intact. The Shepherd told us that his father brought him here when he came to discuss the farm work with Scott. At that time there were two shire horses kept in the stables and half a dozen or so pigs in the sties. Haystacks covered with heavy green tarpaulins tied down to stakes lined the track coming in.

There was always a treat baking in the oven and smoked hams hung from hooks driven into brown ceiling beams. Sometimes a great show was made of bringing down a new ham using a pole with a notch cut in the top. The pole was pushed up under the cord holding up the ham, but despite the farmwife being strong, the ham often came down a bit faster than intended. This had always entertained him as he watched with great expectation as to where it would fall and which precious ornament was put at risk. One of his favourite tasks was to help make blackberry or gooseberry jam on the range.

The Shepherd conjured such charming and evocative images that we really came to like the place. The wooden crosses, he explained, were the last two cats that had lived there. When Scott's wife left he took the cats to the Tower and when the sad days came returned them there to bury them out of respect to the family. He had found it quite lonely after Jeanie and her children left for their new life in Australia.

We had brought some ash keys, hazel nuts and acorns along with three crooks and an adze. To help plan woodland for this valley and the first ceremonial planting we found a high spot that looked over most of the area. This valley was small compared to the others in the Shepherd's domain but still some five hundred acres. Apart from those near the house the only other trees were three ridge line sycamores and a scattering of wind-bent thorns. The Shepherd pointed out where he had been told a small village had once stood. The springing of an old stone bridge still protruded from the river bank. The Ash burn came meandering along a marshy valley floor in convoluted twists and turns. Further upstream it cut through earthy banks swamped with bracken and it sprung from a marshy plateau and scree at the valley head. To the sides, the west rose sharply into a boulder-strewn landscape challenging any creature to climb, and to the east were a series of ridges with small escarpments with a summit encircled by ancient ridges and ditches.

This landscape with its rugged terrain and difficult ground would be a challenge. So would be dealing with the bracken that grew so vigorously to over six feet high. Despite the rough appearance of the place it would improve dramatically with some tree growth. We sat down on a dry area of turf amongst patches of wild thyme and delicate blue harebells, heads rocking from side to side as if chiming our coming to the valley, heralding a time of renewal and new life—silent ringing that spread out from the chosen spot, through the bleached grasses, between the rocks, echoed over the babbling burn and rippled between the tall ferns then became lost in the marshes.

Penny took out her sketch book and started to make some simple background drawings of the existing landscape, noting in her neat italic writing which areas looked dry, marshy, cliffs and so on. She even pencilled in three buzzards flying high overhead to complete the composition. I took some photographs, then we all sat with Penny's sketches before us discussing where to retain and enhance grazing for sheep, which areas to fence off and how to build up woodland types and the best methods to get the trees started. It was an amazing thing to do and trying to project five, ten, forty and one hundred years into the future was fascinating. We all had our personal favourite ideas and parts of the valley. I wondered what the investment company would think of our plans for their land and what the Shepherd had done so far. They obviously did not care for the place as the Shepherd had never seen or heard any sign of them.

As a ceremonial event with the seeds burning holes in our pockets and with the guidance of the Shepherd we aimed for the boulder field and rocky area behind us, where the sheep did not normally go. We chose a sunny spot and Penny pulled out our lunch of fresh bread, ancient looking round cheeses, cold venison and bottles of water from the Tower's well. The seed we had brought would need to be planted in the best soil we could find. As we ate we decided to have one species each and plant the area in randomly chosen clumps as best we could amongst the boulders. It wasn't going to grow into prime timber but was going to become a fascinating habitat. Penny chose the acorns, the Shepherd the hazel nuts and the small sack of ash keys were mine to sow; we set off in our own directions and started a hundred yards or so apart.

I was having visions of delicate ash foliage against the grey of the lichen boulders and was concentrating on getting right down between the rocks; some of the crevices were at least fifteen feet deep. It was slow going clambering up and down, but there were good pockets of soil. Getting tired of climbing I chose a hollow between large angled chunks of basalt with an easier decent down over grassy tussocks to a level area below. I planted maybe twenty seeds at three feet apart using the planting staff and was pushing soil over a planted seed when small stones I had dislodged seemed to flow down a gap between some slabs of stone. I could hear them rattling away like marbles spilt on a staircase. There was a deep cavity of some sort, so getting my fingers around the edge of one of the slabs, gave a good pull. Thinking of my other unexpected find I was getting quite excited but could not shift it. Using the crook I scraped away some of the surrounding turf exposing the corner of a neat hand-hewn stone and wedging the point under an edge, tried to raise it. There was enough movement to show it could be lifted but it was too heavy and I didn't want to break the crook. More stones disappeared into the depths below. I was going to need assistance.

I climbed out of the hollow to ask the Shepherd and Penny to help, but as I came out of the boulder field I heard a cry from Penny in distress. Breaking into a run I found the Shepherd crouched down next to her. Gasping for breath I reached them and asked them what had happened. She had slipped on some loose stones, caught her foot between two rocks and twisted her ankle quite badly. I could see it swelling in front of my eyes. Penny was sobbing and apologising for the hassle she was causing. We hauled her up and propped her against a rock. She wasn't going to be able to walk back so between us we helped her hop along, or on difficult terrain I carried her. I had to wade through the burn with her on my back so I ended up soaking wet. Exhausted and weary we got back to the Tower just before nightfall. Never had we been so glad to see that Golden Tower and its simple comforts. The Shepherd did something clever in the kitchen to encourage a flow of hot water into the bath a little later on and provided a quick meal to satisfy our growing hunger. Penny was bathed and asleep within an hour. When I crept in beside her I lay looking up at the vault above with its many different hues of stone, all leading to the central carving of the Green man. I had to consider where our adventures were leading and thought, perhaps a little pessimistically, that we had better pack up and go home as soon as Penny was able to walk. Maybe we had been getting over enthusiastic about what could be done in these hills. It was time to return to reality.

I did not sleep well that night. I kept waking too hot and stressing about the slightest thing and had nightmares that I could not quite wake up from. There were disturbing Triffid turbines chopping up the landscape, falling like Alice into a cave of wonders and dead cats hauling themselves out of the ground. At one point I thought a helicopter flew low over the Tower. But when I awoke it was a very still humid morning without a sound to be heard.

Casey on the top

They landed the helicopter on site, two hundred yards south of the loch, hidden in a clearing amongst young birch, bright and fresh in the morning light. It was just after dawn. They had come in early to avoid undue attention. Jenny set up a folding table and chairs which Casey L. Pritchard promptly occupied like a Roman Emperor. Jenny placed the estate map in front of him, a laptop computer and a walkie-talkie linked to each member of the survey team.

If there were ghosts within the peat beneath his feet, they would have quivered with such arrogance; they would have felt this kind of presence before.

His team gathered around and he gave his brief. It looked like it was going to be a warm day and Casey was at least going to try to make the best of this horrible experience. He did not enjoy the outdoors, preferring confined spaces with highly technical climate control in the form of central heating or air conditioning. He would tolerate this Godforsaken place in the middle of nowhere for the sake of his personal comforts. He had no intention of coming here again after this visit. There was just too much sky.

The naturalist was given the map of the whole 4125-acre property showing the proposed turbine sites spread across the highest points. Casey instructed him to spiral outwards recording everything he saw, bird, bat, weeds, goats, bugs, butterflies and so on. He was also to take test cores of the peat across the site. All equipment was in the helicopter. The naturalist, young and keen, headed off with a reminder that he was not to reveal his purpose. No matter who asked. "Helicopter leaves at 10pm prompt!" yelled Casey to the man's departing back.

The archaeologist had a lot of research information already prepared and was to report back regarding conditions and likely impact of the proposed development. Martin the hiker was already somewhere in the hills having been sent up a week earlier as a spy. No other members of the team knew he was also involved. He was to walk in the hills observing the people and their movements, farmers, shepherds, gamekeepers, hikers, whoever. He was to remain discreet and preferably invisible, then go to the surrounding villages, make friends and assess the natives.

Elliot listened to the arrogant boy's spiel but said nothing. He did however hoist his rucksack on his back and caught up with Sarah after she had been dispatched by Casey. He asked if he could accompany her and point out a few distant features in the landscape. He had lived in the Borders up till the age of twelve in a village not far from Jedburgh, so had a rough idea of the lie of the land, though he had never been this far into the Cheviots. Sarah was glad of the company. She had an unease regarding this whole venture and a great dislike for Casey. Saying nothing about her feelings she allowed Elliot to lead the way. He headed for the high ridge that the map showed to be the Southern boundary from where he would be able to get his bearings. He was uncomfortable with the financial risk and the potential impact on the landscape and its people.

They stuck to the high boundary ridges as best they could with one precipitous dip down to cross a valley floor along the northern edge of the property. They saw only their own team members, a few sheep, goats and one abandoned farmhouse. They stopped at each hill fort and Sarah took some stunning shots from between great stone gate posts framing the huge rounded slopes with the mosaic of greens, purples and greys receding into the distance. The main thing they remarked upon was the abundance of deciduous trees and how natural the valley looked, for there seemed to be young growth everywhere. When they looked over the neighbouring hills there were frequent angular blocks of ugly Sitka spruce. Sarah took comparative photographs and was rapidly coming to the conclusion that this was one of the most stunningly beautiful areas of hills she had ever been in.

Elliot quite simply wondered who the tenants were and what kind of income was received by his company each year. He knew nothing about this property, but then they had many thousands of farms spread across the whole globe from vast grain estates in East Anglia to virtual jungle in Tasmania. He decided he would have a closer look into the matter on his return to headquarters.

Once his team had dispersed Jenny came up beside Casey and put her hand on his shoulder. He turned to smile at her and put his hand around her waist for a moment. Jenny was his favourite administration girl, always willing to have a bit of fun. They looked over Upper Muirside loch that lay within a shallow scoop on the high Cheviot Hill. All they could see was a muddy puddle and possibly a hindrance to his plans. He thought that it could probably be drained if necessary. Jenny pointed to a large bird that swooped low over the water.

"What's that?" she asked.

"Bloody great big seagull," he replied. "Come on, let's have some breakfast."

Jenny walked over to the helicopter; the pilot had gone off for a wander down amongst young alders and birch by the water's edge. Neither the pilot, Jenny or Casey had any understanding as to what they were looking at. The loch was the remnant of a larger body of water entrapped within the landscape after the great ice sheet retreated. Thousands of years of advancing bog, fen, carr, heather and peat had reduced the quantity of open water to a fraction of its former glory. The land had rapidly become invaded by opportunistic plants. The variety of trees had come and gone along with its associated birds and animals. At its peak there were substantial stands of sizable trees protected from the harshest winds by their adjoining neighbours enabling them to grow well at that altitude despite the exposure and thin dry or waterlogged soils. Rowan, birch and ash grew tall on the drier heights, oak and elm on the deeper soils, willows and alders on the wettest parts. A dynamic woodland and open land developed constantly adapting to a continually changing climate and the pressures of grazing animals. Then along came man with his fire, sheep and goats with the result that all that remained was a few solitary trees clinging to cliff faces or enclosed by the wisest of men.

If a speeded-up film of the last ten thousand years could be seen it would have looked like some crazy chicken-plucking competition where the feathers kept trying to grow back, but eventually the forest lost the battle and the land was laid bare and exposed like the raw skin of the chicken before it is finally cooked and devoured to satisfy man's insatiable appetite. The hand of a simple shepherd had halted this madness and breathed back hope into the land and now the worst of man's behaviour could sweep it away in a few hours. The proposed icons of greed mounted on thousands of tons of leaching concrete displacing peat with its stored carbon; were not to help prevent climate change, to give the earth a second chance, they were quite simply to harvest the associated subsidies, yet again perpetuating the abuse that those reaping the excessive rewards inflicted upon the bruised land.

Casey couldn't care less what wind turbines could or couldn't do for the climate or energy security—he just wanted a safe and lucrative investment that would get his boss off his case.

The walkie-talkie on the table in front of him buzzed and he picked it up and pressing the button said, "Go ahead Martin, what have you got for me?" Martin read out the coordinates and reported, "Presumed shepherd with three black and white dogs walking down into valley north edge of boundary, valley has a couple of hundred white sheep and yesterday evening an old man in the Bleakhope valley, probably a tramp."

"Thanks Martin, keep up the good work, over and out." He took a swig of his breakfast wine which Jenny poured from a bottle picked out of the hamper she had carried over. A bit early considering it wasn't even 8am.

A little later the spotty naturalist radioed in: "This place is amazing. I have already seen an Osprey, otter tracks, a woodcock, nuthatch, tree creepers, orchids that I can't identify and a heap of other things. It could take months to survey this place and there are loads of woods that are bound to be full of stuff!"

74

"Oh," said Casey, barely covering his disappointment. "Photograph, coordinates and names," he replied, possibly a bit more aggressively than he intended.

An Eye and an Arrow

I left Penny to sleep and finding the Shepherd carefully sorting seed at the table asked him about his childhood. We ate a simple breakfast and although to start with he seemed reluctant to talk about it as if the memories hurt, he began to relax (for I must have been persistent in my encouragement) and told me he was born in a farmhouse near Kelso, the third son of four of whom only young Angus and a younger sister May were still alive. She had married a Kenyan and lived on a coffee plantation and had not been over to visit for twenty-five years. Angus farmed the land at the home farm and was married to a distant cousin called Cecelia. They had two boys who he assumed worked the land with their own children, but he had not seen them for a very long time, so didn't really know.

They had had an idyllic childhood and often travelled by horse to visit his father in the Tower. They had played in the burns, rolled down the heather and climbed the sycamores at Scott the Steward's house on many occasions.

Understanding that the Shepherd had said all he wanted to, I went up to see Penny. She was staggering back from the bathroom making a lot of grunts and groans, and I helped her back to bed. Examining her ankle, I could see the swelling had reduced but it was really tender and had turned alarmingly black.

"That looks really bad," I said looking up into her watering eyes. I hated to see her in pain.

"It's very sore," she said, "but it's my own fault for skidding around on those rocks."

"Maybe we should pack up and get you out of the hills," I said, placing her foot back down on the mattress. "I don't want you getting hurt."

"Not on your Nellie," she retorted. "This is going to heal in the next few days. I love this place too much to leave. We've hardly started to explore."

Knowing Penny and her determination I left it at that. Any chance of getting as far as Loch Ness had now receded into another year.

I brought her up some breakfast and we sat chatting about our adventures in the hills. I told her about the hole beneath the slab and we agreed to go back there once she was better. I walked across to the window and looked out across the cobbled yard into the tops of the willows. The air was heavy, hot and humid. There was a haze that hung in the air like a woollen blanket thrown across the land. The weather was going to break soon—its building tension was oppressive and it made me feel exhausted and very sleepy. While I was standing in the window opening I noticed an odd mark on the stonework. At first I thought it was just a bit of vandalism scratched by some bored child, looking out of the window perhaps, also waiting for the weather to change. However, it looked too neat to be casual damage. I took my Swiss army knife from my pocket and selecting an appropriate looking tool, very carefully scraped out the lichen from the grooves. There were straight lines and interesting curves. Intrigued, I scraped away until it was all done. Penny asked what I was doing and I described the neatly carved design to her. There was an arrow and an eye. The arrow pointed slightly up and out of the window; the eyeball stared out from the stone as it must have done for centuries. I wondered if the Shepherd knew about it. I could not make any sense of it but Penny, lying in bed across the room, liking puzzles and mysteries, suddenly declared, "It's a clue, like a treasure hunt leading you to the next one! Try looking along the arrow." I did as instructed and thought it an amusing game and bent down low and moved my head up and down and side to side. All I could see was a tall graceful willow tree about sixty yards away. "Just a tree," I said dismissively, stretching back into an upright position and thinking nothing more of it.

"And how old is the tree?" asked Penny.

"Err, around twenty years I think," I said, still not thinking.

"How old is this tower?" Penny asked, sitting up, fascinated.

Aided by Penny, the penny dropped. "Oh, I see what you mean." Crouching down again I looked down the length of the arrow as suggested by the carved eye and saw only the willow; but sure enough, there was something slightly different about the spot. The haze behind shimmering in the building heat seemed to hold some secret, a darker bit of background held protectively in a humid grasp. "Yes, I think there is something, but it's too hazy to see anything. We will have to wait till it clears."

"How intriguing," said Penny as she leant back onto on the bed. "Another thing to look forward to." She sighed as she plumped up her pillows. As if in warning, there was a long deep thunderous rumble. The air might be clearing sooner than we thought. "The marks sound a bit like those on the Shepherd's crooks," Penny commented and rolled over to find a more comfortable position.

The Flood

The Shepherd and I were sitting in the hall when the rain suddenly began. In fact, hail at first. There was an almighty flash and bang as lightning struck really close. I gasped and we both could hardly see anything for a few moments. The sky darkened to a deep purple grey and then the hail came. Great marble sized lumps of hard ice, pelted down as if out of a shotgun. The hail was so hard we were deafened by it as it rattled on everything outside. I had never seen such an onslaught. Another crash of thunder and a zig-zag of bright white burnt itself into our retinas. It was really very frightening. I rushed upstairs to Penny; she had pulled a pillow over her head, so I tucked her in and closed the shutters and fastened them securely. I returned to the Shepherd in the hall.

Two great banks of dark grey brown cloud met and like two angry bulls that circled each other, charged in, heads clashed like thunder, horns struck together and flashed in the turmoil, snorting and pushing against each other, twisting into swirls of grey. Hard hooves spat up clouds of brown dust against the surrounding blue sky. It was a dramatic storm worthy of any ancient God, which rumbled on all around us, echoing like mortar fire. At one point the air stood still and the hail stopped. We thought it was all over and would clear, but instead there was a sudden chill wind and then the rains came and by God did it lash down! Within seconds the ground, dry from weeks of sun, was awash with rivers of dust-laden water. The storm hissed and spat through the windows at us like a mass of furious cats.

I battled with the hall shutters and discovered for the first time that the back of them were, like the ones in our room above, painted with romantic images. On a background of a multitude of receding green hills paling into the distance, was a great oak tree, golden wavy edged leaves strewn on the ground. Every possible forest creature had been squeezed onto the oak canvas as if hiding from the tempest. A hedgehog lay within the leaves, jays, tree creepers and owls in the brown boughs, deer, a badger, weasels and many other creatures in every nook and cranny. It was worn but stunningly beautiful. On the other side of the shutters the world was currently an unpleasant place to be.

By the evening Penny was strong enough to come down to eat in the hall. We sat in our usual places careful not to touch the other chairs still pushed out from the table. They were ancient chairs, dark oak with a deep reddish patina. Each was slightly different with varying supports beneath the seats and high, slightly dished, backs with finials and a top horizontal bar neatly carved into a variety of shapes. The chairs were clearly a set, but each subtly different, as if to reflect the character of their regular occupants. They seemed to be frozen somehow, caught in a moment of drama, unwilling to be moved back in order against the table. They stood fast, not happy to cooperate until the unresolved was resolved. We ate well that night, comfort food for a stormy night, bolstering us against the chill seeping in around our legs.

Casey's Obsession

Once Casey had latched onto the lucrative potential of wind subsidies he became obsessed. He looked at hundreds of websites and salesmen's brochures. He took Jenny away on a field trip to visit three separate examples of wind power. The first was a single turbine 50 metres high next to a plastics factory where the energy produced was managing to offset a third of the electricity used. The manager explained that the turbine couldn't be connected directly to their facilities due to the intermittent nature of the wind. When asked a bit more carefully he admitted he was not convinced it was such a brilliant investment as he hoped. The maintenance costs were extremely high and they had had a broken blade and worn rotor bearings already. All this had resulted in the overall cost going up, even taking the subsidies into account.

The second was a farm site with three 100 metre high turbines. The posh farmer took them along a dusty track in his new Range Rover and explained that the peasants had revolted at his proposal because they didn't want to see or hear the turbines. When they climbed out and stood next to the giant machines Casey's first reaction was to cower from the huge blades slashing through the air above his head. Aware of the pathetic reaction he then became emboldened and walked up to the tower and placing his hand on the vibrating steel announced, "What elegant structures." Then added, "And they're not really that noisy." He hadn't seen Jenny holding her hands over her ears. The farmer said, "They will get used to them eventually. They whinged about the loss of property value and damaged views, but when the application went to appeal the reporter said they had enough garden screening to alleviate the problem." They walked on to the next machine. Neither Casey nor the farmer had noticed that Jenny had retreated to the car. At the next turbine Casey kicked at a feathery corpse on the ground. "Do you get much of a problem with that?" he asked. The farmer looked slightly embarrassed and wishing he had made a site visit earlier, replied, "A bit, but apparently it won't significantly affect the national population, so it's not an issue." He stooped down and picked up the mangled Barn Owl, walked to some nearby thorns and flung the body of the bird as far under as he could. Casey saw a growing heap rotting within the spiky bush.

Jenny sat in the car waiting for them to return. She had felt ill as soon as she had got out of the car. The whumping, droning and slashing had been enough. She decided she didn't really like turbines.

The third place they visited was a full blown wind farm with twenty-two 125-metre 2-megawatt monstrosities. They were spaced out across a heather-covered hillside dwarfing the nearby trees and village. They noticed a fading sign in one of the village gardens that read 'Stop Highmoor Wind Farm'. It was a sad sight and the profusion of estate agent's 'for sale' signs told a story. This wind farm was more like what Casey had in mind. Mega bucks and he would find a way to get his five percent. Four of the turbines were not turning at all so he asked why. The company man replied, "The National Grid asked us to switch them off as they can't cope with the additional electricity. But don't worry, we actually make more money in constraint payments than we would had they been actually turning." Casey had to ask the site manager to repeat that as he thought he had heard wrong. "No, I'm serious, you can't lose once they are up. It's the getting through planning that's tricky with endless surveys and protesting locals. They are wasting their time though as once somebody decides to apply for a renewable energy project they almost always get the go ahead."

Jenny who had refused to get out of the car asked Casey if they could look at one of the houses for sale in the village. Initially he said no, but after a few hundred yards he thought that it might actually be an interesting exercise, so they stopped at a rather nice Victorian villa with fine turbine views and both walked up to the front door. A pleasant housewife-type answered the door and after saying "Please excuse the mess" about a dozen times allowed them in. The house was just immaculate, gardens mature and well laid out, but the noise from the turbines was grim. "Is it normal to hear them that clearly?" asked Jenny. The lady tried to evade the question but then had to admit you could. She burst into tears and explained that they had been trying to sell and move away since the wind turbines went up, but nobody would buy for obvious reasons. They had been close friends of the landowner but now they wouldn't speak to each other. The village was divided and nobody was happy despite the £20,000 bribe the community received from the power company each year. The parish councillors had argued endlessly about what to do with the money and resentment and anger built further, damaging the social fabric. In truth the village had been a more wholesome and enjoyable place to live before the wind farm proposal. Now they were all stuck together, unable to sell their over-mortgaged properties, stewing in their petty differences that were all brought to the surface in the ensuing debates and campaigning. Casey listened to the whine from the lady, then the constant whine of the turbines and had to admit there was an eerie discomfort about them, both of them. Jenny chatted to the lady trying to console her. They went inside to make tea leaving Casey sitting on a garden chair staring at the whirling blades. He would not want them so close to his home if he lived there. But then he remembered that he didn't like the countryside and thought the woman was just being pathetic. All she needed to do was plant some Cyprus hedging across the end of the garden and the problem was solved. Jenny and the lady returned with tea and Casey suggested, "What if you put a panel fence and some hedging up, surely that would help?"

The lady started sobbing again. "We came here to get away from noise and hassle and industry. This was our dream house, nice village, good people, glorious setting. I really don't think the Government realise what they are doing to people. Either that or they don't give a toss about a few damaged individuals. For the greater good and all that! We have been miserable ever since we first heard about the proposal, spent a fortune trying to protect the countryside and we just get kicked in the teeth. Nobody ever seems to care other than those who are going to be directly affected by the turbines. It's not right that these things are allowed to happen especially when they aren't even efficient or good value for money."

Casey listened carefully, stood up and announced, "We have to go." He jerked his head at Jenny and marched off. Jenny was shocked and tried to comfort the poor lady. "Come on Jenny, I've heard enough, let's get out of here." Jenny obeyed but was fuming. She patted the poor lady on the shoulder, apologised and left. In the car she folded her arms tightly and said, "You're a cruel sod, Casey"—and pouted all the way home. Casey just thought 'Stupid bloody women' and returned to thinking about what he was going to do with the large amounts of money he was going to get from what he called his Cheviot Mountain project.

Stacking Logs

The next day it was still raining. And the next. It rained on and off for four days. Penny stayed inside mostly cooking and reading. I helped the Shepherd with his sheep. Billy Tolk would come down into the valley after the rains to buy those to go. I helped with firewood and was shown the second vault and was impressed by the volume of dry logs stored. The vault was around thirty feet long by twenty wide with logs stacked at intervals along both sides. Light came through a high narrow slit window and the heap of un-stacked firewood beneath it showed how he delivered the logs. He told me that he simply slotted them through the window and they tumbled down the long steep sill onto the floor below. At times of inclement weather he would devote some time to stacking. This increased the amount he could get in. The logs had to be really dry before being stored as there wasn't a lot of air flow. The Shepherd explained that he stacked them in his coppice woods for a couple of seasons before bringing them here or selling them. I helped carry a dozen baskets up to the hall where they were stacked either side of the large stone fireplace.

Penny declared she was better so came down to the vaults and asked to be shown how to stack the firewood. The Shepherd said the way he liked to do it was to separate off the different species as they burnt in different ways and were needed for different purposes. He showed us the types in the unsorted heap beneath the slit window. Ash with its smooth grey bark, bright white timber and fresh smell. We each picked up a log and sniffed. Penny found it easier than I did. Oak was heavier, pale to dark brown, had radial markings and smelt sharper. Elm with its distinctive brown grain, Hornbeam dense and covered in steely grey bark. The Shepherd selected a point along a wall for a new stack and demonstrated the best ways to proceed so it would stay up, allow air flow and yet cram enough in to make the best use of space. I selected elm and began to build what I thought was an excellent stack rising slowly towards the curved vault above. Penny seemed very quick with her chosen Ash and the Shepherd worked on the Hornbeam. We got pretty good at sniffing and looking at the logs to select the right species though I think a few strays got into my stack. The stacking proceeded with great enthusiasm till we had each raised our heaps a foot or so off the floor. Feeling the need of sustenance we stood back to admire our work. Penny looked at my effort and laughed. I had to admit it was a bit higgledy-piggledy but it was at least up. But as we all looked on there was slight movement and suddenly a corner gave way and half of my stack flowed across the floor. This was met with much hilarity. "Well, I'm just a beginner, I'm still in training," I said indignantly. Penny hopped up onto her stack and stood looking down on us—logs moved a little but held. "Well how about this?" she declared in her cheekiest voice, chin turned up in mock pride. Her ash logs were beautifully flush at the front edge, cross stacked at the corners with neat small logs filling the gaps between the larger ones. "Humph!" is all I could manage and Penny put a hand on each of our shoulders and jumped down. Clearly her ankle was better. "I'll go and make some lunch," she said and wriggled her hips provocatively as she disappeared from view.

I Fall Ill and Penny listens to the Shepherd's Tale

By the time the rain stopped Penny was better, but I was sick. The chill and constant damp brought on a nasty cold that laid me low. My nose ran, my head thumped and I developed a nasty cough. I felt terrible. Penny and the Shepherd ensconced me in a deep high armchair that magically appeared beside the hall fire. The fire was lit and the wood heaps I had stacked so neatly on either side of the fireplace started to diminish.

It was Penny's turn to help the Shepherd. They met Billy Tolk and between them and Tolk's dogs herded the sheep some five miles over the old drove road down into Tolk's first enclosed field. Penny thought fifteen pounds per animal a bit mean, but the Shepherd took the wad of notes and carefully put it in a pocket inside his waistcoat. It was more than he needed.

She also helped in the vegetable patch digging and hoeing. She lifted potatoes and took the filled hessian sacks into a corner of the workshop vault for winter storage. The Shepherd opened up to Penny more than me and told her a little about his long lost wife and daughter. He described his wife as a golden star who he had met quite accidently by giving her a lift on the back of a cart laden with sacks of seed barley he had purchased from a merchant in Kelso. She needed a lift to the first village on his route to visit her uncle who was a doctor there. They had only spoken briefly and he didn't expect to see her again, though secretly wished he would as she was a charming and pretty girl. On his way to town a week later there she was in the doctor's front garden pruning roses, or at least pretending to, as he got the impression she had been waiting for him. She smiled and waved and asked if she could catch a lift again. This happened on three occasions but on the last they arrived back just as the good village doctor returned from his work. There were ugly looks and stern words. He never saw her again that summer and when he plucked up enough courage to knock and ask some months later, he was quite clearly told that Mary had returned home to Perthshire. Feeling hurt and disappointed he spent a lonely autumn dreaming of her and walked in the hills thinking of her, sat next to brown burns skimming stones thinking of her. His father at the Tower picked up on his mood and accurately deduced a girl was at the bottom of it. For a seventeen-year-old boy it was difficult to talk about such things, but his father was a warm gentle man who made everybody feel at ease.

The next time the Shepherd saw Mary was when Scott the Steward first fell ill with pneumonia two years later. She was training to be a nurse and had come out with the local doctor to gain some experience. His father had engineered a couple of hours for them to get together and they had an unforgettable walk up onto one of the hill forts and Mary described the hills as surely heaven itself. They had fallen deeply in love and returned to Ashburn big eyed and it was difficult for them to part. That year war had come and he heard Mary was in France tending the wounded. He was in a reserved occupation and was obliged to stay on the land. He got twelve letters during that awful time and sent dozens. At the war end she finally wrote again explaining that she was back in Kelso but had been injured and was concerned as to his reaction. He was working the home farm at the time and sent a message back immediately and with the good doctor as chaperone had met on the cobbles beneath the town hall clock. Mary was beautiful, just as he remembered with golden curls dancing down her back. She was facing the doctor as he approached and when he called her name did not immediately turn. It wasn't until he was within reach that she did. The same golden girl was there, the lovely smile, great big blue eyes and hair framing her high cheek bones, slim and elegant. But she looked worried, they both did. The doctor explained that the war had taken its toll and brushing the hair to the side of her face exposed a nasty red scar stretching from her hairline down her forehead, across her left eyebrow, where it expanded into a mass of scar tissue across her temple and ear which was much reduced with a ragged edge. It was a nasty wound caused by shrapnel. The doctor explained that it would settle to less noticeable white scarring and that her hearing was impaired on that side. But to the Shepherd it was the same Mary and he loved her just as much. He had given her a huge hug and she became overwhelmed with relief and her eyes came to life full of love and gratitude. They had courted for a number of months and married at Oxnam Kirk the following May, the brilliant white of the Kirk dazzling in the fresh sun. His ancestor's gravestones proudly looked on from either side as he crunched up the gravel path.

Penny had listened quietly to the Shepherd's story and did not dare interrupt his flow for fear of stopping him. It was fascinating and he seemed intent on telling somebody and clearly would stop when he had said enough. He looked at Penny with his huge brown eyes and she could see great passion and sorrow all tangled up together and understood why he gave so much to the world through his planting. Every shoot and leaf reaching up to the sun's warmth was an expression of the Shepherd's love and grief; its power drove him on, sowing each seed with deliberate care, giving the world another chance, the opportunity to be reborn, to relive and share his joy. A verdant explosion of his depth of feeling that carpeted the barren earth with life and new hope. The Shepherd sought no recognition for what he did. He simply knew what was right and how to bring the world back into balance.

The Ghost

Now, I must make it absolutely clear that I do not believe in ghosts or any other such nonsense. However, while Penny and the Shepherd were out for the day I suddenly felt better. My head had cleared and the cough stopped. I hauled myself out of the armchair, stretched and went upstairs to refresh myself. I ate some bread and cheese left out for me, had a deep drink of water and decided to go exploring.

I took my allocated planting crook and marched off in a direction I had not been before, drawn in that direction by some strange feeling that I was going to discover something really special again. And I did. I walked along a path that ran parallel to the steep adjacent hill. The route undulated through small dips with downy birch and ridges with silver birch. It was very attractive and the trees looked amazing against the bright blue sky. Insects buzzed and flitted as if accelerated by the heat. I stopped after about a mile or so next to a tumbling burn that came steeply down between cliffs and scree. There was a large moss-covered boulder so I sat a while listening to the gurgling water and birds twittering in the delicate branches above. It occurred to me that this was the first time I had been out alone. While I was sitting there, eyes half closed, enjoying the sun's warmth and woodland noises, I began to feel really sleepy and was just thinking that perhaps I should not have come out, when I heard a very faint noise, a delicate pretty rhythm, which sounded like a child's voice. It vanished but I had heard enough to suddenly become alert and, thinking that it came from further up the burn, began to climb and clamber over the large rocks, using the crook to help me up the steepest parts. Each time I was just beginning to convince myself it had only been my imagination, I heard it again and each time I was more certain it was a child singing. After a difficult ascent the ground levelled out and before me lay a little ravine, the burn flowing enthusiastically between rocks in a series of drops tinkling merrily as it did. The grass was scattered with unusual flowers that grew to knee height; they had few leaves but tall delicate cone-like spikes of violet flowers, giving the ground a beautiful sheen of colour, while the scent was subtle but alluring. The little valley was particularly sheltered and I thought the conditions must be just right for this plant to flourish, as I had not seen it elsewhere. The odd thing about this place was the absence of young trees; there was only one old twisted bird cherry growing out of the top of a cliff between the waterfalls, with its twigs and leaves defiantly held just far enough out over the drop, to be free of the nibbling of goats and sheep.

The waterfalls were very musical in as much as the multitude of little drops, pools and rocks played with the flow of sparkling water in an ever changing composition. It could almost be the sound of singing amplified by the crescent of cliffs and rocks surrounding the old cherry tree beneath which the water flowed. Feeling quite exhausted from the steep climb and still weak from the bug I was recovering from, I decided to lie in the sunshine and have a rest before heading back down.

Now this is the tricky bit. I fell asleep in the warm sun with my head on my rucksack. I know that much. I was really quite exhausted and the earth seemed to hold me, a million fine tendrils creeping up through the grass and flowers, massaging my tired back, the warm air caressing my skin; it was so comfortable I wriggled down into the turf to enhance the feeling. The scents of the unusual flowers seem to intoxicate me and my eyelids gradually closed in blissful peace.

I was woken by Penny in the Golden Tower the following morning.

Penny was really pleased that I was waking up and gave me lots of hugs and kisses. She said she had been really worried about me. It took about ten minutes for me to come to completely and even then I was struggling to remember anything from the previous day. Penny fetched me a cup of tea and some toast as I was truly famished. While I was eating she explained that the Shepherd and she were coming in from the north and saw me staggering around in the Tower's cobbled yard and then quite simply I collapsed in an unconscious heap near the door. My clothes were wet, torn and muddy and the planting tip of the crook had broken off. They hauled me up to bed where Penny stripped me and tended to my cuts and bruises. I told her I had no recollection of my return to the

Tower but did remember a lot but could not separate off what might be real or a dream. I told her that I had seen a ghost or at least dreamed about one. Penny asked if she could get the Shepherd as he should know what happened and I nodded. She scampered off all excited and eager to hear about the ghost.

I was not entirely sure that either of them would react well to what I had to relate. I lay there staring up at the stone face looking down from the vault above. "What would you do?" I whispered. The face just stared back without the slightest hint of an answer. Outside the wind had picked up and it felt as if the rain was going to start again.

Some thirty minutes later the Shepherd and Penny returned. Penny sat beside me on the blankets and the Shepherd on the large studded chest at the end of the bed. I told them everything up to the point where I settled down for a sleep by the waterfall. When asked, the Shepherd could not pinpoint where I had been. I had awoken from my nap to the sound of the child singing again. This time it was not the water but was without doubt a child, a young girl whose melody and words were clear and close. Not daring to move I pretended to be still asleep and kept my eyes closed so as not to disturb her. She sang of the river describing its power and beauty, its clarity and taste, the brown trout and flowers on its surface, pretty white and yellow shifting in the flow. She sang of the marigolds tumbling over the banks and the skylark above. She sounded close so I just had to open my eyes. I sat up and though I could not see her I could tell she was sitting beneath the ancient bird cherry. Her song continued but neatly included "Come see, man who has awoken, come and see me beneath this flowering tree"—so I stood and walked cautiously forward and there she was sitting beneath the shade of the broad boughs. She was a young girl, blue eyes and curly blonde hair around her sweet face. She smiled up at me, eyes narrowing in friendship; I couldn't help

91

but smile back. She was holding a bunch of the unusual violet flowers and beside her lay a planting crook identical to the Shepherd's one and a small hessian bag with a white drawstring, inside which I could see hazel nuts. She was wearing a white dress with a lacy pattern at the neck and hem; she had bare feet and earth between her toes and under her fingernails. She had been planting. She stood up using her crook as a prop; behind her the water poured down in a neat narrow waterfall where it plunged into a turbulent pool, held in place by the grey broken rocks of the cliffs, then became another waterfall plunging down another ten foot. Heather and bilberry clung to every available scrap of soil within the rocks.

"Let me show you something," she said leading me across to a small deeply divided cliff. She speared her crook in the ground at the bottom of the rock leaving it standing and climbed from ledge to ledge, her fine fingers clinging to the rock face. I followed, acutely aware of the precipitous nature of the climb. She came to a deep dark hole in the rock face and she pointed to something within. Peering over her shoulder I could see a tiny oak sapling only four inches high.

"I planted that acorn last year," she said looking up at me, clearly very pleased with herself. Not knowing quite how to respond I smiled at her and said that it was a good spot to choose. She led the way down, was clearly nimble, obviously used to the outdoors life, and she sat down on a broad ledge, patted the stone and I sat down next to her. She pointed downstream and I noticed for the first time that there was a clear view across the wider valley; somehow it didn't look familiar and I realised it was bald, no trees and there were a lot of white sheep. For a moment I thought we were somehow seeing over into the next valley, but knew that could not be the case as the Shepherd's valleys were nearly all enclosed by high ridges.

"What we have begun is so important. We can show the world a better way. There is no need to strip the land bare." She spoke softly, as if reminding me of something we had already agreed on.

I looked across the landscape confused by what I saw and somehow felt at that point that it was a dream, what with this strange girl, the wrong landscape and the oddest feeling that my brain wasn't quite functioning as it should. But when I pinched myself I found it still hurt.

The girl reached the grass, pulled her crook from the ground and picking up the tune again, skipped away along a sheep path following the water in an upstream direction.

"Hey," I shouted after her. "Who are you and where are you going?"

She did not pause to respond and soon we were leaving the waterfalls and violet flowers behind. The land opened up into a broad expanse of undulating bracken and the girl kept appearing and disappearing in the high foliage. I stumbled along following the wisps of her song until I found her standing very still holding the crook upright in front of her. She was staring intently at or through the scrolled iron.

"The crook has many uses, you know," she said, moving her head slightly from side to side as if trying to line up some distant object.

"Who *are* you?" I asked again.

She simply laughed and suddenly pointed to something moving on a hillside.

"A deer!" she exclaimed. "Watch how it moves."

The deer seemed to be following a sheep track diagonally down the heather-clad hill. It then did something odd—it walked in a neat circle, then simply stopped and stared back at us across the valley. It looked like a well-practiced manoeuvre, the purpose of which was unfathomable.

The nameless girl was off again.

"Hurry up, old man, don't dawdle," came echoing back to me.

Admittedly I did feel tired, but 'old' was cheeky. I looked at the back of my hands as I waded through the bracken and thought that perhaps to a young girl they probably looked ancient. But I couldn't remember noticing the wrinkles or grey hairs before. Frowning I puffed on behind her. She came to the heather and disappeared over the ridge ahead. When I caught up with her she was standing, arms angled out by her sides, a brisk cold wind making her white dress flap wildly about her, the crook discarded at her feet. She was crying, tears pouring down her face. In front of her was a scene of devastation. I knew this place—it was the high loch. To me I hadn't walked far enough to find it, or high enough. I had imagined that this place by now, five years since I helped broadcast willow and alder seed and use the planting crook to plant hazelnuts, followed by the dedication of the Shepherd, would have been flourishing with fresh new woodland and indeed it clearly had been as the large noisy bright yellow machines were making short work of scraping them away.

We were standing at the lowest part of the loch looking over the grey chopping waves next to the point where the water flowed out into the burn. To one side there were willows of several different kinds growing tall and green, bending gracefully in the wind. Directly across the water a huge bulldozer snorting black smoke out of its exhaust pipe was going back and forward flattening young trees and shoving them onto a smouldering heap. Bitter smoke stung my eyes, for part of the growing stack had spilled into the water and grey ash and dark brown peat was staining the surface. Behind the bulldozer the long angled arm of a large excavator was digging a deep hole in the peat, a mound of ancient accumulation piled darkly nearby. Beyond that an earlier pit full of steel mesh was being filled with concrete, a queue of white cement trucks waiting their turn on broad dusty tracks cut through the moorland; framing them and receding into the distance, giant turbines loomed dwarfing the yellow machines busy below, making it look like children playing with dinky toys. A vast red crane was hoisting up a giant steel column onto a section already bolted to the concrete. Men in white hard hats and yellow high visibility jackets crawled around like ants below.

I was so shocked and horrified by what I saw—the sheer scale of devastation formed a boiling mass of anger and despair within me. I grew very cold and felt as if I was growing taller and wider as I watched the evil scene before me. Never had I seen such wrongdoing in the name of saving the planet! This was so blatantly evil and misguided it caused my head to throb like a million diesel engines, more powerful than any greed-driven plan. I stood there like a mighty oak, branches reaching taller than any turbine, trunk broader than a ship, buttresses like steel leading to roots that spread and penetrated the soil, ground and earth, embedded in reality, sense and a passion to do the right thing, the welling emotion forming within me like a lion ready to roar. As the power built within me I felt the small hand of a young girl grasp mine. I held tight, then unexpectedly my other hand was also held, and glancing I saw a boy, not dissimilar to the peculiar girl, who smiled encouragingly; and as I looked forward again I caught in the corner of my eyes other people, a mass of them all in turn firmly joining hands behind and beside me. I was not alone, far from it, for hundreds were there with me, thousands, tens of thousands, millions, all joining together across the land, driven by the same desire to stop this unnecessary devastation. This was not the way to save the planet, destroying the very thing they claimed to be trying to protect; this was not remotely

Green, this was Greed, repeating the same mistakes as before just in a different guise, ripping the trees from the ground, the lungs of the planet and replacing them with inefficient, offensive ugly intrusive industrial monsters, like leeches sucking every last bit of available blood from the people to pay for them, driving them into poverty with the ever-present threat of cutting off their source of heat or ability to function as part of a productive society. This was a crime so heinous, cruel and misguided that it had to come to an end.

I could feel the overwhelming mass of people behind me, a collective force calling for justice, sense and a genuine passion to protect the earth, its people, plants and animals. Standing there faced with the mess before us and the need to rethink, our lungs filled, our hearts beat faster and with an enormous bellow we all shouted...

"STOP!"

The sound was like a canon going off, a Mons Meg fuelled by the souls of many. The men working across the water stopped, took of their hats, some scratching their heads; others clambered out of their machines and stared over the grey waves to where we were standing, a hoard of hearts standing firm. Then behind them something odd began to happen. The furthest turbine with its white blades relentlessly slashing at the landscape and swiping at the circling seagulls started to pixelate. Pieces of blade started to break off like a spiralling swirl of confetti whipping away into the breeze until the blades had gone; then the nacelle and tower suddenly collapsed like a Lego construction hit by an errant child, pieces spilling across the ground and soaking into the dark exposed peat. The little men dropped their hats, discarded their high vis jackets and ran for their lives as the next, then the next turbine began to do the same. Before the men had reached the horizon they had become translucent, mere wisps of their corporate selves, fading until they vanished. Their machines slowly sank into the ground turning stiff and rusty as they did. A warm green skin crept over the land, flowing over toppled machinery, site huts and vehicles; it seemed to stretch and squeeze the foreign bodies into its flesh below to be broken down by the earth's immune system.

I watched the trees re-grow and became aware that I was alone, a simple small insignificant human staring across a loch twinkling blue in bright sunlight. My hands were old. I felt old and ached in every joint. Grey hair whipped around my face and across my balding head. The small hand reappeared in mine and then like the others I became translucent and was fading. The girl tugged at me. "It's time to go," she said.

I felt my legs stumbling along; then I tripped, falling on hard cobbles...

"Wow," said Penny, "that's one hell of dream."

We both turned to look at the Shepherd. He was staring out of the window, focusing on nothing. His lovely brown eyes were full of sadness, a line of moisture hanging along the bottom lids. After a long moment, in a very unaccustomed way, he turned and looked me straight in the eye as if reading my soul and equally rarely, asked a direct question.

"Did the girl wear anything around her neck?"

I struggled for a moment trying to recap the images of the girl in my head. Frowning briefly I suddenly pictured again the girl as I first saw her beneath the bird cherry. I was standing some feet higher than her and had looked at the dress she was wearing with interest, as it looked so old fashioned. The lace neck was high but I could remember something glowing at her neck suspended on a fine gold chain. It was a tear shaped stone that glowed in the light, warm and orange.

97

"She was wearing a pendant, a gold chain with an orange stone."

There was a long pause and the Shepherd slumped back down on the chest. He reached into his shirt, undid the chain and held out his large brown hand. Within it lay the very same pendant.

"Oh my God," I said wide eyed.

"That was more than just a dream," was all he said.

Then he suddenly looked much older, a tired wizened old man. There was a pause; then his shoulders sagged and he started to sob, great big heart-rendering sobs, salty tears tracing the creases down his face and dripping down onto the curved top of the chest where they puddled against the iron studs.

Martin Recruits a Gamekeeper

It didn't take long to find a dubious gamekeeper in need of some extra cash. They met in a pub and Martin described briefly that a bit of discrete conservation management was required and was worth quite a bit to anyone prepared to help. Dougie the gamekeeper introduced himself as 'Jed'. Martin called himself 'Kevin' and a pact was made. They agreed to meet accordingly and 'Kevin' left 'Jed' a handful of ten-pound notes to help keep him focused. Martin could tell the gamekeeper had given a false name but it didn't matter, the guy was dodgy enough to get the job done without drawing too much attention to himself.

Journey to the High Loch and towards our Future

After my strange dream I thought it was essential to show Penny the high loch and after a few days helping the Shepherd in his home valley, we decided to make the climb and see how my planting of several years earlier was doing. We packed our rucksacks early and headed off into a glorious warm morning. We were in no hurry so ambled up the Bleakhope track taking frequent detours to explore the smaller paths, rocky knolls, the remains of old farmsteads and ancient cultivation terraces. The Shepherd had been very careful not to plant where he found archaeological remains or other evidence of man's travails on the land. He had developed a great respect for and understanding of the toil of his forbears, and the ancient artefacts and features in his patch of hills. He selected species and locations to highlight and focus on these features, enhancing their setting and hinting at how the earlier landscape may have appeared as early farmers opened up the woodland to cultivate their crops.

We came across a wonderful plateau with low ridges around the outside edge and circular scoops within its levelled surface. The outlook was amazing and indeed we had looked across to this site on an earlier day out and wanted to have a closer look. You got the impression that the former inhabitants had selected the place to be able to oversee the whole valley and high hills around. It lay about half way up the Bleakhope valley on a natural spur that thrust out into the landscape, with high defensive crags behind and below to the north, but with a wide scoop of gentle ground to the south where they had formed cultivated terraces to provide the food they required.

Penny stood looking over this scene, closed her eyes and imagined the people from the past. "You can almost hear the bustle of daily life," she said, pretty eyelids kissed by the warm gentle breeze. She looked truly beautiful standing there with the golden sun on her high cheekbones and dark silky hair waving softly, as if tousled by passing ghosts. From where we stood you could see how the God-Shepherd had applied his planting, like an artist's brush to a freshly primed canvas and in bursts of colour and texture created a wonderful world, beautiful in so many ways. I held Penny's hand to share the moment and we gazed over the Shepherd's work. "This is so perfect I wish I could do the same," I remarked. Penny nodded, and after a few moments replied, "I think you will. I really do. This place has really captured us and it will be difficult to leave."

As it was around midday we decided to eat, so selected a spot in dappled shade beneath tall birch and rowan trees along one side of the old homestead. I unpacked a rug and laid out our picnic, including the bottle of ancient red wine that the Shepherd had insisted we take. He had said it was from his father's era and was endowed with magical qualities befitting a scene from Shakespeare's 'Midsummer Night's Dream'. I had seen him wink at Penny. They were often naughty and I felt they were quietly planning something together for some unknown and mischievous purpose. We lay there enjoying the idyllic setting and took our time eating our lunch and trying the vintage Claret. It was perfect, the food simple and nourishing and the day, dreamlike. Penny lay back in her primrose dress. The sun and fluttering leaves above conspired to make her even more beautiful than ever. The warm light made her glow and the translucence of her dress showed the fine outline of her legs. She was watching me through half closed eyes. "And what are you looking at, young man?" she teased. I moved closer and bent forward to kiss her perfect lips and as I did she grasped me and with one of her most disarming smiles said, "Come here, you gorgeous man."

100

We left the plateau a little later, slightly ruffled around the edges and continued up through the Shepherd's Eden amongst changing woodland and steep scree-covered slopes. The air was kind and it was like a walk in some endless garden. There were different flowers and fascinating rocks and butterflies and bugs around every corner. Penny couldn't get enough of it and we stopped on many occasions so she could do a quick sketch to capture a particularly attractive vista, beetle, or such like.

After several hours we made the final scramble up to the high loch past a series of tumbling waterfalls and gurgling pools. Green ferns adorned the banks fresh and bright. Penny and I stood on the shore looking across the sparkling waters and I have to admit the trees had done well. Like my dream, the birch and alders were some fifteen feet or more high. Along the leeward bank young willows erupted with their customary vigour and I described to Penny how we had teased out great handfuls of fluffy seed and threw it up into the whistling wind. It had obviously worked. We set off to walk around the loch and I showed Penny all the interesting things I had noticed before, like the deep peat hags with dark pools within, the remnants of ancient trees preserved, white and pitiful. I didn't mention the gold coins. The hazel and even some oak were coming away steadily showing that the valley had promise to become yet another success for the Shepherd. I could see how he had carried on planting along the meandering burns that came across the wide scoop in the hill before the peripheral ridge, where the full force of the prevailing wind would make tree growth difficult.

What we both noticed was that the place had been visited recently. There were bits of peat cores lying around, a lot of footprints, a discarded empty bottle of wine and a large patch of mysteriously flattened grass we couldn't explain. I suggested that perhaps it was a wildlife survey team and didn't think a great deal more about it at the time.

Penny was desperate to do some drawings but the sun was too low in the sky so we reluctantly left and headed back down to the Golden Tower, where the Shepherd had created the most delicious lamb casserole. "All home grown," he said. It was exactly what we needed and we all slept long and well that night.

The Gamekeeper

Martin took Jed, the hairy scary gamekeeper with an assumed name, up a forestry track as near to the high loch as they could get, which was about three miles downhill from the ridge bounding the estate. Jed said he had been up there shooting geese a number of years ago but found it too windy and cold and difficult to walk to. He didn't know who it belonged to so hadn't known who to ask permission from, but took the risk anyways. Martin said it belonged to his great uncle and he had a number of things to do to improve its value for shooting events, one of which was to eliminate certain competing species. Jed seemed to accept that and with Martin's promise of further work and maybe the opportunity to join a shooting party, expressed his enthusiasm. When they reached the loch Jed was surprised just how fresh and green it was. He couldn't recall there being any other vegetation than rough grass and heather. They found a spot to sit and Jed lit up a cigarette and offered Martin one. He declined and discussed the list he had copied out from Casey's text. There were three species of bird, Curlew, Golden Plover and Osprey. Jed flinched a bit at the mention of the latter.

"Do you have an issue with that, Jed?" Martin asked watching him carefully.

"Well, I wasn't expecting that." he said wide eyed.

"Ok, if that's a problem we can cancel now," Martin said crisply.

"It's just that they are... er... tricky to shoot," he said, regaining his composure.

"Okay, I understand, I will give you another three hundred per Osprey corpse."

"Deal," said Jed, hiding his anxiety. This guy was serious and was clearly loaded.

They went through the list and agreed on shotgun for the bats, glyphosphate for the wildflowers and rifle for badgers or any other unwanted critter. That should get the clear up started. They agreed to meet at the Horse and Plough at 8pm the following Friday for a progress meeting and a couple of pints. A few fresh twenty-pound notes were exchanged and Martin strode off towards Bleakhope. He had a tramp to track down.

The gamekeeper settled himself down in a peaty hollow overlooking the loch to see what birds were there. He was pretty keen on the bonus idea so would see if an Osprey appeared. He also knew that a big seagull would probably be enough to fool Martin and there were a few of them around. Shooting endangered species was a big gamble; the consequences of being caught were dire. Trying to fool Martin was also risky. He needed the cash, so made himself comfortable and decided to see what came by.

Two and a half hours later Jed woke up. He had dozed off and had so far done nowt. He sat up and gazed across the waves. In amongst the smaller seagulls a large bird swooped down low, talons at the ready. Fumbling for his rifle he slid around in the wet peat, managed to grasp the gun but was too late, the bird was gone. That was a huge bloody great female

Osprey worth three hundred squidlies. Frustrated he settled with his gun waiting to see if the bird would pass again. Twenty minutes later he saw it coming from the far shore gradually coming lower and closer. He got it in his scope and followed its movement. Finger on the trigger. Steady now. "Patience Dougie, patience," he murmured to himself. Slight pressure on the trigger. Just before the point of no return when the trigger cycle would suddenly be released, causing a steel pin to strike the rear of the bullet, igniting a contained explosion initiating a lightning quick piece of hot lead to scorch through the air and penetrate the innocent flesh of his feathery target, something bright caught his attention moving below right of his target. A human.

"Jesus, that was close!" he whispered to himself, slowly releasing the trigger and putting the safety catch on. He ducked down, invisible in his head to toe camouflage gear. He froze and watched carefully. A young couple had just appeared by the far shore. A girl in a silly yellow dress and a tall dark curly haired, rugged looking guy, carrying a small blue rucksack. Walkers. He waited for them to pass. But rather than striding by they idled around looking at the trees and pointing at the birds and stuff. They were not going to disappear so he beat a retreat before they got too close. Crawling through the tussock grass keeping his head down he managed to get over the high ridge where he could bed himself down in the heather. He watched them through the scope. The girl was kinda cute so he didn't mind them taking their time. Why they were spending so long he couldn't understand. "Patience Dougie, think of the cash."

Martin and the Tramp

Martin spotted the tramp in the distance through his binoculars. He ducked into the cover of the trees and slunk along the shadows, glad he hadn't been noticed. The tramp must be a couple of miles off anyway, by a stone barn near the river. However, the Shepherd was already aware of Martin. He had been setting up wood pigeons all the way down the track and King Tut, as the Shepherd called him, a particularly bold roebuck, had moved off the heather into the bracken and set up a woodcock. That in turn had caught the eye of a goshawk that was perched high in an ash tree near the Shepherd's wood shed. The whole valley was on alert. The Shepherd knew all this before Martin had got his binoculars to his eyes; he had lived here a good long while and didn't miss much even with his aged eyesight. Being wary of the occasional visitor the Shepherd lured Martin down towards the little steading and, being suspicious of his slinking in the shadows which is something a normal walker would not do, doubled up behind him to watch what he was up to. The Shepherd sat behind an ancient storm-damaged ash tree and looking through a gap in the tree roots quietly observed Martin poking about. He kept in close to the stone walls creeping around like some character in a Bond movie. After looking in and around the buildings he marched off down the track that led to the Tower, as if he were just a normal hiker. 'You don't fool me,' thought the Shepherd and followed him closely on a parallel sheep track some hundred yards up hill. Martin stopped to look at his map. He was obviously aiming for the Tower.

The Shepherd needed to get ahead so created a diversion. Pushing a large stone over a bit of scree the ensuing flow of noisy stones was enough to get Martin to clamber through the scrub to take a look. An old badger-faced goat bleated at him from further up the slope. Martin paused to get a photograph. Enough done, the Shepherd managed to cut around him and get along the twisty half mile to the Tower first. All he needed to do was lock the front door. He pulled closed the oak door and the iron yet, slipped on a large rusty padlock and vanished around the side of the Tower just as Martin arrived. The well-kept veggie patch and yard was a bit of a giveaway, but there was no evidence that anyone actually lived in the Tower. It was after all just a roofless ruin with a great big rusty padlock that looked like it hadn't been opened for fifty years.

Martin had a wander around the Tower, surprised at how much remained. He had seen the wood yard with the stacked firewood, tractor and equipment at the farmyard at the bottom of Bleakhope and concluded that the tramp was in fact an old woodcutter and just used the Tower's sheds and things for storage. But he still wanted to find the old man and walked back along the rough road in the direction he had come. At the farmyard there was still no sign of the woodcutter so he took the track that headed past and soon came to the Shepherd's stackyard where dozens of tee pee like stacks of coppice firewood poles were built to allow them to dry before being logged. It was like a deserted Indian camp. Still no woodcutter, so he followed the narrowing path beyond. The goat appeared and skipped along in front. "Hello friend," he said and wandered on behind.

The Shepherd followed for a few minutes as Martin headed off to Jake's hag. This was a long maze of marsh and peat hollows that gathered the water from a scoop in the hills. Once you went in there it was tricky to get out. The Shepherd headed back to the farmyard and carried on servicing his saw bench.

It was getting dark when Martin returned. The Shepherd watched him from behind his tractor. Martin had indeed had difficulties in the mire, for he was soaking and covered in mud. He was very grumpy and turned back up Bleakhope; he had one hell of a walk to get to the nearest inn.

The Shepherd's Brothers

Penny and I passed a very wet and miserable walker just before we got to the Bleakhope farmyard. We said "Hi" as we passed but only got a grunt and some grumble about a goat in response. The Shepherd met them at the buildings and they all walked together back to the Tower. Penny was bubbling with enthusiasm over the sheer volume of planting and the wonderful woodland. She had seen loads of wildlife including stag beetles, small copper butterflies and nuthatch, and tree creepers, and long tailed tits, and a massive dark green dragonfly, and, and, and... This made the Shepherd laugh and he nodded. He could see what his planting had done for the valley, hills and indeed wildlife. He had planted every seed or sapling hoping that he was giving something back. He had reaped the rewards from living there and wanted to leave the world a better place. Each time his planting crook broke the soil's surface and he dropped in a seed he planted that hope, giving it the chance to germinate and grow and this simple act made him happy and little did he know would do the same for many others too. He liked to think that everybody would have the chance to plant at least one tree in their lifetime and enjoy watching how it could, like hope itself, grow, flourish and in turn produce seed and multiply. He also felt that all landowners could do their bit too by planting up less productive bits of land or setting aside substantial areas to provide wood fuel or for wildlife and to enhance the landscape. There was nothing more rewarding than walking through a wood you had planted yourself listening to the birdsong, seeing the buzz of life in its myriad of forms, the tall straight, or the gnarled twisted trunks, but also knowing how productive it could be with careful and sensitive management providing timber, firewood, game, fruit and an amazing place for people to learn about the world around them.

Penny's enthusiasm and my deep admiration of his Herculean task gave him some positive feedback that confirmed his feelings about his dedication to, what to others seemed obsessive madness, a task that in no particular way benefitted him, or at least not in comparison to the volume of planting he had done. The amount of coppicing he did was minimal compared to the sheer potential within the woodlands as a whole.

They got to the Tower and the Shepherd explained why he had locked up and where he hung the key in the doghouse, should they ever need to do the same. I told him we had passed the walker and suggested that maybe he had something to do with the people who had been doing the peat coring up by the loch. The Shepherd listened carefully and thought things seemed quite busy in his neck of the woods all of a sudden. I said we would do some research once we were home in front of a PC.

Penny insisted she cooked that evening and the Shepherd and I sat at the carved oak table and I told him about my trips to the Bialwieza forests in Poland and described to him the wonderful variety and density of trees and wildlife and how, although much planted up with conifers like everywhere else, it did preserve some pristine forest. The Shepherd asked a lot of questions about the trees, species, management, wildlife and a number of ecological questions which I had great pleasure in answering with a degree of confidence, having studied for three months in those woods. The Shepherd mentioned that his oldest brother had been in Poland during the war and that gave me the courage and excuse to ask more about his family. I asked him what had happened to his other brothers. It was a sad and fascinating tale.

The Shepherd lit the candelabra and said nothing in response for a long moment, seemingly unsure whether to tell his story or not. But I think that probably after I had told him of my peculiar dream he felt he could trust me.

"Both my elder brothers disappeared without a trace," he began, his eyes becoming distant reflecting the flickering candle flames in their pupils, as though the memories and emotions within him were rekindling and fluttering in and out of his focus. I could sense this was going to be painful for him and hoped the flames would not flutter and die away within his soul.

"It was a frightening and disturbing time at the end of the war," he continued.

"I can imagine," I said encouragingly, eager for him to continue.

"None of us quite knew how things were going to settle down after the war. I had been tied to the land along with Angus. We worked like slaves with the guidance of father who had already semi-retired up here in the Tower and with the farm hands too old to join up, we kept things going. There were land girls too who provided most of the labour and entertainment. There was a strong community feeling and we all worked side by side as a team with a common goal. My two elder brothers William and Maurice would have been due to take over the management as partners of the home farm and the Cheviot lands when father was to retire fully. Angus and I were to be paid off and given a cottage to make our own way in the world. But all that was to change."

Penny came in from the kitchen and laid out cutlery, glasses and side plates. The Shepherd paused while she did this and he prepared the next part of the story. Penny kept looking at him until she caught his eye.

"I hope you're going to like what I've created," she asked. He gave her a big smile and patted her hand.

"You know I will," he said.

They had bonded so well those two that sometimes I felt a bit excluded. But he would not continue relating his memories until she was safely back in the kitchen. He was saving this story for me. Penny seldom told me what they talked about when I wasn't with them. He stared at a knot in the hard oak table and continued.

"Before the war both William and Maurice had established themselves as capable officers in the KOSB and of course they were instantly absorbed into the great war effort. They saw near constant action except for time out for recovering from a variety of wounds. William got badly mangled in barb wire resulting in multiple lacerations and a couple of years later, lost two fingers in a close encounter with a German's bayonet. Instinctively he had grasped the blade as it was plunged towards his belly; he had deflected the lethal weapon, shot the soldier at point blank range with his revolver but left two fingers trampled in the mud. That was the luck of war.

"Maurice got a fractured skull from a bullet penetrating his helmet. The bullet had stopped short of mortally wounding him but to be honest I didn't think he was quite right after that—he was moody and couldn't remember the fabulous times we used to have up here in the hills. To me that loss of shared experience made him seem half dead to me. By the time the war ended they were both physically and mentally wrecked. There were plenty around like that then—half of them didn't know what to do with themselves and the other half wouldn't have been able to do much work even if they wanted to. Frustration and nervousness dominated and squabbles between William and Maurice were commonplace. Angus and I were pretty scared of them. Maurice kept to his uniform most of the time, complete with medals. William settled into country tweed and poised to become the next Laird displacing us as managers, and we had no choice but to move over. We didn't really know what was going to become of us."

The Shepherd sat back in his chair when Penny returned with a tray of steaming bowls. "Pheasant and vegetable soup," she announced. It was really a stew and we ate quietly together. Deliciously gamey—Penny had made good use of readily available supplies. Again the Shepherd did not continue until Penny had departed.

The Shepherd drank some water, placed the glass back on to the table and staring into the heart of the remaining liquid let its gentle movement help him pick up the rhythm of the story again.

"It was around that time that May left the household to help out on the Bentrayne Estate in Argyll. She was seventeen and was to assist Lady Margaret to run the huge shooting lodge and estates in the absence of his Lordship who was still campaigning in the Far East somewhere. It was a brilliant opportunity, but our housekeeper, who had brought her up since the age of five after Mother's death, was heartbroken. May left with her numerous crates, chests and packages in a battered army transport wagon. Letters came regularly describing the adventures she was having. Lady Margaret was very sociable and when his Lordship returned it seemed like non-stop parties. It was at a highland ball that she met her future husband. Apologies, I digress." The Shepherd paused as he looked at me.

"Please carry on," I said, desperate to hear more. But Penny returned with her sketch book to show the Shepherd her work and we got absorbed in woodland matters again. Penny said she wanted to stay into the autumn to experience the colours and help harvest seed. I had to remind her that we were both meant to be pursuing serious career paths. When Penny departed to have a bath the story was picked up again.

"William did not take to estate management well. He had a brisk authoritarian military style that the men on the farm didn't take to at all and some left after a year or so and losing our key people meant that margins dropped, buildings fell into disrepair and there was an underlying discontent. It was a tough time anyway. In truth Angus did most of the day-to-day management and appeased most of the staff's issues. I on the other hand was happily distracted with family life and Heather was growing up fast. We spent more and more time up here with my father, the sheep and these amazing hills. I helped with the hill farming, Mary busied herself in the Tower and Heather became one with nature, outside at every opportunity. However, William had started to put pressure on us at the Hall because he suddenly decided he should benefit from living in the grand house. There were more and more of his officer friends who were marrying and breeding and he couldn't possibly house or entertain them in the Gatekeeper's house. We began to feel like caretakers and had to accommodate his friends and the Hall kitchens were busy providing for an increasing quantity of idle bachelors and raucous families. He was clearly heir apparent and began to come up here more often to have private discussions about succession with father. In a way we just wanted a decision one way or another so we could make appropriate plans. We accepted that a move was inevitable and had made enquiries as to renting a house in Kelso. Maurice slunk around in the background, having taken residence in the groom's flat to the rear of the Hall. He had odd friends and he was becoming more and more difficult with William. We all knew that the whole property, from arable to hill top was to be left to them. But they both wanted to live in the Hall and wouldn't hear of staying in a smaller residence on the lowland farm and had a dislike for the hills. The lack of certainty increased and something had to be done." The Shepherd paused at this point, drank some more water and said he would tell me more another time. Somehow I knew the next part was going to be emotionally difficult for him so did not press him further. Retiring to bed, I explained to Penny that there were a lot of family struggles coming to light. She was pretty much asleep and mumbled, "And they are not over yet, it's all mixed up in the hills." She drifted off again and I was left unable to settle, worrying about everything I had heard, including Penny's odd comment.

Auld Elliot

Thomas Elliot had left his family home many years ago to make his fortune in London. The investment firm he helped establish did well and surfed on the waves of enthusiasm he and his partners brought together. They grew rapidly with an excellent reputation to become serious players in the financial world. They employed fifteen hundred people across the globe with a portfolio including property, insurance, industry and finance. Of course they had many years of ups and downs like everyone else and had been hit hard by the recessions and the more recent credit crunch and banking failures.

He was wealthy, a father of two boys and grandfather of six boys, one hell of an Elliot tribe currently devoid of girls. He had had a good life in the south. But deep within him there was a twelve year old who yearned to return to Jedburgh and settle into a simple retirement enjoying the local life, attending the ride outs, shows and maybe a bit of walking, shooting and fishing.

So having recently returned from the Scottish Borders and been reminded of its outstanding natural beauty he decided to go back up north with his good wife Lizzie to prospect for a place to settle for the remainder of his life. He had two weeks' leave and telling nobody at work about his proposed destination they set off for Jedburgh.

On the way up they had passed through many areas blighted by wind turbines and it did not take long for Lizzie to decide that they were excessively intrusive and quite often completely stationary. "How could this possibly be a solution for climate change or fuel security?" she asked. It was clearly a huge scam brought on by greedy landowners and the opportunistic behaviour of the energy companies. He didn't mention to Lizzie that they had a department working on plans to do the same to some nearby hills. Secretly he was not happy with the concept but had to keep his business head clear on that one. The Government had indeed set it up so big reliable money could be made by trashing the landscape regardless of local opinion. Those that had their views blighted were termed NIMBYS, despite the logic that everybody would react in the same way if they thought their back yards were being so threatened. It was a childish school playground chant.

They stopped at Carter Bar, the famous gateway to Scotland, climbed out of their Jaguar, walked over to the edge to take in the panorama of the Scottish Borders stretching before them and were frankly shocked and disappointed at the scattering of turbines they could see clashing harshly against the superb views. They looked down on two huge arrays of turbines to the west and one to the east, trying without success, to hide within a dark Sitka plantation; the contrast was ridiculous and a scattering of miscellaneous individual turbines made focusing awkward. Lizzie said they made her feel sick and was clear she did not want to live amongst them. They had

114

an extraordinary effect on the landscape; indeed all they could focus on was the white spinning things. The feeling of this being a great frontier between historic warring nations and the images of Border Reivers was dead. Replacing this image and experience of wilderness was a gross industrialization dominated by great icons of greed, subsidy mills. The great rolling mounds of the receding Cheviots were stunning, unique and glorious in the evening sun, but were invisible as all the eye could take in was the incessant chop chop chop of the blades, great grey shadows of doom stretched over the undulating folds, flickering across the green as if flailing the earth of its last vestiges of worth and dignity.

A large blue and silver tour bus pulled into the viewpoint behind them, glistening in an expensive way, its sleek lines and antennae-like mirrors giving it the look of some kind of android wasp. With a great hiss the suspension lowered and the door slid open, as one might imagine a UFO would before abducting the unwary. There was a moment of near silence after the engine was switched off, then out spewed the contents like the bright entrails of some unfortunate road kill, moist and colourful against the drab tarmac. High voices of excitement flowed across the car park and toppled over the edge to float down into the jaws of the waiting Triffid mass, where they were lost, meaningless amongst the rhythmic 'whumph whumph.' There was a time when the enthusiasm in the tourist's voices would have been nurtured by the natives, leading them to the woollen mills, shortbread, Abbeys, Peel towers and iconic destinations across the Borders. The strong open, tartan clad arms of the nation had embraced them, greeted them with genuine care, offering them an experience to match their expectations, images within them built up over their years and extent of travel across the globe. But now the welcoming gesture was replaced, one as much held towards the south as seen by those looking north, a long broad arm came down over the Border hills, stretching over the land, casting a dark shadow over David Robert's Jedburgh Abbey, and Walter Scott's lochs and towers like Kilnsike, Mervinslaw, Slacks and Dykraw and the ancient Southdean Church; this time there was a reiving of a different nature, one that delved the pokes of the poor, a clearance of their highlands of natural beauty and wildlife. This time the arm terminated in a hard white fist, one finger extended upwards in a gesture the whole world recognised.

The excited gabble of tourists flowed to the northern edge, cameras and digital phones rising to their eyes, but then there was a collective gasp, only a couple of clicks and the remainder held in falling hands to look at the gesture they knew too well. Met by the whirling turbines, their faces fell, towers, tartan, abbeys, shortbread and even the thoughts of whisky seeped out of their temples and were wiped away by worried hands stroking down their cheeks to their chins, where the hopes dripped to be lost and trampled in the dust below.

Thomas and Lizzie watched all this with a kind of morbid fascination; the flock of dollars all faced towards a tall red haired lady, possibly of local descent, clearly their leader. She raised both her hands and quite simply announced in an amplified voice: "Geez, I'm sorry guys, it's not what I thought it was going to be." She turned and marched back to the waiting wasp. "Driver," she yelled, "change of plans, let's try France." The flock followed, bleating as they did, complaining about what had become of their beloved Scotland. The door hissed, the suspension raised, the coach turned and quite simply went somewhere else.

Thomas loved the Americans, their positivity and enthusiasm was to be admired, but he also knew that they had high expectations and did not like to be disappointed.

Elliot and Lizzie based themselves in a comfortable hotel nearby and collected brochures from the local estate agents. That night they arranged a table in their hotel suite with maps of the area and heaps of estate agent brochures for them to read through. They graded them in order of attractiveness, suitability of accommodation, location and value. Not that the latter really counted. Money was no object. With highlighter pens they made the map very colourful with scattered circles around properties to view. They decided to reconnoitre first so as not to waste their time with visits to properties in unsuitable areas. With a piece of string they drew a circle centred on Jedburgh Abbey out to thirty miles. There were properties near Bonchester Bridge, Roberton, Denholm, Ancrum, Roxburgh, Mindrum, Morebattle and Crailing of various styles, sizes and values. This was going to be fun. They were staying for ten days so would spread the visits evenly and fine tune their list. If none were suitable then they could always rent a place. There was no desperate hurry to buy.

The following day they decided to tour the whole thirty mile zone they had circled to get a feel of the area. Elliot and Lizzie had not been up to the Borders for about fifteen years, other than Elliot's Cheviot trip and that had been a rushed affair attending the wedding of a distant cousin at Dryburgh Abbey. It had been cold, wet and windy; they had flown to Edinburgh and used a hire car to travel down for the event. They had been late and had had to rush back to catch a flight back to London. It had not been a pleasant experience so taking their time and savouring the towns, villages and landscape was a treat. They felt that when one is looking for a place to settle down one wants to feel safe, to blend in and enjoy one's twilight years so they were aware of the need to find out about likely developments such as roads, railways, supermarkets, chicken farms and of course so-called wind farms.

Penny and the Gamekeeper

In the knowledge that we were going to have to return to our suburban existence soon I offered to help the Shepherd with the rest of the roof repairs. This involved cutting turf from a handy bit of ground preferably containing a lot of drought resistant wildflowers and grasses, carting them to the base of the Tower, hoisting them up onto the vault then laying them as and where required to stop water dripping through.

Penny decided that as it was such a perfect morning she was going to walk up Bleakhope and do some sketching. She packed some food and spare clothes and with a quick kiss on both our cheeks skipped away in high spirits to corner some wildlife to draw. She was going to encounter more than she was expecting.

The Shepherd and I set to and managed to cut and move about half a ton of turves and stack them up against the Tower wall. It was hard work but he took the opportunity to tell me a little more of his story.

Penny wanted to capture the best of Bleakhope and had taken a set of graphite and watercolour pencils to do some quick sketches. She would then use the initial drawings to develop into more substantial paintings once she returned home. The track was dusty as she headed up the valley and birdsong echoed brightly through the branches. It reminded her of a trip to a deep rugged gorge in Corsica a few years back. The shade was cool and welcoming and the sunlit clearings surprisingly hot. Clear bright water rushed and plunged from pool to pool, dancing from deep browns to translucent turquoise. She was a capable artist and saw detail and colour that most would miss.

Somewhere ahead she heard a cuckoo call, its evocative sound reminding her of its crafty technique of laying its eggs in another bird's nest. Intrigued and puzzled that she should hear one so late in the year she followed the call and was led up a minor track through a young oak and holly wood. She had never seen a cuckoo though heard them often enough. She felt like a proper twitcher and as she drew near, she slunk slowly from tree trunk to shrub to dip until she was very close. Then suddenly she saw it, the classic profile upon a moss covered oak limb. It called and moved on. Penny sat and did a quick sketch of the outline from memory and added blues and greys by wetting the watercolour pencils between her lips and added neat sparrowhawk-like bars across its chest. Pleased with her work she followed the track she was on and found it rose steeply for half a mile before levelling off to follow a contour line with intermittent views over the valley. She did several landscape sketches and one of a beautiful red and orange butterfly she could not identify. Inquisitive as to the destination of this unexplored route, she went further than she had intended. She found that the track joined up with the main route and realised she was not that far off the high loch and thought she might as well go all the way to get a quick sketch.

The loch looked amazing with the bright blue sky and willows and alders swaying gently in the breeze. Penny couldn't believe that her husband had really helped sow the seeds and hoped they would be able to do more of the same. There was something really satisfying about the potential of a seed so small and simple becoming so large and significant. She felt the warmth of the breeze and closing her eyes for a moment placed her hand over her belly and repeated the thought... 'so small... so significant.'

She walked around to the southern edge to get the light behind her and found a neat scoop in the peat where she could sit within shelter and enjoy the view over the loch's glinting surface. She made herself comfortable, laid out her pencils and started to sketch the scene before her. She was hidden from view and it would have been difficult to spot her even from the far side of the water. Bright Blue damselflies skimmed over the small peaty pool at her feet. Her sketch developed and she added wispy lines to represent the damselflies and when a large Osprey came to fish she sketched it in as a focal point. The peaty hollow was very warm and slowly she relaxed back into her soft mossy seat. Her eyes closed and she drifted into a wonderful daydream, totally alone and at peace with the world around her.

But she wasn't alone. Close by, too close, somebody lurked with evil intent.

Down at the Tower we had rigged up a pulley system and were hauling up turf one piece at a time in a bucket. The Shepherd below loaded them and I hauled on the rope above and when the bucket was in reach tied off the rope and using a planting crook caught the rope and drew the bucket towards me, unloaded the turf and repeating the procedure. This way a neat stack was accumulating on the vault ridge from where we could collect them for the various patching. It was warm up there amongst the dry grasses and there was a wonderful buzzing of bees visiting the myriad of wildflowers that thrived on the vault's surface. I was quite tired, getting sore hands and needed a break. I wondered how Penny was doing and hoped she hadn't gone too far in the heat.

The gamekeeper, with his false name, raised his rifle and watched the Osprey approach through the sights. He was keen to obtain the three hundred pounds offered by the man. He had got over the guilt of killing these birds, justifying it to himself that there were now plenty of them around. The large beautiful bird swooped low over the water. He steadied the gun but the bird suddenly lifted up as it got close and flew off to the north shore. Having failed to spot a fish it tried again, this time flying

120

straight towards him. Gun up, moment chosen, trigger pulled. Bird dead.

Penny in the hollow only twenty yards in front jumped out of her skin. She had been watching the Osprey through half closed eyes dreaming about the freedom of flight and the stunning movement of its wings, when suddenly there was an almighty bang and the bird simply dropped into the water in front of her. Shocked and very, very angry, she bounded out of the peat hollow to see who had murdered the bird. The gamekeeper, not expecting company, was reloading his gun and not aware of the maddened Penny, but once he heard her splashing through muddy pools towards him, he looked up to be encountered by a mad woman bearing down on him, face blackened by peat splashes, eyes wide and dangerous. The gamekeeper raised his loaded gun in defence but Penny was not going to stop. She grabbed the gun barrel, wrenching it out of his grip, swung it out in a wide arc and it sailed through the air to land with a splash in a deep mire. The gamekeeper fell back in horror, terrified. Penny grabbed him by his collar and despite the obvious danger pinned him against a birch tree and yelled at him: "What the hell do you think you are doing? Do you realise what you have done? That was an Osprey trying to feed its young! Now you've probably killed its babies too!"

"Er...er, didn't think of that, who... what are you?"

Penny realising just how thick this guy was, spat at him: "I'm the guardian of this loch and these hills and you are trespassing!!"

The gamekeeper was shaking with fear. Believing she was some kind of demon, he stammered, "Sorry.... sorry, I didn't know." He twisted out of her grip and quite simply ran, careering through peat puddles, bashing his head on alder branches and tripping over grassy tussocks. He was genuinely terrified.

"And don't you dare come here again as I will be looking out for you!" yelled Penny to his retreating back.

Penny returned to her hollow to find her neat sketch lying at the bottom of the pool, peaty water dissolving the blues and browns of the image of the Osprey. Out in the rippling waters a feathery corpse bobbed in the sunshine.

Later in the pub Dougie described his experiences to his best mate. His mate said there were stories of an auld hag in them parts. The gamekeeper, reunited with his real name, decided the deal was off. He didn't want the man's money and wasn't bothered about the gun; it was just too risky going back up there.

I almost had a bucket loaded with a heavy turf at the wall head when the loud crack of the rifle shot echoed down the Bleakhope. It was a still quiet day at the Tower and the sudden noise made me jump; the rope slipped through my tired hands, burning them till I had to let go. I shouted to the Shepherd as the bucket plummeted down. He had already seen it coming; stepped back, caught his heel on a turf and toppled over backwards. The bucket crashed to the ground just missing his feet. In a split second I was bounding across the vault, dived down through the ruined turret, leaped the spiral stairs four at a time and came tumbling out to find the Shepherd sitting up but looking rather shocked.

"Go and check on Penny!" he grunted.

I grabbed a crook and dashed off up the Bleakhope track. After thirty-five minutes of jogging I was completely out of breath and was exceptionally glad to see Penny marching down towards me. She hugged me and burst into tears, told me the story and I had to laugh at the description of the gamekeeper fleeing for his life. "That's my girl!" I said, comforting her.

She smiled up at me and said, "Yes, it was rather funny, but I'm all shook up and am worried he will come back."

We returned to the Tower to find the Shepherd in the hall. He too was a bit shook up.

Martin and the pubs

Martin was pissed off. The gamekeeper had scarpered with the money, job unfinished. But then he hadn't paid him that much. He was determined to track him down and confront him. Perhaps he was ill or had run out of phone credit. Time would tell. Martin decided the best course of action was to cover all the local pubs to firstly track the missing gamekeeper but also to recruit an alternative if necessary, ask about the woodcutter of Bleakhope and generally get a feeling of local opinion about wind farms.

There were twelve likely pubs, inns or hotels that he thought would be near enough to the hills. He ringed them on the map and crossed off the one he was staying in. The evening before he had already started making enquiries. The only gamekeepers referred to seemed attached to the big estates so he didn't follow up on them. He needed some less well paid scoundrel like his first man, but more reliable. He subtly introduced the subject of wind power to a well-dressed gentleman buying whisky at the bar, who then spent five minutes pontificating about the great benefits of wind power to landowners enabling them to diversify their businesses and actually make decent money for once. Martin felt a degree of encouragement from this and was about to go outside and report to Casey after the man left, but a pretty young lady caught his eye and said, "That's Lord Munfry you know.

Twelve thousands acres and moans about being broke. He drives an Aston Martin for Christ sake and owns a chain of jewellery shops across the country. Wind turbines don't work efficiently and are just a subsidy scam!"

Martin became flustered. He was caught between the need to support wind power and the desire to continue chatting to this rather sexy young filly. The latter won and he sat back down on the bar stool. The lady moved over next to him and he bought her a gin and tonic. They spent the next two hours getting tipsy and discussing renewable energy. She was very green; all in favour of saving the planet etc etc but could not reconcile chopping up birds and despoiling the beautiful Borders landscape to provide intermittent spurts of excessively expensive electricity that she, along with all other consumers, were paying for. Martin, not really knowing what to say, just nodded lots. He hadn't actually given the issues much thought but he was enjoying being close to her and took every opportunity to check out her legs and slim body. She was a brunette with chocolate brown eyes and long dark lashes. By the time they parted he was in absolute agreement with her—wind power was an economic disaster waiting to happen, splitting communities and blighting the countryside wherever the turbines sprang up. He saw her again at breakfast. She didn't even smile at him. She sat down opposite Lord twelve thousand acres and sipped tea delicately with her pinkie raised in dainty acquiescence to the company present. Martin's only thought was 'dissention amongst the ranks perhaps' and he ate on in disappointed silence.

He was going to try three pubs a day and stay in the last each evening. The next was a wayside Inn that was actually nicer inside than its exterior indicated. There were three men at the bar and two couples eating. He tried a direct approach this time asking the barman quite clearly "What do people think about wind turbines around here?" That had an interesting effect. Talk about getting caught in the crossfire! The barman said, "They create jobs and money for the community." One of the gentlemen eating at a table piped up declaring, "Yes, but the developers offering so-called community benefits are effectively paid by the community through their electric bills. They would be better off not allowing the turbines and keeping the money in their pockets. Turbines ruin the landscape scaring off tourists, reducing business so the end result is negative."

"Oh, I never thought of it that way," replied the barman, now looking puzzled and concerned for his business.

"But surely we all need to be green and support these things," the gentleman's lady said.

"So I pay the landowner to get mega-rich while I lose my tourist trade. That's nuts," said the barman.

"Err...sort of," said Martin, becoming more concerned by the minute.

"You can't get away from them," said a stocky man at the bar. "Every valley has them and they spoil the area."

"The ice-caps are melting and the Polar Bears have nowhere to go," said the lady.

"Rubbish!" said the other man at the bar. "There has been no global warming for over fifteen years! That's why they call it climate change now and there was more sea ice in the Baltic last winter than the last fifty years! Any colder and the Polar bears will be on Shetland eating sheep before the end of winter."

'Ooops,' thought Martin, 'hornet's nest, time to depart.' He knocked back the pint. Three miles to the next pub. Offski. He was glad to escape. Perhaps a more subtle approach was required.

Turfing the Tower

After a day's rest the Shepherd felt strong enough to resume our work on the Tower. Penny was going to go to Ashburn to sketch the ruined cottage and secretly plan its restoration. We took spades up onto the vault and the Shepherd demonstrated what was required. The trick was to undercut the existing turf enough to prevent the new bits slipping down the roof or drying out too much. Ideally rain straight after laying would help get roots to grow through into the existing layers. We had already decided where additional work was required and we worked as a team to speed things up. After a couple of hours we took a break and sat with our backs to the exposed wall that rose up enclosing the Shepherd's private quarters behind it. I took the opportunity to prompt the Shepherd to reveal more about his brothers and family. He smiled and after chewing on a long bit of grass for a minute or two, started to tell me about the fateful day.

"My father was a clear thinker. He could sense the rising tensions and knew he was going to have to make a decision. That autumn he got a really bad chest infection and lost weight rapidly. By the following March he was desperately thin and we knew he would not last much longer. In the end it was he who called a meeting asking all his children and his lawyer to attend. It was to be on the first of May when the Tower was a bit more hospitable and everyone could convene. We met and sat around the hall table waiting patiently for him to speak. Rather than telling us he asked us each in turn what we thought should happen to the estate. Millie, a maid from the hall and Scott the Steward's wife Lily served wine and a cold meal of ham and salad. William was asked first and he put it quite plainly that he should inherit both hills and arable by Kelso along with all houses and buildings. He was then prepared to let his other siblings become tenants so as to provide the estate with income and give them a livelihood. That resulted, as you can imagine, in some gruff comments from Maurice. He in turn said the estate should be split so each could then sell up and move on if they so wished."

"And what about you and Angus?" I asked.

"I was happy to take the tenancy of the hills and Angus the arable farm at the Hall. I knew his would be a more valuable farm but I just wanted a simple existence with my family in the hills. Heather and Mary loved the place and would rather be tenants in the hills than rent a place in Kelso."

"How about your sister, was she there?"

"No, she replied in writing saying she had all she could possible want in Kenya so didn't come over."

"So what conclusion did your father come to?"

"He didn't. After lunch he announced that he would think upon the matter and we were all to join him at the same time the following day. He retired to the library and was last seen puffing away on his old briar looking concerned. A bottle of port had appeared on his reading table and we all knew to keep well out of the way."

"Did you meet up again the following day?"

"Well, fate took a hold and we all accumulated in the hall from our various chambers and the lawyer appeared and stood at the head of the table with his fine handlebar moustache and after a minutes silence, which was a painfully long time, announced that our father was dead. Quite simply he was found that way by Lily early in the morning. Briar on the floor beside him, port hardly touched. The poor soul, it had all become too much for him."

"That's really sad, I'm sorry," I said quietly. The Shepherd shrugged and said, "That's life."

The two resident jackdaws flew down from the crowsteps and pecked away at the new turf we had just laid at the other end of the roof. We watched them for a few minutes and the Shepherd said it was probably full of disturbed insects.

I could tell he was brooding about the events back then so didn't pursue the story any further. We carried on turfing and spoke merrily about what we were doing and his plans for the Ashburn valley. We stopped for lunch and when we returned to the roof he continued.

"It was a very sad time, the end of an era. Father was a true nobleman of his time, well respected by all those that knew him. After the funeral we were all summoned again to the Tower to hear the reading of his last will and testament. None of us had a clue what to expect. William had visited the lawyer in his office in Kelso but extracted nothing from him. He said he was following instructions and nobody would know until the meeting in the Tower.

It was raining heavily on the day we met. The lawyer had ridden in early with Millie, from the hall. Scott and his wife were there to help out and we four boys accumulated and jostled nervously in front of the fire in an attempt to dry and warm up. It was tense and we spoke curtly to each other. William was dressed in his best riding gear, Maurice in his army uniform complete with medals and Angus and I in our best tweeds. We took our places at the table and eventually the lawyer began. We had, as before, wine and a light meal provided by Millie and Lily. The lawyer rambled through lengthy preliminaries then came to the critical bit. He explained that this will had been written in the last year of the war when nobody knew what the outcome might be or which sons may still be alive. Put in the simplest of terms it stated that the eldest living son would inherit the whole estate with the option of tenancies and cash for the younger siblings. Well, that was it—Maurice went mad. He swore at the lawyer saying he was incompetent. William sat at the head of the table with a smug look on his face and Angus and I looked on with horror. All the noise attracted Mary and Heather in from the gardens who witnessed the distasteful scene unfolding from the hall door. Lily took Millie, who had started crying, through to the kitchen.

William tried to calm Maurice down, saying, "That's enough Mory, that's enough, calm down man." Maurice turned on him and started ranting about how unfair it was and how hard he had worked, how he deserved a fair share of the estate. Angus and I couldn't recall any occasion when Maurice had helped out. William stood up in a tall threatening way, Maurice stood too and started thumping the table. He grabbed one of father's treasured wine glasses and thumped it down aggressively. It broke the base off and cut Maurice's hand but he kept stabbing the wood creating a harsh gouge in the timber which accumulated a disturbing mix of red wine and the blood that dripped from his hand. Angus and I left and I suggested to Mary that she ride over to the river Kale, pick up our Riley and drive herself home with Heather."

The Shepherd fell silent. He was re-living that awful time. I could tell by the way he stared sightlessly across the hills, eyes damp and sad.

Everybody had gone and he was alone in the Tower. The echoes of the chaos had faded away. Mary and Heather had ridden off in the damp afternoon. The lawyer had calmed the brothers down and departed into the dusk taking Millie back to the Hall. Maurice and William had apologised, shook hands and appeared to be civil towards each other. The Shepherd had stood in the hall with his hand on the back of a carved oak chair staring at the scene. The chairs had been pushed back in anger; the table was a mess with raw damage where Maurice had stabbed at it with the broken wine glass. He had sent the shocked Scott and his wife back to Ashburn saying that they would work together clearing up the following day and they had been glad to leave. That night he slept fitfully waking at the slightest sound. Something had gone horribly wrong with his family; the loss of his father had left a vacuum that somehow refused to be filled by anything secure and stable. Worse was to come.

The next morning nobody came, neither Scott nor his wife. By noon he was anxious; by one o'clock he was worried about them. At two he watched a lone rider come down the drove road. He didn't recognise the man so walked out to greet him at the barmkin entrance. The rider halted his bay gelding, took off his broad hat, pulled out a letter from his waistcoat pocket and lent down to hand it to him. It was a moment the Shepherd would never forget. He took the letter smiling up at the rider; the rider didn't return the greeting and looked the Shepherd in the eye and simply said, "I'm so sorry," straightened up, put his hat back on, turned his horse and made his way back up the drove road. The Shepherd had been left in the silence of the valleys staring at the black rimmed letter in his hand.

His whole existence was shattered when he read the words. He collapsed in disbelief on the hard ground staring at the memories replaying on the cobbles. He had risen to his feet and spent hours striding back and forth in total horror. Dusk came and the sheer desolation overwhelmed him. He could not understand why his father had abandoned him; he swore at his brothers' stupidity, blaming them for the chain of events, begged to, then cursed the very God that neglected his need, then prayed to be taken back in time to prevent the awful things happening. Darkness fell and in despair he howled at the deep fathomless sky. His broken heart was like a black hole sucking in the Tower, his bleak hope, the surrounding hills and valleys, the whole world, moon and stars, all was black. Fate had removed everything and crushed it to a dark destructive seed within him, his pain and his loss. He lent against the stone wall surrounding the Tower well then clambered up onto the wallhead and grasped the iron bar with its coiled rope. He sobbed above the murky depth, his mind scanning for a solution, a way to bring them back, to say sorry and to hug them once more. He hung on to the bar till his fingers grew numb and his whole body chilled and he shivered with the cold, exhaustion and trauma. He resolved to do the only thing be thought that would take him to them: he moved his feet closer to the edge while grass and stones crumbled and fell rattling and echoing ending in eerie splashes far below. He edged closer preparing to release himself, to let go of this world and fall to greet his family, for the chance to hold them even one last time. His tears fell to the spring water below and spread like the iridescence of oil upon the surface.

But something changed. His tears had awoken something deep below, moved the tiniest quirk in the strands of time and space. Just as he reached the point of no return a tiny voice came floating up that well, the sweet voice of Heather: "*Be strong Dad, be strong and hold fast!*" That was enough. His hands held fast to the hard cold bar just as his feet slipped over the edge and with a sudden jolt of reality he was left dangling above a painful and unpleasant end, broken and freezing to death far below in the deep cold water. With eyes wide with sudden awareness he wriggled and swung; his hands began to lose grip and in desperation he twisted back and forth trying to reach the opposite wall. He just managed to get a toe on a solid stone, then the same with his other foot, then with an almighty lunge he flung himself over the edge falling and rolling onto the cobbles beyond. He staggered to his feet empowered by the gift of a second chance and all the grief, pain and hurt erupted.

131

He stared at the dark sky above the Tower well and it all came out; the desperate seed within his soul exploded in an infinitely vast blast of emotion releasing like a rising, boiling mushroom cloud through the empty void returning the world and heavens to their place. He gasped the cold air in, like an almost drowned man and watched the sky brighten as the grey clouds parted revealing a bright and powerful moon, followed by its accompanying stars. The sky cleared, the dust settled and the wind stopped. The re-born Shepherd collapsed unconscious to the ground.

Scott the Steward found him the next day, a sad heap, cold and grey in the pink dawn. He had scooped him up and taken him up into the Tower where he remained for many days tended by Scott's wife and little Mille.

He made it to the funeral but visibly shook through the ordeal.

I sat quietly aware of the Shepherd's pain, waiting patiently to see if he was going to say more. I knew I wouldn't hear the entire story, but enough to understand what drove this God-Shepherd in his amazing work.

The moment was broken by an odd noise from behind us. We turned and with a funny little bleat the badger-faced goat appeared, hopped over the vault and started nibbling precariously close to the edge. Penny then followed full of smiles and laughter. "You've met my new friend then?" she said. We both had to smile at her enthusiasm. Penny sat on the far side of the Shepherd and we all gazed across the God-Shepherd's creation. The day was bright, the breeze warm and all was well with the world. As I looked forward I became aware of another person with us. In the corner of my eye a flash of white caught my attention. I looked across but could see nothing, but if I looked slightly to the side I saw the lacy hem of a white dress, a pair of dirty feet and when I moved my head up a tiny bit the complete image of a pretty young girl hanging onto her daddy's arm, golden locks flowing over her shoulder, blue eyes gazing lovingly into her father's large brown ones. I did not dare move and watched the girl for a few minutes until Penny noticed my odd stance. I moved, the image faded and despite trying again, I could not see Heather. I felt so moved by the devotion of this spirit I could have cried. An hour later I doubted I had seen anything at all.

A Close shave

Elliot and Lizzie had viewed a three-bedroom modern ranch style house with ten acres near Crailing. It was not quite their taste and too close to the river, but a good starting point to gauge what they were likely to get for their money. It was almost two in the afternoon and they were famished. They found a small hotel with great views over the valley. They parked up next to a tatty old Landover that had dead things in the back. Hares, Elliot thought. The hotel had a bar and adjoining restaurant area. It was busy and they got some drinks and a menu. Two hairy men dressed in camouflage sat drinking and chatting on high backed pews. Elliot thought they looked like gamekeepers. Elliot and Lizzie sat at the only available table and watched the people come and go at the bar. A pretty girl with alarmingly pink hair took their order. They were surprised at how busy the place was and assumed the food must be excellent.

A tall figure came into the bar; he had particularly curly dark hair that made him stand out in a crowd. Martin leant forward and quietly asked the barman if the owner of the Landover in the car park was there. "Yep, Dougie the keeper, just behind you." Too loud—by the time he had turned the gamekeeper without his false name was up and out the door like a shot, his friend crashing out the door behind him. Martin made pursuit but he was not fast enough; he was met with gravel flying up from the off-road tyres. He returned to the bar and ordered a pint of Best. The barman grumbled about Dougie not paying, so Martin said he was happy to pay if he found out the gamekeeper's full name and address. The barman took the twenty-pound note and wrote: 'Douglas Kirkwall, flat behind the high street, Jedburgh, exact flat not known.' Martin nodded in thanks and sat back on his bar stool to relax at last. He became aware of being stared at by a couple on the far side of the restaurant; he took a furtive look and turned to face the other way. 'Hell, that looked like old Elliot, what's he doing here?' Martin took care not to look that way again and left the hotel as quickly as possible. Before he departed he wrote a note for the barman. Using the false name he had given the gamekeeper he indicated that if Dougie or anybody wanted to make contact that they should call him on the mobile number provided. The number was a fake, but if Elliot thought he recognised him it would put him off the scent. He couldn't work out why he might be there.

The pink haired girl was serving Elliot and Lizzie their food and was blocking their view. The man at the bar took advantage and disappeared. Next pub a mile and a half.

"That really did look like that Martin chap from investments," said Elliot.

"Maybe he's on holiday up here," replied Lizzie

"What are the chances of that?" mumbled Elliot, thinking of Casey.

Casey makes plans

Casey had calmed down. Jenny had fallen out with her almost ex-Bertie. Their reunion hadn't worked. That pleased him, for he could now invite her out hopefully without her whimpering on about her ex. She was very flirty and good fun in the office and they had a laugh most of the time. Casey was sitting in front of his PC typing 'demolition using explosives' in the Google tool bar. He had decided to at least consider more seriously doing the 'clearance' work himself. The agent's words echoed in his head and he knew it was the safest option. However, anybody that really knew Casey would recognise that to carry out such a mission, especially when he was a bit of an indoor boy, wasn't really that clever. Casey had already worked through his list of Biodiversity Action Plan species, writing next to them means of elimination. He had to admit that the naturalist had produced an extensive list. Casey had his 'Observers Book of Birds' and a similar one for butterflies and one called 'Rare Upland Plants'. He would take his time, learn everything necessary and proceed in the spring. This would allow plenty of time for the agent to do his prep work and for the Government policies to settle. This project was potentially so valuable that waiting a few more months and being better prepared was going to be worth it.

"Jenny, can you see if you can get Martin for me or the agent?"

"Yes boss," she said, clip-clopping across the floor in her high heels. Casey watched her every move. Yep, she would do. He hadn't seen Rosie yet; she was coming that evening to collect her CDs.

When Jenny got Martin he was sounding nervous; she put her hand over the mouthpiece on the telephone and in a loud whisper said, "He sounds in a panic."

"Hi Martin," he said with confidence but dreading the news. "Tell me all about it."

"I think I've just seen Auld Elliot and his Mrs in a pub quite close to Jedburgh, is that possible?"

After a pause he replied in his brisk business-like manner: "Well, he is off at the moment, didn't say where he was going though, not that he would tell me anyway. I want you back in two days. Can you now concentrate on identifying the woodcutter tramp guy, where he lives and the young couple you saw? Ask at the pubs, village shops or similar."

"Yep, that's fine, see you soon," Martin said with relief and hung up.

Casey looked up at Jenny. "Fancy a drink tonight?"

Last day in Eden

Penny was up first. She had woken too early but had a spring in her step and a smile that held a secret. She walked along the track towards Scott the Steward's house, her white dress fluttering around her calves and the funny old goat skipping along behind her. There was a soft early light piercing through the green, illuminating the path ahead of her in dappled disarray. When she came to the spot where the tumbling cottage came into view between delicate rowan trees, she sat on a moss-covered log and the lack of sleep caught up with her, blurring her eyes slightly as she let her imagination feed into the view. Soft swirls of mist meandered around the house, slates, sad and chipped wafted up over the roof slipping back into place, broken bricks healed and rose to straighten up the crumbling chimney stack. Windows with bright paint and sparkling panes of glass shimmered into the blind openings.

The goat stared forward as if he could see it too. The grey walls became washed with white and a neatly trellised porch grew out from the dark doorway. The ground shrank back and peonies, aquilegia, poppies and a jungle of foxgloves, deep blue delphiniums and lilies spread up around the edge of a cottage garden. The mist cleared beyond the blossoms and a tall, dark and handsome man came into view, a pretty clear faced young lady beside him. Between them, arms raised, holding tight and chuckling, was a pretty little girl dressed in a cream lace edged dress.

Penny had already chosen: Heather.

The Shepherd and I ate a leisurely breakfast and he said he was ready to tell me more. He poured out a second cup of steaming hot tea when all the toast was gone. He lent forward on his elbows, rested his chin in his hands and with head bowed, closed his eyes. I thought perhaps he was praying. The steam rose from his tea adding the finest gloss to his balding scalp. He stayed so still for several minutes he resembled a stone effigy from a Cathedral grave of polished grey marble, solid and reliable in the sculptor's hands. I had never looked quite so closely at him before. He was old, very old. His large sunburned ears, hooded eyes and long crooked nose chiselled chip by chip from a rough-hewn block. Each scar and pock mark carved in a memory of some distant happening. His wonderful bushy grey eyebrows added to the warmth of his character and his furrowed brow reflected decades of toil upon the land. I could see a master mason taking this job in hand, perfecting the God-Shepherd, choosing a niche high above the alter, an example to us all.

When he started to speak he spoke so softly I could hardly hear. "Of course I never saw them again," he breathed. "The Riley had spun off the road and tumbled over and over down a steep escarpment onto rocks washed by the river Kale. I used to take a pilgrimage there each year and stand on the bridge looking down at the spot. I willed with all my broken heart to stretch back time, to pull on the strings and draw them back, reach out and place the deep blue car back on its road, to propel it across the bridge like a toy to reach the Hall by nightfall. They were buried at Oxnam. The Minister's words were kind; he described how those that drifted from view would always be at our side sharing our lives. I returned to the Tower and Scott and his wife were incredibly supportive. I worked extremely hard, too hard really, to drown out the pain. I resolved to plant trees, to enhance the place where we had been so happy together. Key moments in my life always happened in or near the Tower and this place became my base. I was happy for Angus to be at the Hall."

I asked, "What became of William and Maurice? Was the estate sold?"

"Well, this is the odd thing. At the time we understood that William had departed with the deeds and the Solicitor to sell the Estate to a London investment firm. We never received confirmation or otherwise, nor saw or heard of them since. The letters we found indicated William was heading for South Africa and Maurice for Singapore. No amount of detective work ever showed them up. It was as if the earth had simply swallowed them up. The Solicitor wrote to the investment company on several occasions and the response was always the same: "The conveyance was pending." As nothing seemed to happen we carried on as normal, farming as we saw fit. The years went by; the solicitor with his handlebar moustache passed away, his firm absorbed by a bigger one and we forgot about the ownership issue but had assumed that someday we would be served notice and because of that kept our heads down and said nothing. Angus dealt with any official sort of stuff at the Hall."

"So you lost two brothers, a wife and child on the same night! How terrible."

"Yes, it was surreal, like a higher being had picked up a rubber and cleaned half of the blackboard. It left voids that still gape and threaten to swallow me whole. I would like to know what happened to them. I was furious with them at the time because Mary and Heather would not have driven off that day if they, my brothers, hadn't been so badly behaved. But I have forgiven them since; we were all very young in hindsight and they had been through such horrors in the war. I threw myself into creating woodland and the rewards have been endless. Not a day goes by when I don't appreciate the miracle of nature in this place; the more you plant the more nature flows in and multiplies."

The Shepherd raised his head and sipped his tea. He seemed to shimmer between ancient man and the God-Shepherd as if his power were fading. But despite this I knew that he would put every ounce he had into his Eden. Penny came skipping up the stairs exclaiming that it was a fabulous day and what good company the goat was. She then went to the kitchen and came back with a plate with really quite a lot of toast on it. The Shepherd simply looked up at her and said, "You are done here; I hope you will return soon." I didn't really understand the comment until we were back home.

"I want to show you something special before you go." We packed some lunch into a rucksack and headed out. The Shepherd led us up a path in the Bleakhope valley through a mixture of oaks and alders, then up into a large expanse of silver birch, all places we had not been before. We stopped beneath some larch for a break where the track split off into two. All these trees must have been from his earlier planting as they were really quite substantial. The larch rose fifty or sixty feet above us from a bed of mossy needles and soft grasses below. They all grew parallel with a graceful curve for the first eight feet, then strove upwards, rocket like, to spread their broad boughs above. Harebells were scattered liberally beneath the trees; the goat nibbled at them until Penny chased it off and we sat amongst them looking down over the direction we had come. The different species were planted in large blocks but carefully blended together at the edges.

We chatted about what our plans were going to be when we got home and knew that we had some big decisions to make. We were at a point in our careers where the options opened up so we had to choose the right route and get our heads down and work really hard. Penny was watching me while I was saying all this and somehow I knew she had different plans but could not guess.

The Shepherd opened up one of his cloth bags and showed us masses of ash keys. He told us that ash trees were related to olives and that there was an opportunity just to scatter these on bare soil on the higher slopes we were heading for. We left the larch grove and Penny chose which track to take as the Shepherd said that each led to the same destination. She took the right option and of course later I understood the symbolism in what we said and did on that final trip. We rose up through the larch, then rowan and scrub willow to a steep hill rising above us. It was mostly heather with outcrops of grey whinstone around which pipits and wagtails hopped. Skylarks sang above us against a deep blue sky. The steep slopes were cut into by a lattice of gently angled sheep tracks where a million ovine feet had tramped for millennium leaving bare soil, peat and scree ripe for sowing. The Shepherd gave us each a bag and we spent an hour walking our own chosen routes back and forth broadcasting the seed in hopes of some falling

140

on fertile ground. Once our sacks were empty the Shepherd led us to the summit. There was the remains of an ancient hill fort with clearly defined ridges and ditches. We sat in the warmth and enjoyed the far reaching views over the Shepherd's Eden that formed a sea of frothing greens. Beyond, the bare hills were beautiful but bleak, exposed to the harshest of conditions. The effect this man had upon the landscape was incredible. I truly hoped he understood the significance of what he had achieved and the influence it would eventually have on other people who really cared about their land. Even if one person planted one tree as a result and that in turn inspired another, then the world would indeed become a better place.

After we had eaten he led us up onto the ridge that encircled the hillfort and pointed out the different species planted in the vista stretching below. This was, he explained, the spot where he and Mary had truly fallen for each other so many years before. He came to the part where the ridge was almost at its highest and asked us to look over the woodland to see if we could see any pattern or shapes in the planting. We had to admit we couldn't really. He walked on another few paces making us wait till he was ready and then beckoned us forward asking us to keep looking for something in the trees. It was quite surprising for every step we took an image began to come into focus across the slopes below. By the time we reached the Shepherd we could see it. The layout of planting took on the form of a mother holding a child, a Madonna of his own Mary and his beloved daughter Heather.

"In autumn the larches turn golden like their hair and the fresh birch greens slowly turn to rich yellows, then when the leaves fall to leave purple branches and white stems they resemble a finely embroidered dress. Every time I come up here, which sadly is not so often nowadays, it has changed."

Penny and I were overwhelmed; not only was there magnificent woodland full of wildlife, there were unexpected dimensions layered upon each other. The ancient hillforts, the flow of man's impact upon the land, terraces, ridge and furrow, quarries, dykes and the latest planting that put the life back. This image, we found, could only really be seen from one ten-yard circle, a bit like Fukuda's piano—you had to stand in an exact spot for the image to work well. We tried walking in all directions to see what happened and the image quite simply went out of focus and became nothing more than mixed woodland. In time the dynamic nature of woodland would blur the edges as trees came and went dissolving the image as surely as the memories of the Shepherd would dissipate over time.

Penny did a sketch of the Shepherd and I sitting on the fort embankment with the image beyond us. She said she would do a watercolour once she was home. Her composition of the view was amazing and she really caught the ruggedness of the Shepherd with neat short strokes of a soft pencil. I was gazing across the vista, soaking up the view and suddenly remembered the threat of the turbines. It made me wince, for if they were to go up near the high loch they would completely overshadow the Shepherd's domain and completely destroy this incredible remnant of wild land. Penny who was sketching me at the time asked, "Are you okay?" She must have seen the cloud pass over my face. She knew me well and would extract the truth later, but I just replied, "Sure, I don't want to leave, that's all." The thought of returning to our suburban existence pained me. "Would it be possible to come back next Easter?" I asked.

The Shepherd laughed and responded, "I think you will find that Penny is the one to ask about that."

I was confused and Penny looked suspiciously at the Shepherd and thought, 'How does he know when my own husband hasn't a clue?' She quickly recovered, beamed at us and said, "I am most definitely coming back sometime next year if at all possible. Now that I have met you and been in your world I am completely hooked and there will be no stopping me."

We took a zig-zag route down paths we had never been on before. The Shepherd described this as the well walk as there were three ancient wells; each he had restored and built a neat stone dyke around and installed simple mechanisms with bars, handles, ropes and buckets to raise water from hidden depths. He said that if you drank slowly and savoured the water you would find each well's water tasted slightly different and it was especially noticeable from one valley to the next. At the last of the three wells the Shepherd made a comment that really nagged at the back of my mind.

"This is where William and Maurice's horses were found."

I didn't pursue it further but it was odd.

That evening we ate a feast of cold meats, home grown salad and potatoes. I was concerned that we had eaten him out of house and home and offered to make a trip to suppliers to stock up his basics. He wouldn't hear of it and said he would be taking a load of firewood off to Jedburgh in a week or two and would replenish then. He opened a fabulous bottle of white wine of unknown origins and age; the label was too faded, but it must have been old because the cork and bottle neck seemed to be wrapped in thin lead. As we sat chatting in the flickering candlelight and glowing fire in the hearth I felt a combination of extreme contentment and deep anxiety. I was in the presence of somebody who had settled his differences with the world, a man who had embraced fate and in doing so had found a peaceful purpose.

However, the anxiety was nibbling away at the edges as there was a feeling that the Shepherd's Creation could be wiped away in seconds by the greed of individuals many miles away. The thought of the marching turbines creeping up into the Cheviots like great white aliens and spewing over his boundaries on the pretext of saving the planet was thoroughly disturbing. Such erections destroyed the environment; they were grim inefficient industrial monsters: what a complete load of nonsense—carbon dioxide only made 0.04% of the atmosphere and had become a mere gaseous excuse to rape the planet yet again, to extract money from the masses enriching the few. I vowed I would do everything possible to prevent any intrusion upon the Shepherd's Land, regardless of ownership.

Later that evening I was watching Penny sitting on the bed brushing her long auburn hair. She was very careful to look after herself and insisted on brushing her hair before bed each evening, one hundred strokes as her granny had taught her. The result was great hair and generally a happy and healthy wife. I was so proud of her and her many talents. She smiled at me and asked, "You don't want to leave, do you?" She was right—neither of us did and we agreed to return as soon as things were settled in the spring.

Penny cried when we left the following morning. We left the Shepherd at the Tower door. After a few hundred yards before we were lost amongst the willows Penny looked back. The Shepherd was still there, small and wizened. She hoped he made it through the winter.

Coming down out of the Cheviots was an odd experience. Every step of descent was like waking up from a bizarre but wonderful dream. The odd experiences I had had became more and more unlikely and surreal as civilisation approached. We descended from the heights through layers of wafting mist and dropped into bright sunshine below. After a mile or so we stopped for a rest, jumped up onto a big round straw bale in a recently harvested field and took in the vastness of the landscape. The lower enclosed fields gently lifted up towards the hills which rose in a multitude of soft greens and buffs and layers of cloud clung to the highest tops making it difficult to distinguish between dry land and the moist blanket draped over. Indeed it was easy to imagine the Cheviots rising several thousand feet higher into great Alpine peaks. The whole picture gave the impression of a gigantic floating island gently moving on a sea of mist. It was magic, an almost real and difficult to get to land, full of unknown wild places untouched by the harshness of the modern world.

We walked the home stretch towards Jedburgh in silence, deep in our own thoughts. We passed beneath great industrial leviathans whump-thumping, blades chopping in vain, great shadows swiping the fields, slashing at the natural balance around them. We suddenly became anxious about the date: would our car still be there, the bills laying in a heap at home, the worried parents, friends and neighbours. The stress of modern existence returned hard and fast. We got to our car to find a 'police aware' sticker on it, a partially flat tyre and a cracked rear light lens. We opened her up, started the engine and dug out our mobile phones. The next hour we spent calling the most critical people and listening to dozens of messages and did a blanket response text to all our contacts. Some replied with relief and some responded saying they didn't know we were away. The impact of reality was jarring and it took a while to settle back into it. We went to speak to the police about retrieving our car, got the tyres all checked, filled up with fuel and headed south. At Carter Bar we stopped and admired the amazing outlook into the highest Cheviots, but squirmed with horror at the mess of turbines in the other direction. We could just feel the Shepherd's Land somewhere east amongst the sun kissed summits poking above the mist and hoped they would remain turbine free.

145

I hugged Penny's shoulders and commented, "Were we really up there living in a castle with an ancient shepherd? It sounds really unlikely and I don't think people will believe our stories."

"Yes, I know what you mean. It was all a bit surreal, wasn't it?" Penny said. "I'm coming back though. Someday soon. If the Shepherd and his wonderful trees are under threat I will be first in line to defend them."

We took one last look, returned to our car and headed off. By the time we reached Bryness it was raining and did so all the way home. Penny spoke of all the paintings she was going to do and I promised to write down all our experiences lest we forgot.

The Shepherd felt lonely that evening—something he thought he had successfully eradicated many years before. He knew they would return but probably not for a year or so.

Elliot requests a board meeting

As the oldest remaining employee and a founding member of staff, Elliot was much respected but was becoming out of touch. He knew it was time to retire. He and Lizzie had decided to move to the Borders and they wanted to do their bit to protect the landscape not only there but also across the whole country from the ridiculous turbines. They spent a lot of time researching the issues and followed a number of wind farm planning applications up and down the country, along with the substantial daily coverage in the press. Any intelligent person could see that a system driven by such blatant greed on false pretences of saving the planet, that damaged the landscape and wildlife, was completely unjustifiable.

The board gathered and Elliot spent thirty minutes outlining his concerns about wind power from a personal and then an economic point of view. Grimms suggested gathering more evidence before committing any further resources, Brighstone agreed and the remainder followed leaving Auld Elliot feeling old but not entirely defeated, for a glimmer of hope to halt the project had not gone. He then announced his intention to retire the following Easter which was met with comments like "You've certainly done your bit" and "You have definitely earned it." They may think he was past it and would have no influence upon company policy but he now had a clear aim for his last few months, to prevent the support of the wind power scam. Later, feeling tired, sipping a malt with ice, he summoned Casey.

Casey eventually appeared and presented his report. Elliot sat and paged through the seventy pages quickly and sitting back in his chair said to Casey, "You know I'm not comfortable with this, don't you?"

Casey shrugged and responded, "I was asked to come up with an investment that was both lucrative and safe. For a minimal input there are guaranteed riches..." Elliot interrupted him.

"Yes, but the impact on people, the landscape and wildlife is unacceptable for no guarantee of protection against climate change and certainly no meaningful energy security."

"What, an ancient wood cutting tramp that is about to peg it, a few seagulls and it certainly won't affect badgers or otters, will it? As for landscape its miles from anywhere and they will only appear as little white sticks in the distance and only if the weather is clear, which, let's face it, hardly ever happens in Scotland 'cos it's always pissing down with rain."

They glared at each other, each trying to protect their cause.

"I will read your report Casey and we will reconvene soon." Elliot carefully held back his anger.

Casey was glad to escape. He was nervous as he had had to fill in a few blanks on the report. There was nothing back from the legal department or an indication of the current return on the property. God damn it they were being useless! When he got back to the office he slammed the door making Jenny jump. He said nothing, stood in front of the wall mirror and preened himself, smoothed back his gelled hair above his ears, twisted his neck in his collar and bared his teeth. He was thirty-five and didn't like the signs of aging. He was overweight, had excessively rosy cheeks and nose, wrinkles at his temples and grey creeping into his sideburns. Somehow he felt time was running out. Jenny appeared in the reflection behind him. She put her hand on his shoulder and beamed a huge smile. "Surely it can't be that bad?" she asked. Casey stared at himself a moment longer, then regaining his composure turned to face her. "I need Martin now!" he snapped. She stepped back, somewhat alarmed, and minced back to her corner to phone Martin. She called him and arranged for him to come up in an hour. She put the phone down and let Casey know. He nodded. She felt deflated; she was attracted to his power and confidence but found him so bad tempered sometimes. Sulking somewhat, she got on with her typing and said nothing.

Martin arrived looking flustered and sunburnt. Jenny pulled out a chair for him and went to make them all a coffee. Martin did look wild with his height, reddened face and shaggy curly hair. He had only been back a day and hadn't had a chance to tidy himself much. Still living with his parents at twenty seven was bad enough but the ridiculous fuss his mother had made over him was just daft. He had eaten too much and told most of his adventures to his parental audience late into the night with frequent gasps and sighs. Having never ventured far from home they didn't really have much concept of the world beyond. Martin's hiking had grown out of a need to escape the oppressive attention.

"I need a comprehensive report about your trip, Martin." Martin pulled out a scrappy, muddy and torn notebook and held it up. Casey waved his hand at it. "A proper professional document. E-mail it to me as soon as you can. But tell me about the tower and ruined cottage—is there any chance the tramp or young couple were living there?" Casey asked thinking 'rock shattering ka-boom!' Martin responded as professionally as possible. "The cottage is pretty much roofless and the tower impenetrable. The only other shelter is the occasional old railway wagon. The ones I looked into were stuffed full of foosty hay." Casey pondered the matter and asked him to write it all up, tidy himself up and come back at the end of the week, complete with the spare cash and expense receipts where available. Martin nodded and left. He was feeling guilty about how much he had *not* given to the gamekeeper. But hell, he had earned it; he had had a tough time.

As soon as Martin had gone Casey looked up at the sheepish Jenny. "Fancy going to a club tonight?" She nodded eagerly and like a sunburst, her broad smile and bright blue eyes lit up the office. All was not lost.

Penny's Pregnancy

A quick test two days after Penny and I returned home was all it needed to send Penny into a whirlwind of excitement and happiness. Not having the remotest idea that she might be pregnant, the news hit me like a missile. Penny spun out of the bathroom brandishing what looked like a toothbrush screaming, "I'm pregnant, I'm pregnant! Can you believe it?" She covered me in kisses and hugged me till it hurt. Penny overflowed with sheer exuberant joy and I had to physically hold her till she settled. Of course I remembered our moments of passion in the hills a few weeks previous but I was not remotely prepared for the news. I had to get a stiff drink and sit down to take it all in. There were serious consequences as we were trying to plan our next career move. It looked like I was going to be working and Penny being a mother at home which was fantastic and scary at the same time. She said she could work from home while she could. Of course we had often discussed having children but always assumed it was something we would do in a few years' time after settling into serious careers.

"You know, the Shepherd knew. He knew that I would get pregnant and knew when I was. I don't know how but he seemed to be willing it to happen. He would ask subtle questions about our plans for the future and I know it's a girl and it just has to be called Heather." She lifted up her top and held her slim elegant belly and I laughed because there wasn't the remotest hint of swelling. She was naturally slender and I thought she would still look fabulous even with a baby bump. Penny being Penny was buzzing with it, talking faster than I could listen. She had remarkable passion for everything she did and I could tell being pregnant was going to be met with the same enthusiasm and motherhood would come naturally to her. My main task was going to be trying to moderate her into not doing too much.

"I assume the choice of 'Heather' is because of the Shepherd's lost daughter?"

"Yes of course it has to be, she is going to be reborn, deserves to be reborn."

150

"You know I don't believe all that rebirth stuff, don't you?"

"Yes, not normally, but think about it, she was still very much present in that valley. I could tell you could sense her too."

I shrugged but knew exactly what she meant. I was the one who kept seeing her. I was the one that knew that where the badger faced goat was, the spirit of Heather was nearby too. The Shepherd couldn't see her, or Penny, but she could feel Heather in her own funny way. We sat quietly contemplating these strange ideas for quite a while until Penny announced her hunger.

Such is pregnancy.

Heather's world

Death to Heather had been weird. She had been wrenched from one world to another like being dragged through shards of glass. The pain was brief, intense and thoroughly unpleasant. Within seconds her mother's face appeared and faded before her. They were standing together on the fresh green bank of a fast flowing river, feeling pale but not uncomfortable. Her mother had grasped both her hands, looked deep into her eyes, whispered the words *'I love you, be strong Heather'* and with eyes full of sadness and adoration dissolved before her. Feeling oddly light Heather instinctively walked back to the Tower. She didn't look back at the smoking car half stuck in the water. She didn't see the sightless corpses draped across the submerged bonnet or the blood seeping away into the flow. She did what any child would; she sought out her remaining parent. She couldn't really sense movement nor understand time, she just found herself back in the hall next to her Dad. She knew she wasn't what she was before, but she did know she was still needed. Her father only heard her words once shortly after her 'change'. Her Dad was distraught wanting to see her and Mum and thought he could come through too, but Heather knew he would just fade away like her mother had, so she stopped him and told him to be strong. It worked, but he never heard her again.

After a while she got used to her new existence. She began to explore, to relive her times in the hills or indeed anywhere she had been before. She found she didn't have to actually walk; all she needed to do was think herself somewhere. Once there she could do anything she wanted, but she could never go beyond her former territory. She grew accustomed to the other 'people' who were there with her, but she faded them out and didn't see or hear them any more unless she let them in. There was only one boy that looked like her that she could take with her sometimes. He was very like her in so many ways, but seemed to struggle to stay looking like a boy. Sometimes he would simply blur and vanish. Other times he would wail like a new born baby and become helpless.

Heather learnt from her father, helped him choose what to do by moving things a little, just enough to hint at things, make a pebble drop or blow on his cheek. She had no energy for anything more or able to repeat it very often. It did have an effect and as such she engaged with his new passion of tree planting; she knew it was for her and her mother so she was fully committed. Time was odd; she flitted around helping him plant seeds only to be climbing the resultant forty-year-old tree the next day. Sometimes her Dad was young and strong, sometimes old and wrinkly.

It wasn't until Penny and her man came that she focused and followed them in any kind of meaningful sequence. She became super alert as the tingly man came into the valley the first time and completely overjoyed when he returned with Penny. She felt Penny was really important, somehow critical to her own existence. She followed them a lot, helping them, teasing them and took every chance to be noticed by or felt by the funny man who slowly came to be able to see her.

Heather had discovered the truth about the family and what had really happened that September night so long ago. She had shown the funny man a few things but didn't know whether he had taken notice or not.

Her goat was much the same as ever, following her most of the time. He was fully aware of her and didn't change his behaviour at all. Oddly though, he was with her regardless of time. Sometimes he was the young Billy she had known, sometimes very old. Time didn't seem to behave itself in her new world unless she really focused her mind. She never grew older and just felt like a normal child, for decades.

She listened closely to Penny and the tingly man and never heard them say a thing against her father. Indeed they had nothing but awe and admiration for him. She smiled when they called him the God-Shepherd. She felt like that as well, seeing what he had been through and how much he did for the countryside. She was deeply proud of her dad and hugged him tightly and cried with him when he was upset. Nothing was going to separate her from her dear old Dad, even if he was completely unaware of her.

Jenny

They had a fantastic time out together. Casey was completely different out of his work environment. Jenny had glammed herself up and he was in jeans and a casual denim shirt. They had had drinks at a cocktail bar followed by a tavern meal where they had both had the beef and ale pie, then went to Casey's favourite nightclub. He didn't talk about work and she forgot about Bertie. They talked of their ambitions and disgust at how religions were constantly wrecking the world. He told her about his dream of owning dozens of apartments in exotic locations and having a mega smart yacht. Jenny glowed with the idea and imagined herself dripping with bling and showing off to her old schoolmates. In particular that snooty cow Angelique.

At 3am she gave him a huge hug, a kiss on the cheek and disappeared in a taxi. They were both revelling in the chemistry building between them.

Jenny returned home to find her cat munching the last of her three goldfish, the smashed bowl lying against the radiator. Casey found his flat door open and a caustic note from his ex.

Winter in the Shepherd's Land

Autumn colour rolled into the monochrome of winter. Eden became dormant except for the hardy. Grey geese roosted on dull water, bobbing in the silver ebb or huddled in a thawed puddle amongst gathering ice. Intermittent bright days harboured the harshest of turbine tempting winds. Crisp snow came and went filling in between pale tussocks of grass. It was a harsh place in the depths of winter. Its blessings were the most incredible skies with trillions of stars sprinkled above like sugar and the solitude, the sheer emptiness of the place. After all, who would be daft enough to stay up so high at that time of year?

The Shepherd. Over many years he had perfected winter survival. He was well prepared as always with stores of food, meat hanging from the beams, dry goods on the shelves, apples wrapped in paper and a vault full of dry logs. The sheep had hay that he exchanged for logs at Cessford each November. He loved his isolation and let the solitude and independence waft around him. Of course Heather was there huddled next to him by the great old range in the kitchen. She had watched him stuff sheep's wool between the ceiling beams and nail up an old fishing net beneath to hold it all in place. She had laughed silently at his ingenuity making insulated inner panels for the windows to seal out the bleak. His box bed built halfway up the wall next to the range was his winter den when the upper rooms became too bitter. He had his current books and the long portraits of his family around the kitchen. Black and white enlargements framed in gilt pine. The one of Mary holding Heather like a Madonna and Child was his favourite. Mary in an evening gown and one of his father smoking a pipe next to the Hall portico. Penny was the only person he had let into the kitchen. His quarters above, reached by a narrow turnpike, were unvisited by anyone other than himself. There were five rooms stacked at odd levels in the Tower above. His library was his sanctuary. The lighting and outlook was amazing; many thousands of books were his intellectual indulgence and his means of transport to different times and worlds. Occasionally he would add to the sagging oak shelves with a detour to a Jedburgh shop or antique warehouse. Reading became the mortar between the blocks of day-to-day life.

The Shepherd's winter routine was simple. He awoke naturally at daybreak, added kindling and logs to the embers in the grate of the great black kitchen beast and put the kettle on. By the time he returned from the bathroom above, dressed and ready for the day, the polished black kettle with its elegant curved spout had performed and he fried bread in lard which he stored in a large brown ceramic jar. Without fresh dairy produce his diet was limited. Powdered milk sufficed. Normally he kept chickens for their eggs, but without Pip to put off the foxes he didn't have any that winter. His sheep were his morning priority. He walked down the track to their paddocks, slid back the heavy door of one of the old railway wagons and hauled out several bales. He toppled them over the fence, climbed over the style, cut the strings and filled four hayracks with enough to keep the sheep going. He was finding the bales heavy that year. He thought it was a combination of poor hay and his creaky joints. If there was grass available the sheep ignored the hay so he didn't need to add some every day. He would return to the Tower, top up his wood supply in the kitchen, pile up the grate and prepare some soup or stew that could last a couple of days. He would then settle down to catch up with his diary, which he had kept up with reasonably well since he was seven and read his latest book.

Despite his many years in the Tower, his library still came up with surprising titles that had not been devoured. There were books behind books, books in trunks, books in cupboards, books on the floor and on every available surface. Occasionally he would dust the small amount of space between them but inevitably got bogged down in some ancient tome, duster poised, then abandoned. There were quite a few such dusters to be found in odd places around the room. Two ancient mariner's globes sat by the single north-facing window. The shutters when closed in winter showed beautiful paintings on their inner sides. On the left a regal young lady sat reading a book on her lap, long dark hair falling against a fair complexion and down over a fine blue dress, gold jewellery at her neck and wrists. The book upon her knee was open showing fine Celtic illuminated script relating some ancient tale. The writing was decipherable but nobody had ever translated it. Beyond the reader a scene of Cheviot Hills receding blue and purple to a sun-kissed horizon. Primeval looking white cattle, with great curving black-tipped horns stood around a gnarled oak that rose behind her carved chair. The second shutter showed a tall king with golden crown and long brown beard trailing down his red robes. He was standing by a river holding a salmon like one would a baby, a neat coronet depicted on its steel grey head and a string of pearls loosely bound around its silvery flanks. Despite his extensive reading the Shepherd had never extracted any significance from this image. It was just another part of the great mystery he found in his Tower and valleys. In the centre of the room he had rigged up a chandelier to hold six candles which he lit when daylight did not suffice. The library steps were normally left beneath so he could climb and light them when needed. The elm plank floor had a collection of tatty Persian rugs overlapping at odd angles. The cats Archie and Archimedes had added to the worn appearance many years before. On sunny days when the shutters were open they would lie on the stone window seats squirming in the heat and occasionally bat at the moving shadows cast by Virginia creeper leaves outside. In autumn the leaves would turn crimson adding to the warm leather backs of the books and reds and browns of the rugged floor. The room was magnificent in its ramshackle way, a book lover's dream come true, more than enough to make a dealer drool. Volumes long lost to the outside world waited quietly in cobwebbed corners.

The Tower, like any building without central heating blasting away, was generally cold. The kitchen and the Shepherd's quarters above benefitted from the range's constant warmth rising through the Tower. This kept the damp and frost at bay, but only just. The Shepherd was really glad to have managed, with help, to re-turf those parts of the stone vaults that had been leaking and so far the repairs had been successful.

One bright January morning he sat on an old velvet armchair in his library gazing at the painted shutters admiring the artist's skills as he always did. He felt that at last he had found a charming couple to take over the place once he could work no more. Knowing that he was now struggling with the upkeep of the Tower and finding his tree work slower and slower, he really needed to have the young people back. He looked at his leathery hands with their huge knobbly knuckles. Where had this aged body come from, why had it happened so fast? He still had so much more planting to do, so much more to give. He wished he could contact them, to ask them to come quickly, that the place was theirs. But he didn't even know their full names or where they lived and with a baby on the way they would be gone a while. He just hoped they would return before it was too late. He was not comfortable with his nephews at the Hall taking over as they had already shown a total lack of interest or for that matter some London investment firm. These people had no understanding of the Tower or hills. The young couple were ideal; they loved the place and were fit and strong enough to make a difference. He spoke to the elegant figures on the shutters.

"I do hope you come back."

Heather, who was standing in front of the shutters trying unsuccessfully to make one of the globes turn by pushing it with a finger, looked up to find her father staring at her; for a second she thought he could see her, but soon realised he was gazing at the paintings through her. She rushed over to him and reaching up to kiss his bristly cheek, misinterpreting his words, she said, "Oh Dad, if only I could show you that I have *never* left you!"

Sometimes it could be so frustrating being a ghost.

Casey and Jenny Plot and Plan

Casey was using Jenny, not only in a physical sense; he needed an accomplice to help him through the current crisis. So it was Jenny who arranged instruction for the safe and effective use of high explosives with the oily burley Derek Demster. As manager of one of the company's UK quarries he felt obliged to help out, but was suspicious of the motivations of this pretty little filly, so made sure he protected himself just in case whatever they were up to went wrong. She had treated him to a ploughman's lunch in a nearby hotel, chose the same to make him feel comfortable, despite her dislike of the offering and managed to come to an arrangement. It had taken a lot of flirting and resulted in dirty marks on her red dress, but she came away with a deal costing only £4000, whereby Jenny and Casey would receive two weekends of discrete intensive training and enough stuff to fell say a couple of tall buildings. Jenny promised to wear something tight.

Casey was very pleased as should anything go wrong it was Jenny who had neatly implicated herself.

Pregnant Penny

Penny was finding being pregnant fairly tough. She had suffered every form of morning sickness available and was hugely emotional with the hormones. I was finding it difficult too. I had Penny to look after and had applied for six ecology positions that interested me. I had invitations to two interviews, one in Exeter and the other in Edinburgh. I received no response from the other four. With the pressures of Penny's pregnancy and the inevitable house move and possible new career, tensions grew. The grandparents fussed and generally interfered. When Penny had a minor bleed they had a major panic. I found a voice of confident authority held the chaos at bay, but in truth I was deeply concerned and was doing a lot of frantic internet research in the background. Finding the need for distraction I joined the local squash club and spent two evenings a week de-stressing and socialising. Penny wasn't impressed but a man needs space from such things and the exercise was keeping me trim.

One evening I tucked up Penny on the sofa in front of our gas fire. Penny stared at the repetitive flickering.

"I wish we had a real fire," she said wistfully. "I would feed it ash and hornbeam logs and learn to distinguish between the different scents they would give off." I smiled as I knew she was harking back to when we were stacking logs in the Shepherd's vault. I missed the old man, the Tower and the amazing hills too. We were so detached in our protected suburban world, our Cheviot experiences seemed so unworldly, a different reality. We listened to the harsh wind blowing outside, battering at the fabric of the building.

"I'm worried, it's so nasty and cold out there; do you think the Shepherd will be alright?" Penny asked.

"Of course he will—he's been doing it for dozens of years."

"But I'm really worried. What if it all goes badly? Don't you see that if the slightest thing goes wrong it won't work?" Penny looked up at me with a wrinkled brow.

I brushed a strand of dark hair off her pretty cheekbone and reassured her. "I'm sure everything will be fine, you'll see." I was beginning to become a bit confused by what she said and put it down to her exhaustion.

"What happens to Heather if we lose the baby?" Penny persisted.

160

"I really don't think we will, but I suppose we would just have to keep trying."

Penny was getting quite agitated so I knelt down in front of her and gave her a comforting hug. The baby bump pressed against my chest.

"We would have to go back, otherwise it can't work, and what if it was a boy?"

Somewhat losing her train of thought I decided to go and make some supper. I wished I had paid more attention.

Target Practice

Casey, surprisingly, was a good shot. He held the gun correctly, aligned the sights how he had been shown, pulled the trigger slowly and hit the chest of the paper target 150 yards away. He was pleased. Everybody around him was scared. He was a good shot but everything else was disastrous. He couldn't load the gun, tripped over the stairs and generally pointed the gun at everyone in the vicinity. Alarming to say the least.

Jenny was competent. She knew the gun well, how to handle it carefully and safely but seldom hit the target. She found as soon as she pulled the trigger the gun moved and the bullet whizzed off into the distance. The instructor would have to step in behind her and demonstrate the methods required to improve her performance. Jenny asked the instructor to join them for a snack and a chat in the clubroom afterwards, but he was too busy the first time. Mysteriously he managed to fit it into his schedule in his subsequent weeks. Casey would ask him a series of practical questions. Jenny would just sit there, nod occasionally, gaze at his twinkling hazel eyes and think about his strong brown shoulders.

She managed to arrange a thirteenth lesson.

The Wind Turbine Meeting in East Yorkshire

Elliot followed a number of applications quite closely and visited several public meetings. The proposal in Yorkshire particularly disturbed him, as the effect on the landscape would be dire. The infinitely wealthy and powerful energy company felt obliged to put on exhibitions so as to deceive the unwary natives. It was underplayed with quiet advertising. Elliot wandered around the exhibit where there were a number of posters. The first tried to frighten the public with the prospect of a dramatic rise in global temperatures, the second was a map with tiny black dots showing the proposed positions of the 125-metre tall turbines. It did not indicate the sheer impact they would have on the surrounding three villages.

The next talked about noise and shadow flickering and how only a very small percentage of the surrounding dwellings would experience anything detrimental and only then at a very few times of the year. Elliot was no fool, it was blatantly obvious that the two offending turbines would be removed from the scheme to pacify the pathetic and irrelevant concerns of those living nearby, leaving their original plan in a better position to get past the local planning authority. The fact that the residents would have their expensive views blighted for at least a generation and probably longer was not even mentioned.

The poster showing a Zone of Theoretical Visibility was suspect. Elliot thought it was based on the central and lowest turbine, but even so the area affected by that huge turbine was vast. He doubted their advertising of the meeting reached as far as the map showed.

Six photo montages showed the huge industrial beasts looming over tiny village houses. In each photograph foreground clutter such as road signs or silage bales were used to distort the scale or distract the viewer from the true horror.

The last talked about the bribe money and the beneficial effect on the pitiful sums in the parish council's coffers. A village hall would be re-roofed, post offices and village shops would have additional car parking and tourist interpretation boards installed. Elliot was not impressed—there was no mention of the effect on the local tourism businesses, house values and the fact that people would drift away from the gross industrialisation of the countryside. It would become a wind factory.

Elliot gave the pretty boy and girl peddling the lies a dirty look but said nothing. Instead he went off to write some stern letters.

One of Life's Strange Coincidences

Bertie was feeling morose and depressed; he missed Jenny but didn't want her back. He took to frequenting the bar in the basement of the office block where she worked. It was a young and trendy place where futuristic white and purple lights lit crisp minimalistic edges. On Friday and Saturday nights the ambience was enhanced with live music. Bertie was a bit mixed up with his feelings about Jenny and wanted to see her at the bar, but feared rejection again or seeing her with somebody else. One evening he plucked up courage to buy a drink for a girl who looked equally moody at the other end of the bar. Rosie was grateful but not initially particularly talkative until Bertie started mentioning Jenny. Rosie started paying more attention and they very soon realised they had lots in common. Rosie knew the flirtatious Jenny, having met her when visiting Casey in his offices. Jenny at the time worked as part of the administration team and was noticeably attractive; she had had a few conversations with her and had swapped phone numbers with the intent of a shopping trip sometime. Bertie explained the demise of their relationship and Rosie told him about Casey. They both had lots to talk about so agreed to meet again.

My Dream

By late March Penny was finding her bump quite difficult to sleep with, and moved around a lot in the night. To enable one of us at least to get a good night's sleep, I took to sneaking out to the spare room. However, I wasn't always the one that benefitted. The spare room was too stuffy with the windows closed and often too cold if it was left open on its narrowest setting. On a particularly warm night I forgot to open them.

I found myself walking on a blue grey day, along a leafy path between tall oaks. They were too mature to be planted by the Shepherd, but I recognised enough to know it was Bleakhope. A cord across my shoulder cut into my blue and white striped pyjamas; it supported a sack full of acorns at my waist. I held in my hand the planting crook that I had used in the Cheviots. I looked at its beautiful ornate top and felt its planting spike striking the ground as I walked along. I was on a planting trip and was at peace with my purpose. A clearing opened up where a giant ash tree had finally succumbed to its age and lay prone across the ground. I opened the sack, spiked a hole in the ground and dropped in an acorn, moved on a yard and planted another, then another. A young girl sat on the huge ash trunk and watched me; pleased with my progress, she smiled down at me and I smiled back. After a while she patted the trunk next to her and I clambered up to sit there. We sat there watching the man in pyjamas planting. Any moment could have been captured in paints and proudly hung on any wall, the man's attire complementing the blue greens of the lichen-covered trunk and the trees beyond.

"I hope to live along enough to appreciate them," I said.

"You already have," the girl laughed. "You don't have to be here forever. What you have begun is enough."

I looked down at the figure sowing the seeds; he was determined and focused on his task.

"Many will follow you like those that you follow, followed the Shepherd."

It sounded like a line from a prayer I once knew.

"Would you like to see them grow?"

I nodded and we both stood up. She waved her hand across the scene in front of us. The familiar Mr Pyjamas vanished and a soft pulsating light began. Most of the acorns germinated and pushed up through the fluctuating grasses; animals came and went, the occasionally human flitting in and out, deer nibbling most of the seedlings. A dozen out of the fifty planted reached head height; fast moving critters rushed around devouring rotting wood, and the trunk beneath our feet gradually subsided. After a while only two oaks remained. A great storm had flattened the others. The two twisted and danced around each other as they struggled towards the light. A crude wooden bench appeared on one side of the clearing and a faint image of an old man with a broad-brimmed hat flickered, becoming

165

clearer as he frequented the spot; then as the oak canopy closed overhead and the image shrank, faded and finally vanished.

I awoke, sat up and stretched, rubbed my eyes, pulled back the duvet, swung my legs over the edge of the bed, wriggled my toes into my slippers and stepped into a cool misty morning. I walked further along the path beyond my ash tree planting, finding the increasing slope harder and harder to climb. I was hot, sweaty and finally giving in to my exhaustion sat upon something hard and angular. My head dropped towards my knees and I could hardly breathe. I stared at my left hand; it was gripping the harsh angular edge of a block of concrete. I flinched as such things did not belong in the Shepherd's land. A steady whump-whump noise began in front of me which increased in volume until it controlled the rhythm of my heart. A great anxiety grew over me as I believed that should the whumping cease, or indeed got too fast, then I would surely perish. With a horrible crunching I pulled my neck up to see the source of the sound: a great white metal tower loomed in front. At its base a small oval door beckoned and I staggered up and wobbled towards it. I knew I needed to get through it and fast. A brisk wind pushed me back. The giant above struck at me with grim blades, trying to swat me out of the way. Its noise grew and grew controlling my body. I had to cover my ears and held my eyes tight shut to try to blot out the monster. Bearing it no more, I collapsed on the gravel just a foot away from the door, the beast above drumming at me: "You're beaten—you're beaten—you're beaten." Tormented by the words I forced open my eyes and with a final burst lunged forward with my hand, struck the door which clanged open before me. There was immediate silence, not a swish from above or a thump. Penny appeared before me in the opening and mouthed something. Thinking she was in danger I clambered through the door. A glow surrounded me and I saw the bottom steps of a spiral stairway. I climbed up into the dim above, at intervals around the curved tower, conduits as thick as my arm were clamped to the metal; black pipes bulged and receded like leaches swallowing great globules of blood. Other tubes pulsated, lights stretching up and down. It was if the whole tower was an artificial tree, plastic xylem and phloem keeping the organism alive.

As I steadily rose the four chrome wheels of an office swivel chair appeared above me, then sensible shoes, tidy legs, a skirt hem, then a complete receptionist sitting behind a clean desk. She looked up at me through horn rimmed glasses and said in a clear crisp voice: "Thank you for choosing Eternal Energy to save the planet, please indicate the reason for your visit today." A white form was pushed across the plastic desk. The writing offered three options....

The first read: 'To get rich quick and to hell with everybody else.'

The second read: 'To show everybody how green I am.'

The third: 'To destroy landscapes, blight homes and kill wildlife.'

I didn't like any option but the receptionist drummed her fingers impatiently and waggled a red pen beneath my nose. "You must choose before you can proceed." So I ticked option two and clambered on up.

A caped figure appeared before me and held out a glass. It was the one that held my toothbrush at home. I drank heavily and could see toothpaste marks in its base. I lay back on the bed; Penny adjusted my pillows and pulled up the blanket to make me comfortable.

The blanket overheated me again and I woke up on a damp metal landing. I clambered to my feet, my movements echoing above and below me. I felt as if I was halfway up a giant empty tube of toothpaste. On the far side of the landing a small oak table supported a Gothic collection box; it had a neat scroll ended slot in its top panel. A sign in front declared 'Please pay here so I can get rich at your expense and go to heaven for saving the world.' I pulled out a large gold coin from my pocket; it was familiar somehow and I dropped it with a clunk on top of the other coins in the box.

I carried on up and after a dozen steps the underside of a glass table appeared. As I rose to its level a long room emerged and filled with a bustle of smartly dressed people who milled around roulette wheels and croupiers dealing cards. It was a casino. Every so often a gleeful cry would go up from a table. Signs above declared things like 'In scoping', 'live application' or 'Anti-anti action.' Elsewhere moody silences slunk under low level lights.

In the heart of the room a vivid three-dimensional holographic display of Scotland appeared. Around the periphery technicians watched screens and punched urgently at keyboards in response to the gambling at the tables around them. At the head of the display a large fat toad-like man with bushy eyebrows oversaw the activity. Assistants brought miniature wind turbines with black swastikas as blades and dropped them into the display, where the software grasped them and stuck them in the allotted place amongst the thousands already swamping hills, valleys and lochs. Miniature displaced swans flew up from the display and vanished forever in little puffs of soft white dust. Each time a turbine joined the ridiculous fairground in the display, a target indicator behind the toad chimed and blinked up a level towards the words "Independence". The toad wore a peaked visor and his rear flippers sat in a pool of black sticky oil. Every so often he declared: "They're getting them like it or not." I was so horrified at the destruction, I faced up to the toad and blocked his view of the display. "Out of the way man!" he croaked. I stood my ground and staring him hard in the eye said, "No, this has gone far enough, it has got to stop!" He glared at me dangerously. "What you are doing is wrong," I said. "You are taking advantage of a questionable policy, penalising the poor, destroying landscapes and tempting the greedy." Warts on his back oozed frothy slime.

"And you have a better way?" he croaked.

Everybody went silent and stared; we were left each side of the glowing image. I stepped back and pulled down a projector screen by its cord; an image came into focus of a simple lowly shepherd planting a sapling tree. The toad was mad and roared as a mad toad does. He pulled down his own projector screen and a scratched black and white film began to roll, showing an army of giant swastika turbines on caterpillar tracks advancing ruthlessly through the Shepherd's Eden, mincing up giant beech and oak trees with razor sharp blades. Slug-like trails of chippings followed the devastation across the hills. I was horrified and shouted at him: "You must stop! You are doing this for your own gratification, a way to your own coronation. You are destroying the very thing you declare to be trying to save!" The toad reared up, its eyes turned red from green and its front claws lashed out at me; its jowl swelled, till stretched and translucent, it issued an alarmingly loud "Groalk" as it lunged for me; but the black oil beneath its feet lubricated its downfall and it fell forwards into the hologram. The software sizzled in an attempt to process the creature. Steam rose up from the twitching toad and pink bled into the oozing froth.

The image disappeared and Penny was there in front of me. She looked worried and said, "You *are* having a rough night, aren't you?"

169

"Tell me about it," I said and drifted back onto the soft mattress.

I walked up the last few steps in the narrowing tower towards a deep humming sound, clearly the monster's lair. I carefully proceeded and emerged into a large well lit room. In the centre was a great machine that thrummed away menacingly and threatened me with ugly words; its top was covered in a mass of leaching tubes swallowing great globules and odd mechanical devices with flashing lights. At its front end a great shaft a foot wide stuck out into the open air, like Pinocchio's nose trying to pretend its honest purpose, but I knew the truth about that nose.

Advancing to the great muscular neck twisting and groaning, I pulled a sacred sword from my waist and drew it up to slay the beast by severing the mighty neck; but before I could strike, words written on the side of the shaft caught my attention, feeding a seed of doubt: 'But—what—if—wind—power—works—and—saves—the—planet?' My slight hesitation gave the beast time to react and behind me the humming and grinding increased. I turned to see an android toad forming from the pipes and wires from the monster's back. It rose together, large and dangerous, a metal bar appearing in its wiry claw and it advanced flailing with deadly intent in its rubbery eyes. Not seeing a way past it I turned and like an Olympic athlete dived over the shaft. The metal bar crashed against the turning neck in a cloud of sparks and the toad screamed as you would if you hit your own thumb with a hammer. Then I saw the beast's weakness, a large engorged crimson pulsating organ that lay within the skeletal core behind the toad, the heart of the matter. I lifted my trusty sword that glinted in the light and, seeing my intention, the android toad flung a mass of cogs and circuit boards at me. But it was too late! I made a great dive and my trusty blade was whistling

170

through the hot tense air and met its mark. With an explosive gush the organ was destroyed! The toad's projectile debris flew over my head and smashed an external fibreglass panel, exposing the giddying height I was at. The wind seemed to howl 'Freedom' as it streaked by. The android toad collapsed in a heap of useless, lifeless components.

I lay gasping and kicking at my covers. I had slain the dragon but was awash with sweat and exhausted beyond belief. Penny laid aside my sword, took off my battered helmet and mopped my heated brow. Grateful for her loving attention, I muttered "Thanks" and rolled over into the recovery position.

The early pre-dawn was cool. I stepped along the path satisfied with my kill, but to my horror as the view opened up rows of sad grey turbines appeared, stretching to the far horizon. Not one moved; they were frozen and dormant with no fuel. I came up to the first and a noise above startled me. A brown rope came whistling down from above, and before it reached the limit of its length an object appeared on the end. With a thump it twisted grimly on the taught rope. A figure, neck caught in a noose, head at an odd angle, came to rest, its body draped in yellow and two dirty feet dangling in vain above the firm soil. A brown label was tied around one of its big toes. I stepped forward despite the macabre scene and read: 'I thought I needed the money.'

When I approached the second turbine the rising sun splashed a pink warning up into the sky, making the industrial protrusion darker and more menacing. Again a rope came down with a thump leaving a large sack on the end. It had writing on its side, so I stepped close to hold the sack still and read it. In large gold letters the word 'SWAG' declared its contents. A large rat ran up my leg, across my chest, over my shoulders and leaped onto the rope above. Eyeing me suspiciously it negotiated its way down to the sack using its fat tail for balance. It started gnawing and a trickle of golden wheat grains fell to the ground, then as it tore away at the weave two gold coins fell and rolled to my feet. The rat, with increased enthusiasm, tore away at the hessian until a great gash appeared and the remaining contents slumped unpleasantly to the ground; a streaming, stinking pile of horse manure rested beneath the empty sack. The rat jumped down, sniffed at the heap, gave me a dirty look and undulated away in front of its unpleasant tail.

As I walked along to the third turbine, Heather reached up and took my hand. It felt like the most natural thing in the world. We stood before the dark silhouette of the machine and I braced myself for its gruesome package; but for a moment or two nothing happened. I looked up at the towering grey edifice, its height lost in wafting mist. The rich man's folly seemed to be thinking, like the wait in a game of chess, then it made its move, the whipping sound of the rope, but this time instead of an offering, the rope came to rest at my shoulder with nothing but a loose end. It hung there as if asking *me* what should hang there; it was waiting for *my* answer. I hung onto Heather's hand tightly. Then, as I watched the rope, it began to twist and turn as if an invisible seamanship student was demonstrating their knot tying skills. The vacant noose came to rest and through it the brink of the rising sun hesitated as if fearing the result. On the furthest ridge the air began to stir as the rays blessed the hillside with its warmth. The forlorn branches of great felled oaks and beech stretched up into the morning pink, hoping in vain to be returned to their former glory.

Wanting to see more, Heather tugged on my hand and said, "Shoulders, shoulders." I reached down and with the normal protest "But you're so heavy" hauled her onto my shoulders and held her legs where they hung over me. The distant turbine, awoken by the stirring of the morning air, creaked a groan and began to turn with its damp blade tips glistening in the sunlight.

Heather on my shoulders played with the twisted rope.

As the earth tipped towards the sun the next turbine began to turn. I watched them as one after another began to harness the breeze. It was heart-breaking to see the total devastation of the Shepherd's Eden, harsh tracks cut through the land leading to each turbine that would be there for ever, even if the towers rusted away. The trees were gone and the scarred land bled dark peaty fluids into the once crystal clear burns.

"Make a pretty necklace," Heather said from my shoulders.

The next turbine in front of us flung down a rope in earnest, then those leading away one after the other. Grim packages bumped down. As the sun's light caught the blades the meagre flow of air gave its life to the subsidy mills and the hanging figures were each in turn given a sudden yank as if to seal the deal with death. The valley became Gibbet Valley, making the former name of Bleakhope serene and gentle in comparison. The sun was almost upon us.

Then there was a sudden lightening of my load and a horrible thud as a package banged into my side. In sudden realization of what was happening I grasped the swinging bundle and lifted its weight and struggled with the noose at the neck, but it was too tight and as a great grieving sob rose in my soul the reluctant sun touched the evil blades above and yanked the rope and bundle from me. I froze in horror. I had slain one beast but how could I protect the Shepherd's Eden if I couldn't even protect an innocent child? I needed help and lots of it. I quivered in horror as the hanging bundle faded into the white above me.

Heather's hand grasped mine. "Look, Daddy, isn't it pretty?" I looked down in tearful relief at Heather holding up her daisy chain. She was standing amongst the bright white flowers scattered through the sunny grass. They all looked up at me with bright enthusiasm.

Never have I felt so good hugging someone.

Penny, hearing my sobs came through. Properly awake, I looked into Penny's eyes. I now knew for sure that Heather was going to be fine. Both Heathers.

"Can I get you anything?" Penny asked.

"Yes," I said, "...a very strong coffee, a pen and some paper."

Elliot Retires

The overwhelming thing about retiring is just how difficult it is. Elliot had dozens of 'signing off' reports to write including that referring to Casey's Cheviot proposal. He spent several days and time at home sifting through Casey's papers. He had to lay aside his personal bias and assess the information in a professional manner. Despite this he still wrote a hefty report. There were questions relating to every aspect of Casey's work. The report needed to be in before the next board meeting. However, he would have retired before then so decided the best course of action to emphasize his concerns was to have a private meeting with Brighstone.

He met with Brighstone in his top floor office and after a coffee and lengthy chat reminiscing about the good and the difficult times, he produced his report and asked him to look at it with great care and not to let Casey make any more major blunders. Brighstone was polite, understanding and reassured Elliot that he would pay particular attention to the project.

Elliot left feeling he had done his bit and felt confident that Brighstone had paid attention. He would be gone in two days and be able to put his mind at rest over such matters.

Brighstone leafed through Elliot's document stopping at only two places. The first was in the ecology section where Elliot had noted he thought a number of pages had not been submitted from the original survey, as the grammar just did not make sense when you turned from one page to the next. Brighstone huffed at this thinking it a weak comment. The second was underlined stating that Elliot had not been able to find evidence of the £45000 annual rental income from the property. Brighstone pondered for a moment on this, but then thought about the complexities of the finance department and his own difficulties extracting information. He got up from his desk, picked up the report and walked across to his blue tinted floor to ceiling glass windows and looked out across an urban and industrial landscape. He spoke to his half reflection in the glass: "I don't see why Elliot has such a thing about wind turbines, they're better than having nuclear power stations scattered across the countryside. He's just a silly old soul." He looked down at Elliot's report, hefted it in his hand, walked back to his desk and placed it in the filing tray. Busy times, busy times.

The Shepherd's Knees

All of us will from time to time suffer from some form of infirmity of the joints and all will agree that such ailments can be horrifically painful and incapacitating. The Shepherd had had his share and suffered from regular bouts of rheumatism since his thirties and a degree of osteoporosis in the last fifteen years, but generally, considering his advanced age, kept remarkably mobile. Changing weather at any time of year could, in a matter of only a few hours, immobilise him. The winter with its fluctuations from rain to clear frosty weather had been very tough on his knees, to the extent that going up and down to the cellar for logs was becoming unbearable. He was almost unable to feed the sheep and had taken to giving them double quantities to last them longer when he could get down the track to see them; new growth in the pastures had begun which was a relief as his stock of hay was running low. He had almost run out of anti-inflammatory medication and was becoming worried.

One night, sitting very close to the range in his kitchen, trousers rolled up to warm directly from the fire, he feared for his wellbeing and became acutely aware of his deterioration and mortality. Some of us, especially men apparently, get into this state during a bad cold, getting a splinter or after a night out. The Shepherd was made of sterner stuff. He had trees to plant for Heather, for Mary and for the hills. He had seen the winter through and it was almost May which would bring better weather, so he could continue as normal once his knees recovered. April was proving to be a vicious month with cold lashing rains coming in from the north east.

Heather, who had become his constant 'would be companion' in the recent months, hated to see her dad so old and frail. Sometimes it pained her so much she would go for a walk up in the hills till she found her dad at half his age and spend time with him there to make herself feel better. She did however, spend most of her time with him at his maximum age, as that is where she felt she was needed most and it was easiest to find as that's as far as she could go in that direction. On other occasions, if the anticipation got too much, she would just step forward in time a little to see what happened next. A bit like flicking ahead when reading a book. If she went back she could get as far as the time she last saw her mother on the banks of the river Kale. Latterly she had been saddened by his discomfort with getting old and nearing the end of his life.

She sat next to him by the range watching his worried brow and her aged father rubbing his sore knees and she had tried to rub them too, although she knew it would not be noticed. She hugged him a lot of the time. She would sit next to him with her arm round his waist or over his shoulders chatting away to him about who was in the valley that day, what birds or animals she had seen or about what he did forty-two years ago. On occasion she knew something bad was going to happen so would try desperately to warn him, but it never worked. The physical things she could manage were pathetically small. But sitting there watching him in pain with his knees made her think a bit more clearly about trying to do something. Somewhere within her strangely displaced mind she remembered her mother's voice and like a silent echo you listen very carefully for; it said 'You are a grown up girl now, it's important that you learn to do things for yourself.' Feeling that she now had a very grown up and important job to do, she stared at the old man's knobbly knees as if the grey bristly hairs would give her a clue.

It was during these strange moments that the Shepherd came to a very important decision. There was absolutely no doubt that he needed help and soon. He had to be realistic about his predicament. What he really wanted was Penny and her young man back. He had had a number of visitors over the years but these were the ones that clicked with him and everything he had worked for. They seemed to understand him and his woodland passion. Heather could see he needed help too.

"I wish Penny were here now," said the Shepherd to his knees. "She would find a way to help me."

And that was it. Heather would find a way to help him by fetching Penny and her husband. She spun out of the Tower in an excitable state trying to decide what to do. She knew the tingly man was important from the moment he came into her world, he felt different as if he wanted to speak to her. So the first thing she did was go right back to the moment he looked down into the valley from the windswept ridge. She saw the moment he paused and considered which route to take. She had jumped up and down next to him pointing and shouting, then stood right in front of him waving her arms trying to tell him why it was so important to come that way. 'My father is sick don't you see, he needs Penny now, you must come and see my dad then you need to go back and get Penny.' The tingly man didn't see or hear her, but he did look down both valleys and something made him more comfortable about choosing that route. Thinking excitedly that she had done something, she had gone down the valley with him chattering about everything around them. It was Heather who had been worried about him getting too cold so she showed him the pigsty and when he had settled down did everything to keep him warm in the cold of the night by lying next to him. She had followed him everywhere and found bit by bit he began to react just a tiny amount, not so much to what she did, but more to what she was feeling.

The Shepherd knocked down the embers in the range and watched the orange glow come and go in the grey ash; he stacked another six ash logs in behind the bars and listened to them slowly ignite and crackle into life. He really appreciated the extra boost of heat on his sore joints and took great satisfaction from the knowledge, that while the tree had been growing, it had provided great beauty and a place for wildlife to flourish. Anything that went up the chimney was quite simply reabsorbed by his trees.

Heather returned from studying Penny's man and sat on the hot plate to the left of the grate and swinging her legs over the side told her dad that she was doing what she could and that help was on its way. The old man cupped his old hands over his old knees and lent towards the friendly flicker of the flames. For him the sounds of a fire were company for him; sometimes he imagined he heard a voice or the soft singing of an old song Mary used to sing to Heather to lull her to sleep. He raised his dry white palms in front of the fire for a few moments, then rubbed them together to get the blood flowing. Feeling hungry, he dragged his pot of stew over the heat and rising slowly organized a bowl and spoon on the edge of the range, a wooden spoon for stirring and his current book.

Heather returned to the young man when he was standing at the top of the scree, before he had started down into the valley and met the Shepherd for the first time. The man stepped onto the scree to make a careful descent just as her father was about to turn back from the tall stones. She was so determined to get them to meet, she tried to get the scree moving to carry the man down to her dad. She knelt down and with all her energy tried to tip a stone at the top of the slope, but nothing happened. Feeling desperate she suddenly had an idea; her companion the badger-faced goat was casually nibbling nearby. The goat being the only creature that fully sensed her and followed her most of the time, could actually do things for her. She ran across the scree calling the goat; the first time the goat simply went up hill and around the top of the scree jumping from rock to rock. So she went back over slightly lower and called again, and this time he crossed over the stones some of which began to move, but not fast enough so she did it again and again and on the last the scree began to flow and rapidly avalanched down to the tingly man who couldn't react quick enough to get out of the way and found himself swept down to the Shepherd below.

Heather returned to the old Shepherd and told him what she had done. Of course her words were silent to the old man, who now sat with his back to the fire and was strapping his knees tightly in the hopes that it would at least give them some support. Heather stood next to him looking at his bandaged knees and became really worried. For the first time ever she wondered what would happen to her if her father died. Would she be left alone in the hills if her father vanished like her mother had? She couldn't bear the thought of either her father being in pain, losing him entirely or not being at the Tower or in the hills where she belonged.

With increased urgency she returned to her study of the young man.

Operation Elimination is Ready

Casey stored the explosives and equipment in two sports bags at the back of his wardrobe at home. Jenny had the sense to carefully remove the as yet unused new rifle from Casey, to stop him playing with it, because she knew he would only do something stupid. She said she needed to take it home to practice holding it and get used to its weight. Casey's initial reluctance was soon dissipated with a hip wiggle and a smile.

They had both kitted themselves up with camouflage jump suits and mountain gear, rucksack, maps, compasses, binoculars, books, emergency food packs and first aid kits. They agreed that they should get themselves fit so Jenny had joined a regular dance class and Casey his local gym. Jenny was also jogging around her local park at least three early mornings each week. She was sleek, strong and sexy, melding with the Bond girl images in her head. Casey said she was looking better and better. She was getting a lot of whistles on the street and would deliberately take routes past building sites to attract such attention. If she saw scaffolding or a skip, a detour was essential to test her latest outfit. Her work colleagues noticed her increased confidence and tongues began to wag questioning her relationship with Casey, although they did take great care not to be caught in any compromising circumstances at work. Only Li, the very small and cheerful office cleaner, noticed stray red undergarments under a desk in Casey's office one evening. Nothing was said but Jenny found them neatly folded in a desk drawer the next morning. She didn't tell Casey.

Casey had joined the gym, gone through the initial health and fitness assessment and began on a twice weekly regime on the extensive range of the shining equipment available. He would arrive with steely determination, dress the part, approach the chosen device with great aplomb, mount it, grasp it and apply the force of his ample limbs. However, two minutes of effort turned him very red, four minutes sweating profusely and ten minutes in the shower feeling like he had done a good job. The gym instructor had encouraged him to do more, but Casey could only pant a wheezy, "Yes I'm building it up slowly." In truth he was not progressing and would compensate with exaggerated claims with his new gym mates in the bar later. He told them he was preparing for a great adventure in the Scottish mountains in a few weeks' time. They listened with interest, envying the excitement that he exuded and encouraging him on his secretive mission. He would not divulge details but with the aid of trying to impress them, a glass or two of wine and a large amount of stupidity, he said he had been allotted the mission to bring down two large structures, under the cover of darkness to prevent nationally sensitive documents falling into the wrong hands. Each time he saw them he added some detail to keep them interested. He hadn't even asked them what they did for a living.

Both Jenny and Casey had booked the same two weeks off at the beginning of May. They were both becoming more anxious about what they were trying to do, but there was a thrilling anticipation that bonded them and their shared aim to get rich quick was clouding their judgements and the delusion built between them, left them neglecting the consequences of their actions, if things went wrong. To them nothing could or would.

A New Romance

Bertie and Rosie became an item. Perhaps to some they were an odd matched couple. She was trendy and overdid the eye make-up and piercings and was a partner in a nearby clothing boutique, whereas he was smarter and gave a more traditionally respectable impression. They grew to love each other and saw each other several times a week. They shared a deep resentment and even hate towards their former partners Jenny and Casey. They would plan imaginary ways to seek revenge and laugh about their failings. Jenny was pretty but a complete tart according to Bertie. Rosie said Casey was evil who quite simply used people and spat them out when not needed anymore. They were both right.

Then one evening Rosie bumped into the lovely Li who she had met in Casey's offices on a few occasions and Li innocently said "I hope you got back your red lingerie that I tidied up for you." Rosie stammered a response, "Oh yes, that was really kind of you." Well, that was it, she went home seething and swearing about Casey and just how quickly she had been replaced. Forgetting just how quickly she had got together with Bertie. She wanted to know who his new woman was and when and why and where. Red lingerie, how horrible, she was a black lingerie girl and Casey had always told her he hated red! She brooded at home and was determined to find out more and thought that Jenny, who she knew and had befriended at Casey's offices, would probably know something. Casey was useless when it came to secrecy and subterfuge. She looked through her mobile phone contact list and found Jenny's number. They had exchanged phone numbers on the premise of a future shopping trip together. She was just about to press the button, but at the last second decided not to. She needed to speak to Bertie first.

Heather Learns More

As time went on, at least for the tingly man, as time for Heather was an odd dynamic, she found she could attract his attention. He would catch her movement in the corner of his eye but less when he looked directly. She trained the goat to be more obedient and come to her call and settle down on the ground when she asked. She discovered that if the man was tired, just beginning to wake up or in particular ill, he was more receptive and sometimes impressively so.

The other thing that occurred to her was that she had once been aware of other changed people in the valley who she had quickly blanked out as they disturbed her, so she tried to find them again and eventually came across the boy who looked like her. He was odd to speak to and often just vanished in front of her and she would have to go back and forth in the valleys and time to find him again. Slowly she learnt that he could speak to many other people like them and they in turn could communicate with others. Like a global network of drifting souls reaching back and forth in time.

Elliot's Contact

Sarah the photographer was a good person. She was kind to just about everyone, always giving the benefit of the doubt. She was also exceptionally good looking with curly rich auburn hair and deep sparkling brown eyes. She never believed people when they commented on her looks. Her nature was to look out and not at herself. As official photographer on Casey's Cheviot project she had produced a well presented and accurate depiction of the features she and Elliot had visited on her trip to the Cheviots. She made it clear that she had only skimmed the surface and hadn't reached the tower remains or ruined cottage in Ashburn. What she had photographed was the broader landscape views from the highest parts of the estate and the archaeological features encountered. She recommended a return visit of up to five days to do a more comprehensive job. Casey had sneered at the stunning portfolio of the Cheviot Estate and squirmed at the volume of hill forts and other notable ancient features and her photographs showed an amazing loch with fresh young trees growing round its shore. Graceful birch and alder framing views of unusual waterfowl. There were shots of receding drystone dykes tracking field boundaries or snaking along the spines of the hills. Surprised looking hares and hawks that had been caught in her lens. All in all, considering it was such a brief overview, it illustrated the sheer quality of the place.

Casey had thanked her curtly and decided to be more careful with his instructions to her successor. He needed drab photographs, not postcard stuff.

Before Elliot retired from the company he had had a number of meetings with Sarah and she had produced several sets of photographs for him including some blown up to poster size. They got on really well and he learnt a little of her background. She was thirty-five, had grown up on an equestrian centre in Devon and had many years of riding experience. The photography had grown out from a desire to capture those great moments when horses cleared a high fence or a rider came tumbling off, preferably unharmed, into a muddy pool. She was good at her job, owned most of her own equipment and had the opportunity to travel far and wide across the world. Sarah had a long term boyfriend but no plans to marry or have children. When Elliot and Lizzie had a private leaving do at home Sarah was invited too, though her man decided not to go. Sarah knew a good number of the faces from work but had not talked to most of them before. She was pleasant company and Elliot asked her to keep him in the loop with anything to do with the Cheviot property and she said she was happy to do so, though doubted she should after he retired. But what the hell, she didn't want to see turbines in the Cheviots either.

Elliot was pleased with this contact and they agreed to communicate using private Skype accounts that were secure from IT watchdogs at the company. This would ensure Elliot would be kept up to date with Casey's tricks as he was suspicious when he discovered that both Casey and Jenny were both off at the same time in early May. He encouraged Sarah to take the same weeks off too and join him for an all-expenses paid trip back to the Cheviots. How could she refuse?

Heather uses the goat

Heather was having fun with her goat. The goat seemed to enjoy the additional attention. When Martin came nosing around the Bleakhope farmyard and the Tower she managed to encourage the goat to follow her into Jake's hag. The goat in turn was followed by Martin. She didn't like Martin, he was sneaky and nosy and was annoying her dad, so she and the goat moved daintily along the path stepping neatly or leaping over deep marshy holes. For some reason Martin was foolish enough to follow and very soon was slipping and sliding into the sticky mires. It was amusing and she thought a fitting thing for someone who seemed to threaten her father. Eventually the goat had had enough and looped back home to the farmyard. Martin used shocking words and Heather had to cover her ears. The nasty man went away after that.

My Interview

I was to leave London the morning before my interview in Exeter so as to be on time and fresh for the occasion. I was very keen on the proposed position and had done a lot of research into their organisation. The area was rich in woodland and I was keen to work and live there.

The day before Penny had sat at the kitchen table while we talked about the opportunity. I stood behind her massaging her neck and back, squeezing and rubbing on demand. Penny sat upright in the chair with her fine fingers resting on the Heather bump. The reality of the bump turning into a screaming demanding child was looming. My friends at the squash club warned me at regular intervals that my life was about to change in a dramatic and irreversible way. I had half laughed and tried to imagine what it would be like and then worried about it.

The prospective grandparents had bought a pram, pushchair, cot, bottles, changing mats and numerous toys and mobiles. They insisted when I said there was no need. Penny and I laughed about it as we could see they were quietly competing with each other. Toys became more and more expensive as the weeks went by. I lent down and kissed Penny's slender neck; she raised a hand and hung onto my upper arm in a loving way.

"Do you think we could get a message to the Shepherd once the baby is born?" Penny asked.

I knew how important the link between her baby and the Shepherd's lost girl was to her, but didn't have a clue about sending a message. I thought the only way was to get the map coordinates and hire somebody to ride out to him with the news.

"Don't worry I'll think of something," I responded kissing her neck again.

Penny didn't seem too confident about my response, withdrew her loving hand and went quiet on me. After a while she turned around to look at me.

"I know—we could take Heather there after she's born."

I knew she was trying to gauge my reaction. Actually I thought it was daft taking a newborn on such an adventure.

"I think it's a great idea, but being realistic, I think it would be completely impractical until she was a lot older. Imagine carrying her in your arms over that distance. You would need to keep stopping to feed her and if the weather was nasty you and the child would be at great risk." She didn't respond so I changed the subject and said I would stay a couple of days in Exeter looking at rental properties just in case we were likely to move there.

The next morning she drove me down to the station and I headed out on my Exeter expedition. I said I'd phone or text once I was settled in a bed and breakfast establishment and insisted that she called her mum if she needed anything.

On the journey I reviewed the woodland ecology experience I had gained in various locations so as to be prepared for interview questions and scribbled notes about my European visits and finally came to the latest experience in the Borders. I underlined the words 'Establishing Native Woodland in the Cheviot Uplands' and somehow seized up. There was so much I could write. I put my pen down and watched the countryside rattle by through the train window. There was a lot to see, thick hedges, scattered woodland, cows in fields, then a grim emergence of a wind farm rising above a long attractive ridge; it was sickening to see and not one blade was moving. As I stared my focus changed and I found I was looking at the reflection of the pretty lady sitting opposite me; she likewise was staring out of the window at the wind farm. I watched her expressions and could read her distaste of the scene. As I looked out at the gross turbines through her reflection another image formed in my mind, one of the ghostly Heather standing before the devastation at the high loch in my dream, turbines going up before her, her golden curls whipping around her face, tears streaming down her cheeks, arms out to her sides, wrists exposed to the wind as if allowing the wind to slice them, sacrificing herself to protect the hills.

I gradually got the impression the lady opposite was watching my reflection in a similar manner. I looked away slightly embarrassed and returned to the sheet of paper in front of me. I looked at the heading and wrote down in large urgent writing *'Heather – Ghost – Turbines – Help!'* Then sat there unable to write more. I had been disturbed by the wind farm, the lady opposite and the words on the page in front of me. I was worried that my desire to see an increase in deciduous and native planting in the UK was up against a really evil force. Greed. I had heard of great forests being stripped aside to make way for wind farms. It seemed ridiculous for them to be claiming to be installing them to reduce the impact of climate change when leaving the tree cycle in place would have worked just fine, unlike the grossly expensive turbines. I was in a negative mood and the lady opposite must have noticed.

"We fought against a wind farm for six years in Cornwall," she announced, snapping me out of my trance.

"Oh," I said, unaccustomed to fellow travellers actually being human.

"Our village was threatened by a proposal to erect seventeen one-hundred meter high turbines within only eight-hundred metres of my house."

She seemed really nice and had seen what I had written.

"That's far too close, they should be at least two kilometres away and preferably not put up at all," I replied, now interested in her story.

"We got over six-hundred objections, the parish council against it and the county council planners recommended refusal." She leaned forward in a more engaging way. She really was quite good looking.

"That must have been a huge relief for you," I said.

"No. The planning committee gave them the go ahead. They are building them now."

I was shocked. Really shocked. I was hooked and wanted to hear the whole story.

"Why?"

Penny and her Moment of Madness

Penny didn't sleep particularly well on her own. It was odd not having her husband at least somewhere nearby. He had called her just as he was settling down for the night. He had been away before and she didn't like it then either. This time she knew it was critical for him to get a job and quickly as she could see the reserves in their bank account dwindling fast. She was not going to disturb her mum in the middle of the night so tried watching the telly for a bit, then read a magazine, but she was fidgety. She tried to analyse what was bothering her, thinking it was just because she was on her own, but then began to think about the Shepherd in the hills and the threat to his lifetime's work and how much it meant to him and the amazing things he did. She thought about his great loss and how he had chosen to give, rather than live a life of misery and bitterness. She was also stressed about her baby and the link with the Heather in the hills. Sometimes she laughed at herself for being so daft but then felt guilty as she thought about her Cheviot experiences. She had never seen Heather but *felt* her there. It was as if the Shepherd had a double shadow like an actor on a stage lit from both sides. There was something that accompanied him and in places like his kitchen it felt particularly strong. The more she thought about him the more she felt a growing sense that something was wrong. It felt like the Shepherd was calling her, was in distress and needed her urgently. The more she fought with the feelings the more her concern grew. Something was happening and she needed to go to him. She talked herself up, then down about it to the point of exhaustion.

As the night moved on she began to feel really tired so had a drink of water, put the light out and soon drifted off to sleep.

But then woke at four in the morning, eyes wide, feeling completely sane and rational and came to a decision. She was going to visit the Shepherd *before* the baby was born. She was going to go there immediately and would not have to carry the baby in her arms after all. If she went now, several weeks before her baby was due, it would be much less risky. She could also flit before her husband or family could stop her. Mad she knew, but she was determined. She just had to go to the Shepherd without delay. She clambered out of bed, packed her rucksack with food, medicines, first aid kit, and extra clothing, along with a map, her mobile phone, purse and cards. She had a strong cup of coffee, some toast and leaving a 'sorry' note rushed out to the car. She drove off and was north of Birmingham before her husband had woken up.

Interview Panic

I woke later than intended. The sweet bed and breakfast host knocked on the bedroom door and announced that if I wasn't down for breakfast very soon I would have to help myself as she was going out. I apologised profusely and looked at the clock... 9.45am... panic... interview at 11.00am. I had forgotten to set my alarm on my mobile phone like I normally did.

Actually I had slept in late because after checking in and phoning Penny, I had summoned a taxi and met my new friend from the train, Kerry, at a wine bar in the heart of the city. She got off the train with me and insisted we met later. She said she had loads to talk about and I agreed, justifying the somewhat inappropriate and clandestine meeting on the pretext of fending off turbines. This was true, but she was also a charming and pretty girl. I seldom got the opportunity to meet new people and being miles from home thought no harm would come of it. I was wrong; I did indeed learn about wind farm campaigns, but also just how predatory some women can be. A couple of hours later I politely explained to Kerry that I was *very* married and my wife was due to give birth in a week or so. Kerry apologised and we exchanged phone numbers and parted company. I returned to the B & B, my tail between my legs trying not to wake the occupants with the jangling keys. I made it to the room, had a quick bath and threw myself onto the bed with a huge sigh. It had been a tiring and unusual day to say the least. Later, settling down, I muttered, "Sorry Penny, I won't do that again."

I ate hurriedly, paid the host and called a taxi as I stumbled out of the door and sent Penny a text while I was in the taxi as I was too nervous to phone. I made it to the interview three minutes early, hot and uncomfortable. I then waited forty-five minutes before being summoned. Such is life. There were three people on the interview panel, all middle-aged and excessively serious. They asked me numerous questions and it actually went really well. I knew what they wanted and had prepared appropriately. They seemed to like me and I left feeling happy about how it had gone. That is, until I went into the toilet before leaving the building; while washing my hands I looked up in the mirror. My hair was a mess! I looked beaten up and, worst of all, had dribbles of my rushed breakfast on my chin and collar. My confidence ebbed; I cleaned myself up and headed out to find some letting agents. I wasn't going to go home until I had at least looked at what was available in the area, just in case they could forgive me for being scruffy. I phoned Penny but got no response so sent her a text saying the interview went fine and that I was off to look at rental properties.

Penny was only an hour from the Border and was feeling physically tired but otherwise fine. She pulled into a motorway service station and sat on her own eating fish and chips and stirring the ice in a polystyrene cup of fizzy orange. She was nervous and kept muttering to herself, "Why am I doing this?" She got odd looks of concern and pity from nearby customers, but she ignored them and focused on her mission. She aimed to get to Jedburgh that night, book into some accommodation and head out the following morning into the hills. She sent her mum a text saying she was visiting a friend in Salisbury and one to her husband congratulating him for a successful interview, saying that everything was fine except for losing her voice. Catch up soon xx.

Sipping the sickly fizzy drink she considered the risks of walking into the hills. She would take enough food, stock up with medical supplies and have her phone fully charged but switched off except when she needed it. She didn't know what to expect when she got to the Tower, but mentally braced herself for any eventuality. She knew at the worst she might find the rotting corpse of the Shepherd in his kitchen chair, or broken body in the hills somewhere. But this was why she felt she had to go, to make sure these things didn't happen, if it wasn't already too late.

Penny knew her husband would go ballistic when he found out she had driven off to Scotland risking herself and their unborn daughter, but she did know the risks. She might have an accident or something might happen with the baby, which she knew would be awful but she was still determined to check the Shepherd was alright; he was fairly ancient and there was nobody there to check on him. She knew it was going to be a long hike but was going to drive as far up the roads and tracks as their mini would allow, park up leaving a note to fend off farmers and head out on foot. She was fundamentally too honest to deceive her family for long so planned to send explanatory texts once she was almost there, probably from a hilltop before she walked down out of range of the phone network. She finished her drink, tidied up the plastic tray in front of her and headed out to the car. She got in, fired up the engine, then started having doubts. This was the opportunity to turn around and go back and nobody would be any the wiser; she could say she had turned back from going off to Salisbury. She put the car into gear and drew out of the car park, then remembered that she had no choice but to go north as there was no sliproad enabling her to turn south. That finalised the decision and she was out onto the motorway heading towards the Shepherd.

Bertie and Rosie Become Suspicious

The next time they met, Rosie asked Bertie if she should call Jenny to see if he knew anything about Casey's new woman. Bertie squirmed a bit at this, imagining the two of them starting to talk about him, sharing notes embarrassing him and possibly jeopardising his new relationship.

"I'd rather you didn't, sooner or later she will find out about us and could turn bitchy."

Rosie thought about this for a moment or two trying to find a way to find out about Casey's latest.

"Why does it matter anyway?" asked Bertie. An ex is an ex, he thought, forgetting how much hurt he felt from the way Jenny had treated him.

"I just don't want any new wench touching my stuff. I've still got to get the rest of my clothes and books at Casey's flat, including some nice black lingerie that you will like." She smiled, lightening the conversation and trying to divert Bertie from his train of thought.

"Why don't you get it over and done with and demand your stuff back?"

"I've already got my CD collection, but I left a bit of a nasty note last time, so he's probably either chucked everything out or changed the lock."

"Have you still got a key?"

"Yes I do," replied Rosie, now seeing a way to find out who the new woman was without upsetting Bertie.

"I've still got a key for Jenny's flat and some of her stuff which I want to get out of my place so I could ask her then," he said trying to help Rosie but also looking forward to telling Jenny what he now thought about her. It would be cathartic for him to rid his home of the last traces of Jenny and to clear his mind, so he could focus completely on the delicious Rosie.

"Why don't we do it now? You go to Jenny's and I'll go to Casey's place. It's Friday night, Casey will definitely be out as he loved to on Fridays and you might catch Jenny; if not, you could use your key and just dump her stuff. If she's there ask her about Casey's love life but don't let the bitch touch you."

"No chance of that, I can assure you! I have met the perfect woman now."

They finished their drinks, agreed to text each other at 10pm to swap notes and disappeared into the half-lit street.

Bertie stood on the street opposite Jenny's flat. He wasn't sure he wanted to see her. He was carrying two large bags of Jenny's clothes and miscellaneous belongings. He was watching the windows of her flat. He could see her moving between the bedroom and bathroom. He was about to walk across the street to go up and see her when a broad man in a greatcoat and trilby stepped up to the intercom of Jenny's block of flats and pressed a button. Upstairs Jenny's lights went off and the man below spoke to the gadget and a moment later Jenny appeared. Bertie ducked into a darkened doorway and watched with interest. The broad man stepped back, greeted Jenny who then linked arms with him and they walked away down the street. Bertie was unsure whether to follow them to see who the man was, or to dump Jenny's stuff and just get back to Rosie. The latter option won; he didn't want or need any confrontation with Jenny or her new man. He wasn't entirely surprised that she had hooked up with someone else so quickly. Tart!

When the coast was clear he made his way up to her flat. His keys still worked and he opened the door, punched in the alarm security code and gave her cat lots of attention. He peeked out of the window to make sure Jenny wasn't coming back up the street, then feeling confident put the hall light on, dumped her stuff against a wall and was just about to depart when the cat started rubbing up and down his leg and meowing for food. He couldn't neglect her so he went into the kitchen and found a sachet of food and put the food in her bowl. The cat was pleased. He found a used envelope and a pen and wrote a quick note. 'Brought back your stuff, fed yer cat again, don't starve her! Hope you have fun with your new man. B.'

Bertie stood up and was about to depart when he noticed a picture missing from the wall in front of him. It was a photograph of Amsterdam in winter with frozen canals, bridges and a rusty bike sticking out of the ice. It was a photograph he had taken himself and had blown up and framed after he and Jenny had had a romantic trip to Holland. He felt hurt that it had been taken down but accepted that's what happens when you split up with someone. He looked around and saw it stuffed next to the flip-top bin. He went over and pulled it out. The frame had slight damage where it had been dumped down but was fine otherwise. 'I'm having that back thank you very much,' he thought and walked out of the kitchen switching off the lights; he was heading to leave but then thought 'maybe she's chucking out other stuff of mine too.' So he put the photo on the floor by the door and decided to have a quick poke around. Nothing much jumped out at him as he had already cleared out, but then he remembered his dinner jacket bought by Jenny, so he opened up her wardrobe and found the jacket. He pulled it out and it caught on something that came tumbling out too. It was an odd canvas case. He unzipped it and picked out a gun, a brand new, totally unused rifle; a secondary case held expensive looking sights. He weighed them in his hand thinking it all very odd and not the sort of thing Jenny would have had for she was the cuddly bunny fanatic who wouldn't hurt a fly. He packed it away and got out of the flat quickly, having sacrificed his DJ and hung it back in the wardrobe, otherwise Jenny would know he had been in there and seen the gun. He walked off with the picture under his arm to find a safe comfortable place to send Rosie a text from. He was really confused about the gun.

As predicted, Casey was out. Rosie didn't care. Her keys worked and she didn't hesitate to scan around looking for traces of the new woman and collecting anything of hers she still wanted. She couldn't find a single bit of evidence which surprised her, no red panties, no lipstick and no girlie stuff in the bathroom. Puzzled, she started opening cupboards in the kitchen—nothing. Then the bin—nothing. She even opened the dishwasher and saw nothing, well almost nothing, there were two wine glasses, two cups, in fact two of everything. That would figure. The place was odd because it was too clean and tidy. Casey was normally messy and didn't even bother filling up the dishwasher let alone switch it on. So the new woman was the clean and tidy type, got him all organised like his personal assistant, secretary or something. She stopped for a moment as an image of Jenny at Casey's office flashed into her mind closely followed by one of Casey looking at her backside. She had jabbed him in the ribs at the time and given him a dirty look. 'I just wonder.' she thought and went through to the lounge. It had been moved around a bit, the glass coffee table had been pushed diagonally into a corner and a new wooden one had taken its place on the red rug. She walked around sneering, then something caught her eye: through the glass table she could see, barely hidden, two sports bags. Odd. She pulled out the table and opened them up. She lifted out a heavy package; not knowing what it was she turned it over then saw the label 'Danger high explosives'. She put it back very carefully and looked in the other bag: electronic switchgear and a big coil of wire. Somewhat alarmed, she put everything back in place and retreated without taking anything with her. 'I bet this has something to do with that Cheviot Mountain project,' she thought. She walked a couple of streets then paused to check her texts. Bertie's read: 'Found something odd we need to meet.' She sent one back: 'Me too, my place thirty minutes.'

Part 3 – Madness in the Mountains

The Shepherd in Need

The Shepherd was exhausted; he had slept in well past dawn, not raised from his bed, got dressed or eaten. He lay sleeping fitfully. His knees were agony and had woken him frequently in the night. He had become confused and drifted back to sleep each time. He didn't want to move because of the excruciating pain and had finished the glass of water within reach.

Heather fretted, walking up and down in the kitchen then around and around the hills looking for a clue of how to help.

She looked down each valley and over every hill to see if there was anybody heading that way. Nobody except Billy Tolk and his dog in the distance checking his sheep, too far out of her range even if she could do something. She went up to the high fort from where she could see the portrait in trees of her mother holding her when she was tiny; she loved the view and drew great comfort from it. She returned to the Tower kitchen and listened to her father's laboured breath on his box bed. She scanned her memory for help and the only clue she had was to speak to the boy. She had to go back ten years and to the high loch to find him. He was sitting on a summer's day looking at two lads fishing without permission in the bright waters, not that anyone would have cared but they were furtive all the same. The boy listened to her plea for help then agreed to go back with her; he held her hand so as not to get lost and they were back in the kitchen next to her father. The boy looked around him and said, 'I've been here before, I came with father to see auntie Mary.' Puzzled, Heather asked if he could find somebody to help. He vanished and then reappeared seconds later. All he could tell her was that a pregnant woman in a hotel in Jedburgh was coming soon. He vanished again leaving Heather hopeful at least. She fussed around her father telling him help was coming and not to worry. The Shepherd rolled over at one point and said something in his sleep that sounded like a 'thank you.'

Penny Prepares for Adventure

Penny arrived in Jedburgh before 1pm. She booked into a tidy looking hotel and ate lunch in the bar. She was ravenously hungry and was glad to eat something better than service station junk. She ignored those around her who stared at her bump and told the concerned receptionist that her husband was going to meet her the next day. This of course led to more accumulated guilt, so she sent him a text saying her throat was bad but everything else fine. A long soak in a bath helped soothe her sore back. She felt bad about her white lies but knew nothing was going to stop her reaching the Shepherd. Anyway everybody knew just how strong minded she could be. She lay amongst the bubbles contemplating the inevitability of the changes that were coming. To her the idea of moving out of suburban London to Exeter was fine as it was a beautiful area to live, but if they could move north nearer the Cheviots she would be happier. She had bonded so well with the Shepherd, his God-like task and the quality of the hills was outstanding. The Shepherd had demonstrated just how a huge diversity of life could be returned to the hills through something as simple as tree planting; his reduction of livestock and introduction of simple coppice rotations kept the landscape and environment a dynamic place and provided a healthy income free of subsidy.

Penny loved the concept of being able to appreciate and benefit from a small thing like a seed or sapling planted and watching it grow over the years. Each tree would be part of the cycle in the woodlands, filling the niche that the nature around it allowed. She lay back in the bath head resting, eyes closed with the scented steam rising deliciously around her. She felt the familiar little movements within her womb and stroking her hands gracefully and softly down her body to her swollen belly she pressed against the little kicks, encouraging more. She spoke softly to baby Heather stirring within her, as she often did. "Not long now baby, you stay safe there till I'm happy about the Shepherd. I need you to be strong for me for a few days. We've got a lot to do and a long walk ahead of us so please lie still and be patient.' A reassuring flutter beneath her hand made her smile. Pregnancy could be absolute bliss. It was a privilege that was to be savoured and to most, something that didn't come around very often. Penny focused on remembering the experiences good and bad, even the morning sickness and bleed was part of the journey. She enjoyed the slow swelling of her slim figure, its potency, the potential of new life and like the growing saplings, filling the niche available. Penny longed to be there in the hills tending her young trees. "I'm coming to the Tower tomorrow," she murmured into the hot air as she pushed herself forward, eyes slowly opening. Somehow there was a parting in the steam, a clear space with spinning eddies up and down its edges. A movement of cooler air that she assumed was due to her own movement. She looked around, grasped the golden towel and dried off her face, then sighing, sank back into the comfort of the bath, eyes closing to let her mind lap up her happiness and peace.

Tomorrow was another day.

Casey and Jenny up a Tree

Bertie met Rosie at her flat. She had a pot of tea ready and a pizza in the oven.

"Tell me all about it, what did you find?" asked Rosie as Bertie settled into the chair opposite.

202

"You won't believe it Rosie, I found a brand new rifle, sights, ammunition, everything! She is not remotely that way inclined, so I can't understand it at all."

Rosie froze with the teapot hovering ready to pour. Several things began to slot into place. Jenny had a gun? Jenny had a *gun*! She also worked alongside Casey—and Casey fancied her. What was going on? Had they got together for some evil mission, were they lovers? They were lovers! She'd been replaced by that tart, Bertie's tart!

"She's with Casey, they've got together. That's funny, considering that we got together too. But I'm pissed off and really worried too! Did you see her there?"

"I saw her upstairs before she left with some chubby geezer wearing a greatcoat and trilby."

"Were they *together* together? You know what I mean; did it look like they were an item?"

"Er, I'd say so, they linked arms and she hugged into him," replied Bertie.

"So, Casey and Jenny got together. The stupid cow, she will come a cropper. Casey won't give a monkey's about someone like that. You know what I found?"

"Tell me," said Bertie fetching a cloth to wipe up the spilt tea.

"Explosives!" ejaculated Rosie, well mad.

"A new rifle—and explosives!" Bertie replied. "This is getting serious. Have you got a pen and paper? I need to analyse this." A seeping concern entered his mind. He still cared for Jenny despite what he said.

The Gym Mate

Casey didn't know that one of the guys he drank with after his somewhat feeble gym sessions was D.I. Johnson from the MET. He had listened to Casey's bragging, initially thinking his stories were just made up to impress them all at the bar. He hadn't paid that much attention to start with, but several days later he was walking through the open plan office adjoining his own on the fifth floor when he heard a young assistant answering an incoming call, saying, "And what quantity of explosives have gone missing?" Nothing clicked at the time but he was good at absorbing information and being observant. The words sat, poised somewhere, waiting in his neat memory.

A week later he was coming out of the gym and he saw Casey dressed like a 1930's gangster in a greatcoat and a trilby. He had a pretty blonde on his arm dressed in a tight red number; she was fit looking, too good for Casey, he thought. The image stuck—it just looked suspicious. He imagined a hidden gun beneath the greatcoat and chuckled at the image.

It wasn't until he read a report about Red Kites being found poisoned at a proposed wind farm site in Lincolnshire that the little pieces of information began to topple and fall. Casey had also talked about his wind power project and how much money he was going to make.

The pieces of information coagulated into an odd image that hadn't quite been projected onto his conscious screen—yet.

Jenny and Casey Depart

The red Ferrari didn't have much space for baggage so they had to pack it and unpack it several times to get it in successfully. The bloke at the newsagents on the corner watched them and thought it served him right for having such a yuppy car.

Casey said he had to use his own transport as he couldn't use a company vehicle to go on holiday. Jenny didn't drive. Once everything was on board they slipped quietly out of Canary Wharf and filtered their way out to the M25 and onto the A1. Jenny was buzzing with excitement. She had packed her little black number in the rucksack and her favourite red lingerie just in case a casino trip was involved. Casey laughed with her and with perhaps too much enthusiasm, sped up the motorway.

The Perfect Cottage

I had looked at four properties, none of which struck me as the kind of place where Penny would want to raise a child. She needed green space, so I looked further afield. About twenty miles from Exeter I viewed what I can only describe as the perfect cottage. It was an old miller's house built onto the side of the adjoining bridge. It was beautiful with gushing weirs and pools of deep dark water slipping quietly beneath the stone arched bridge. There was a large secure and secluded garden with established flowerbeds and trees. The track that went over the bridge led to low lying meadows along the riverside and being too narrow for modern tractors, served livestock and the occasional walker only. The cottage itself had three charming bedrooms squashed into a beamy roof. Leaded dormers framed vistas of trees and the river. Convinced that Penny would love it I took lots of pictures and texted them to her. The kitchen was small but well fitted out and the main living room had a large inglenook and a creaky staircase leading to the bedrooms above. Outside there was a workshop and rickety garage covered with Russian vine.

I tried phoning Jenny to see if she had got the photos but got no response, so sent another text asking her to call me back later. I was really excited and was hoping I had made the right impression at the interview.

I phoned the letting agent and asked how long the property had been available and would the owner accept fifty pounds a month less to suit my budget. What I was thinking was the fifty pounds a month saved could go into making the place really special for Penny. The agent said he would phone back in the morning. I returned to my bed and breakfast and leafed through the other available lets. Somehow they paled in comparison.

Jenny and the Police Officer

A very shiny red Ferrari with an exceptionally pretty blonde in the passenger seat was going to attract attention anyway. The same travelling at one hundred and fifteen miles an hour near Durham was asking for trouble. The flashing of blue lights behind them brought on a series of bad words from Casey that even Jenny was shocked by. He pulled over in a skidding stop. He wound down the window and waited for the worst. The Durham cop smiled politely and asked him to accompany him to the police car. Casey reluctantly stepped out and followed the copper. But Jenny got out too and trotted past Casey and got to the policeman first, and Casey stopped to see what she was doing. They were having words, strong silent ones that Casey couldn't hear. He watched how she moved and smiled, then the policeman's voice dropped; she was flirting with him, offering him something. Casey hesitated and hung back. Then Jenny turned and stomped past him back to the Ferrari saying "Good luck" as she passed. Casey went on and got into the police car puzzled as to what was said. The police officer did the normal, told him off and gave him a handful of points to decorate his licence.

Casey returned to his car, pulled out cautiously past the cop car and demanded to know what Jenny had said.

She went quiet then after a while said: "Just our luck, a gay copper."

Elliot's Expedition

Before Sarah joined them in their accommodation near Chesters, Elliot and Lizzie made contact with three local anti-wind turbine groups. They were passionate about preserving the Borders landscape and wildlife but were up against a mixed council who felt obliged to let some schemes through, a government hell-bent on independence riding on the back of renewable energy and local apathy and distrust of anything associated with the words 'anti' or 'protest'. Elliot listened carefully, then suggested to each to meet him for a pub lunch the following day. He indicated that he wanted to help them but needed bringing up to speed.

They met as agreed and he was horrified by the persistent dishonesty of the developers, both corporate and individual. He heard about the poisoning of wildlife, false noise reports, proximity to people's houses and the bombardment of the population by the government with lies and threats. He took notes about bird and bat deaths and test masts going up without permission and agreed to visit the various sites. He said he had a lot to offer both from a business expertise point of view and financially. The three group leaders looked very pleased and they all exchanged email addresses and phone numbers. Elliot was upset by what he had heard and took his notes back to his hotel to make plans.

Sarah was coming the following day so he set about planning a walk into the hills at the weekend. The forecast was for bright clear weather with little wind. He laid out his map of the estate as provided by Casey and marked on a proposed route cutting up and down the main valleys taking in the ruined cottage in Ashburn and the tower in Bleakhope. They had already agreed to camp for at least one night to ensure adequate time for Sarah to get enough photographs. She was looking forward to the whole experience as she hadn't been camping since her schooldays. Elliot felt he was too old but was on a mission and anyone that knew him was aware that he quite simply never gave up.

He had spent a considerable amount of time looking at the economics of wind power and was shocked at just how completely unviable it all was. Without the huge consumer funded subsidies the industry wouldn't have got off the starting block. It was clearly more intelligent to invest in something that worked efficiently such as hydro, tidal and wave power or perhaps more significantly clean gas power stations or the safer nuclear energies that were low carbon technologies. The government seemed to have got caught up in the whole green thing without really knowing what it was getting into. Nobody had foreseen the rise of the greedy to take advantage of the seductive subsidies. The result was a damaged economy and despoiled landscape and ironically a huge risk to wildlife that surely the greenies were trying to protect in the first place.

Lizzie was going to stay at the hotel and carry on collating information about the health issues with wind turbines and make contact with more objectors in the area. She had bad hips so was unable to walk very far. She teased Elliot about going camping with a thirty-five year old. He replied that it would get the blood pumping, but assured her that they would be using separate tents.

My Concern about Penny

I had no idea at the time what Penny was up to. If I had known, perhaps events wouldn't have unfolded in the alarming way they did. I was so thrilled about the cottage I had found I didn't pick up Penny's nervousness when I spoke to her that evening. She phoned me at 8pm and was about to tell me something but in my enthusiasm I spoke over her, describing the cottage and its many attributes. After I had finished I asked her how the Heather bump and her throat was and to say what she was going to say before I started chatting. She said that her throat was fine and that she was going to go to see Susan in Salisbury but changed her mind. I didn't doubt her and went on to tell her about the cottages I was going to visit over the weekend. I wished her a good night and we agreed to speak again the next evening.

It wasn't until I was having a bar supper later that evening that I felt that Penny had wanted to say more. There had been a hesitancy in her voice that concerned me. I tried phoning when I returned to the bedroom but only got her voice mail service. I sent a text letting her know I would keep my phone on all night if she needed me. I still felt concerned so phoned Penny's mother and asked if she could check up on her when she could. She told me that Penny had said she was going to Salisbury to see a friend, but when I pointed out Penny had changed her mind she said she would pop around in the morning.

Feeling happier I continued to look at the cottage brochures and ran a hot bath to relax in.

A Saturday in May

Casey and Jenny had stayed in a hotel in Wooler and were heading towards Hownam to park up and head up to the high loch to do some weed killing. They had masses of time so were going to do a little each day and decided that killing the rare plants was a good starting point. Jenny had planned the route and directed Casey to Hownam, then up a smaller road that got progressively rougher and bumpier as they went. Casey became more and more concerned about his Ferrari as stones pinged on the underside.

"Why the hell did you bring us this way into the mountains?" he snapped. "These stones could damage the sump!"

"I'm really sorry," Jenny whimpered. "It's just a map, it doesn't say anything about the road quality." She found him really difficult to be with when he was grumpy. They had had a wonderful night in Wooler making the best of the hotel's facilities and she had fallen for him more and more. He could be so sweet and loving, so perfect in many ways, then turn like this.

Seeing a car park with a number of four-wheel drives in it he decided that was far enough. The Ferrari did look a little bit out of place in the hills. They acted according to plan. They were bird watchers going up into the hills for the day. They donned their rucksacks and locked the car. As they walked off up the track an ATV came bumping down towards them. They waved politely and Casey lifted the binoculars that were hanging round his neck and mouthed 'bird watching'. The gamekeeper just smiled and drove on. 'Idiots,' he thought.

Penny had had her breakfast, paid with her debit card and was driving up some rough tracks to the west of the Shepherd's Eden. She was desperate to get to him, but knew it was going to be one hell of a hike. Fortunately it had been dry for a couple of days so the track she was on should take her deep into a Sitka Spruce plantation where she could hide the car. After a couple of close shaves with deep ruts she thought it best to stop. She wedged the car into some young trees virtually hiding it from view but also scratching the sides quite badly. 'Oh dear, will have to confess in due course,' she thought. She checked her location on the map and reckoned she was five miles off the Shepherd's boundary. A steep and tough walk, but if she was right it would be an easy decent from the high loch. She hauled on her rucksack for the first time and found it particularly heavy. Having second thoughts she almost took it off to give up, but then thought of the Shepherd lying somewhere with a broken leg and with a grunt set her determination. Heather kicked within her and Penny said, "We are going to do this baby just hold tight." She clambered over a wire fence snagging her trousers in the process. Not put off, she strode out across the rough grass aiming towards a small cliff she had located on her map. The ground was fairly bumpy and she found it slow going. Frequent boggy areas meant she had to make a number of detours. The rucksack was cutting into her shoulders and she was getting too hot.

When she reached the cliff she collapsed panting on the grass, pulled off the rucksack and lay back staring up at the blue sky. "Oh why, oh why am I doing this?" Then she recalled a long time ago when she was eight; she had been on a Devon beach collecting shells and stones in a bright yellow bucket. She had wandered off while her parents lay back on their beach towels dozing in the heat. She had been focusing only a few feet in front of her and only needed a few more things to fill the bucket, when she heard shouting from the beach behind her. She had looked up and saw people waving and pointing in her direction and not recognising them she looked away and spotting the remains of a sea urchin and a dead starfish carried on regardless. It wasn't until the volume of the shouting increased and water started lapping around her ankles that she had any clue to what was happening. She looked around her and suddenly realised that the rising tide had cut her off; she was absolutely terrified despite being a strong swimmer at school. She dropped her precious bucket and started trying to wade back, but she was on a high spit of sand and the water was already a couple of feet deep around her. She wailed "Help Dad!" at the top of her voice but they were too far away to hear. Then she saw someone running down the beach towards her; a tall grey haired man plunged into the sea and diving into a crawl, swam over towards the rapidly diminishing spit. By the time he got to her she was up to her tummy screaming and panicking. She would never forget the man; he was old and weather beaten, but he came steadily out of the water gaining a grip with his toes in the soft sand, pushing the water heavily in front of him, arms flailing. His face was pale despite his tan and his eyes looked like they were popping out of his head. He had a horrible rasping breath and he was choking on the salty water. She was pretty terrified of him too, but he simply grabbed her around the waist and dived back into the water towards the beach. He swam on his back doing a kind of half sideways stroke. To start with she had struggled in panic and at one point ducked right under the water and came up coughing and spluttering; he had shouted at her to stay still and then she had hung on to him tight. As they reached shallow water strong hands grabbed and lifted her up, and by the time she reached the beach her mum and dad were there to take over. She had hugged them tighter than ever before, crying and shaking with cold and shock. The man who had rescued her, noble duty done, staggered back up the soft sand and just as her dad scooped her up to take her back to the car she saw the man quite simply crumple to the ground. She had shouted: "The man, the man!" Her mother had rushed over to help. Back in the car they waited for mum to return. With chattering teeth she asked, "Will he be alright dad?"

"I'm sure he will be fine, just exhausted I expect," her dad had said, his tone betraying his concern.

Then they heard the sound of a siren and saw the flashing blue lights of an ambulance as it manoeuvred its way through the car park. Mum came back looking very pale. Penny asked her "Is he okay mum?"

"He just needs a check-up, that's all," she said looking up at Dad. Dad had said nothing and drove off to our holiday house.

Penny didn't think they were telling the truth. "He saved my life, didn't he?" she asked.

Mum nodded. From the back seat Penny could see her dabbing away the tears.

The memory dispersed amongst drifts of white cloud high above. Nothing was going to stop Penny from saving the Shepherd.

Elliot and Sarah bumped along the track in a hired four-wheel drive. They passed the small clearing where Penny had hidden the Mini. The track took them to within four miles of the Shepherd's boundary. He had a copy of a letter from the Forestry Authority giving him permission to park in the woodlands. He wedged it onto the dash, visible to any interested party. They clambered out and loaded themselves up with the rucksacks prepared with tents, lilos, food and everything else deemed necessary. They agreed to take turns with the holdall carrying the camera equipment and headed for the ridge to the south of Upper Muirdean Loch. Elliot was slow but steady. They found a sheep track that took them upwards at a gentle incline. Despite that they both needed frequent stops and drinks of water. If it wasn't for their need to keep moving, Sarah would have had her camera out snapping at frequent opportunities.

Casey and Jenny had gone the shortest way. But it was also the steepest, their legs ached and the sweat poured off them. Jenny didn't feel sexy anymore. Casey was annoyed and worried about his Ferrari and racing heart. When they stopped his heart just kept thudding heavily in his chest. Jenny recovered quickly and he felt obliged to keep up with her, being the man of the mission. It took them two hours to reach a gentler ridge that would lead them in the right direction. He was annoyed that Jenny was so much fitter than him. She paused often to let him catch up, but pretended to be admiring the view. They stopped for lunch and Jenny lay back in her tight camouflage jumpsuit looking gorgeous but feeling sticky and unpleasant within. Casey swallowed large chunks of chocolate and drank an excessive amount of coke. He was moaning about the useless gamekeeper and was longing to be back with his pet air conditioning. But they had to get phase one complete so packed up and moved on. He felt completely sluggish and progress was slow. They saw nobody in the hills except on a far ridge beyond the high loch where a couple laden down with rucksacks moved slowly east. They waited till they had gone before heading down into the young woodland to make a base. They had granules of concentrated glyphosphate and a small sprayer hidden in a rucksack to do the job. Armed with the naturalist's map and his botanical notes they started to seek out the evil weeds. Finding them elusive, he realised the task was going to be greater than he expected. Jenny did exactly as she was asked.

Penny was truly exhausted. Her body was not prepared for the steep inclines. She was worried about baby Heather inside her. There had been no friendly kicks or wriggles for several hours. According to the map she had only covered a mile and a half; she had sore feet, back and legs already and should have been at home resting. She staggered up onto her feet again, reminding herself that once she reached the ridge it would become much easier, as it would be downhill all the way to the Tower. Her next target was a small hunt gate that led through to the higher heather-clad land. She could see the thin grey line of the stone dyke in the distance but not the actual gate. She took a bearing and headed in what she thought was the right direction, but it wasn't so simple; the rough grassland undulated as it rose higher, so she very soon lost her line of sight and became disorientated each time she negotiated a marshy area or rocky slope. Penny was a tough character but she was also intelligent enough to realise she was putting herself and her baby at risk, especially if she didn't find a way to get to the Tower before dark. Her progress was just too slow. She stopped on a hummock in hopes of identifying a landmark to aim for and unfolded her map to help. As she was sitting studying it, something caught her eye moving some five hundred yards away. Looking up she saw two horses grazing casually on a fresh bit of grass near a stream. Now there's an idea, she thought and although it was down the hill she thought it worth a try.

She approached the horses and whistled to see what would happen. Both horses looked up at her then carried on grazing, so she walked closer making friendly clucking noises. The largest was a bay gelding of the heavy hunter type with a white blaze down his face; the other was a black and white gelding cob with great shaggy fetlocks. They stepped away clearly not wanting to be caught and taken off the spring grass. Then Penny thought that an apple from her food supply would do the trick. She took off her rucksack, took out an apple and her first aid kit. She took a bite out and put it on her flat hand and approached with the offering; the bay stepped up to her and took it willingly. The cob, feeling left out, nuzzled her and she bit off another piece for him. She gave them lots of attention with enthusiastic stroking. Keeping them interested with promises of more morsels of fruit she knelt by the first aid kit and took out a fabric bandage and held it in her hand. She bit off more apple and as she fed it to the cob slipped the end of the bandage through the horses head collar and tied a quick knot. Sensing he was being caught the animal threw up his head, but Penny was ready and as the bandage dropped and unrolled from her hand she caught it before the horse could step away. Once finding resistance, he stood still and Penny rewarded him with more apple. She had only a little riding experience but enough to tie the bandage onto the head collar to make simple reins. She shoved the first aid kit back in her rucksack, wriggled the arm straps back on and hoisted it onto her shoulders, keeping her eye on the horse at all times to watch for sudden movements. She was gambling on the horse being used to being ridden and so far that looked likely. She led him to a bit of bank where sheep had eroded the soil and aligned him as best she could, then holding tight she climbed above him, rubbed his back and pulled the bandage reins over his head. He startled a bit but clearly knew what was coming. She lent on him to test for his reaction; he stepped sideways a bit but was still within reach. Then taking a huge risk she pushed her bump over his back, then quickly and quietly swung her leg over and pulling back on the reins sat down in a riding position. The cob jolted and leapt sideways almost toppling Penny off, but she hung on and said soothing words and managed to right herself and after a few more scary moments she calmed him down. She relaxed, lent forward and his shaggy feet stepped out; he knew the score. She found she could steer him with gentle leg pressure and occasional tweaks on the bandage reins. The whole experience had left her feeling beaten up but relieved as, so long as she took it steady, she could make good progress. The bay followed behind his companion.

Sarah had set up her tripod and camera with a big lens to take shots of distant features and pull in the background for dramatic affect. She took a photo of a couple walking down by the loch with the pretty white trunks of fresh young birch and a super shot of a lone rider as they came up onto the horizon across the valley. There were lots of cliffs and forts catching the light that made great pictures. Elliot, glad of the rest, finally encouraged her to pack up and move on. He wanted to camp part of the way down the Ashburn valley to be off the exposed heights.

Casey had identified one of the orchids on his list and with Jenny as a spotter he was following with the pump action

217

sprayer. Once they knew what they were looking for they were finding dozens. He was worried about this but felt sure concentrating on the most sensitive species first was the best course of action. They had found a small burn trickling into the loch that was deep enough to fill the sprayer. The sachets of weed killer were convenient sizes to carry and handle. Jenny stuffed most of the empty sachets into her rucksack.

D.I. Johnson was jogging down to the gym for a quick Saturday morning workout. He loved being physically fit and enjoyed the social times associated with the gym. His wife had said as long as he was back by two to take the kids to the movie, that was fine. He did some stretching and then chose the rowing machine for a quick blast. He had big arms and shoulders and always felt great on that machine. Last time he had used it that Casey bloke was struggling on the next one. He had been puffing and groaning. As Johnson thought about this he remembered Casey's words 'got to take a building or two down'; this memory went pinging up like a ball in a pinball machine and rapidly bounced around hitting the other memories that were waiting and like a great window opening the image of Casey and explosives and buildings shone bright and clear. The gym manager was surprised to see him leave so fast.

Johnson got to his office with only an hour to spare before having to leave to take his children to the latest Disney flick. He grabbed a new notebook and wrote down...Casey *who*? *Which* investment firm? Explosives missing from *where*? *Which* wind power site? He fired up his PC and within ten minutes with the aid of Google identified Casey Leonard Pritchard, 35 years old, DZY Investments. He ran a search on internal records and discovered the explosives were missing from KL Quarries, a report from a Derek Demster, KL

Quarries was owned by Fox Group who in turn was owned by DZY Investments employer of Mr Pritchard. How interesting. He phoned the investment company and asked to be put through to Casey. The security receptionist obliged and a voicemail declared his absence till 17th May. So he was on holiday, was he? He would have to wait until Monday to find out more about the wind farm site. He emailed 'traffic' asking them to run a check on Casey Leonard Pritchard to see if he could identify a vehicle associated with him. He knew they would be short staffed on a Saturday so left his initial research there. He had a cartoon to watch and Monday would be soon enough.

I had tried phoning Penny several times on Saturday morning and left her a message. By eleven I had reached the next house on my list. It was a charming Vicarage at the end of a busy little village. I pulled up outside and tried phoning again, but had no response, so sent a text asking her to phone as I was concerned. I then phoned her mum and again no reply so left a message asking if she'd been over to see Penny yet. The Vicarage was actually quite large for what they were asking per month which immediately made me suspicious— what was the catch? As a student I had been caught out by renting a flat in a tenement near Uni that seemed so ideal, only to find I had to put up with nightly disturbance from the student bar below. Fine while you were being sociable but hellish if you wanted to study or sleep. I walked up to the Gothic entrance to the Vicarage and pulled out the beautifully ornate, somewhat oversized, key.

Mr Cob

Mr Cob, as Penny called him, was brilliant. He had obviously had reasonable training and responded well to her crude riding. She managed to negotiate the rough land and Mr Cob kept out of the marshy places. Each time she had a clear view of the landscape she guided him in the direction of the hunt gate. Although it was difficult riding with a rucksack on, she was feeling confident about her progress. When she reached the gate she had initially planned to let Mr Cob go to return to his grazing, but thinking that he was such a blessing she thought she could just borrow him for a day to get her safely to the Tower and the chances were that a couple of horses put out to grass like that were not going to be checked by an owner that often, so hopefully nobody would notice. She slid off Mr Cob's back with a bit of a thud not welcoming the thought of trying to remount. She tied him up to a fence post and went to open the gate. It was bound up with several bits of old baler twine, so she had to find a sharp stone to saw through them and even then the gate was so bedded into the turf she had quite a task opening it enough for Mr Cob. He came through willingly enough but then she had difficulties stopping the bay coming through too. Apologising to the bay she pushed him back and dragged the gate shut. She joined the old bits of twine together and refastened the gate.

She patted the bay over the wall and walked off with Mr Cob, looking for a handy mounting place. Seeing a bit of post and rail fencing blocking off the gap left by a bit of collapsed wall, she aligned Mr Cob and hauled herself onto the wooden fence. Finding it hard to balance with the rucksack on and keep Mr Cob in place she had to take a chance and as she pushed against the fence Mr Cob stepped sideways, forcing her to have to push harder; a rail snapped and she plummeted to the ground with one foot caught between the rails. Mr Cob pulled away and walked off to talk to the other horse over the wall. Penny had landed badly, bashing her wrist and head on the ground. She had twisted awkwardly and had to struggle to release her foot. Feeling a bit worse from the fall she had to sit there for a few minutes to recover.

She took off her rucksack and lay back on the turf, pulled out her phone and checked the reception. Nothing there, but she was sure there would be at the high ridge. She returned her phone to her pocket and put her hands on her baby bump, worrying about the affect all this rough activity was having. She felt a movement and smiled to Heather. "Glad you're okay in there baby, we've done the worst." She stood up with great difficulty and caught Mr Cob and tied him up to a rail. She pulled out a packet of digestive biscuits and fed him a couple and ate several herself. She wiped mud off her forehead and out of her hair and straightening herself out and repositioning the rucksack, prepared to mount again. She checked her map, selected a new target, successfully clambered onto Mr Cob and set off up the hill.

Heather in a Spin

Heather was fretting. She hadn't seen her dad move since midnight. Even the old wooden framed kitchen clock had stopped in the early hours. The Shepherd hadn't had the strength to wind it up. She could see that he was still breathing but he looked deathly pale. The fire had gone out and he was cold, extremely cold.

Heather knew Penny was coming and kept going up to the highest hill in her territory to see whether she could see her.

She scanned in all directions and saw two people at the top of Ashburn so went to see who they were. She found a tall man with a kind face walking with who she thought must be his daughter. They had large rucksacks on and looked tired and hungry. They sat down for a snack and she sat opposite them completing a triangle and listened to them talk. The old man was explaining to Sarah his concerns about the proposed wind farm in one of the most stunning parts of the Borders and how the trees would be felled and cruelly pushed aside, and how tracks would be laid using stone quarried along the route followed by impossibly huge wind turbines that would be bolted to massive blocks of steel and concrete poured into giant holes. Cable trenches would scar the hills and hundreds of men would trample the ground.

Heather was absolutely aghast and horrified and she sat mouth open and eyes wide listening to them. She had seen the white things spinning and spreading from the distance and they had made her feel uncomfortable and nervous. The man then described how the huge propellers could kill bats and birds and scare others away permanently. Sarah said she felt it was her duty to record and present visual evidence why the project should not go ahead. There was not only an amazing array of features and wildlife but also the potential of more enhancements throughout the hills with the careful integration of woodland and agriculture and she was determined to demonstrate the potential and reasons for preserving the hills. Elliot said that wind power would ultimately fail and the machines would rust away and crumble to the ground and be swallowed by the earth like so many follies of mankind.

Heather stood up and with hands on her sides, elbows out, shouted at them: "Well come on then, what are we going to do about it? We need to get a move on and I've got to find Penny so she can save my Dad." The images they had created in her head were dreadful—she could not believe that anyone could suggest destroying all her father's planting and scar and trample the ground. She spun off back to the Tower to tell her Dad, to wake him and get him to stop them doing it. Didn't the evil people know just how many had lived and worked in the hills, how much history lay just beneath the surface, how the bare land could be transformed into something truly amazing?

Her dad just lay there looking grey, so she went off to find Penny's man. She knew he would be most receptive when he was ill and could see her especially when half asleep, so she followed him back to when he was at his worst when getting over a bad cold. He had gone off on his own exploring before he had fully recovered. He had laid down to rest and she had managed to lure him by singing and once she had his attention had taken him all the way to the high loch and with the help from the boy who looked like her and his ability to link with other changed people, had manipulated his mind to see images of what Elliot had described to Sarah, as the potential fate of the hills. She had had problems getting him back to the Tower but the task succeeded as the following day he described his 'dream' to Penny and the Shepherd.

Penny's Dilemma

Two things happened as soon as Penny reached the high ridge. Firstly her phone went *ping, ping, ping* as it came into range and the emails and texts rained in and secondly Heather moved suddenly within her and gave an almighty kick. She clutched her bump in front of her letting go of the reins. "Ow Heather that was sore!" she gasped getting really concerned. "Don't come yet babe, you've still got two weeks cooking." Heather wriggled in a more normal way. "Sorry, it's being a tough day for you," Penny said reassuringly.

Heather inside her womb had a very good reason to kick. Heather of the hills had just become aware of Heather the bump. It was a strange experience for them both. Heather the bump felt a pulse of energy from outside her mother's body, like nothing she had felt before. All she knew to do was kick and she had kicked really hard. The pulse had been frightening.

Heather standing by the high loch had been scanning the horizon for Penny and suddenly she was there sitting on a horse. She could feel Penny immediately she came over star knoll and rushed to her in earnest, but as she drifted towards her something odd happened; the first thing was that she could sense there was someone else there she couldn't see; it was immensely powerful and potent in a calm strong way. It was like a warm red glow emanating from the centre of Penny and it drew her in close and for a split second she saw another face staring right back at her, the face of a baby with large bright blue eyes; it seemed to say, 'I'm here for you.' Heather of the Hills reeled back in shock and confusion; she stood some fifteen yards away staring at the Penny she had hoped for so much. The soft breeze ruffled her once golden curls. This was the Penny who was coming to save her Dad. She smiled and stretched out her hands in front of her to Penny in greeting and desperation, pearly tears sliding down her pale cheeks. 'Thanks for coming but please be quick.' The red glow receded within Penny and Heather felt more comfortable to approach. She floated around Penny and the horse, aware of the new person; it was like a cautious stand off and there was a strong mutual attraction and slight fear of each other all at the same time. Neither had felt this before and an odd tension fell into place. It was like two magnets circling each other that had equal ability to attract or repel each other.

Penny rode up to the remains of a weather-beaten thorn, slid off to the ground and shed her rucksack. She was exhausted, bruised and dirty. But she really didn't care—her baby was fine and the Shepherd was priority and she knew she could get to the Tower safely. She sat and drank some water and ate a tuna sandwich she had brought from the garage in Jedburgh. She thought she had better inform hubby, so she took out her phone and checked her emails and texts. The emails were the normal sales stuff she ignored, but the two texts alarmed her. The first from her mum said: 'Been to your house dear and discovered you've gone. Did you change your mind again and go to Salisbury? Couldn't understand your note, who was it for? Contact me please. Mum x.' The second one she was scared to read: it was from hubby and was predictable. 'Just had a text from your Mum saying you're not there! Where the hell are you? Are you okay? Please contact me ASAP!'

Penny sat gazing across the hilltops. After a while she texted them both saying 'Hi, baby and I are absolutely fine so please don't panic. I have to confess I am visiting the Shepherd as something tells me he needs help. I'm sorry I didn't tell you, I just knew you would try to stop me. I have used safe transport and will be at the Tower by sundown. My phone will go out of range as I go down the valley and I will switch it off anyway to save power. Please don't do anything till you hear from me, I shall be in touch about midday tomorrow. xx'

Withdrawal from the Hills

Jenny and Casey hadn't seen Penny or the horse. They had run out of orchid spray so were heading back to the car. Tired and hungry they were pleased to have achieved something at least. They were going to stay in Kelso that night and stock up with weed killer in the morning. They thought there would be a handy garden centre somewhere. Jenny had enjoyed working as a team with Casey and very much looked forward to Day Two of the mission. They did however agree to find a gentler route into the hills. Jenny suggested they hired a large four-wheel drive and sleep in it somewhere. That way they could achieve more and have less walking to do. Casey didn't like the idea at all, finding daytime in the hills an unpleasant experience, let alone night. He felt that if he was to put up with this whole event he would at least have to have a comfortable place to stay and decent food. But by the time he got back to his car Jenny had made enough seductive promises to bring him round. Furthermore the little rash of chips in the blood red paintwork of the Ferrari bumper and sills sharpened his thinking. He was furious and grumbled to Jenny all the way to Kelso.

Good Company

Sarah and Elliot were getting on like a house on fire. They discovered they had a mutual interest in travel, especially Eastern Europe. Sarah had insisted on stopping at every possible photo opportunity and Elliot put numbers and arrows on the map for later reference. They found a small plateau halfway down the Ash burn, hidden between short steep banks of crumbling clay. It was sheltered and gave them easy access to fresh water. They pitched their tents with the openings facing each other and built a fire using a ring of stones between the tents. Elliot had matches and managed to get a heap of dry grass to smoulder then eventually burst into flames after a lot of earnest blowing. Sarah collected twigs and bits of broken fence posts to feed it, but with the scarcity of trees in that valley there wasn't much to find.

They were really enjoying the whole experience and they settled down to an evening of trying to cook sausages on the fire and chatting about childhood experiences, their mutual love of landscape and just how important it was to preserve and enhance it. Sarah had produced an exhibition of landscape photography as a post grad student in Gloucestershire, based on the area from Tewkesbury to The Forest of Dean, illustrating the variety of landforms and the importance of trees and hedges in maintaining the attractive quality of the countryside.

Elliot was much more relaxed having retired from the company, felt he could explain to Sarah his misgivings about wind power, its effects on the people and the damage to the country they lived in. He expressed his feelings about the company getting involved with something that was so clearly disliked by the majority, the pointless political gesturing and as all things effected directly by politicians well worth avoiding. Sarah said she would present a portfolio to her company superiors that would be difficult to ignore.

Penny Finds the Shepherd

At the Tower there was silence. It clung to the beams and hung quietly in the cobwebs. The Shepherd didn't move. The fire had long gone out. The Tower had had continuous occupation since it was built over five hundred years ago, whether that was by great Border barons, tenant farmers or squatters. There had always been the voices of humanity bouncing around inside its vaults. The building had changed like most, but its heart, its integrity as a place for the living had been intact. The Shepherd sometimes felt like a last bastion of support, a buttress of human flesh and bone propping up its walls. It had been such an amazing home for him for so long his every fibre had intertwined with its masonry like the whole of his woodland and hills outside. When you have loved and cared for something for so long you become part of it. The Shepherd was the current 'laird' and indeed was the master of everything he looked out upon. His only wish was to have shared it with Mary and Heather.

Mr Cob wasn't so good coming down the Bleakhope track. His hooves slipped and stones jutted against his frogs. Penny let him walk on the grass where possible, but then found he would pull his head down to graze and she would have to tug on the bandage reins and kick him on. She had spent two hours negotiating the slope and there was a hint of dusk in the sky. She wanted to move faster but knew she had to look after the horse. She was going to need him tomorrow to regain enough height to get phone reception. At last she came to the sheep paddocks where she slipped off and removing the reins set Mr Cob loose to graze. The sheep stotted off to the far end and watched carefully at the odd animal. Mr Cob buckled at the knees and Penny watched him roll over and over in the dust, then stand, stretch and do that wonderful horse shake thing. Penny loved to see horses do that and wished she could do it too.

Leaving the paddocks she only had a few hundred yards to walk to the Tower. She was feeling sore from riding bareback and her anxiety was building, making her heart beat faster in dread of what she might find. She glanced in the direction of the Tower and scanned the skyline for a trail of smoke that would indicate a healthy fire and Shepherd in residence. She had brought firelighters and matches just in case. The familiar old goat appeared and bleated a welcome. Seeing the Tower again made her heart leap with excitement, both from the joy of seeing it but also the fear of what lay within.

She reached the door and looked up at the ornate crest carved above it before stepping cautiously in. The Shepherd's crook was just inside the open door. She shouted up but it was quiet, far too quiet. She called "helloo" as she made her way up the curved stairs, but this prompted no response. The hall door was closed so she knocked and entered quietly. Everything seemed in place. Portraits, furniture and the chairs still at odd angles. She dumped her rucksack on the table and feeling sick with dread rushed into the kitchen.

At first she couldn't see the Shepherd, so she ran to the base of the turnpike leading to his private quarters and yelled up them. A cold empty echo came tumbling back down. She thought about going up them but then as she hesitated thought she heard a movement behind her. She turned to see the Shepherd's hand hanging out of his box bed next to the range. 'Oh my God he's dead!' she thought, seeing the greyness of his fingers. She stepped over and peered in. The Shepherd's face was turned away from her so she cautiously placed her hand on his head: stone cold, she got a kitchen chair over to stand on so she could reach further over him; she started to cry and wished she'd left sooner. "Oh, I'm so sorry, really, really sorry, I should have come to you last week." She stroked the old man's hair and leant over to see his face. His eyes were closed but just as she was going to retreat and rethink what to do, she thought she saw the slightest twitch beneath his left eye. With raised hopes she started to gently shake his shoulder and said, "Wake up, wake up, it's me, Penny." Then there was a horrible wheeze as the Shepherd's body responded to her touch. His head turned towards her and his pale fingers clenched the edge of the bed. He tried to open his eyes but they seemed gunged up and his lips were dry. She jumped down. "Water, you need water!" She grabbed a mug and filled it from the brass kitchen tap, clambered back up and putting an arm under his bony shoulders, she managed to get his head high enough to get the cup to his mouth. She had to pry open his jaw with her thumb and crudely tip some in. It was an unpleasant thing to do but she could see it was critical.

The Shepherd gulped and the cold water splashing down his shirt made him start and seem to wake him more. He coughed and choked and she feared she had made things worse, but she could hardly call an ambulance. He grunted and seemed to become aware of her; a shaky hand moved and touched her arm in acknowledgment. Hugely encouraged, she gave him some more water that was received more enthusiastically, several heavy gulps and the Shepherd rested his head back. Penny could feel how cold he was so quickly laid the range grate with paper and kindling and finding the matches in the normal place got some flames flickering. Once she was happy she loaded up the fire with small dry logs and returned to the Shepherd. He looked so cold and pale she was really worried; she had to get him warmed up as his own body wasn't generating enough heat. "Only one way to solve that," she muttered, then sat down and took off her boots and coat, stood on the chair and pulling back the blankets, pushed him over to the far side and managed to climb in next to him. She spoke all the time reassuring him that he would be fine. She pushed her bump up against him, rubbed his arms and chest vigorously to get the blood flowing, then hugged him tightly to share her heat. He didn't and couldn't resist, but after a while he started to shiver and twitch as if his body had remembered what to do. His breath quickened and she could feel him trying to move. She lay there warming him for more than an hour until she felt too hot beneath the many layers of blankets.

Eventually the Shepherd's shivering subsided and she could tell he had fallen asleep. His breaths became heavier and much more regular. She hugged into him praying he would recover and then extracted herself.

The next thing was food, so she scanned around to see what the Shepherd had. The bread was stale but there were vegetables that looked fine. A joint of ham lay beneath a mesh dome on the windowsill and some apples in a bowl on the table. She pulled out her own food and got to, chopped up the ham, carrots and potatoes to create a nourishing soup. She ate a bread roll from her own supplies and laid out some chocolate bars on the kitchen table. As she added more logs to the fire she became even more determined to save the Shepherd and longed to hear him speak. She selected a black pot from the sink drainer, added some water and returned to the table to put in the ingredients. She seasoned it with salt and placed it on the hot plate. She pulled over a chair and grasping a large wooden spoon stirred the broth at regular intervals and kept herself warm by the fire. She was too exhausted to stand. She listened to the faint breaths from the box bed and if she thought she couldn't hear anything froze with ears pricked. She thought this is what she would do once baby Heather was born and lay in her own cot.

As she sat there in the warming kitchen she was overcome with exhaustion and without realising it sat back and her eyes slowly closed. The next thing she knew was being woken by a great hissing from the fire. She sat up quickly struggling to remember when and where and why and seeing the soup boiling over, grabbed the spoon from the floor where it had slipped from her fingers, poked it through the pot handle and dragged it off the heat. She stumbled over to the sink, washed the spoon and returned to stir the pot to prevent it burning. The regular breaths of the Shepherd gave her some comfort. Once she was happy the meal was cooked she ladled some into a bowl and placed it on the table to cool. She returned to the old man in his cot-like bed and hauled him around till she had him propped up enough to feed. First she gave him another cupful of water and fetching a tea towel dabbed the gunk off his eyes and wiped his face. She felt so sad seeing him like that, in bed in his clothes, unshaven and uncomfortable. She would get him sorted out in the morning. The soup had cooled, so she spooned some into his mouth and he swallowed heavily. After the bowl was empty she stroked his forehead and heard his stomach gurgling which sounded promising. Thinking he now felt clammy she found some paracetamol and ibuprofen in her first aid kit, took out two tablets of each and ground them to a fine powder, added it to a small amount of water and with some difficulty managed to get the Shepherd to swallow it. She followed it up with chopped up chocolate to chase away the taste of the medicine and give him some more energy. She smiled at the thought of human life as being a great cycle where you start off as a helpless baby, only to end up so dependent again in later life.

The Shepherd just managed to open his eyes a tiny bit and look up at Penny. She gave him a huge smile and rubbing his shoulder said, "You'll be fine by the morning, you'll see." Feeling she was about to collapse herself, she went up to her old room, quickly washed, cleaned her teeth and changed into a tracksuit. She returned to the kitchen, loaded up the fire with ash logs as high as she dared and clambered up into the box bed next to the Shepherd. He stirred briefly as she hugged into him.

"Heather and I are going to keep you warm."

Indecision

I didn't know what to do. Penny had gone gallivanting on her noble quest. I was in Devon worried sick. She was only a couple of weeks off giving birth and was putting herself and our child at risk. What if she started to give birth early, who would know and would they be alright? At least there was a chance the Shepherd would be there and he would have enough experience with sheep and cattle births. But then James Herriot images of calving ropes and the like alarmed me. I knew just how compulsive Penny could be, but also that she wasn't completely mad, she would be well prepared and judge the risks for herself. I spoke to her mum and explained what I thought. We agreed to contact the Jedburgh police explaining the circumstances and primed them for action should Penny not be in contact before 1pm the following day. When I phoned them and told them what was happening, they thought the best course of action was to warn the mountain rescue service. They did that on my behalf and suggested I did everything through the police service to keep them informed. I thanked the officer profusely and returned to my lodgings. There was one more property that I wanted to view. It was a modern house on the outskirts of Exeter that the agent insisted I viewed. It wasn't our cup of tea as a dwelling, but it had five acres of garden and paddocks attached. I was unsure whether to just head north on the train immediately, so I could be close at hand if Penny needed me, or to complete my mission in Exeter as planned. In the end I stayed giving Penny and fate the benefit of the doubt.

Happy Heather

The spirit of the Shepherd's Heather was overjoyed; she had accompanied Penny all the way down the track to the Tower and had been at her shoulder ever since. She had encouraged Penny at every opportunity and had become used to the baby inside her. The baby pulsed with the potency of young life and Heather grew to appreciate its company. To her it felt supportive, as if it too was encouraging them to help the Shepherd. However, if she got too close or was too direct in her approach, she felt pushed away in a blunt harsh way. She was so glad that Penny had come back; she wanted to help her and encourage her to stay. Thinking about this she decided to try what the boy that looked like her had helped do with Penny's husband, she wanted to know what would keep Penny there, but was severely scolded by the baby as soon as she tried. She drifted ghost-like out of the Tower feeling a bit hurt and leant against the well to think. She decided to go back to Penny when she was last there and see what she could do. She watched Penny for a few days and on one occasion came upon her skipping along the track towards the tumbled down cottage; she had sat on a moss-covered log and started thinking about restoring the cottage. Heather gently infiltrated Penny's imagination and very quickly began to enhance and project her ideas into the scene before her; it was fun and easy surfing Penny's imagination, but when the image of a toddler appeared between Penny and her husband, she suddenly became aware of the tiniest spark of red glowing within Penny's belly. Fearful of being rejected she retreated and stood next to the old goat to see what happened.

Hotel Plans

Jenny had selected the most expensive hotel in the area. Casey could afford it and he was enjoying her company. She spent an hour getting dressed, doing her hair and make-up. She had selected her little black number, high heels and a simple string of pearls at her neck. She looked perfect. She fluttered her eyelashes at Casey and asked, "What do you think darling, is this going to turn heads?" She swung her hips from side to side, looked up at the ceiling with her large blue eyes and put her hand behind her head to complete the picture. Casey was aching; he had sore legs, stretched lungs and the start of a blister on his right heel. He would have preferred fish and chips and a cheap B & B, but knew he had to feed Jenny's delusions to keep her on board. "You look absolutely stunning," he said genuinely impressed. She did and she knew it.

They descended for dinner, entered the dining room and there was a satisfying lull in the general chatter as all the warm blooded men paused with cutlery poised in odd positions, looking over their wine glasses or accidently dropping their napkins on the floor, to gaze at Jenny's figure, starting from the perfect feet and working gradually upwards. In a strange almost choreographed way the female proportion of the room, aware of a pause from their male counterparts, all looked up, saw their menfolk's distracted eyes, looked in the general direction of distraction, perceived the goddess Jenny and struck out neatly with a foot to refocus their loved ones on the consequences of such foolish thoughts. A hum, sounding a bit like 'Tart', reverberated across the fine linen tablecloths, but then they could have just been ordering desert. Male cheeks flushed and female eyes glared as Casey and Jenny were shown to a seat in the bay window, enjoying prime views over the Cheviot Hills. They looked amazing, a billowing mass of fading blues rising up before them, framed by the fine veteran oaks on the silken lawns of the hotel's grounds. "This is absolutely perfect!" breathed Jenny, enjoying the setting as she placed her perfect derriere upon the tapestry seat. Casey looked out upon the beautiful hills and imagined a thousand turbines with twenty-pound notes fluttering up into the evening sky, then caught in the jet stream being sucked away into his private Swiss bank account. He didn't give a monkey's about views.

By dessert, with the help of a couple of bottles of excessively expensive Claret, they had decided to do the exciting bit of their mission the following day. They were going to hire a four-wheel drive, prepare for sleeping in it and spend the afternoon shooting birds and then at dusk Jenny would do her commando bit with the explosives.

The Shepherd's Strength

When the Shepherd was a teenager he had boundless energy. He loved the farming and estate management. His ancestors had become great landowners through hard work, clever marriages and plenty of luck. They had expanded their acres by being decent honest citizens. They had not sunk to manipulation, cheating, reiving or turfing out tenants when it happened to suit them. However, if crossed they were a serious danger, for if anybody stole from them they would be effective in regaining their property by whatever means was necessary, violent or otherwise. They were typical Border survivors and loved their land. The Shepherd was true to his family and directed his energy into protecting and enhancing what he knew they were lucky to have. So many estates dissolved after the war and perhaps theirs would have too if William and Maurice had taken over. The mysterious disappearance of those brothers had changed the fate of the family. He would love to know what had happened to them as no hint of their whereabouts had ever materialised.

Heather knew though, it was a deep dark disturbing place, something she refused to think about, somewhere she pretended didn't exist. It was too close to why she had 'changed'. She had sensed the horrors within and kept away. It had become a Pandora's box. Not to be opened. But like a swelling mosquito bite it was also urging her to itch. So she would sort of avoid it, sort of not look at it, sort of not think about the place that screamed and howled. It was dark in there and she felt the echoes of violence and struggle. When she had led the tingly man a merry dance up the burn to the loch, she had given him a clue of how to find the place. Hinting that it was something he could look at on her behalf, like an adult checking if the ice was strong enough before allowing children to skate. A deep dark cave, a mass of odd shaped stalactites each brewing disturbing thoughts, drip by steady drip falling through the black to plink and plonk below, splashing out niggles and worries that run together in little rivulets, that if not dispersed quickly would become raging torrents of torment.

The Shepherd's Strength was his undying faith in his love of his wife and child, the ability of life to persist despite death, to spite death. The Shepherd had evaporated his torment in a night of madness, teetering above the abyss of the Tower's well many years before. His proven strength now grew around him, thousands of acres of life-giving trees, so beneficial in every way. Like the bare hills his soul had become re-clothed in a forest of faith, nurturing the world's potential and demonstrating to those that dared to look, that there was indeed, a different way.

Penny Wakes Up

At two in the morning Penny woke up. She was horribly uncomfortable; she was lying up against the Shepherd and was too hot and damp. It also smelt pretty bad. The Shepherd breathed steadily beside her. She clambered out of the box bed into a chilly kitchen. A few embers in the fire soon caught scraps of kindling; she shivered in front of the growing flames till she could pile up some logs on top. She went upstairs to see if there was any hot water for a bath and finding it just bearable washed away the smell of sweat and urine. She knew she was going to have to clean up the Shepherd and do something about keeping his bed dry. She got dressed, laid out her clothes on the bed, selected her spare tracksuit that would do the job, took a large pile of towels from next to the hot water cylinder in the bathroom and returned to the kitchen. She stoked up the fire, lit a couple of candles and had a closer look at the Shepherd in his bed. The mattress was an old-fashioned one of horse hair and noisy springs covered with an underblanket and sheet. Six other blankets of various colours lay over the Shepherd. The Shepherd had collapsed in bed with his day clothes on so she was going to have quite a task sorting him out.

A Cool Bright Sunday Morning

Elliot woke early. He was cold and seriously stiff. He now remembered why he had sworn never to go camping again. He was way past the age he should be roughing it on such an adventure. He struggled out of his sleeping bag and shivering violently put on his damp clothes. Dawn and dew were cruel things when camping. To get the blood flowing in his old body he walked off uphill to look for twigs and sticks to relight the fire. Very soon he was puffing and he could feel his warmth coming back. He headed for a patch of hillside where the sun was shining and stood with the heat on his back.

It was then that the full impact of just how stunningly beautiful the Cheviot Hills really were, hit him. Across the view from where he stood the sun was catching the higher slopes and wafts of mist were rising up turning the whole scene into the most magical place. It could have been the setting of any mystical adventure—he could well imagine knights riding out of the mist, or a fearsome dragon swooping out of the sky to devour innocent lambs and it was so incredibly quiet. Not the tiniest movement of air. Elliot thought he would be able to hear a pin dropping anywhere in the valley. Ashburn was a stunning place, even without trees. The burn flowed north east and the boulder field and high crags framed it to the west and contrasting this to the east were soft green, gently rolling hills. The ruined cottage stood half a mile downstream from their camp. The two huge sycamores sheltering the cottage rose majestically through the shrouding mist, bright and fresh in their cloak of spring. Every so often Elliot could see the hint of a chimney or bit of old roof. The way the mist rose almost made him feel he was standing on a land that was slowly sinking, tucking its head down as if to avoid trouble.

Then he thought of that idiot Casey and his foolish turbine plans. Greed was a dangerous thing. He could see the cancer spreading across the land, a fungus eating at the hearts of once decent men. Landowners, who took pride in their agriculture, showing off their pedigree stock and caring for their crops, hedges and woodland had become blind. Once touched by the prospect of easy money, they could not see past the pound signs in their eyes. Now the same men were out at dusk clearing their rare bats with a little shotgun 'practice' before calling in the windy agent. Fine ash trees they climbed as children greeted with a chainsaw to clear the way for poles and cables, all done before the council knew anything about it. Now there was a new dinner table subject: 'When are you putting up your turbines?' Well, shame on them, thought Elliot; they have exposed themselves as being the worst in society. They bemoan the loss of their farming subsidies and justify their greed forgetting the effect on other people, wildlife and the amazing landscape. Farmers have survived thousands of years without turbines and have endured the ups and downs of their trade with honour. There is no honour in raping the countryside under the guise of protecting our world. Nothing was more obvious to Elliot as he gazed upon that morning scene.

Sarah woke sometime later. She was blessed with that ability to sleep through most things, but the crackle of a real fire and the smell of bacon and eggs penetrated her defences. Finding herself suddenly ravenously hungry she was out of her tent surprisingly quickly, stretching her teddy bear print pyjamas to the whole valley. Strangely, she went over to Elliot and hugged him. "You're just like my poor old dad," she said. Elliot, having only sons, wasn't used to such affection and blushed outwardly but beamed inwardly. Sarah was a smashing girl, he would be proud to have her as a daughter. She crouched by the fire and absorbed the welcome heat. Smoke drifted past her making her eyes water. She didn't care; this trip was bringing her to life.

The Shepherd Speaks

Penny slept till ten. She had done wonders with the Shepherd. She left him bed bathed and redressed in her tracksuit lying on layers of towels to keep him dry. She had made herself a bed of blankets, pillows and cushions on the floor in front of the kitchen range so she could re-stoke frequently. She was woken by the Shepherd; he was moving around his bed and saying, "Hello, who's there?" Penny was up in a flash. Dizzy and wobbly, she got to the bed as the Shepherd started to clamber out, and Penny helped him down. "Thank you," he said, "back in a mo." He staggered off up the stairs to his private quarters. Penny was amazed that he could even stand up. She stared at the door he had vanished through, then turned to prepare to feed him. She could hear the gurgling of plumbing above. She cleared away her bed and dragged the kitchen table over to the range. By the time he came back down she had the fire blazing, the soup bubbling away and the table set. He appeared fully dressed in clean clothes, his hair brushed, face shaved and looking remarkably well considering. However, he was still pale and was visibly shaking. She rushed over to him, gave him a quick hug then seated him at a chair nearest the fire. He said nothing till he had drunk three glasses of water which Penny kept topping up. "You came straight from heaven," he said. Penny smiled thinking about the rough journey in she had had the day before. "I'm just amazed that you are out of bed considering..." Penny didn't need to say anymore. "Soup?" she asked. He nodded and she dished some out. He ate quickly and quietly. He had two bowls before looking up at her. "I was in a sorry state, wasn't I?" Penny nodded.

"Did you come here alone?"

"Yes," replied Penny, suddenly remembering her promise to call her husband. "Once I've got you comfortable I'm going to ride up Bleakhope till I get a signal for my phone and let everybody know we are all fine."

"Ride? All?" asked the Shepherd.

"Err...I sort of borrowed a horse. But I'm going to return it soon. All, as in you, me and this special person," she said stroking her bump.

"Of course." He tried to smile. Then looking suddenly very tired he said, "I need to rest some more."

Penny could see that. She helped him climb back up into the bed, pulled the blankets over him and he quite simply rolled over and went to sleep.

"I will be back soon," said Penny kissing the top of his head. She could see past the wrinkles, scars and grey hair to the real person within. A man of deep love and understanding.

The Shooting Party Depart

By eleven Casey had persuaded the hotel manager to lend him his four-wheel drive. He exchanged it for £100 cash and the use of his Ferrari. Casey lied about the insurance saying it was an 'any driver' policy. He could see the fellow was very steady and sensible and he had promised not to do anything stupid in the sports car. By twelve they were kitted out for a night or two sleeping in the vehicle and drove up the same forestry track Penny and Elliot had used. It was getting busy up there. They saw Elliot's Land Rover and took a branching track to get further along the wood. It took them about half a mile further over some very rutted terrain. They found a hollow to tuck the vehicle out of sight and Casey spent the next thirty minutes putting the sights on the new rifle. Jenny packed a rucksack with her demolition kit and another with clothing, food, maps, binoculars and of course make-up. They were both dressed in their camouflage jumpsuits and looked like a professional hit squad. Jenny had 'knock 'em dead' lipstick on. She hung a plastic-covered map around her neck along with her compass, took a bearing and led them off in the right direction. Casey couldn't read maps, let alone understand a compass. They had parked three miles from the high loch and the going was difficult over rocky ridges and around marshes.

When they reached the loch they found a hidden spot overlooking the sparkling water. They bedded in and Casey took his new rifle out of its canvas case. He loved the feel of it, the smell of residual mineral oil and wood polish. It made him feel powerful. Jenny extracted a pack of laminated sheets showing large photographs of the birds they needed to eliminate. Osprey, Golden Plover, Barn Owl, Goshawks, Curlew and others. She looked out her binoculars and started scanning the water and the sky above.

Casey loaded the gun and thought he needed a practice shot. A flock of gulls were dancing above the water so he aimed carefully adhering rigidly to his training and selecting a slower moving bird, aimed just in front of it and pulled the trigger. The sharp crack made Jenny jump, the bird flew on but a feather floated down, rocking to and fro to the water. Half the birds on the water flew up and away.

"Clipped the end of its wing. I'm sure I was lined up for its body."

"For goodness sake Casey love, be patient and don't waste ammunition!"

"I had to test it, remember that's the first time I've ever fired it. It's louder than I expected."

"You're telling me!" replied Jenny rubbing her right ear. Earplugs hadn't been on her list of equipment.

They decided to eat their lunch to allow time for the birds to come in again. Casey told Jenny how as a kid he had loved to play with plastic soldiers in a sandpit in his back garden. He used to line them up along the sand and invent different methods of dispatching them. Some, he said, he would throw stones at, some would be tortured with a penknife until they talked. Others got the water drip treatment, but his favourite was to hold a soldier's arm on the wooden board holding in the sand and with his dad's hammer beat it until the limb was squashed flat. If Casey had looked he would have seen a moment of horror on Jenny's face. She was a softy at heart. That was a long way off a clean kill of a bird with a high powered rifle. She regained her composure and said, "That was a bit harsh wasn't it?" Casey looked at her trying to gauge how serious she was being and not finding a clue laughed it off, saying, "It didn't matter, they were my brother's toys." Jenny found his whole description and reaction somewhat disturbing. She went quiet and ate her sandwich looking at Casey holding up his rifle and pretending to fire at things. "Bam, bam, bam." Jenny realised she didn't know Casey as well as perhaps she thought or ought. Sometimes she was a bit worried by what he said.

A Long Journey

I changed my mind. I woke with a jolt at five in the morning. I must have been mad to trust fate. I woke after having had horrible dreams about Penny losing the baby. I sat up and tried to clear my head, but the images were disturbing. I realised that if something went wrong the chances were that the Shepherd wouldn't be able to help her, or he might be sick or even dead. I was going to have to get there, quickly, and hope Penny managed to get back up the hill to reach a point where her phone worked. I washed and dressed in a state of stress. I packed and quite simply walked out of the B&B leaving a short message and a handful of notes. I used my mobile phone web access to get a taxi and was at the airport at 6.30am. The next flight available was 8.30am. I got something to eat and read a book from my rucksack. By 11am I was climbing into a hire car in Edinburgh airport. I found the nearest shopping centre and equipped myself at an outdoor store, chemist and supermarket and sped off towards Jedburgh.

A Steep Journey

Penny was feeling really heavy when she left the Tower. She had only a few things in her rucksack this time but the bump was really weighing her down. She had felt Heather stretching and squirming within her and spoke comforting words to her as she often did. At the paddocks she hauled out a bale of hay from the old railway wagon and with some difficulty managed to get it over the fence. The sheep came close and Mr Cob came up to the bale for a sniff. She climbed over and gave him a lot of attention. She had a chopped apple in her pocket from the Shepherd's table and fed him pieces as she quietly tied on her makeshift reins. She led him along the fence line, out of the gate and mounted from an old bit of farm machinery. Mr Cob wasn't hugely impressed with being used again but acquiesced because of the frequent apple treats. Penny really felt she shouldn't be doing this, but knew her message to her husband was critical. She pointed the horse in the right direction and kicked him on. She pulled out and switched on her mobile phone. The time was 12.15pm, a bit later than ideal but she should be able to get a message through before anybody hit the panic button. Where she could she trotted Mr Cob on the grassy parts of the track but had to let him take his time if there were stones.

Despite the anxiety of her circumstances she absorbed the sheer quality of the woodland and landscape around her. The Shepherd really knew how to plant; he had learnt what grew best where, but also how to plan a wood so it came up looking natural. There was as much skill deciding where not to plant as there was where the trees were encouraged to grow. The gaps allowed distant features to be enhanced by subtle framing. Sometimes he had used low growing shrubby trees and in others tall clean growing beech or ash to allow views through the trees to something beyond. He had the ability to project ahead ten, fifty or a hundred years to visualise the ongoing dynamic nature of the woodland.

Completely absorbed by her admiration of the sights and sounds around her she jumped when her phone started ringing as they reached the top of the valley. She pulled the phone from her pocket and saw it was her mother calling, but it cut out before she could answer. She slid off Mr Cob's back and patted his neck. He put his head down to graze. She wrote a text to her husband and mother: 'Don't worry folks all is well, I have visited the Shepherd and he is ok, but does need help for a few days. Baby Heather is happy squirming inside me. I'll call or text again the day after tomorrow.' She didn't want to ride up the valley every day.

Satisfied that she had done her duty to keep her family at bay she gathered up the bandage reins and led Mr Cob towards a handy boulder to remount. Her phone started ringing which was not entirely surprising and she fumbled to get it out of her pocket, turned it over to see who was calling and seeing it was her husband, she pressed the button and lifted the phone to her ear, but just as she said "Hi", but before she could say anything else, there was the crack of a gun further into the hills that made Mr Cob jump in alarm; the jolt on the reins dislodged the phone and it fell forward onto the grass. Thinking that it was lucky it hadn't hit a stone she said, "What's all the shooting about? Steady Mr Cob, steady now." Mr Cob lent towards her and shoved her away from the phone. "Mr Cob, stop being so pushy. Ow, stop it!" She was just about to grasp the phone, when the great big hairy hocked hoof of Mr Cob came gently down on the device. It simply shattered with a horrible crunching sound and Mr Cob took another step forward lowering his head and continued to graze. Penny looked at the mangled mess and swore. She knew it wasn't the horse's fault but was angry with him anyway. The animal gave her a casual glance and returned to his grazing. He had heard it all before.

That was a large chunk of her security removed. All of a sudden she felt marooned, remembering conversations with her husband about how we rely too much on our phones and the state we get into if they don't work, or if we lose them. She had said she would not be in contact for two days so if something went wrong it would probably take three days to reach her. She thought she should just give in and head for Jedburgh, but she did not want to abandon the poorly Shepherd. A memory flash of an old man's face so pale and worried on a beach years before haunted her. So standing there holding the reins and picking up the mobile carcass, she had to make a difficult decision. She thought returning the horse and getting off the hills was the sensible thing to do. The emergency services would deal with the Shepherd. She had her baby to consider too, so she started leading the horse back the way she had come up into the hills the day before.

Penny Calls

I was so relieved to hear Penny's voice, but then there had been a noise that sounded awfully like a gunshot followed by a lot of odd noises and Penny talking in the background in a defensive way to some bloke called Mr Cob. It sounded like she was trying to defend herself. I became very alarmed and started driving dangerously fast. I had a reasonable idea where she would have called me from, at the head of Bleakhope, but was completely confused about who this Mr Cob was. I was panicking about Penny and the baby being hurt and fretted about whether I should call the police and activate the rescue services. I tried calling her, but a message came back indicating that her phone was switched off. It would take me four hours to get there. A rescue helicopter would take an hour but cost thousands and it could all be a misunderstanding anyway. I drove on doggedly.

Desperate Heather

The spirit of the Shepherd's Heather was distraught. Penny looked like she was going away. She was leading the horse towards the gate in the stone wall. Heather knew that it marked the boundary of her territory and she was unable to go beyond it. If Penny went through all she would be able to do was watch helplessly. All she could think of was to try to get the baby inside her to stop her. She spun around Penny waiting for the opportunity. As she drew closer she could feel the baby's defences go up, pushing against her like a repelling magnet. Penny and Mr Cob had reached the gate and she was fumbling with the string. Heather just had to do something so she made a sudden dart in at the baby knowing she was going to get hurt. She was right; she was soundly kicked back like an electric shock and retreated thirty yards, feeling thoroughly bruised.

Penny clutched her belly and lent forward breathing hard. Her baby had just given a tremendous kick and it had been quite a shock. She stood up straight again feeling more familiar movements within her. She looked at the gate, then turned back to look at the route she had just come up from the Tower. She was worried.

Sarah, Elliot and the Ashburn Hill Forts

They wanted to photograph all the hill forts. There were three to the north of the ruined house in the Ashburn valley. They decided to walk down to the ruins, leave their camping gear there for that night and do the hill forts with the bare minimum of food and equipment. Sarah took a selection of lenses including a wide angle and her biggest telephoto. They found the remains of an understairs cupboard in the ruins and hid their remaining things there. All three hill forts were on a high ridge that formed the northern boundary of the estate. They hadn't quite got that far on their first trip with Casey, so were keen to see them, but it was quite a climb for Elliot and even Sarah had to stop frequently.

As they rose the sheer impact of the Cheviot Hills emerged. They were bold rounded hills with rocky cleughs and cliffs. A landscape of surprises. A tinkling burn gushed half buried beneath the turf, noisily warning the walker of its presence. A deep peaty pool surrounded by soft mosses. Sharp rugged gullies, like cat scratches down the back of your hand, oozing and flowing with the mountain's lifeblood between steep crumbling cliffs. A handful of dark goats watched warily through devil's eyes. Raptors in the long grass leapt into the soft breeze, prey still wriggling in its talons. Sarah photographed it all.

At the first and highest hill fort they collapsed hot and tired. Elliot extracted their lunch and watched Sarah do something clever with her phone and camera. Being aware of Elliot watching she explained, "I'm sending all the photographs to my computer at work from where they are automatically backed up in two separate archives and another copy goes direct to my pc at home. There, job done." Elliot nodded still amazed at modern technology. "That didn't take long."

"I'm taking the opportunity to empty the memory while I'm in range. I'm taking loads of pics."

"Can you set up the telephoto on the tripod and let me take some long shots?

"Yes off course, you'll be impressed by what you can see."

And surprised.

Towering Follies

The old man in the Tower was tired. He was weary. He had slaved away for decades with his livestock and planting. He had transformed more than a quarter of the land he cared for from being bleak, windswept and over grazed to a productive, beautiful and magical place. While other farmers farmed subsidies he had tended the land. He had more cash than he would ever need, a cold rickety fortalice that he called home and he had found a way to be at one with his life and the environment around him. Like blowing slowly and from deep within one's lungs to start a fire, he had breathed across the hilltops and through the valleys awakening the memories in the ground. The gradual degradation and acidification of the layers of abused soil was paused. A new life began, leading to ecological and economical sense. His firewood had become as valuable as lamb. When he sold his neat dry logs people paid double the going rate as they knew what be offered was going to keep them warm, unlike the green logs supplied by others. The rising trees drew in numerous creatures and a balance evolved.

The Shepherd woke hungry. He drifted in and out of nightmares of Triffid-like turbines marching through his woods crushing his efforts in thoughtless, mindless dishonesty. He did not believe felling trees to put up windmills made sense. At least water mills worked all the time and returned the water unharmed to the river. Large fish couldn't pass through the lade grills and small fish tumbled through the slow moving mill wheel buckets without damage. He remembered Penny's man relating his dream and feared the worst. He was beyond stopping the invasion of the towering follies because he thought the land belonged to somebody else and he didn't even have a tenancy agreement.

He then woke a little more and tried to piece together the last few days. He had been ill, stuck in bed, desperately thirsty and weak. Then Penny was there bustling around making him feel comfortable. She was heavily pregnant, but then he knew she would be. Where was she now? Why was she on her own? What had she said about a horse? He stretched feeling better than he had, clambered out of his bed very carefully and headed for the bathroom. When he came back down he piled logs onto the fire and sat in the armchair that Penny had put there. He lent towards the fire, joints cold and aching, staring into the flames. He considered what he really wanted, trying to clear his mind and plan a way forward. He was a survivor and had a steely determination. He accepted his age and condition but did not want to be dragged away to some nursing home where the inmates dribbled and muttered around him. If he was to become a mutterer and dribbler he was going to do it in his Tower, even if it meant shortening his life. Even if it meant somebody eventually finding his decomposing corpse in his bed. He shivered at the image and rose to eat. He found some of Penny's broth in the pot beside the range and pulled it onto the hotplate. What he wanted was Penny and her man to move in, but how could they with a young baby and their own lives to lead elsewhere? But he did know that they would have a better idea of how to deal with the threat of the towering follies.

Elliot's Photographs

Elliot needed the camera to be mounted on a tripod as his hands shook too much. He showed Sarah just how much and she laughed in agreement. He said it was because he was alone in the hills with a beautiful young lady. Looking through such a powerful lens, he found it astonishing how detailed the images were and the way the perspective was drawn together exaggerating the height of the hills. He spotted a deer across the valley and took a beautiful shot as it negotiated its way down a steep heather-covered slope. As he scanned across the hill tops he photographed a kestrel hovering above a grey cliff. Further round to the south west where the Bleakhope valley lapped at the high ridge a rider slowly made their way towards a narrow gate. In such a vast empty scene it was a lovely lonely movement, zig-zagging up a slope adjacent to a long scree of purple-grey stones. It was the only sign of humanity they had seen all day. Elliot wondered who it was and why they were there so took a photo. The rider dismounted near the wall and once off Elliot could see several things: the rider was female, she had no hat and when she moved it was slow and awkward. "Come and look at this, there's something not right." Sarah stepped over and looked through the view finder. She adjusted the camera settings and held her finger on the button to take series of photographs in very quick succession. "She's been riding bareback," Sarah said, then after another few pictures, "It looks like she's going to go through the gate." More bursts of the camera. "Hold on... she's doubled up... she looks sick... she's stood up again... no, not sick."

"What can you see?" said Elliot squinting in the right direction.

"Uh huh... you know what... that's all a bit strange... I think she's heavily pregnant!" She stood away from the camera.

"Do you think she's in need of help?" asked Elliot.

"Looks like she is off to get help on horseback."

A sudden sharp noise echoed over the hills. A gun had been fired somewhere in the general direction of the woman and horse.

"I wonder what they are shooting at," said Sarah looking worried. "There is more going on up here than we expected."

Sarah returned to her camera to scan the horizon. "I can't see anybody, but they are probably in the next valley." She pulled the camera around to look at the rider again. "Now the pregnant lady has gone—must have got through the gate and away over the horizon. All very strange up here today." She turned to look at Elliot; he was gazing down the valley and she followed his line of sight.

"And I've noticed something else too," exclaimed Elliot.

"Smoke," they both said together. A thin tendril of smoke was winding its way upwards from a dense patch of willows beside the river, midway between where the Ash burn met the bigger river coming down from Bleakhope.

The March into the Hills

I stopped in a car park and bought a burger from a van selling miscellaneous heart-clogging food. I needed plenty of energy for my climb and was very hungry. I returned to the car and carefully balanced the polystyrene cup of tea on the dash and quickly ate the burger. Junk food just tasted so good when you are starving. I unfolded the map of the hills and looked for the shortest route to the Tower. The only two options worth considering were either long or steep. Perhaps over-estimating my fitness I chose the steeper route thinking I could put the

254

pressure on getting up the sharp gradients, then recover while traversing the gentle slopes further on. I put on my new walking boots and walked up and down the car park to test them. They were nice and at that price they should be. I packed my rucksack with medical supplies, first aid kit, matches, food, water and clothing. Satisfied that I had the critical things organised I drove off into the hills.

But part of the way up the sharp slope I was struggling, my heart was thumping away and my muscles weren't getting enough oxygen. Playing squash kept me fit for squash but not for jogging up Cheviots. I had to stop frequently and finished off the first bottle of water within half an hour. I was grumbling about Penny's madness, but hoped she was okay. I was really concerned about the mysterious Mr Cob and why she hadn't called back after the gunshot and other strange noises. What on earth was going on? Was I going to find a trail of tragedy? It was despite the circumstances a beautiful day. At each rest I made the point of looking around and appreciating the landscape. It was a stunning place to be. It didn't take long for my hire car and the small winding road to become toy-like far beneath me. Each step separated me from my normal reality. It was like climbing into the sky to another world, somehow unreal. It refreshed the soul and actually in many ways it felt more real than the urban environments I was used to. The higher I climbed the more I remembered how I felt about the hills, the Shepherd and his Tower and all the weird and wonderful experiences I had had in those hidden valleys. The nearer I got to the Tower the more I agreed with Penny that we should do everything to protect the old man, his woodlands and the amazing buildings and archaeology. I grew more and more frustrated and angry that someone living many miles away could propose industrialising those extraordinary hills by taking advantage of a misguided energy policy. But first things first, I had to make sure that Penny and the baby were okay, then the Shepherd and only then would I be able to focus on protecting the hills from turbines.

Casey and Jenny have a Tiff

Jenny had become irritated by Casey, more so after he asked her if she was premenstrual. He could be so tactless sometimes. She had asked him to have a go with the gun to get a feel of it. He quite simply said "No!" She couldn't work out what had got into him; he had gone quiet and broody while waiting for the birds to settle back on the loch.

Casey was irritated about her over reaction with his tale about the toy soldiers. He had then begun to think about his brothers. His oldest brother was four years his senior, tall, handsome and a hit with the girls. He had admired, envied and hated him all at the same time. His parents had always focused on their first born golden child who could do no wrong. Casey and his little brother were dragged up in the wake of this super being. All three had done okay though, got through Uni and landed reasonable positions in reputable firms. But his oldest brother was still one step higher than him. He was now the CEO of a private pharmaceutical firm specialising in cancer therapy drugs. His younger brother worked as a chef in a leading restaurant in Soho. Although Casey was reasonably content in his work he had recently learned that both his brothers actually earned almost twice what he did.

But he was going to show them, he was setting up the wind farm deal so he could filter off "management fees" to a company he had set up called CLP Environ Ltd. The company would only take 5% of the millions the agent had indicated would be realised from the project each year. Jenny had fine-tuned the arrangements to appear legitimate and reasonable. She was getting good at faking paperwork.

"I would like to get used to the gun too," said Jenny looking at Casey.

"Just wait till I've got a bird on our list," he responded looking through the gun sights.

"Well here's your chance, that's a Curlew coming in from the east."

Casey swung round. "Where, which one is it?"

"The Curlew-shaped one," jibed Jenny.

Casey lowered the gun and gave her a dirty look.

"Come on Casey love, we've got to work as a team," said Jenny smiling in the hopes he would soften. Her smiles were pretty disarming.

"Okay but this bird is mine—point it out to me."

"Please," suggested Jenny.

"Pretty please, sweet Jenny, tell me which one," Casey said sarcastically.

"Over there just coming over the tallest of those white trunked trees."

He'd seen it, took his time, aimed, followed, waited and *bam*, the loud crack of the gun sent hundreds of birds off the water again. The Curlew dropped like a stone into the long grass behind the birch trees.

"Brilliant, right through the heart!" exclaimed Casey. "Bull's eye—all that training has paid off." He was very pleased with himself and passed the gun over to Jenny. He became buoyant and enthusiastic. "We really can do this babe, we really can."

The Curlew struggled in the grass, heart intact. The bullet had smashed one of its wings. It hopped around distressed. Fox fodder.

Penny's Retreat

Penny disliked shooting. Being pregnant and highly aware of the value of life, she felt particularly sensitive about the subject. She was on the ridge of the hill and felt exposed and in danger from stray bullets. She headed downhill immediately. Halfway down she heard another shot. She was feeling vulnerable and was stressing about the decision she had made on the ridge.

Sarah and Elliot return to the Ruined Cottage

Photography was Sarah's passion. She had been inspired ever since she put up posters of Madonna and another of dolphins leaping out of the sea on her bedroom wall. She had fallen asleep and woken up with the images and began to wonder how they were taken. On her twelfth birthday her parents bought her a good quality second-hand SLR camera and that was it, everything was photographed. She learnt how to use the camera and focused on the horses and riders jumping in their equestrian centre. It wasn't long before she was winning prizes at school for her work and then extended to local fêtes and shows. By the time she was eighteen she was being invited to do wedding photography.

Elliot didn't think he was arty enough to take photographs, but had to admit to Sarah that now he had used her zoom lens he was rather taken with the idea of getting a good camera of his own. He was also keen to have an excuse to get out and about with Sarah again. Despite his aching legs she made him feel younger.

They reached the ruined cottage at four o'clock and chose a grassy patch between the two sycamore trees to pitch their tents. Elliot got a fire going and they had a cup of tea and a snack. They decided they were going to reconnoitre the peel tower afterwards, before the light faded.

Penny locks up

Penny was feeling uncomfortable. She was becoming scared about having the baby. She had tried not to think about the forthcoming event and had heard and seen enough to know it was never an easy or pleasant experience. She wasn't a huge fan of hospitals anyway, they made her nervous and the smells and sounds were often distressing. There was the possibility that she could get caught in the hills and all the riding, hauling the Shepherd around, general physical abuse and mental stress could bring on an early birth and then she would have serious problems. The increasing nervousness made her twitchy and furrowed her pretty brow. She was suddenly feeling very alone, tired, dirty and really needed a bath followed by a long undisturbed night. If only.

When she got down to the paddock she released Mr Cob amongst the sheep, their funny horned brown heads all turned to watch for a moment then resumed their grazing positions. They had sussed Mr Cob already and didn't need to again. She turned to walk down the track to return to the Tower thinking she was really going to have to take things easy from now on; then there were two sharp cracks of a gun that sounded alarmingly nearby. Birds lifted from the trees and departed. Penny was beginning to feel like she was being hunted. The shooters were definitely in Bleakhope and far too close for comfort. She remembered her fray with the brainless gamekeeper and wondered if he had returned to scare her, or worse. She hurried through the willows and panting heavily soon reached the Golden Tower. It looked stunning in the late afternoon light, glowing majestically as it must have for the past few centuries, but she had no time to admire it; she knew what to do and had to be quick. The iron yet moaned as she pushed it into its stone recess; she fitted the large padlock and was glad to hear the satisfying click as it locked securely. The oak door swung round to blank off any views of crooks or boots that would give away the occupants. The latch closed and she slid the heavy oak beam from its slot across behind the diagonal studded planks into the corresponding hole opposite. "There," she sighed, sweating and breathing hard. "That will stop them." She ran up to the kitchen, closed the door and leant her back against it for a few minutes so as to catch her breath.

The Shepherd was snoring gently in his bed. She could see that he had been up by the bowl and mug on the drainer and the soup pot was empty. She was glad to see he had been well enough to get up and eat. Her first job was to douse the fire so as to stop the rising smoke giving them away. She grabbed a jug from the sink windowsill, filled it quickly from the tap and poured it onto the embers, and with a great sizzling of steam she put it out. Another jug and there was nothing but a few wafts of steamy smoke meandering up the broad flue. There was however, a nasty ashy puddle seeping across the ancient stone flags. The Shepherd slept on and she pulled his blankets well over him and then ran upstairs to find a point from where she could look out for the gunman. She looked out of her bedroom window but it wasn't facing the right direction. The bathroom was no good either, so she went on up the twisted stone stairs and flinched when another two rifle shots rang out clear and powerful. He must be really close. Physically shaking now from fear and exhaustion, the only place to see what was going on was the turf covered vault. She climbed out of the top of the roofless turret and gingerly clambered across the sloping turfs to the gable remnant. She could hear talking now, muffled voices somewhere nearby. The grass roof was dangerously steep and she knew if she started to slip it was a certain death drop of thirty feet or so. If it had been raining she wouldn't have even tried.

As she crouched tight behind the crumbling gable, her boots wedged into the wild flowers and tufts of grass, she heard the voices stop in the trees at the end of the track. She was sure one of the voices was female. Peering around the edge of the stones down to the ground she waited to see who appeared. Thinking that she was going to see a burley gamekeeper and maybe his girlfriend she was surprised to see a stunning blonde stride confidently from the trees. She was undeniably beautiful, slim figure in a tight camouflage jump suit, long real blonde hair, big blue eyes, red lipstick and manicured fingernails. The catwalk image was disturbingly contorted by the high powered rifle slung over her shoulder. In surprise Penny ducked down quickly and in doing so the turf she was standing on moved slightly. Having only been laid the previous autumn its roots had not yet intermeshed enough into the existing turf to be secure. It slipped some more and Penny had to make a dive for a safer place. She grasped handfuls of grass stems and kicked herself up the dangerous slope. She only just managed to reach the level ridge of the vault and sat there panting and shaking. However, her desperate movements dislodged a trickle of pebbles from the turfs and she watched helplessly as they tumbled over the edge. They landed with a rattle directly in front of Jenny. Her reactions were quick and she looked up at the roof where Penny clung tight to the vault. Two jackdaws returned to their perch on the crowstepped gable recovering from the disturbance of the rifle blast. Seeing the two black birds high above her, Jenny relaxed; she was canny though and spent a moment scanning the tower's dilapidated roof. If she was a few inches taller she would have seen the sole of Penny's walking boot. Penny held her breath, too terrified to move. Her face was tight against the turf and between clumps of purple thrift she could see the two jackdaws strutting up and down one of the protruding crow steps. How appropriate, she thought.

Jenny below was irritated by the crows and by Casey who had just managed to miss an easy shot at a fat wood pigeon further up the path. She wanted to prove to him that she was a good shot too. She took the gun off her shoulders and raising it took careful aim. It wasn't a great distance so the glistening black feathers of the bird's chest filled the scope—an easy shot. She pulled the trigger and the gun made a harsh noise echoing around the Tower and the remains of its barmkin wall. Both birds flew off. 'Why did I miss that?' thought Jenny. Casey came running up behind her doing up his jumpsuit zip "What are you shooting at?" he asked.

"Practicing on some bird," She said. "Pretty sure I got it though. It landed in the grass up there." She pointed to the turf-covered vault. Penny who had felt the bullet whistle past her head and seen the impact on the bolection moulding of a fireplace, long stranded above the dry part of the Tower. She was crawling commando style, or rather tortoise style, with her bump scraping along the plants, and she toppled herself into the roofless turret and pushed herself against the stonework and swore quietly to herself. These people were vicious killers.

Downstairs the Shepherd had woken and was trying to work out what the loud noise was. He sat up and saw the grey wet ash puddles on the floor and the wet prints of boots heading towards the hall door. He could tell something was going on, so he hauled himself out of bed, staggered slowly through the hall following the footprints and started up the stairs. He was met by Penny rushing down them. She grabbed him, more to stop herself knocking him over and with wide eyes put her fingers to her lips. "There's some daft woman out there taking pot shots at me and I don't know why." The Shepherd nodded and whispered, "Follow me." He wobbled a lot in front of her but managed to lead her back down through the kitchen and through the elm-planked door to his private quarters. Penny had never been through it out of respect and as they rose through the Tower twisting with the stairs she counted five closed doors; she was intrigued and amazed at how much more there was to the Tower. She really had no idea. They came to a final small door which the Shepherd opened revealing another small turret room. It had two narrow windows, one of which looked down over the Tower entrance and barmkin arch beyond. She could see that the blonde lady had now been joined by a slightly overweight red faced man. They stood under the arch looking like a pair out of some Die Hard film, on a mission to eliminate. To eliminate Penny, her baby and the Shepherd. A strand of anger begun to form within Penny; this was not a healthy thing for a pregnant person. A few yards behind she could see the badger-faced goat watching them. The couple were talking but not loud enough for Penny to hear.

Casey who was six inches taller than Jenny had seen Penny's boot disappearing over the ridge and mistaking it for Jenny's bird, said, "Well, you may have hit it but you've not killed it, as I can still see it hopping around up there." Jenny who knew she'd missed it and seen the two birds fly off was confused and embarrassed so changed the subject. "Why did you take so long having a pee?"

263

Casey responded, "Cos that bloody goat kept staring at me and I just couldn't go." A few yards away the badger-faced goat glared at him.

The Photography Team become Spies

"More shooting and close, what do you think they are doing?" said a worried Sarah.

"I don't know, it's not a normal shooting season I don't think, I thought most species were left alone at this time of year," replied Elliot.

"And I thought you weren't allowed to shoot on Sundays," added Sarah.

"It's coming from the direction of the Tower. We were going to have a look anyway. Bring your camera with a couple of lenses."

Sarah finished her tea and organised her photography gear while Elliot studied the map. He could see that the tower was only about half a mile and although the map didn't show so many trees, the main tracks were shown. He reckoned that if they went uphill slightly to the south of the tower there was a small crag from where they would get a decent view.

They walked towards the tower and cut up the hillside to the left where they could walk along a narrower path that soon led them up into the most amazing area of apple and pear trees. In all directions the pink and white blossoms covered the craggy twisted trees. It was an amazing place to be; the trees were spaced so that they could grow to their full potential forming a full broad head, each holding its floral display to the buzz of thousands of bees. After a few hundred yards they found themselves completely lost as the trees seemed to go on for ever in each direction. It was as if they had stepped into a different world where the humming of insects and chatter of small birds was overwhelming in the warm evening sunshine. Where they had walked in Ashburn and up to the hill forts was quite devoid of tree growth, open and beautiful in its own way, but this was like paradise. Sarah stopped, pulled out her camera, put on the standard 50mm lens and took dozens of pictures. She got Elliot to walk on a bit, then return to her through the blaze of colour. The gnarled trunks contrasted with the delicate fresh flowers. It was like a study of youth and age; only when old, twisted and craggy from the rigours of life could you hold aloft and really appreciate the most perfect and beautiful display of love and understanding, drawing in the bees to perform a subtle and incidental act of reproduction. The insects, seduced by the nectar of their desire, were unaware of their crucial part in the age-old act; they did not know just how important they were, keeping species alive on the planet for millions of years, more important than they could possibly know. The understanding of bees and a colony as one organism was to understand the true cycles of nature.

Sarah asked Elliot to take photos of her walking away and skipping back through the trees. He obliged and laughed with her because the whole scene would have been more effective had she been wearing a summer dress rather than jeans, a t-shirt and clumpy walking boots. They walked on, clambered up on to the stony crag at the top of the orchard and managed to find a spot where they could just see the top of the tower. Sarah set up the tripod and long lens and zoomed in to see what was down there.

The Tower glowed in the lowering light, almost throbbing with golds, browns and buff tones. She could see the upper ruined remains of private chambers, fireplaces high in walls exposed to the weather, the crow stepped gables and the soft sheen of grass covering the vaults. A roofless turret clung on to the side of an exposed lower vault and she could just see the slates and narrow window of a higher turret beyond the wall with the fireplaces. The whole image sat in a soft sea of white willows like a ship lost in a distant ocean, green and blue waves keeping it afloat, giving it a chance to sail to its misplaced harbour.

They took turns taking photographs of every detail. "I wonder who lives there?" said Sarah, zooming in on the tiniest drift of smoke coming from a high chimney.

"Maybe someone camping like we are at the ruined cottage," remarked Elliot. He took a turn with the camera and caught a pair of jackdaws standing on a wallhead, bold and dark against the soft mellow stone. He widened the view then caught a movement to the right of the frame; somebody was climbing out of the roofless turret. "Oh my God, it's the pregnant girl!" he said in surprise. "What on earth is she doing there? I thought she'd ridden over the hill towards Jedburgh. Why on earth is she clambering around on top of the Tower? Looks mighty dangerous to me." He let Sarah take over and stood back in shock. What was going on here? 'She should be in Jedburgh having a baby by now,' he thought.

"She must be completely crazy—that roof is steep; she's now walking across it and if she slips there's nothing to stop her going over the edge!" Sarah watched in horror as Penny ducked down behind the crowsteps and peered over the stones. The chimney had stopped smoking and it had suddenly gone deadly quiet and still. It was almost like the whole valley was watching and waiting with bated breath. Their whole future held within those moments, held within Penny's swollen belly, everything willing her to be careful not to slip and plunge fatefully to the hard cobbles below.

"Oh no! She's slipping Elliot, I can't bear to watch." He took over and could see Penny's feet losing their grip and her desperate struggle to the top of the vault. Sarah watched Elliot's furrowed worried face as he took a stream of photographs. "She looks terrified and exhausted, what's she so worried about?" The two jackdaws returned to their perch. "She's lying on top of the Tower looking pale and scared; I bet it's something to do with those Sunday shooters." And if in response to his comment, there was the horrible retort of the gun again. Elliot and Sarah jumped. Elliot's finger was on the camera release and he took a flow of shots; he had seen the burst of dust as the bullet struck the fireplace behind Penny. "Jesus! They're trying to kill her! They're shooting at her. No wonder she's scared trying to hide on the roof!" Sarah took over the camera and was just in time to see Penny's back disappear through the turret. The tense silence returned. They saw nothing and heard nothing for a number of minutes. Sarah scanned around with the camera, then something caught her eye, the flashing of something in the higher turret. She zoomed in and saw Penny, then briefly the face of an old man through the small window. "They're holed up in their tower like something from the middle ages!"

"They?" asked Elliot.

"There's an old man there too. Come on, we need to get closer to see if we can help."

Heather and her Goat are upset

The goat and Heather the ghost were highly agitated; they had been following Casey and Jenny disliking their every word and move. When Casey was standing against a tree trying to urinate, Heather was jumping around on the other side of him trying to get the goat to butt him; she was beckoning him and dancing around but all the goat did was watch and stare. Then Jenny had shot at the jackdaw and Heather went mad rushing up to Jenny trying to hit and scratch her, kick her shins and push her over. Of course nothing happened so she burst into tears and screamed at her. Only the goat heard and he came closer looking a bit more defensive this time. He eyed up Jenny's backside and thought about a good run and thud but then Casey returned and presented a more interesting challenge.

Return to the Magic of Eden

I heard the gunshots and saw the smoke rising from Ashburn as I came over the northern ridge and stood gazing down onto the Shepherd's lands. The view was just amazing and uplifting. The silky spring greens of the rolling Cheviot slopes eased into the richness of Bleakhope beyond the Tower. Blazes of bright greens bubbled into the sea of delicate pinks where the Shepherd had concentrated his fruit trees. There they benefitted from a southerly aspect in a sheltered pocket protected from the rise of land that lifted up between the smaller valley where the Tower stood and the wilder Bleakhope. I breathed deeply catching my breath and I was sure I could smell the blossom mixed with the eager growth of the sward beneath my feet. Despite my urgency to find Penny I soaked up the strength-giving sights. 'This is what life was all about, being within and helping protect these wild and remote places,' I thought. The Shepherd's touch showed just what could be done.

I saw some people moving around on a rocky place just above the orchards and assumed they were the people firing guns and thought it odd that the Shepherd allowed such activities, especially in the breeding season. Thinking that I had better go and see what was going on I set off.

"All downhill from here," I said to the warm breeze.

Little did I know what I was going to find.

The Demolition Team

Jenny and Casey had retreated to the trees some two hundred yards from the Tower. This was the maximum length of the detonator cable. Jenny laid out the kit in a neat and orderly way. She was a secretary and PA so was good at that sort of thing. She had spotted a good crevice in the base of the Tower's nearest corner and knew what she had to do, destroy that corner of the building and the rest would surely come tumbling down and if not she had plenty spare explosive and detonators. They were completely unaware of the tower's inhabitants.

Sarah and Elliot were making their way down a fairly rugged slope of hawthorn and blackthorn having to avoid being scratched to bits. The blackthorn had an ability to create particularly dense impenetrable copses so it was slow going. Sarah was following too close to Elliot and got swiped across the cheek and jaw by a branch. She yelped and sat and cried while Elliot dabbed at the bleeding welt with a handkerchief. They slowed down after that and left more space between them. When they reached the woodland edge they could hear voices, so crouching low, hid behind a bit of the barmkin wall.

Sarah took her camera out of its case and poised ready to see what the people she could hear were doing. She looked through a gap and saw nothing from the track or tower but thought she could hear footsteps approaching. Clearly the gunman was dangerous with intent to kill so they had to stay hidden, but she was determined to record everything whatever the outcome. She had spare memory cards in her pocket for the camera so could take as many pictures as she needed.

Jenny appeared looking stunning and efficient, like a model advertising the armed forces. She was carrying a rucksack and walked nimbly to the large stones at the base of the Tower.

"What the hell is *she* doing here?" said Elliot. "This is all something to do with Casey and his turbines I bet!"

"A bit beyond the call of duty I'd say," said Sarah.

"Well, I'm going to put a stop to this nonsense right now," growled Elliot, standing up to go across to the girl to ask her what was going on.

"No you can't," squeaked Sarah. "Remember they were shooting at the pregnant lady. If they think you saw them they'll need to eliminate you as a potential witness!" Elliot sat back down, heavy hearted and very alarmed.

"Okay, we will just have to observe—take lots of pictures, won't you?" Sarah nodded and patted him on his shoulder.

They watched Jenny packing something in a gap between the Tower's masonry, then she was up on her feet, clicked in the end of the cable and ran back, reel whirring.

"I don't believe it, they're trying to blow the place up! They're crazy, there are people in there!" She was about to rush out herself when Casey stepped into view, rifle at the ready.

Heather also saw what was happening. She'd seen pictures of this—how dare they try to damage the Tower and hurt her father and Penny! Knowing she couldn't stop them herself she dived over to the stuff packed into the crevice and started tapping at it and calling the goat over as urgently as possible. The goat saw her and trotted over.

Elliot could see what he could do and before Sarah could stop him he was off. He forgot about the risks and was running round the barmkin wall and at his age shouldn't have been. Sarah could see what he was doing. If he got behind the Tower he could sneak round and pull out the cable before the charge was detonated. She thought if she could distract Casey it would give Elliot some protection. She peered around the wall to see the goat doing something odd; it was nibbling at the explosive as if it too was trying to protect the Tower and those inside. Sarah watched fascinated, picked up the camera and took some photos. Casey was furious and tried to chase off the goat. The goat backed off. Casey turned away. The invisible Heather ran over to Casey and screamed and flapped her hands as if Casey were attacking her. The goat was not impressed and took aim. Every moment was caught on camera. The goat was remarkably nimble and by the time it reached Casey, head down, it was traveling really quite fast. Casey screamed like a girl when he was propelled across the ground. Sarah laughed as the camera snapped away. The goat backed up preparing for another go. Jenny ran back down to see what was going on and found Casey swearing in the dust. She saw the goat coming again and swinging around with a karate kick caught it on the side of the head. It toppled sideways and retreated to Heather who stood at the corner of the Tower. She was looking at the explosives desperately trying to think of what to do. She spoke kindly to the goat. Jenny hauled Casey up from the ground. He was furious and once on his feet pushed her away. "I don't need help from a bloody woman!" As he pushed her she grasped his jumpsuit to try to stop herself from falling but the force was too great and she fell back tearing off half a perfect fingernail. "Now look what you've gone and done!" screamed Jenny. "You better get out of the way 'cos I'm going to blow this place now!" She ran up the track. All she had to do was plug the cable in and hit the button.

Casey blamed the goat. He was feeling bruised and sore and was not impressed with Jenny's attitude. Casey raised the gun and aimed at the goat's head. Heather came screaming towards him trying to block the path of the bullet. The goat lifted its head up to follow. Casey kept it framed in the sights and pulled the trigger as Elliot slid around the corner to disconnect the cable. The searing hot bullet passed harmlessly through Heather's sternum, heart and spine, through Elliot's leg cauterising on its way and lodged in an espalier pear thirty yards distant. Elliot fell down hard catching his head on the corner of the stonework; just as he began to pass out he saw the cable and stretched his hand out towards it.

Penny and the Shepherd watched in horror from the turret not believing what they were seeing. They had seen both Jenny running out the detonator cable and Casey with the rifle and although not understanding why, they could see they were in mortal danger. They were trying to demolish the Tower and they were in it. All Penny could think of doing was getting out of the Tower as quickly as possible. "Where's the key for the padlock, I shut everything up as I came in earlier?" The Shepherd looked worried and said apologetically, "In the doghouse."

"You mean outside, so we are trapped?"

He nodded.

"Damn," said Penny and just as she decided to scream out of the window was when Casey fired at the goat.

I was at Ashburn; I found the campsite with a smouldering fire but no people. Then I heard shouting from the Tower and a gunshot and then an awful silence. I ran as hard as I could but knew I had to be careful not to get caught up with stray gunmen. Before I knew it, in the lengthening shadows I had collided into a woman hiding behind a bit of wall. She yanked me down and put her hand over my mouth. In shock I thought for a moment she was part of Mr Cob's mob! My eyes were wide and I half expected to feel a cold icy blade at my throat. Then I saw she held nothing more dangerous than a camera. "It's okay, I'm Sarah, nothing to do with the guys with the guns." She continued to take photos explaining what she could to me in a whisper. She said they were trying to kill some woman and that Elliot was going around the back to see if he could pull out the detonator cable to stop them blowing up the castle with the pregnant lady and an old man stuck inside. That was enough for me to pay attention. Then there was another shot. We both froze. Sarah could see something lying on the ground. It wasn't a goat.

Jenny had reached the detonator control, plugged in the cable; heard Casey fire at the goat and after thinking for no more than three seconds thought 'What the hell!' and hit the button. There was no explosion, no flying rock debris. She couldn't understand why—she'd done everything exactly as per her training; there should have been a loud bang.

Casey was in shock, his body overloaded with adrenalin. He had missed the goat and felled some old bloke who appeared around the corner just as he pulled the trigger. He assumed it was the tramp that Martin had described until he reached him and pushed his bloody head over with his boot and saw who it really was... Auld Elliot! "How the hell... what the... Why?" he panicked and ran away up the track shouting for Jenny, who was running down.

"Why didn't it blow up?" she said in response to his agitation.

"I've just shot Auld Elliot! I don't believe it, I've gone and killed him!" He had grabbed her by the shoulders and was shaking her violently. "What have we done Jenny? And why did you try to detonate the explosives when I was still down there, you silly bitch?" Casey yelled, his face beetroot red.

Sarah and I heard all this and ran immediately to the man lying on the ground. He was looking pretty rough; blood was seeping through his trousers and from his head where it had caught the corner of the Tower as he fell. "He's breathing," said Sarah. "At least he's not dead." That's when I heard Penny yelling from above: "The key's in the doghouse!" But before I could respond there was a shout from Casey behind me. "Who the hell are you two?" He was lifting his gun up against his red and mad face as if to fire again. Jenny panting behind him, said, "Jesus Casey, they're taking photos, we have got stop them!"

Sarah was taking pictures from her hip before I wrenched her away roughly round the corner, "Run! Follow me!" I urged and we pelted off around the Tower walls. Jenny, seeing what we were doing, told Casey to chase us and she set off in the other direction to try to cut us off at the back.

"The pregnant woman is my wife! Why are they trying to kill her?" I asked as we ran.

"I don't know! We came across all this by accident; we're camping near the ruined cottage."

I aimed for the doghouse. Casey was struggling—he had stopped to catch his breath and was leaning against the wall where nobody could see him, but he knew he could trap them with Jenny's help so needn't rush. Jenny careered around the corner at speed and when she saw us she shouted "Stop!"

We stood still and waited for Jenny to get close. I whispered, "Let her get near to think she's got us, then run when I grab her."

I wasn't stupid. She was trying to slow us down till Casey came up behind. When Jenny was about ten feet away, hands on hips looking nervously over our shoulders, wondering where Casey was, my college days on the pitch came into play and I quite simply dived into a full-flung rugby tackle and caught her round her slim waist. She was down, winded with me and we rolled through the doghouse door. I flung her against the back wall, alarmed at my treatment of this gorgeous blonde and slapped her across the face, hard. "Shut up and stay here till I get back—I'll deal with you later!" And I spun around, grabbed the rusty key off its nail, jumped out, kicked the door closed, fitted the clasp, grabbed a garden fork that was leaning against the shed and plunged one of its tines through the clasp jamming it securely shut. Jenny whimpered like a dog inside.

I shouted up to Penny: "The key is in the wood shed." I knew she would understand and added: "The dangerous blonde is in the doghouse." I flung the key as hard as I could through the arrow slit window through which we had helped the Shepherd load up his cellar with logs. Penny would find it there. I sped off to catch up with Sarah.

Casey came charging around the corner and a bullet came whizzing past us. Jenny started screaming "I'm in the doghouse!" and banged on the door. Casey tried to pull out the fork but it was too firmly wedged and yelled at her: "Shut up, you'll just have to stay there; I'll deal with you later." And he was back on our heels in earnest. 'Great,' thought Jenny and slumped back down onto the dog bed.

Sarah and I were pelting down the track towards Ashburn, Casey firing behind us. I was very aware of the power and potential accuracy of the rifle, although he seemed to miss the goat at very short range. I knew we had to get as far away as possible for our own safety, but also to draw him away from the Tower.

Penny took the Shepherd back to his bed as he was feeling weak. She said she would cook some more food but had something to do first. She found the padlock key in the cellar, then went into the Shepherd's workshop in the next vault and found some baler twine; she was going to pay a visit to the woman in the doghouse. She then opened up the oak door, listened quietly to see if anybody was out there, then released the padlock. The yet groaned as she pulled it open. She stepped out to be met by another groan. Auld Elliot had come to and had propped himself up against the stonework; he was clearly in pain and was holding his leg. Bizarrely he was still clutching the detonator cable as if to stop it snaking across the ground and seeking out its detonator. Penny rushed over to him. "We thought you'd been shot dead!"

"Apparently not," he grimaced. "That Casey is a complete idiot, couldn't even get that right."

"Come on, I need to get you inside quick before he comes back."

"Okay, I'll try, where's Casey gone?"

Penny struggled to get him up but enough to stagger and pull him through the door. He had to drag his foot sideways and they both fell back onto the bottom steps of the stairs. "Casey's gone off hunting my husband, but he's a clever one—he'll find a way to sort Casey out." Penny closed and locked the iron yet and put the key carefully in her pocket. She was glad to close off the oak door and replace the securing beam. The Tower had become a place of refuge and defence as it must have many times before. They battled up the stairs and Penny got Elliot sitting on a kitchen chair. The Shepherd pushed himself up in his bed, saw Elliot and said, "Hello, welcome to the Tower nursing home, sorry I can't help." Penny laughed and replied, "Don't you two worry, I will have you both sorted out in no time, but first things first—let's have a look at this leg."

Casey's Chase

Heather followed the goat that was intent on pursuing the aggressive Casey, who in turn was chasing the tall curly haired bloke and the photographer woman. She was vaguely familiar to him, some journalist or something. He was in too deep now: they had to be eliminated or his life was over. He had never imagined such a scenario or expected to become a cold blooded murderer; he just wanted to get rich, and it's what he deserved for all his years of slavery.

He knew they were there somewhere. Casey was standing next to the campfire at Ashburn, the rifle reloaded at his shoulder; the smoke drifted up and stung his eyes. He had heard them skirt around the back of the ruined cottage, their feet skidding on the fallen slates.

Sarah was gasping for breath. She wasn't that fit, certainly not for sprinting around the hills in twilight. A red glow stretched over their heads and dappled with a cooling blue sky. The tall man had protected her so far and was standing listening intently for Casey's next move.

Desperation

I was exhausted. Casey was being persistent to say the least, but then he was out of control and trying to save his skin. Ashburn was an almost treeless valley so to make a break for it and try to get up onto the higher ground to get a phone signal was going to be too risky. Then I remembered the boulder field on the flanks of the hill behind—they could easily lose Casey in that maze. "Listen carefully, I need to get you out of this mess, I'm going to get you safely hidden. If you look up there at the bottom of those cliffs there's a whole maze of boulders and dips and hollows. When I give you the signal go as fast as you can, run to the back of the sycamores then go like crazy diagonally up to the biggest rocks you can see. I'll lure him away then cut back. If you hear me call, flash your camera and I'll find you."

"Come out with your hands up and I'll not shoot!" shouted Casey, carefully reloading his gun. I looked Sarah in the eyes and held her shoulders. "You've really got to go for it, don't stop till you're hidden amongst the rocks." She nodded, wide eyed and scared.

"Be careful," she said gripping my arm.

"Right, go!" I whispered, and she was off.

I picked up a slate and sent it skimming through the air over the cottage. It landed on one of the tents behind Casey and he spun around in surprise. "We will come out if you throw your gun down, then we can talk," I shouted. I could see Sarah had reached the second tree and was about to make a dash up the hill; it was then that I realised what an easy target she would be, exposed on the open slope and she had a stream to cross that was going to slow her down. I began to walk around the far side of the cottage to see if I could get behind Casey. I picked up a couple more slates and threw them as hard as I could over the crumbling roof to try to distract him. What I didn't realise was that Casey had snuck forward towards the corner of the cottage. By the time I saw him he had seen Sarah and was levelling the gun in her direction. I grabbed a rock and threw it as hard as I could, but he had already pulled the trigger. The rock flew past him and landed harmlessly in the grass beyond. The retort was cruel in the beauty of the valley, flushed with a blood red glow above. I saw Sarah fall in the distance. Sickened by the sight I slung another stone, and this time it caught Casey's shoulder. He swung round and fired a bullet that bounced off the cottage wall as I dived for cover. 'This is getting a tad hairy,' I thought and made a break for it in the opposite direction. I was thinking tree cover—that way I could lose him and come back to find Sarah.

Casey was not far behind me as I leaped across a burn and ducked and dived to make targeting very difficult, but that didn't stop him trying and bullets came flying by. It then went quiet, so I assumed he had run out of ammunition or energy so I began to circle round in a wide arc back towards where I had last seen Sarah. She wasn't there and I spent a precious five minutes searching, thinking that she must only be injured; then I headed towards the boulder field. I assumed Casey had given up as I hadn't seen or heard anything of him. But I remained cautious so I didn't call until I was well in amongst the boulders. When I felt secure enough I called for Sarah in increasing volume and concern until I got a responding flash. It was slightly confusing exactly where it came from. She began to call too and I was desperate to yell back to quieten her. I did find her, cold and shaking, back against a low cliff. "Thank God you're okay, did he hit you?" She shook her head and just hugged me tight. Poor little thing, she was really scared.

Casey the Killer

Casey had never killed anyone before. Elliot just got in the way, that's all. He had seen him slumped and twisted with blood pouring down his face from a bullet hole in the head. Now that he had killed once he thought another couple were going to make no difference to any jail term—he just had to try to get away with it. He had followed the tall guy, then saw him cutting back. He knew he would have to go back to find the woman, so he pre-empted this and was already searching for Sarah when he arrived. The man kept looking behind him when in fact Casey was in front of him. Casey bided his time—this curly haired idiot would lead him to Sarah and then he'd take them both out. He saw the flash and heard the calling and eventually found them fifty yards away resting and hugging in the shadow of a large slab of grey stone that must have fallen from the cliff face many millennia before. He took his time, got them in his sights. He could see that if he missed the girl he would at least hit the bloke.

He pulled gently and with a horrific bang, that echoed through the rocks and up the cliff above, a bullet was propelled towards Sarah's pretty face. But he missed again. He was just vaguely becoming aware that he always missed to the right of the target and he fired again—but they were already off at high speed.

Trapped

Sarah and I careered between boulders at speed, Casey firing behind. The bullets whizzed and pinged around us. I was surprised that the red-faced gunman could keep up. Sarah collapsed against a grassy bank completely exhausted. "I can't go on!" she wheezed.

"You're going to have to," I said hauling her to her feet, but she really was at her strength's end. Desperate to get away from the hunter, I was looking around for a better place to go and suddenly noticed a tall rock I knew and recalled a discovery I had made just before Penny twisted her ankle on our previous visit. "Quick, this way, I've got an idea." I could hear the gunman stumbling around far too close. We slid down the steep grass into a deep hollow, not a good place to get caught by a hunter, but I had to take the gamble. I remembered the odd stone slab at the bottom where I had planted ash seed and could still hear the sound of the stones trickling down into a cavity below. Now, if that was large enough, we could take cover till Casey gave up. I remembered the slab moving when I last tried to lift it with the planting crook; two of us would manage.

"There's a place to hide beneath this slab, you need to help me open it," I said with more confidence than I felt. Sarah nodded and we both fell to our knees and started scraping away the turf and debris on and around the stone. We were making a terrible noise but had to be quick. As I swept the moss and earth off the top with the side of my hand I saw a carved symbol where the moss still clung, a simple eye staring back like the one on the window surround in the Tower bedroom. "There's something metal here too," Sarah said digging at the soil beside the slab "And here," she said with more faith and hope. Immediately I saw what it was and understood: they were crude hinges of iron sitting in hollowed-out stones on either side to prevent them rusting solid. Last time I had been trying to lift the slab from the wrong side. "Quick, lift here." We both got our fingers under the edge and hauled.

Casey's unfit lungs were making a horrible noise not too far away; he was close and would hear them soon. He was spitting blood, had a burning chest, numerous cuts and bruises and a horrible throbbing in his head. But he knew they were hiding nearby. He was going to get them this time, he could sense it.

A strange thing happened when we opened up the slab. It was too heavy for one person and teetered precariously on its thick iron hinges. There was an odd movement in the air and the distinct feeling that perhaps we were disturbing a place we should not be. Something slipped, bumped and rattled down the darkness beneath us. We looked up at each other in alarm. Nothing could be worse than stepping into a deep dark void of the unknown with things that might lurk there. Sarah was petrified of the dark in normal circumstances, but we had to do it and quickly. She took off her rucksack and handed it to me, then felt with her feet in the cool inky pool of fear. She found a sound footing, then another. "There's a step... yes, there's definitely more... a proper way down." She reached up for her rucksack which I had ready for her and as she grasped it she flinched in horror as she saw four odd white stick-like things embedded in the soil, where the stone slab had rested. I saw them too, four skeletal fingers, human and tragic. A sudden movement behind me and I shouted: "Go!" Sarah vanished and I could hear her clambering down, then gasps and sobbing below. Poor Sarah.

"Freeze, you bastard!" Casey screamed at me. "Got you at last!"

He had his rifle up and trained on my head. There was no way he could miss this time, even with the misaligned sights. I raised my hands and as he pulled the trigger dropped to the ground out of the way. The bullet skimmed across my scalp and ricocheting around the enclosing stones, it scared the hell out of me. I fell backwards and blood trickled down into my eyes. I couldn't see what was going on so made a lunge for him. I brought him down with a thump but he kicked away and was on his feet again. I struggled up and staggered backwards wiping the sticky blood out of my eyes. The gun barrel was only a foot from my head. "This time mate, I've got you!" Casey snarled and pulled the trigger. *Click*—nothing. He knew a split second before I did, grabbed the barrel and swung the gun around like a club.

Casey stood over the cocky tall guy—there was blood all over him. He kicked him in the side, no reaction. "Dead as a Dodo," he laughed. "Got you that time, didn't I?" He spat on the man and turned to the dark hole beside the slab and looked down into an abyss of horrors. He was so far outside his comfort zone he didn't care anymore. He reloaded his weapon, pulled out a pen torch from a small pocket on his jumpsuit and illuminated the steps descending into the murk. He put his hand on top of the raised slab and stepped onto the stone below, then moved down onto the next. "I'm coming to get you bitch, you shouldn't have been snooping around taking pictures." It was at that point that his torchlight caught the four finger bones wedged into the soil and his hand tipped the balance of the raised slab causing it to collapse on top of him, pushing him down the steps.

Sarah, shaking in the pitch black below, had heard the shots and shouting. She knew her knight in shining armour was dead and she was crying, full of self-pity huddled against cold damp stones. She didn't want to die, she didn't want to die in this terrible place, and she didn't want to die at the hands of such an evil man. She didn't want to die. Then she heard Casey scream. The slab had fallen on him with such speed, he hadn't quite managed to get out of the way; it had caught his shoulder forcing him down and the edge of the slab had landed on his right forefinger, crushing the nail and trapping his hand. He screamed in shock and pain and dropped the gun and torch. In reaction he shoved up against the slab and just managed to move it enough to pull his finger free, put it into his left armpit and rocked forward in agony. He then realised his mistake. He was trapped beneath a slab that was too heavy to lift on his own; and he had dropped his torch and gun down to the photographer below. If he had simply closed the stone lid she would probably have been trapped and would have perished in time. Too late, he was now at the mercy of the woman below, caught in a tomb, escape from which was impossible without her help to push up on the slab. He had to force her, so made a mad dash for the gun and torch below.

Sarah had seen the torch come rolling down the steps, but hadn't realised the gun was there too. She made a dive for it, grasped it and using it managed to navigate her way further away into the cave. It was vast, much larger than she had imagined. The collapse of the cliff thousands of years ago as the ice retreated and relieved the pressure on the land had left a long series of cavities beneath a field of giant rocks and boulders.

Casey was completely in the dark. He saw the torch light receding into the depths of the cave and fumbled around for the gun in hopes she hadn't taken it. At that point he thought the torch was the more useful of the two. He could feel stones, then sticks, some fabric and as he patted his hand along the material came to a rounded object that had something taut stretched across it. Its shape was familiar somehow and he explored it with his good hand; fingers finding voids, he gripped it and his thumb popped through something in an unpleasant way. Then he realised in horror what he held—a skull! He shook it off his hand in alarm and could feel the spine and ribcage beneath the fabric. He stumbled back in the dark and tripped backwards over something much more familiar; sitting up and feeling around, he found his gun.

Sarah and Casey were trapped. Unlikely cooperation was their only way out.

Heather's Dread

Why anybody wanted to go to the chambers underground baffled her. Heather had avoided the place ever since she had had a quick look there many years ago. It scared her, there was still a lot of pain and anger, all bottled up ready to explode. When they lifted the slab there had been a sudden rush and two people she recognised came out; they stared at her, then at each other and dissolved before her like her mother had.

Nurse Penny

Elliot sat in the armchair Penny had dragged in for him from the hall. He had been tidied up, leg wounds cleaned, smothered in antiseptic cream and bandaged tightly to stop the bleeding. The cut in his head had been stretched by the egg-like swelling on his skull beneath. It had two pieces of waterproof plaster crossed over it as if marking the spot. It was still bleeding and he dabbed it with a small blue handtowel. The fire was blazing, but Elliot was quivering violently from shock and anxiety. He was really worried about Sarah and felt responsible for drawing her into the mess.

Penny was in a state about her husband and was keeping herself busy and trying to hide her concerns, but was jittery and clumsy. The Heather inside her was squirming too, making her uncomfortable. She checked on the Shepherd who had fallen asleep and returned to her cooking. She had a pot of vegetables simmering on the stove and was chopping up a ham she had unhooked from the ceiling above.

To distract herself she had been asking Elliot about Casey and his wind turbine plans. She had a pretty good idea what was going on and she was fuming inside. "So this ridiculous government policy is driving people to split families and communities, shoot at each other, slaughter wildlife, fell mature trees, blow up ancient buildings, plough unique archaeology from the ground and blight our stunning landscapes with an industrial mess to satisfy individuals' greed? So landowners get super-rich quick at our expense and you see the future of energy as gas and nuclear because there is no real choice? Wind power is just too feeble and intermittent to be effective?"

"Yes, if it wasn't so awful it would be funny," growled Elliot. "People like Casey are out of control, driven by greed and the great Wind Rush overcomes them. They erect these ivory towers and inevitably they will come crumbling down! In the meantime we all have to suffer."

It was dark outside and Penny lit another lamp and took it upstairs to their bedroom window. She was hoping it would help her husband find his way back. She looked out but couldn't see any lights or hear anything unusual.

Surely she would have heard something by now?

Goat Rescue

Heather and the goat looked down the deep hollow at Penny's man lying cold and twisted in the pale moonlight. *They* knew he wasn't dead. Now that the two spirits trapped beneath the slab had escaped the place didn't feel so bad for Heather. She had to help the man so he could get back to Penny and the Shepherd. She floated down next to the unconscious living body and the goat hopped nimbly down beside her. She fussed around the man's head looking at the blood matting his hair; it wasn't bleeding much but looked sore. The top of his scalp had a gash across it and his head above his ear was swollen and messy with blood. She needed to wake him so encouraged the goat over and flapping her hands around a lot managed to get the goat to tread gently on him with delicate hooves and sniff around his face. After a while there was a flicker of his eyelids and quite a long time after that the man's eyes flew open and he sat up quickly to protect himself. But he couldn't recall what from.

Concussed

I found myself sitting up staring at the black and white face of the Shepherd's old goat. Or was it Heather's? Who was Heather? My head was incredibly sore; I sat there feeling the damage, remembering loud noises. I could see the carving on top of the stone slab next to me knowing it was important, but couldn't for the life of me remember why—I think I had tried lifting it before but it had been too heavy. I knew the symbol from somewhere too. I lent forward and held my head trying to remember what I was doing there. I was walking down from

287

the high ridge to meet Penny at the Tower—that much was clear. Perhaps I had accidently fallen down there in the dark. But I couldn't recall it being dark. I slowly clambered to my feet. 'Must have whacked my head on the rocks. Got to get to the Tower to save Penny.' The goat sprang up the way it had come down. I followed and when I stood around getting my bearings I could see the tops of the two Sycamores by Ashburn cottage so staggered off in that direction. Why had I wandered off my planned route? How long had I been lying there? My mind was a muddle and my head really throbbed. I knew it was concussion from the fall. Penny wasn't expecting me, so I realised I was lucky to have woken up, as nobody would be looking for me. The air was chilly and I relied on the goat to lead the way. From time to time I thought I saw a pale figure ahead of me, though sometimes right next to me, so I put it down to the moonlight catching things and my confused state of mind.

Heather ran back and forward keeping the goat moving in the right direction. She didn't want the tingly man to collapse and not reach the Tower. An owl hooted and that seemed to enliven him. At the burn he waded in and spent two minutes washing his hair and face. It clearly was a cold and unpleasant experience, but it seemed to help as his pace quickened afterwards. He found the campsite and glowing embers but no people. He crouched and warmed his hands for a minute, then forced himself up to go. The track to the Tower was eerie in the moonlight with the willows above making the moonlight dazzling as it filtered through the foliage.

When I saw the Tower, somebody had placed an oil lantern in the bedroom window. I called but there was no response. I reached the door and found it locked. I knew it was only locked if strangers were poking about and had seen the campsite, so assumed they must have been spotted by Penny and the Shepherd, but then why have a give-away lantern burning at a window? I shouted but my voice was hoarse and weak and I knew banging on the door was a waste of time, but tried anyway. Then I remembered where the Shepherd hung a spare key. I walked around to the doghouse, pulled out the garden fork, which I thought an odd way to secure it, opened up the door and was met by the piercing scream of a woman from the darkness within.

Deep Desolate Despair

Sarah hugged the torch close to her chest. She knew the power of light. She also knew the power of the dark. As a child growing up she had always had a night light. The first was a plastic moulding of a cow jumping over the moon. It used to fade at bedtime and brighten in the morning to simulate natural dusk and dawn. Her last one was a pandrop shaped alarm clock with a dimmable light. She had drawn a likeness of her first boyfriend on that one. It was dumped when the boyfriend was.

Casey was a scared wimp. He had always chosen easy options; his elder brother had worked extremely hard at his academic studies and his younger was hugely dedicated to his passion of cooking. Casey had got average results at school, slobbed around being a lad at Uni and had been lucky in the exams. His jobs were gained through a combination of the 'gift of the gab' and dishonesty. His skills were being able to convince people he was better and more able than he really was. He was a bluffer, an actor. Something he needed to apply to escape from his current nightmare predicament.

He had the gun, it was loaded, but if he shot her, then he would be stuck and die a slow miserable subterranean death like the corpse he had found at the door. Alternatively, perhaps somebody would find them and he would spend many years in jail.

He thought if he fired a shot the light from the gun would at least give flash illumination to give him an idea of the layout of the void he was within. He held the gun up in front of him and then thought of a bullet bouncing back at him if he were to shoot directly at a rock. He thrust the gun forward into to the black and it seemed clear, but changed his mind—he didn't want to shoot himself. He knelt down and scraped up some pebbles and standing again, carefully threw them at different angles away from him and that way managed to discover what he thought was the greatest space before him.

Sarah had seen the sheer scale of the void and was terrified of getting lost. She was squeezed into a tight corner and had her rucksack open before her, pen torch switched off and gripped in her mouth. She pulled out a fleece top with a furry lined hood and put it on to try to warm up. Digging deeper past her photography cases she found her favourite woolly jumper and some bars of chocolate. She closed up her rucksack and put it on her shoulders. She ate one bar of chocolate very quietly and listened out for movement. If she had to move on into the cave to escape the gunman, she needed to be prepared. Despite herself she was shedding the victim status and going into survival mode. She wasn't going to be beaten by this madman, there would be a way. She heard the man throwing stones and after a moment or two realised that he was stranded in the dark and like dropping stones down a well he was assessing the blackness before him. She thought that perhaps he would have a mobile phone to provide backup light; she did, but she was saving that. If she had the torch she had a tool every bit as useful as a gun. She imagined being a character in a video game collecting bonuses and equipment. She'd had her chocolate bonus and now was the time to consider her kit bag. She had her camera with a flash, food, clothing, the man's torch, but no map. This is where the camera and jumper were going to be useful. She had the camera hung around her neck and jumper in her hands. She was thinking about a logical way to rid herself of this stupid wild idiot.

"If you come out now I won't shoot!" Casey called into the nothingness in front of him. "If you come out in the count of ten I will let you go."

"Not on your Nellie," breathed Sarah.

"One...two...come on, you know it's for the best... three... four... you're going to get hurt unless you come out now... five... six... this is your last chance.... seven............. eight.... you silly cow, you're going to die in this hole tonight unless you give in NOW....... nine......... right, you've had it... ten."

Casey had a good idea of the direction the cave led. He raised the gun, having to use his second finger as his forefinger was too swollen, and keeping the gun level, fired. The flash was brief and illuminating, burning a useful image of the way ahead into his retinas, but he was completely unprepared for the volume of the shot that bounced back at him at short range off the rocks. He collapsed with his hands over his ears. The bullet had whizzed through the cave, then bounced a couple of times before sizzling in a stretch of still water seventy yards further in.

Sarah had jumped at the noise but knew she was relatively safe where she was hidden. She chewed at the jumper trying to keep calm and apply logic. What was the man going to do? Why did he want her dead?

"There's no escape, all I want is your camera then I will go!" Casey yelled. He would nibble away at what he wanted.

Destroy the evidence first then force her to help him lift the slab, then finish her off. He would shove her back down the hole to rot.

Sarah thought about his words and doubted that would be the end of it; she had also seen too much and realised that he and the girl thought he'd killed Elliot. She knew they hadn't, but having thought that realised Elliot might die of his injuries and shock later. A useful element of doubt lurked there.

"If you throw me the camera I'll go now." He knew she wouldn't know that he was trapped beneath the slab too and wouldn't be able to escape without her. The last thing he wanted was to have to go further into the cave. Too many bats and things.

Sarah thought it might be worth a try to see if he would go. She took the camera out of its case, laid it on the ground in front of her, took off her rucksack and pulled the other camera equipment out. She could feel the wide angle lens, took it out of its case and wedged it into the lens opening of the camera case; she then took a plastic box containing cleaning fluids and brushes, forced it down behind the lens and closed up the case. If seen or picked up it would resemble her camera. But he must be stupid because all she needed was the memory cards anyway and photographers don't part with their cameras that easily. She repacked her bag and put it onto her back. She kept the fake camera at her feet and carried on the job with her jumper.

In the Doghouse

Penny had heard Jenny scream and rushed up to the high turret to look down on the sheds. What she saw was scary and funny at the same time. There was a lot of noise and commotion in the shed—she feared it might be Casey back and her husband and Sarah lying dead or injured out in the cold of the night. But after a few more bumps and squeals, a tall figure staggered out into the bright moonlight. She could see it was her husband. He seemed to be carrying a large bundle under his arm that wriggled and screamed and bit and thumped. Its beautiful blonde hair shook and flapped in the eerie light.

"I'll open up the door!" Penny yelled and flew down the stairs as fast as she could.

I was having a strange night. Not only had I suffered extensive head injuries, I had been attacked by a rabid woman locked in the doghouse! Something appropriate about that I thought. I was cold and wet and couldn't work out what was going on. The little monster was scratching at my eyes the moment I walked in and swearing and shouting about somebody called Casey. I wasn't in the mood and wanted to check on Penny and the Shepherd. I simply scooped her under my arm and hung on. It was like a more interesting game of rugby and thought it was a great idea to pass onto the Olympic committee. A pass, a try and conversion would take on a whole new meaning. Very watchable.

I heard Penny shouting from high up in the Tower and headed around to the entrance.

Penny meets Jenny

Penny opened the oak door as quickly as she could and fumbled madly undoing the padlock. Her husband appeared with his unusual bundle. The blonde just hung limply propping her head on her hand and pouting. The yet swung open, he strode in and kissed Penny on the cheek. She swung the yet closed, locked it and secured the oak door.

"Boy, am I glad to see you!"

"What shall I do with this?" he asked, hefting the grumpy girl under his arm.

"Get her arms behind her back; I've got something for her I prepared earlier."

He lowered her to the ground, neatly flipped her over and brought her arms together behind her back. She spat and swore but they both ignored her. Penny pulled out the pieces of hemp twine from her rear pocket that she had collected from the workshop earlier and quickly tied her thumbs together. Her husband lifted her onto her feet and held her to let Penny have a look. An onlooker would have seen two very good looking women eyeing each other suspiciously. They were the same height and build, although Penny's bump distorted this image. Penny had large brown eyes, Jenny had large blue ones. Their hair was the same length and they both had a splattering of freckles on their cheeks.

"Who the hell are you lot?" asked Jenny.

"Secret Service," replied Penny.

Jenny suddenly kicked back at the strong guy holding her. He winced in pain as her boot caught his shin. He let her go and Jenny stumbled forward. Penny stepped aside and she fell through the doorway leading to the vaults.

"Right, let's get upstairs. I need to get cleaned up, fed and get my head sorted. Have you got some ibuprofen and some strong tea?"

Penny led the way and took him straight to their bathroom and left him in charge of running himself a bath. "I will be back with my first aid kit in a mo, please tell me what happened to Sarah just in case I need to break bad news to the others."

"Err, I don't know," he said thinking 'who's Sarah, what others?'

"Right, I better go, I need Elliot to stir the stew," Penny said rushing through the door.

Penny reached the kitchen to find Elliot had already moved close enough to the range to look after the meal.

"Brilliant, just what I was going to ask you to do." Elliot grimaced; he disliked cooking at the best of times—that was Lizzie's department. But cooking after being shot in the leg was beyond the call of duty. "Any sign of Sarah?" asked Elliot looking concerned.

"I asked my husband but he seemed not to know who Sarah was. He's had a hell of a bash to the head and seems confused. I need to get him cleaned up and bandaged."

"Ask him again, I don't want her getting hurt."

"Okay, will do. By the way, we've brought Jenny in from the doghouse; if she comes in, pay no attention. There's no escape from the Tower, it's all locked up. She's in a bad mood and might bump around for a bit. I'll talk to her once she's calmed down."

Elliot smiled at her relaxed attitude.

Down in the Dumps

Casey was becoming depressed. Now that all the fast action was over and his adrenaline was dropping he was shaking and miserable. Sarah had gone quiet on him and he was tired and hungry. He went back up the steps to have another go at the slab, but however hard he pushed, it only moved a quarter of an inch at the most.

Sarah had heard him go up the steps and took the opportunity to set up her fake camera and lay a trap. But first she tied the end of her unravelled jumper round a large stone on the floor. She didn't know how far the wool would stretch but it would allow her to go a certain distance without becoming totally lost. She broke about a five yard length off to attach to her the torch and tied the other ends to her belt and picked up the fake camera. She flashed the pen torch just enough to get a bearing then groped her way across the cave floor and placed the camera where Casey would see it. She then took out her remote control flash and set it up at ninety degrees from the fake camera, un-clicked its controller and flashing her torch again moved back into the cave about fifteen yards; she could feel a large boulder and managed to duck down behind it. She flashed her torch again to orientate herself to the flash unit.

"Oi, what are you doing back there?" Casey had seen the torch flashing.

"I'm really cold, I want to go home, I've decided to give you the camera. I've put it on the floor," said Sarah selecting a handful of fist sized rocks. She was full of chocolate and warm in her fleece.

"Clever girl, now you're coming round to my way of thinking," Casey sneered; he had to get the gun barrel poking in her back to get her to help with the slab.

"How am I going to find it?" shouted Casey.

"I'll shine the torch on it," replied Sarah.

"Okay, go ahead but no funny business, right?"

"Do you want it or not?" Sarah replied.

Casey saw the torchlight come on and he could see the camera and approached carefully gun at the ready.

Sarah had undone the wool from her belt and secured it to the torch. She moved to the other side of the camera opposite the flash and switched it on, then ran quickly for cover. She wrapped the wool around her left hand and was holding the flash controller, finger on the button ready to press, in her other hand a stone ready to throw. The torch shone in Casey's eyes as he approached but he wanted to dispose of the camera first before going for the stupid woman.

Sarah thought it was a bit like fishing. She watched him come slowly forward dazzled by the torch. She could see be had the gun up ready to shoot. She waited patiently—it was all about timing. Casey wanted the torch so desperately he was going to grab the camera then go for the torch. He stooped forward for the camera and as his hand grabbed it Sarah hit the remote flash button; the sudden flash surprised him—he jumped around and aimed the gun towards the place where the flash came from. Perfect, thought Sarah, and slung the rock as hard as she could towards his gun now held at right angles to her, nicely lit by the torch. The stone caught his arm and another was already on its way. She set the flash off again to confuse him and the stone hit his knuckles. The third missed, flash, flash, the forth caught the gun and knocked it out of his hands—and the gun went skidding into the darkness. Maddened, Casey swung around and flung himself at the torch. It flicked out of the way towards the boulder. He tried again; Sarah went around the other side and ran for where she thought the gun would be; the torch followed skidding sideways with Casey close behind. Sarah pressed the flash button again and it illuminated the weapon lying against the cave wall. She just managed to grab it, but the pause in movement was enough for Casey to get a hand on the torch. He found the wool and had broken it before she could yank it away. She flew past him at speed grabbing her flash as she did.

Casey could hear her disappearing into the depths of the cave. He turned to see if he could find the gun with the torch; when he couldn't, he realised what she had been up to. But he had the torch whereas she only had two bullets in the gun and was unlikely to be able to use it. He shone the light on the camera, picked up a rock and smashed it to pieces, plastic and glass scattered across the floor. Next task, find the woman. He wasn't scared of her now he had the torch. He followed in the direction she had gone and was overwhelmed by the cave, which extended well beyond the light from the torch with a jumble of large slabs leaning at different angles, a maze of tunnels and chambers. He shone the torch all round him and up into the cathedral-like space. He thought he could hear Sarah so followed the sounds. He didn't notice the wool lying in the dirt.

"Give up now you stupid, stupid girl." His voice filtered through the space and echoed back at him. Sarah, ignoring him, was crouched out of range of the torch trying desperately to find the safety lock on the gun. When Casey got too close she scooped up some stones and seeing a lowered opening opposite started throwing them in; it was just enough to make him head that way. Once he had moved far enough away she grasped the wool she had retied to her belt at her waist and as the torchlight receded she began to reel herself in using the wool. This led her back almost to the entrance steps. She rolled up the wool and taking off her rucksack, stuffed it in for future use if required. She searched the rucksack contents and found her mobile phone. She switched it on and checked the battery level—half full. Finding the steps, she walked up to see if she could open the slab. She had heard the resounding thump just before Casey had screamed. Putting her shoulders against the flat stone and pushing up with all her might achieved nothing. As she came down she realised the only way out was either with his help or waiting to be found. She switched off her phone and put it into a back trouser pocket, then retreated further into the cave and finding a slight recess crouched down to think about her predicament.

Where's Sarah?

The Shepherd was awake sitting at the table eating stew with Elliot. Penny was making a strong black coffee for herself. Her husband was prodding the fire with a poker. "So you're telling me that I have already been here and was seen running off with a girl called Sarah being pursued by this Casey nutter, with bullets whizzing all over the place. Is that how I got this?" He said pointing at the gash on his scalp.

"Yes, he was definitely trying to kill you! That's why we are so concerned about Sarah and she was taking a lot of photos of what was going on. He will want to get rid of her camera and probably her too."

"Then I must go out and look for her as soon as possible."

"None of us are in a good enough condition to go searching tonight."

"I think you might be right there." He gently touched the side of his head. He closed his eyes and tried to remember what happened.

"If you can recall where you woke up that would be the first place to start looking," suggested Penny.

"All I recall is standing looking down at a moss-filled carving on a stone, following the goat and then collecting the mad woman from the doghouse."

"If you draw what you saw I might be able to help," suggested the Shepherd.

299

Penny found a pencil and a scrap of paper and her husband sketched a lens shape with a circle inside and a dot in the middle. A simple eye stared out of the pages at them. The Shepherd looked at it and replied, "That symbol is quite common here; I think it's a kind of family motto or device. It's on the crest above the door when you come in, on some old books, my crooks, boundary stones of the estate and even some of the dishes in here." He stood and took a couple of old plates off a shelf and put them on the table. Each had the symbol glazed in blue against white, the only difference being a triangle at one end making the images fish like.

"My older brothers had invented an adventure game that they used to play up here together. Angus and I were told we were too young to join in. We felt left out but used to listen to their stories of secret meetings, dragons, knights in armour, Border reiving, damsels in distress, secret caves and that sort of thing. They would disappear into the hills with great excitement on some quest or other. Angus and I copied them but nearer the Tower. We collected locations of that symbol and made up our own games. Though ours were more like cowboys and Indians."

"What about the books?" asked Elliot. "Is there a record of where these symbols are?"

"Not exactly, but their club book is still here. I've got it in the library somewhere."

"Could we see it?" asked Penny

"You'll need to help me get it."

The Shepherd stood and Penny followed him up his private stairs. Elliot and Penny's husband looked at the sketch and plates trying to think where these clues might lead.

Jenny Calms Down

Jenny had fallen through the door towards the vaults. Her captors had just walked off as if nothing had happened leaving her there. She had struggled to get up; having your hands tied behind your back makes things very difficult. You have nothing to push against the floor with. She shoved herself against a wall and kicked herself up with her feet. Once up, things were easier. She was standing in a long corridor with a curved stone ceiling; there were two doors on her right and a third straight ahead. Each door was made of broad planks of hard grey oak with studded nails criss-crossed over them. All the doors were closed and the one straight ahead was padlocked. The two to the right had wrought iron latches, the kind where you have to press down hard with your thumb. Not handy if your thumbs are tied together behind your back. Jenny thought they might lead to an escape route. She tried getting her elbow onto the workshop door latch but wasn't tall enough. She tried then to push down with her chin, but wasn't strong enough. She thought the next door might be easier so tried there too, but the same problems availed and she failed to get into the wood store. Frustrated, she wandered off to look for a sharp edge in the stonework to rub the string on to cut it off. At the bottom of the stairs a sharp edge might have worked but when she reversed up to the stone and tried she only grazed her skin and broke a thumbnail. Cursing obscenities she advanced up the stairs. She found the place spooky and scary. She never had liked old places.

Jenny was sulking. She wasn't remotely happy about Casey; he had turned from a loving friend and co-conspirator to a sharp tongued, aggressive and thoroughly unpleasant killer. She was now wandering around a cold stony castle; she was starving and seemed to have ended up with members of the

Secret Service. When she reached the hall she could hear talking through a half open door to the left; she avoided it and walked towards the door at the far end. She was awestruck with the place and gazed up at the high vault above. She wondered why there were doors and windows halfway up the walls. Seeing the lower windows she rushed over to see if there was a way down, but found it difficult to look down without feeling dizzy; even if there had been a drainpipe or something to clamber down she couldn't without free hands. The goat that butted Casey seemed to be watching her; each time she looked out of the Tower it would stop grazing and look up at her. What she didn't know was that Heather was floating around the Tower keeping an eye on Jenny; she was studying her, seeing what she did and where she went. At the far end of the hall Jenny opened the unlatched door with her foot and staggered and bumped up the spiral stone stairs until she came to the guest bedroom where she went to look at herself in the bedroom mirror. She didn't like what she saw. Ever since her mother had taken her to a beauty contest at the age of ten she had taken great care over her appearance. She was always clean, well groomed, dressed for the occasion with make-up and nails perfect. The mirror reflected back the worst thing possible for her personal self-image and esteem. She was looking dishevelled, dirty, had smudged lipstick and mascara stains down her face where she had been crying. The camouflage jumpsuit was covered in mud and cobwebs from the doghouse. She started crying again and watched the tears rolling down her cheeks. Frustrated and miserable, she kicked out at the mirror stand; she caught it harder than she meant to and it started to topple over.

Penny and the Shepherd returned to the kitchen. Penny had a huge smile on her face. "You have the most incredible library, why didn't you tell us? Just walking through to help get this down I have seen a dozen rare and important books!" The Shepherd chuckled at her enthusiasm and responded, "We have been rather busy with everything else."

That's when they heard an awful crashing from above. "That will be Jenny. I'll go and sort her out," said Penny, handing over William and Maurice's adventure book to Elliot.

Casey Finds the Meeting Room

Casey was working his way through a series of narrower tunnels beneath slabs of dark volcanic rock. It had gone incredibly quiet and he thought perhaps the photographer woman had hidden in a gap somewhere and gone back towards the entrance. There were several alternative routes within the maze of rocks; he stuck to the largest and most obvious. "I know you're in there!" he shouted. An eerie echo, then nothing. "There's no escape," he said more quietly, not liking his own words talking back at him. Their meaning seemed to apply to him as much as the woman. 'Where is the bitch?' he thought. He'd gone off women; in fact he had a long time ago. He just used them. They were guaranteed trouble, which had been proven yet again by that stupid girl Jenny. Yes she was perfect to look at, but didn't have an ounce of intelligence. She'd cocked up the demolition and got herself locked in the doghouse.

After another fifty yards his torch began to dim. Just that slight yellowing of the light. He noticed but didn't react in particular as he had just entered a most unexpected scene. His dimming torch picked up the end of something wooden. He stepped forward and a long plank table stretched out before him with a range of carved chairs down either side. At each end what he thought looked like thrones. They had taller, more ornate backs. He walked down the side illuminating the table and a clutter of things upon it. There was a layer of soft grey dust covering it all. He passed his finger over the back of a chair. The dust was so fine and thick—clearly the place hadn't been visited for many centuries.

He was wrong. There were clusters of tankards, tall church altar candlesticks several feet high, some with the stumps of dirty yellow candles. Further along there was a carved wooden box lying open exposing a number of scrolls. One had turned end pieces. His torch battery notched down in brightness. He rummaged through them searching for something resembling a map and carefully lifted one out, blew the dust off and rolled it out on a space on the table. He pinned it down with tankards and a candlestick; he hoped it was a map of the caves showing a way out. He looked at it carefully with the dimming torch. To Casey it was a possible means of escape from his current predicament but to a knowledgeable historian it was a find of the century. It was a beautifully executed depiction of the Cheviot Hills accurately showing conical hills or great ridges sweeping across the map. It gave a perspective as a bird might view it looking south from high in the sky. The borderline was shown as a red ochre line zig-zagging over the hills. Each town or village was marked with a collection of tiny houses; a church, a neat gold crucifix and places of defence were shown as an accurate portrayal of the main façade of each building. If a tower had two turrets it was shown, six windows, then tiny rectangles depicted them. Some were coloured in red or had gold dots next to them depending on their significance. Rivers and streams were marked as fine black lines, mills as tiny millwheels, arable land as parallel yellow lines and woodland as miniature trees shaded green. Cattle and sheep were shown to illustrate grazing and cairns as triangles. Across this amazing document were marks, arrows and names, muster points and other indecipherable marks. Sweeping sketched lines led from tower to tower marking a line of defence across the map. Some were circled with tiny horses illustrating the quantity of available mounted men. It was the most perfect snapshot of a Border line of defence against raiding English Reivers. If Casey had cared to look he would have followed the raids, the skirmishes and leaders of each troop and tower across the hills. His eyes missed the linking of frontline fortalices across the land, Graden, Thirlestane, Yetholm, Mow, Corbet, Whitten, Gateshawtour, Bierhope, Hownam, Hyndhope, Burnepeglo, Giltentour, Okenlee, Knocklawsend, Souden, Edgertoon, Slakis, Mervins, Rucchly, Blackchester, Kilnsike, Dykra, Oulie and dozens more. What he did notice though was a sketch that could have been a map of the cave. He didn't realise it could be useful till later. Elaborate illuminated script in bright colours framed the map with descriptions and notes in Latin.

The torch suddenly dimmed significantly and he took more attention this time. He shook it and swore. He was going to have to go back and didn't have time to look at the other maps. However, he was determined to go all around the room. At the far end his feeble light showed an odd bundle lying across the table. It didn't seem so pale and dusty. He gasped in horror when he realised what it was. A body was slumped forward on to the table, its head still hanging onto tufts of hair. Skin falling away from bone. The person had worn smart clothes. Tweed riding jacket, pale jodhpurs and black riding boots. Casey walked around it. A riding crop lay on the floor. But most gruesome of all, one of the tall candlesticks clung to its neck, a rusty metal spike jammed between pale vertebrae. Casey was shaking. He wasn't the only killer to have haunted this cave. The torch went out. He froze in panic the switched it off and on again. It glowed feebly. Leaving the murder scene he returned to the place where he had come in. But there were two routes, not one, and he didn't recognise either.

Jenny Repents

Penny found Jenny sitting on her bed crying and whimpering. She was looking at the floor rocking back and forward. The smashed mirror lay on the floor, shards of glass scattered in all directions. "I'm sorry, none of this was meant to happen. Casey didn't say anything about people living here," sobbed Jenny.

"It's best if you stop now and tell me what you've been up to. Why you came here to blow up this incredible home." Penny was thinking about the incredible library as much as anything, hidden away for all these years.

"I'm desperate to use the toilet," moaned Jenny.

Penny could see wearing a jumpsuit with her hands fixed behind her back could lead to quite a mess.

"Okay, I'll help you, but any funny business and you will be left to pee in your pants next time."

Jenny nodded. Penny pulled out another piece of baler twine and bound Jenny's feet together so she could only take small steps. She then helped her stand and snipped her thumbs free. Jenny hobbled off to the toilet.

When she returned to the bedroom Jenny asked not to have her hands tied. "Okay, but your feet stay like that; you make one false move and you'll have more than just your thumbs tied together."

"It's okay. I don't care about Casey and his mission any more, I just want to go home or to a warm comfortable prison a thousand miles from here."

"You sit there. I'm going to get a brush and dustpan so you can clear up in here before doing anything else. If you are good we will feed you." Jenny sat down and Penny left to fetch the cleaning equipment from the kitchen.

Jenny was both emotionally and physically exhausted, so much so she could barely keep her eyes open. She let her eyes gently close but then suddenly opened them when she thought someone came into the room. She looked up but couldn't see anyone. She sat there looking at the long shards of broken mirror glass wondering if she could grab a piece, cut her legs free then stab the bossy woman in the guts before jumping out of a window. Better having a twisted ankle from jumping than a lifetime in jail. She looked at the door and thinking it worth a go she dragged a bit of mirror close enough with her foot to pick up. Her hand reached out but then something flashed from the array of pieces on the oak boards. It was fleeting, but just for a split second she thought she'd seen a face looking at her. She reached towards the glass again and stopped; this time the face was back, staring at her. A little girl's face, wide eyed and serious; each shard she looked at showed the same face. Looking around her, then up above, she could not understand where the image came from. A bit freaked out she sat back shaking slightly. The little girl she saw wasn't her but it could have been, blue eyes, freckles and blonde locks. Taking it as a warning, she sat there obediently waiting. When Penny returned she did what she was told and swept up the broken mirror into the wooden box Penny had brought up. The little blonde girl looked back from every piece.

Sarah's Photography Skills

Having got over her initial shock Sarah was now seeing the gruesome corpse as a photo opportunity. She recalled the four bones embedded in the soil. There was no sign of Casey returning. She hoped he was thoroughly lost. The corpse was dressed in an army uniform complete with medals. She assumed that the caverns must have been some sort of secret army bunker and something tragic had happened when this man was trying to leave. She wasn't far off with the secret army bunker idea. Perhaps from a few centuries earlier though. The photographs were amazing if somewhat grim. She took thirty shots then changed the memory card putting the full one in her jeans pocket. She then retreated to a safe crevice nearby to wait for either Casey to return or rescue. She didn't want to perish like the man who trapped his fingers.

The Adventure Book

Elliot thought the book was amazing. On the front cover the word 'mathematics' had been covered over with 'The Ashburn Army', below which was a crayon drawing of the family eye device in royal blue and yellow. In the two bottom corners there were what looked like self-portraits of William and Maurice holding swords. It truly was 'Boys Own' stuff. "How old were they when they did this?" asked Elliot.

The Shepherd had a sip of tea and holding the sides of the mug to warm his hands thought for a moment or two, then said, "I reckon William sixteen and Maurice fourteen." He chuckled to himself, then continued: "Angus and I were too young to join in, but we fed off their excitement and invented our own pretend land."

"Did you make a book too?" asked Elliot with enthusiasm.

"Yes we did in our own funny way." His eyes became distant. "Those were tremendous summers. It was just before the war. There had been building tension nationally and we were all picking up on it. We were the 'Blekhape Boys' and nothing could stand in our way. It did sadly. Our older brothers were soon training to be officers. We all had to grow up fast, too fast really. The Estate needed running as anybody over eighteen had been drafted. Only a very few returned and they never recovered. The Ashburn Army had been disbanded and the Blekhape Boys became part of the Land Army producing food for our men at the front. It was a harsh time for all."

"And the book?" pressed Elliot.

"We had a ceremony and we dropped it down the Tower well."

"Shame."

Casey is Out of His Depth

Casey was lost. The torch had died. He had tried taking the battery out, warming it in his hands, and putting it back in. It helped but only the once. It gained him about thirty yards and he didn't recognise anything. He sat down and simply wept. He couldn't believe how his mission had led to this. His eyes strained to see something. Even on the darkest of terrestrial nights you could still see your hand in front of your face. Down in that subterranean dungeon he saw nothing. He was blind. His mother had become registered blind at the age of forty-eight. He was an angry young man at the time and found her loss of ability stupid and pathetic—all she had to do was try harder. Her advanced glaucoma was inoperable and their relationship had broken down. He had become selfish and his mother sad and bitter. One day she had implied her sight was failing because he was such a difficult teenager. He had run off with an older woman which lasted all of three days. He had had to return with his tail between his legs and became an object of derision to his mother. When University came along it was his 'Great Escape'. Now *he* was desolate, blind. If there was anybody there to listen they would have heard the soft word 'Mummy' trickling out between his lips.

After a while his shivering became more intense and he had to keep moving regardless. He stood up and strained to hear something that could guide him in his hour of need. Just the faintest something led him and it became slowly louder and louder. It came into focus as he fumbled along arms stretched out in front of him. It was the crisp *plip, plop* of water dripping into water. It gave him something to concentrate on. He couldn't believe he'd shot someone and clubbed another to death. He wasn't a killer really. His bravado stretched only as far as killing one or two birds—even blowing up the tower was a bit beyond him. He hadn't expected it to be so large and intact and when he realised it was occupied he had been shocked. Jenny had carried on regardless and had almost blown him up too. Perhaps it would have been better if he had become a cropper under a heap of rubble. At least he would not have shot Auld Elliot.

He stepped into the water and back out immediately and crouched down to listen. The dripping water played a rhythmic tune in his ears calming him. He had to think more clearly. He had to find the woman, disarm her then negotiate his way out. He had to get her to fire the two bullets in the gun or at least show she couldn't. He had about ten kicking around in his pocket so if he could get the gun back it would help.

Plip plop......plip plop.....plip plop. After a while it began to wear him down like some evil torture. He thought he would have to make progress by moving through the water. He didn't want go back to the chamber with the corpse. The thought made him shake even more and he started wading into the pool before him. It got progressively deeper and when it reached his knees he decided to go back, but when he tried the water only seemed to rise up around him. By the time it reached his waist be was shivering so violently he thought he was going to die. There was only one thing left to do. He started hollering. The word 'Help' started to echo through the caverns.

Jenny Confesses

Penny took Jenny down to the kitchen and introduced her to the Shepherd. When she saw Elliot she blurted out, "We thought you were dead!" And started sobbing. "He didn't mean to shoot you, he was trying to hit the goat."

"And how many people would have died if you had detonated the explosives?" growled Elliot.

After that she went a bit quiet. Penny gave her some stew and a cup of black coffee. She sat there, tangled hair hiding her face, eating the food. The tall good looking man, who had pushed her around, was asleep in a kitchen chair by the range, poker still in his hand. He looked pretty beaten up.

Penny added logs to the fire, smiled at her sleeping husband, then found a pen and paper and sat next to Jenny. "You need to tell me everything Jenny, let's start with your name and address."

311

Jenny, still believing Penny had something to do with the Secret Service, confessed to everything. She even signed the bit of paper at the end.

Sarah Listens

Sarah had dozed off. She was completely exhausted and it was very quiet in her part of the cave. She was warm and although not sitting particularly comfortably was tired enough for the fingers of sleep to entrap her.

She woke through a tumble of troubling dreams. She was hunting rabbits, dazzling them with a wartime searchlight, then shooting at them with a machine gun. Then she was holding hands with a tall curly haired guy and running down a hillside only to collide with an old man with only one leg. It was disturbing and she woke with a start. She sat there thinking she had heard something, then the faint cries of "Help...please help me!" wafted to her on the still cave air. Then she remembered everything, the chase, the gun shots, Casey hitting the man who helped her and the struggles within the cave. She picked up the gun at her feet, lit it with her phone and worked out how to release the safety catch and fire it. She saw that there were only two bullets left.

Every so often the distant plaintive cries would echo through to her. 'Tough,' she thought, 'you brought it upon yourself.' But after a while she remembered that if nobody found them, getting him to help push up the slab was the only chance of escape. She would have to go and find him, negotiate and bring him back. Then a little later she became more human and took pity on the pathetic man lost in the tunnels. She rigged up her wool again and began to wander following the sound of the pleading man. She was so glad to have used the wool and could see how easily it would be to get lost, but then her wool came to an end and the cries were very close. She undid it from her belt and laid it in the centre of the passage, then using the gun's barrel marked arrows in the cave floor showing the direction to the wool. This was fine so long as she could see. Her phone was showing a quarter battery power left so she couldn't delay. Beyond that she had her remote flash in her rucksack that would suffice in an odd way if so required.

She considered the gun. What was she going to do with it? Shoot him, threaten him? She had no intention of killing him and injuring him would make him useless for lifting the slab. She didn't want to risk him getting his hands on the gun either. She only had two bullets but he probably had lots.

She had to crouch quite low to squeeze into the space where the calling was coming from. Her phone could only illuminate a small distance ahead but she soon came to the edge of some underground pond or lake. The space it lay within was massive judging by the high echoes. The man fell silent when she came in but she could hear him splashing around some distance away. Not knowing quite what to say to the evil man, she shouted: "Where are you?" She could hear splashing as if he was coming her way. Thinking he might be up to tricks she backed away into the gap she had just come through. "If you don't stop at the edge of the water I'll shoot you." All she heard was his rasping gasps. She raised the gun; if he didn't stop she would fire beside him as a warning. He loomed into the light soaking wet and shaking. Safety catch off. "Stop right there mate!" Sarah said. Casey was so wasted he could hardly speak. He put his hands out to show her he wasn't going to hurt her but she misinterpreted his clumsy movements and pulled the trigger. The bang was so loud they both cringed. The bullet hissed into the water just behind him. "Sit idiot!" she shouted. "The next one's in your guts."

"Okay, okay," he mumbled, sitting obediently. "Please," he pleaded, "can you get me out of this hell hole?"

"That just depends," she replied.

"I'm really really sorry."

"You shot the old man, why?"

"I thought he was the goat... no, no I mean I was aiming for the goat and he got in the way." Casey's teeth were juddering violently.

"So why did you chase and shoot at us if that was just an accident?" Sarah persisted.

"Cos you'd photographed me doing it."

"Yep, and I've already emailed them to my boss so you're in big trouble and there's no point in making things worse."

Casey didn't quite believe her; he knew there was no phone signal in the valley. But then she might be a reporter with a satellite phone.

"What are you going to do with the pictures?"

"My email said 'some bloke is shooting at me, if you don't hear from me by 9am tomorrow morning send in the heavies.' They have the coordinates so it won't take much to find us."

This made Casey think more carefully. Not only did he really need to get out of the dark prison, he also needed to get as far away as possible and get warm and dry and he was so desperately hungry. As he was a bluffer himself he knew that's the kind of thing he would have said. She was annoying him, trying to control him. A woman in charge didn't go down well with him, even in his sorry state.

"What are you trying to do here in the valley anyway? What's all the shooting about and why are you trying to blow up an historic building?"

"I'm starving, got any food?"

"Yes plenty, would you like some? I've got a Mars Bar if you like."

He was being pathetic. So far he hadn't impressed her much.

"Tell you what, you answer all my questions and I'll feed you, okay?"

All he could do was nod. Sarah put her hand down to the camera hanging in front of her, switched it on, and flicked it onto video and clicked record. She then jabbed the gun at him. She was worried about her phone running out of battery power and knew they had to get a move on.

"Anything you want, I just want to get out like you do," said Casey. He shifted his position slightly preparing to lunge for her and try for the gun. He pulled his feet up beneath himself. Sarah sensed something in the dim light and took a step back. "Alright, that's nice, you're going to confess everything to your new girlfriend," said Sarah trying to remain confident and in control.

'Like hell I am,' thought Casey, 'I'm going to give you such a hiding bitch.'

"Sure I will, sure," he said trying to placate her.

"Okay, but I've got one thing to do first." She raised the gun and pointing it as carefully as she could, pulled the trigger.

The Ashburn Army

Elliot paged through the book. It was a lovely record of the two boys' youth. They had imaginary dens complete with dragons, warriors and details of their quests. Each page showed a building, a hilltop cairn, a particular interesting rock or something similar. They had written their tasks and successes or failures at each one. Such as... 'This is where Mori slipped on the old ash tree and ended up hanging upside down caught by the heel of his boot. We didn't catch the Goaders but spied on the Blekhape Boys instead.'

In the very centre of the book was a map of the estate with a picture in the middle showing a dark cave with a long table with chairs down both sides. At the far end sat William depicted as a noble King. To his side a knight in armour. Elliot assumed it was Maurice. The two crude faces stared out of the pages as if haunting the onlooker. Elliot found the image disturbing now that the Shepherd had provided a short potted family history. He swung the book around and flicking through the pages in front of the Shepherd asked, "Are any of these places real?" The Shepherd had never really thought about it. He started at the beginning looking at each sketch in turn. "The Tower well... Mutton Crest... Lily's Leap... The Babbling Bank... yes, I'd say so. There's some I don't recognise but on the whole yes."

Elliot turned the book around and found the centre picture again. "And this one?" he said tapping the page.

The Shepherd looked at it carefully. Underneath it said 'The Meeting Place'. "I'd say it was the Tower's hall here— there's the table and chairs, exaggerated candles, a few tankards for effect." Elliot was still tapping, and then the Shepherd went very still. Under Elliot's tapping finger at the top left corner a neat little drawing stood alone, circled with tiny letters reading 'Secret entrance'. The sketch showed a slab with the family device on it, a neat little eye watching the reader, a stick propping up the stone. "Could this be what he saw before he bashed his head?" asked Elliot. They looked up at Penny who was standing behind Jenny brushing Jenny's hair. "Err...any chance of waking him up?" asked the Shepherd.

"I think we've got a map here, a kind of treasure map that may well lead us to Sarah.

Penny smiled; she had been listening to their musings over the book. She stepped over and shook her husband's shoulder. The poker fell with a rattle to the floor.

Casey Begs

As Casey flinched from the bullet fizzing past his ear his main thought was 'Got ya, that's your last bullet!' And he made his move. What he wasn't expecting was to see the gun flying past his face and splashing into the water some distance away. He just caught her foot as she stepped back and toppled her over; she scrambled backwards and kicked out as he grabbed her. Feeling she was losing her advantage she rolled over and crawled out of his reach. She crouched low and ran clutching her mobile phone. Casey followed the receding light and had not realised that there was a low part of the tunnel: he ran straight into it whacking his forehead into the rock face. He crumpled unconscious to the ground.

Sarah heard him grunt and fall, aware of the deadly silence that followed. She turned and carefully approached him to see what has happened. Her instincts told her to just get away from him, but she still needed him to help open the slab. She found him flat out on the ground bleeding from a swelling on his head. She knew she would have to act fast. She checked he was still alive, then clambering over him pulled off his boots, which she took back to the water and slung them in; then she came back for his jumpsuit which she had to yank off by rolling him around quite roughly. She turned out the pocket contents and finding amongst the coins and bullets a Swiss army knife, she made quick work of slicing the fabric into strips. She kept the knife in her front jeans pocket and then looking at him lying there in his thermal underwear thought 'What the hell' and pulled everything off except his underpants—she wasn't going there, yuk. His excess weight exposed made an unpleasant sight. She rolled him over and tied his wrists tightly behind his back with the strips she had cut. She could feel him coming around so taking the extra clothes with her slunk away into the tunnel, sat down quietly, switched off her phone and waited.

Heather is Excited

Heather was in the kitchen enjoying the company. She'd never known so many people together at the same time in all her time as a changeling. She was satisfied that Penny and her man were there to help her father. She liked the old man who got shot in the leg but didn't like Jenny who had evil thoughts. She couldn't quite understand why Penny was being so nice to her. Penny had finished her hair in a neat plait and fastened it with a piece of purple ribbon. She was now holding up Jenny's chin and dabbing away the mascara smudges on her cheeks. Heather had often watched her mother apply make-up before going out and loved it when she groomed her hair. Heather couldn't help slipping into Jenny and imagining her beloved mother was brushing her hair or wiping her face. She closed her eyes and tried to feel Penny cleaning her face. What she felt was the steady presence of the other Heather within Penny—there seemed to be a mutual respect between them. She watched Penny through Jenny's eyes and saw that she was entirely loving and forgiving. She had listened to Jenny's woeful tale and understood her. She wasn't evil or bad, just misguided and clearly taken in by the trickster Casey.

Heather was feeling sad about her mother so went back to where she last saw her on the banks of the river Kale. She looked into her mother's eyes again then left feeling tearful.

Memories

When Penny woke me I jumped. I was very sound asleep. Something my body and mind needed to do. I sat there somewhat dazed. Penny explained that Elliot and the Shepherd thought they knew where Sarah might be. I wobbled over and joined them at the table. Penny put the kettle on. They showed me the wonderful book; I laughed and wondered how well they had done in mathematics when I saw that the book was meant to be a school work book. Elliot showed me the central depiction of the meeting room. I looked at it carefully and without even trying to recall pointed at the sketch and said, "That's where she went! We lifted the slab and she climbed down." I studied it a bit more closely. "The carving's the same and the way it hinges up is accurate. The stick would have helped as I seem to remember something about the slab falling shut. That's as far as I can remember. If she's in there then at least Casey can't get at her. He wouldn't have been able to lift the slab on his own."

"So where's Casey now?" Jenny piped up. Elliot looked up at her and with a sad expression shook his head and said, "If I know Casey he will be miles away by now probably enjoying a hot bubble bath before leaving the country."

"Do you know where this opening slab is, because I've never seen it in all my time here?" asked the Shepherd.

319

"All I know is that I followed the goat back from Ashburn."

"Can I suggest that we all get some sleep and send out a search party at first light?" Penny said.

There were unanimously nods of agreement. It was past 2am.

Casey Wakes Up

His head was really sore and he was completely disorientated. He was also incredibly cold. He tried to get up but found he was stuck face down in the damp soil, and for some reason be couldn't move his hands. He struggled some more and realised she had tied them behind his back. He started cursing and swearing, managed to roll over and then came to the horrible conclusion that he had nothing but his underpants on. He was shivering and his stomach was making unpleasant rumblings. What had she done to him?

"I'll get you for this!" he shouted into the black void. Sarah, who was quite close, just laughed thinking what he had done to everybody else who got in his way. He froze and seethed wishing all manner of evils upon her. "You do realise we're both going to die in here, don't you?" she said. "The entrance is so well concealed that even when they find and remove your second victim's body the chances are they will not realise this place exists. We will run out of food, go mad, maybe I will eat you to last a bit longer, but ultimately we will both perish like the soldier at the steps. We will be discovered in decades to come, a sad remnant of human suffering."

Casey knew she spoke the truth. He knew they had to do this together.

"I know a way to get out," he mumbled.

Sarah knew he was thinking about pushing up the slab together.

"Back in there before I came through the water I found a big room. It looked like a kind of secret meeting room. There was a table and chairs, candlesticks, tankards and all sorts."

"So?" asked Sarah not believing a thing he said.

"On the table there was a wooden box with ancient scrolls in it; one of them looked like a map of the caves."

"And?"

"Well, these places always have more than one entrance—there's bound to be another way in and out, an escape route."

Sarah wanted to believe him but didn't trust him.

"If we get back to the map we could at least have a look. If we work together we could escape," he pleaded.

"Okay, so how do we get there?" asked Sarah.

"If you feed me and give me my clothes back I can show you." Casey had got up to his feet and was preparing to run and dive on her.

"Tell you what, if you lead us there, I will feed you at the table you describe. If then we get out of the caves I will return your clothes."

It was then that he made a rush for her. She had let her guard down for a moment and his desperation made him quick. Before she knew it his flabby hairy chest was pinning her down, his legs locked around hers like a toad in the spawning season, his bristly chin and bad breath up against her face. In panic and horror she squirmed and screamed, her phone flew into the dark and she was stuck struggling to breathe beneath his bulk. Her boyfriend was overweight in a lovely cuddly kind of way and she loved him to bits. This man was gross. Struggling in the dark she did the only thing she could and that was scratch and bite. She was good at it: her nails slashed at his bare back and sides and her teeth clamped down on something unpleasant and rubbery. The screaming was spine chilling as the man rolled sideways in severe pain. In the pitch black she rolled and fumbled around for the phone, found it and switched it on. She illuminated a sad broken man. He sat there sobbing, blood pouring down his face. The bottom inch of his nose was dangling in a gruesome way. He was quivering in his underpants.

"Well you asked for that, you idiot!" Sarah shouted at him. "We are getting out of here now! Any more funny business and I will bite off your ears!"

"Okay... just get me to an 'ospital."

Sarah was worried about what she had done to him. She was not remotely violent. She had just been defending herself. Now she felt remorseful.

"Right, let's start again. Why did you come to the valley, start shooting things and trying to blow up the Tower?"

This time he talked. Slowly and painfully

"We came to clear the way for a wind farm. The company I work for owns this estate. Our job is to eliminate any potential barriers to the project." He was in serious discomfort but Sarah wanted the whole truth so didn't budge. Her phone was warning her that her battery was about to fail.

"Go on," she said.

"We are here to shoot the rare bats and birds, weedkiller the rare plants and take out any special features of archaeological significance. We weren't expecting a huge occupied castle. Our satellite imagery just showed some tumbled down walls with grass in between. It's not our fault. Can we go now?"

"No, why do you want to put up a wind farm in the most beautiful part of these incredible hills?

He went quiet; his mangled nose was dripping in a most alarming way.

"Well?"

He shuffled on his knees and looked up at her.

"For the money. The subsidies are huge, irresistible in fact; you get stacks of doe for sticking up the turbines. The government are desperate to get them up to reach their targets."

"So in your enthusiasm to soak up the excessive subsidies you destroy everything in the way. Chop down trees, kill wildlife and blow up buildings?"

He looked really sad, tears and blood puddling on the cave floor and just nodded.

"You are not a very nice man, are you? You clearly don't give an ounce of thought to those that would be affected by your wind farm. Those who have their views completely trashed, the noise, shadow flickering, tourist accommodation emptying, bats that get their lungs damaged and birds minced by the spinning blades. You don't care that the rest of the population are broke because of your incredible selfish greed. It's not green energy, its greed energy!" Sarah was mad, very mad. "And you clearly don't have the slightest respect for women. You've dragged that blonde woman into this; I bet she wasn't going to get the bonuses you get, right?"

Casey nodded. "That's about it," he mumbled."

"You want to get out of here?" Sarah shouted.

Casey struggled to his feet.

"Right, the first thing you do is apologise to me, show some respect."

"Okay, I am really sorry, really, really sorry."

"Are you going to respect women from now on?" Sarah wanted to emphasise this point. He clearly didn't.

"Yes, oh please God get me out of here," he cried. What he really meant was, 'Oh please God get me away from this annoying woman.'

"Right, walk through there." Sarah shone the light ahead. She made him walk in front of her following the arrows she had scratched in the floor with the gun barrel earlier. Eventually they found the wool; she tied the end to her belt and made him follow it. Waddling ahead in his spotty underpants, he looked ridiculous. After a few yards the phone battery died and they were plunged into inevitable blackness. Casey mumbled, "Oh god I'm sorry," again and again. Sarah picked up the wool and took the lead. "Touch me and it's your ears, right?" She still had a bad taste in her mouth, a bit like the tail end of escargot. She didn't want to think about what it was, and certainly didn't want grisly ears for afters.

The dark was omnipotent; it was an all-encompassing envelope that drained all hope. Sarah wondered how she was going to be able to deal with Casey at the slab and what would happen if they got out into the open air. That was something she craved more than anything else. Space and freedom.

Casey wanted drugs, anything to take away the pain in his nose, his forehead and all over his body. The scratches stung horribly. He hated this bitch.

When they got to the steps Sarah extracted her flash, pointed it in what she thought was the right direction and pressed the button. Nothing happened. Feeling the unit she felt a crack running across it. Damaged beyond repair. She then tried her camera. Same, she pulled out the memory card and shoved it into a pocket and abandoned the camera. It would make an interesting report on her insurance claim form. She placed it on the ground next to the uniformed skeleton. Her last resort was a small box of matches from one of the rucksack's side pockets. She struck one and it glowed and flickered hopefully in the slightest movement of air seeping into the cave past the edges of the slab. It gave them enough light to head up the steps. When they reached the top they felt more like a team. The match burnt out as she put her hand up to the slab. "We need to get out of here so on the count of three, push!" encouraged Sarah.

"I'm sorry I've been such a bastard!" Casey blurted out. He meant it. Almost.

"And I'm sorry about your nose," said Sarah. She meant it. "One... two... push!"

Casey had his shoulders under it, Sarah her hands. The slab went up about six inches but they were left with no way of pushing it far enough to stay open. They had to let it down again. But they knew they could do it. Now that they had gulped fresh Cheviot air they were equally full of hope. The splash of moonlight blessed them with energy.

"I'm going to cut you free. Stay still and then we can push it up till it stays up and we can get out." She pulled out the pocket knife, released the blade, fumbled with the matches till she struck one, saw the fabric and sawed through it. As soon as she had freed him she dropped the box of matches and penknife and with a joint sense of urgency they both reached up and pushed with all their might. The slab swung up on its ancient hinges and sat open and erect in the glorious early morning sky.

They both scrambled out, one to each side of the inky pool and not knowing quite what to do next glared at each other. They were both terrified of the open hole between them; it was a beckoning jaw leading only to madness.

Casey was shaking violently in the cold air. "Can I have my clothes back now?" he asked aggressively.

"Okay I'll get them out." Sarah took off the rucksack and started opening it. Casey remembered that she had said she had food. He was so desperately hungry and cold he was more than just a little impatient and he reached out over the opening to grab it, so as to get both his clothes and the food. He caught hold of one of the shoulder straps and tugged hard. Sarah hung on, but being wary of the gaping mouth between them stretched her arms out rather than stepping forward. They both then tugged again and the rucksack stretched tense above the void. Casey tugged hardest and wrenched Sarah's shoulder, who then felt the rucksack slipping from her fingers. It was at that moment Sarah saw a rapid movement coming up behind Casey. He was sneering at Sarah just about to be abusive when the old badger faced goat made contact with Casey's moonlit buttocks. Casey toppled forward clutching the rucksack in one hand, lost his footing, stumbled over the edge and he fell feet first into the abyss. His free hand flew up to save himself, but caught the top edge of the slab which then overbalanced and collapsed towards him. Some grain of memory retracted the hand before the slab caught a finger again. He bumped down the steps into the black. His thought, simply, 'Oh no not again!'

Sarah looked at the goat and said, "Bravo." She let the goat lead her away. When she found their campsite she climbed into her sleeping bag in a state of complete exhaustion and fell into a deep dreamless sleep.

Dark Ingenious Madness

Casey landed in a heap at the foot of the crude stone steps and howled. After a while he stopped. He still had the rucksack in his hand. He had to think, so sat up in the dark. He rummaged inside and found the chocolate which he ate quickly, all three bars. He couldn't find any clothes other than his thermals, but he was very happy to get them on. He stood up and fumbled around with his arms out trying to orientate himself. He stepped forward and something went crunch under his foot. He stooped and felt around on the ground and found a rough rectangle that felt like sandpaper next to funny little sticks. He picked one up. It seemed to have a sharp end and a rounded end, and putting it under his mangled nose he sniffed it. Just enough went to the less damaged scent receptors. "Matches!" he exclaimed and back down on the cave floor he picked up another twenty-one. He struck one and held it aloft to light the space. The corpse lay next to him, skull looking up at him grinning as if asking, 'Now what ya going to do?' Just before the flame burnt his finger something red and silver caught his eye lying next to the body. He dropped the match and struck another, saw his penknife that Sarah had taken from his jumpsuit pocket and grabbed it. The match burnt out and he struck another. They weren't going to get him far. He counted how long the match lasted—ten seconds max. Nineteen matches left, one hundred and ninety seconds, just over three minutes. He had to think. He needed a lamp. A container and a source of fuel. He put his hand down onto the corpse and felt the material of the dead man's uniform. It was bone dry. The knife Sarah had dropped was going to be very handy. Grabbing the uniform in the dark, he undid the jacket buttons and hacked at the shirt and vest below it till he could tear off strips. He created a heap, struck a match and gingerly applied the flame whose eager tendrils lapped greedily at the dry weave and after a few encouraging puffs from Casey a glowing mass of fabric was just burning enough to provide a light. He kept blowing now and then to keep it alive. A container? He needed something to put it in so he could carry it with him. He searched in the rucksack but everything was either plastic or fabric. The glowing light ebbed against the corpse and freaked Casey out; he imagined himself dying slowly next to this soldier having fought no battles or earned no medals, desolate, alone and worthless. God, if his brothers could see him now. If his mother could see him. Casey wept sad tears; he missed his brothers, his mum and dad. There had been happy times. Had been. He didn't want to look at the shrivelled head with its taught dark dry skin, the tufts of orange hair falling out upon the floor. The exposed bone glinted, tempting him to look, to face what he didn't want to see. He was shaking, with cold, shock, fear and horror, and he slowly looked up at the grinning head of Maurice and stared into the eyeless sockets, deep and dark, a warning, a reflection of what he had become. "Oh my God, Wind Power has brought me to this," he whispered to the staring skull. "Greed has made me do this, all I wanted was more money and turbines were a giveaway." He shook his head, averted his eyes and tended his fading fire. Then he did the only thing he could think of. He lent forward, grasped Maurice's skull by the eye sockets and twisted the skull sharply; there was a horrible crunching and it nearly came away, but not quite. His fire fizzled out and he had to use the knife to finish the job, sawing in the dark through the remains of a spinal cord. He couldn't see the leather strap of a saddle bag that slipped away once the head was removed. He sat back on the ground holding the skull. He was being punished, he knew it and this was a living hell. Why did he have to do this? He knew why. He had taken advantage of a misguided Government policy that tempted the greedy to ride roughshod over all around to gain excessive amounts of money. He turned the skull over in his hands and felt for the basal opening. He should have heeded Auld Elliot's warning in the board room not to do something that had such an effect on others. Now he'd killed him. Perhaps Elliot had come to warn him, to help him back off. Then the goat, that bloody goat had butted in. What business did it have interfering?

Casey pulled off the remaining tufts of hair from the scalp and pushed them down into the cranial case; he then covered the bristly tinder with thin strips of shirt and pushed it in tight.

328

Using the penknife, he felt for the eye openings and stabbed at the back to make air holes. If he wasn't so busy becoming thoroughly disturbed by the experience he would have been admiring his ingenuity. He thought about what turbines must be like to live next to with the drone of the generators and whump of the blades. Wind Power had sucked him in and the harvest he was reaping was chewing him up. He placed the skull lamp on the floor, struck another match and poking it through an eye managed after a while to light his lantern. It smelt unpleasantly of burning hair and the acrid smoke stung his eyes. He lifted it in one hand and like an inverted Yorick with the flickering within he sneered back at it. "Alas, you will have to do." Somehow reality was too weird for Casey and his mind was slipping into a half real nightmare. With the skull propped on the lowest step he yanked the jacket and trousers off the skeleton, put the jacket on and packed the trousers into the rucksack. The remaining clothes he cut into strips for his lantern and filled the jacket pockets and rucksack to the brim. He needed enough fuel to get back to the meeting room and those candles. He put the rucksack on, collected his skull lamp, hooked his finger under the chin like carrying a freshly caught fish through the gills and headed off deeper into the cave. "You killed someone once, didn't you?" he said conversationally to Maurice's head. "Whoever he was we are off to find him. It would be nice for you to see him again, wouldn't it?" Casey had a new friend. "Don't go near the turbines, mind. We'll avoid those, don't worry." Casey's smile was gentle and friendly. "Who was he? Your senior officer?" Casey walked off into the depths of the cave. "Maybe your brother? Fate got you in the end though didn't it? You got your fingers caught like I did." Casey laughed.

Maurice could do nothing more than gape back, his eyes glinting with the firelight.

The Tower Awakens

Heather the ghost had discovered something. She had been bonding with the baby. She had approached with gentle respect and genuine love. She had slipped gently within to share the space. It was a wonderful experience. It felt right, as if she belonged there in the warm orange glow, with the comforting *thump thump* of Penny's heart and soft breathing. It had been a long, long time since Heather felt so calm and settled. The baby seemed to like it and they comforted each other in a mutually beneficial way. Not really touching, just occupying the same space and being at one with each other. Heather felt she had been there before, protected from the harsh world within the ultimate safe place. The womb of creation. She then did something she hadn't done before. She fell asleep.

I was awake early before any hint of dawn, dressed, had the range fired up and kettle hissing before anyone else stirred. I was feeling thoroughly beaten up but had my energy back. When the Shepherd and Elliot had woken and dressed we joined at the kitchen table. Elliot was in considerable discomfort with his leg wound but the imperative was to rescue Sarah. The only way they were going to find her was to collate and analyse the information they had. We laid out the book and took notes and the Shepherd drew a map of the Ashburn valley. He thought the most likely place was along the boulder field that ran along the west side of the valley beneath the high cliffs, but did point out that it was about a quarter of a mile long with extensive dips and hollows. I had no concept of how far I had walked to return to the Tower but did have a nagging feeling that I had been to the hollow with the slab before. The Shepherd pointed out that if that were the case it must be where we had done some planting of tree seed on our previous trip.

330

This duly noted, Elliot wanted to explore the theme of the family motto.

"There is something about this book that makes you feel like they were following a trail. Can you identify each of the places shown and mark them on the map in the same order as they appear in the book?"

"I will do my best," replied the Shepherd. He took a sip of his coffee, picked up the pencil and started writing consecutive numbers dotted across the map. I watched in the hope of a neat route being laid out but it didn't look like that. The numbers seemed to lead one way for a bit, then suddenly alter direction.

"Some don't mean anything to me, what should I do?" asked the Shepherd, looking quizzically up at us.

Elliot with his analytical mind said, "Number them in the book and put the number in the map's margin so we know we've still to put them in."

"God I hope Sarah's okay," breathed Elliot. He really loved that girl; she was spirited, intelligent, a brilliant photographer and super company.

I had to react so I drained my coffee, stood up to prepare myself to get out and start searching. I was the only one fit enough to do it. There was just enough light from the approaching dawn to see outside. I explained what I was going to do, grabbed a handful of oatcakes and headed for the door. It was then that I heard shouting and the sound of someone running across the stone flags of the hall. I opened the door to be hit by Jenny in a panic. "There's something wrong! I think the baby's coming. Penny's writhing around in the bed holding her belly asking for you." Jenny grabbed my arm and pulled and we both flew across the hall and up the stairs to the bedroom. The abandoned oatcakes rolled across the stone floor like coins, did little loops and settled down waiting politely for the outcome.

Investigative Powers

D.I. Johnson had an inquisitive mind. He hadn't settled on Saturday night at all. His wife and children noticed how distracted he had become, but this was not unusual when he was focusing on a puzzling case. After dinner he went back to the gym and made some casual enquiries. He ascertained that Casey's ex, Rosie had once been a gym member too. An hour later he was at her flat and was welcomed in by an anxious looking Bertie. Half an hour later he had heard enough and set off to make arrangements to search Casey and Jenny's accommodation. He had keys from Rosie and Bertie. By ten he had a response from traffic stating that Casey had been stopped for speeding at Durham. Unsure of their destination he knew he needed information from Casey's employers. He returned home late and had a fitful sleep trying to work out exactly what Casey and Jenny were up to. What nationally sensitive documents would need to be destroyed and why blow up a building to achieve that? What was the rifle for? Taking out guards? Furthermore, what did any of this have to do with a proposed wind farm?

He went for a jog at 8am the following morning and just out of curiosity took a route past Casey's work. A tall fierce looking man was standing outside the office smoking a long black cigar. It stank, but he paused, exchanged pleasantries, then finding the man not entirely unapproachable explained who he was and what he needed to know. The man showing professional caution suggested that he returned in an hour with his ID and the information he had gathered so far.

When Grimms welcomed him into his office a little later, he had already called in his private secretary who was busily extracting files from Casey's office and computer. She found his security a joke. Using his personal assistant's first name was only her fourth attempt. Grimms could sense a potential scandal that could have a severe impact on the company.

By the time Johnson left at 2pm he knew where Casey was going. By 5pm he had tracked Casey to the hotel by Kelso, learnt about the car swap and talked to a policeman in Hawick who had reports of a stolen horse in that area of the hills and a prior notification of the possible need for the mountain rescue services including a helicopter along with the likely coordinates.

Johnson was still confused as to why all this action for a turbine site, but then thought about the dead red kites in Lincolnshire. Wind Power was big business so people took big risks. He looked at the location on Google earth and could only see ruins. Perhaps Casey was going to blow open an ancient vault and shoot kites? Whatever, it was all very odd. He alerted the helicopter crew at Boulmer, a paramedic team from the Borders General Hospital, a selection of his own officers and two from Jedburgh Police who were familiar with the area.

At 11.00pm he and his crew were on the sleeper train to Northumberland.

The Great Rescue

Penny was gasping and grunting, hunched up on the bed. Both Heathers had woken with a start and not being accustomed to each other the reaction was automatic and strong. The kick had ruptured the bag containing the warm protective waters around her and early labour was triggered. Penny's husband strode into the room and seeing the inevitable said the only thing he could think of, "Jenny, hot water, soap and towels! Get loads and quick." He wasn't sure he knew or wanted to know what these were but it seemed to resonate with his mental images. Jenny rushed off to the kitchen and Penny looked up at her man—tall, confident with his dark curly hair held back at the forehead by worried hands.

"It's going to be fine darling; we'll get you through this," he said. Penny's response was neat, to the point, and best not repeated.

Jenny returned with a bucket full of hot water and the half used bar of coal tar soap from behind the kitchen sink. She put them down next to the bed and disappeared into the bathroom. Penny rolled onto her back and winced in pain. She reached out for her husband's hand and grasped it tightly. "Oooh, this is bad, really bad, much more so than I expected." She was crying from pain and worry. "God I hope my little Heather's going to be okay."

"There's no reason why she shouldn't be," he said with only a slight tremor in his voice.

"But this is a fortnight too soon," she screamed as she tensed up.

Heather the spirit stood against the stone wall staring at the scene before her, emotions in turmoil.

Jenny returned with as many towels as she could. Surprisingly, she seemed to have a better idea of what to do than Penny's husband. She told him to attend to Penny's head and she would see to the tail and pulling up the covers laid down some towels. 'I've watched Casualty often enough so I should be able to do this,' she thought.

The throbbing sound came in from the direction of the Eildon hills, their heather-clad sides glowing with the first rays of the day. It was cool, clear and bright. Johnson looked at his team. Four armed officers clad in black combat gear. An experienced crack team he had used before on a number of dockland drug busts. He had briefed them as best he could. They were to expect somebody armed and potentially dangerous, the possibility of explosives and to assist in the rescue of a heavily pregnant woman. The paramedics in bright yellow and green sat with an obstetrician trying to crack jokes over the racket of the engine. They were to rescue the pregnant lady and be prepared for gunshot injuries or worse. The four members of the mountain rescue team were dressed in red overalls and were equipped with a stretcher, climbing gear, emergency blankets, food and first aid kit. The two local police he put in charge of extracting and recording statements from whoever they found in the remote valley. His role was to assess the situation at high speed, control the necessary action and prevent anybody getting hurt.

The pilot and co-pilot communicated with each other and their base. "We are going down into the valley now." The helicopter ducked down out of radar penetration. The co-pilot referred to his charts and pointed at open grassland near the river. The pilot brought down the helicopter slowly trying to select the safest spot and chose a flat area adjacent to the sheep paddocks. The small brown sheep stotted to the furthest corner and turned to stare and stamp their feet at the giant yellow monster.

The helicopter touched down and the teams leaped out. Johnson ran ahead, an odd figure dressed in his city suit, grey tie flapping over his shoulder. Behind him were his armed police, helmeted, black and dangerous, guns up and ready, pointing this way and that. The mountain rescue team red and serious, stretcher between them. The medical team like a bright yellow and green tail. If observed from a distance they would have resembled a strange dragon snaking through the trees towards the Golden Tower.

When I heard the helicopter getting close I realised it could be the Mountain Rescue Service, so apologising to Penny and Jenny I flew down the stairs at speed, unlocked the door and ran out. I was met by a tall sharp looking man with a crowd of medics and police behind. "Are you safe in the castle?" he asked, assessing what he saw.

"Yes, my wife's inside having a baby and there's an old man in there that has been shot in the leg."

'So it's happened,' thought Johnson. "Right, back in the castle please, medics please attend, Jedburgh officers too please."

"We are missing Sarah the photographer," I shouted as I led them into the Tower.

Johnson had spotted the detonator cable. "You two, track, disable, photograph, bag and check all the outbuildings. That explosive could be full of fingerprints." He pointed to the packing between the quoin stones. The armed officers, guns up and ready, tracked the cable into the trees.

"Follow me please," he asked the remaining men and jogged further up the track. Soon the trees cleared as he entered the Ashburn valley and he spotted the ruined cottage. He pointed to the offices indicating for them to split and circle the property. He pulled out his own fire arm and cautiously approached the ruins. He got the Mountain Rescue men to stay back behind an ancient ash tree by the track. On reaching the crumbling building he moved quietly along the wall and quickly glanced in through an old window opening. Empty. Moving to the next. Nothing. His men came round and the taller said, "Tents only Sir. Nobody in the building. Female in a tent looking pretty bad." Johnson shouted to the Mountain Rescue team: "Right guys, all clear, female in a tent needs attention."

They ran around to the tent and found Sarah shaking and unconscious. In reality she had only been asleep for thirty minutes and was physically and mentally traumatised. The men tried to rouse her and all they got was a mumbled, "Case...he...stuck....... underground." She was delirious and confused. She seemed physically in one piece so they zipped up her sleeping bag again, lifted her onto the stretcher and headed back to the helicopter. Seeing no reason to go further Johnson returned to the Tower.

I had taken the medics straight up to Penny who was mid-contraction. Within seconds they were all over her, cases opened with medical paraphernalia. I stepped back to let them do their thing and comforted Penny. She was stifling the swear words and pushing down hard. Jenny scuttled off to get a stack of fresh towels. The team guided Penny with her pushing and were rigging up a drip when baby Heather decided no further help was needed; with a huge groan from Penny the baby took its first gasps of cool Cheviot air and screamed. Loudly.

Downstairs in the kitchen Elliot and the Shepherd both stood with surprise, smiled at each other and sat back down again. They knew their place and they both had sore limbs.

The spirit of Heather stared at the baby. She was awestruck. A new person had entered the world. Somebody she had been getting to know quite well already. Baby Heather was upset and noisy. Heather watched frozen against the stone wall not knowing quite what to do. She wanted to comfort baby Heather but was horrified at the sight. She'd seen plenty of animals giving birth but found the human example somewhat alarming. But watching her friend so stressed made her resolved to help. The doctors and nurses were busy doing something with the baby's umbilical cord and Penny was still trying to catch her breath. Heather closed her eyes and instantly felt the baby's plea for comfort. She had to help so let the baby draw her in; she drifted calmly across the ancient planks and enveloped the distressed baby with love. The crying faded and as they were lifted up onto Penny the midwife in charge said, "What a fabulous child, she's calm already, and just look at those incredible knowing eyes!" The baby latched onto Penny's exposed breast and despite the early birth managed to suckle. Heather expanded her love to envelop Penny who in turn stared down at her little miracle and with a huge smile wept with joy. She was meeting Heather at last.

I went down to tell Elliot and The Shepherd the good news and found the policemen taking statements and a medic attending to Elliot's leg. They both looked up and the Shepherd said smiling, "We heard, Heather has arrived!" I nodded and shook their hands. Elliot, who was wincing with pain, said, "Congratulations, well done son." The medic finished bandaging up his leg and left to find a stretcher and help. "They are going to take me into the hospital with Sarah. She's apparently completely wasted and won't wake up, but other than numerous scratches and bruises is intact."

"Any sign of Casey?" I asked.

"No, but then nobody's had a chance to look," replied the Shepherd.

"Probably done a runner," I said.

I collected a jug of fresh water from the kitchen sink and left them to continue helping the police with their enquiries. Upstairs I found the midwife having a serious talk with Penny. They both looked up at me when I came in and for a moment I thought something was wrong, but baby Heather was still latched on, eyes half asleep. "They want me to go to hospital for checks but I'm not budging." I knew that look.

"Can I have a word?" I said to the midwife and we retired to the hall downstairs.

When we got there I explained to her just how stubborn Penny was, asked what condition she and the baby were in and what were the risks of her staying here. The midwife had to admit they were both healthy but as it was her first child and seemingly premature there was a risk, but she couldn't force the issue. After listening carefully to the list of potential conditions, I said we would stay but would be very careful and respond appropriately to any symptoms. She explained that it was essential that Penny's diet was good and that I react quickly to any concerns. We returned upstairs where Jenny was bustling around tidying up and looking after Penny's every need. She seemed to have forgotten her evil doings and was saying to Penny that she wanted to be a midwife. Penny said, "And you would be really good at it too, you have a firm but gentle touch." The moment of warmth shared between the two women was cut off by the knock of a policeman at the door. They came in and asked to take statements. I steered them to the Tower's window seat and sat in the light of the rising sun. The old grey exterior of the shutters was incongruous with the crisp black uniforms. I began to relate my experiences and became aware of Penny and Jenny confiding together beyond the policeman's shoulders. Jenny opened Penny's rucksack and pulled out a few sheets of paper. Penny tore them in half and gave them back to Jenny who slipped away downstairs to warm herself by the heat of the range. While she was there she stoked the embers and encouraged a little flame. Returning to the bedroom she found Penny talking to one of the policemen with me goggling my eyes and gesturing behind his back. "Here's Michelle, I'm afraid she doesn't speak much English. She's from Toulouse and will be our Au pair for the next six months." Jenny did a little curtsey and said 'Allo' in a very poor French accent. She looked very cute and innocent and clearly the policeman liked what he saw. They enquired as to the whereabouts of the Jenny that the Shepherd and Elliot had talked about and Penny continued pointedly ignoring my frantic gesticulating. Penny said she escaped through a window in the night. She gave a description frighteningly close to Jenny's appearance that, but for the camouflage jumpsuit, was accurate. The policeman did give a final look over at Jenny's features but probably for different reasons. I took my hands off my paling face and quickly ushered them out saying that Penny and the baby now needed to rest.

They met DI Johnson coming out of the kitchen who smiled and stepped aside for the stretcher with a recumbent Elliot upon it. He flapped a hand up and said, "Catch up soon." He looked tired and grey.

A few minutes later the helicopter was gone and a new era began in the Golden Tower.

Aftermath

It took almost thirty-six hours for two things to happen and then they did at the exact same time.

Elliot was sitting in a wheelchair beside Sarah's bed. Lizzie had just returned to the hotel reassured that Elliot was on the mend. He had had to have bone splinters removed. The bullet had just caught the edge of his femur. No wonder it hurt. He was watching Sarah sleeping with her hair scattered across the fresh white hospital linen, thinking it was his fault she had ended up like this. The nurses said she had woken a couple of times and went to the loo with some assistance, then fell asleep again. She hadn't said a lot. Just the word 'trapped' a few times. While he watched and worried, her eyes fluttered and she awoke staring right at him. "Glad you're okay. Casey's trapped, he fell back down the steps and the slab slammed shut. He's not a nice person."

"Sounds like he got what he deserved. Do you want me to tell the police?"

"Yeah, s'pose you better."

But she was wrong. Casey wasn't trapped. Casey was happy. He emerged into the Cheviot sunshine as Sarah woke up. He blinked in the dazzling light. "Sorry I had to leave you down there mate, but I've got a turbine to switch on." He had left his new friend the right way up on the table. He had positioned Maurice's skull facing that of the man slumped at the ancient table deep within the ground. The two sets of sightless sockets stared at each other as Casey wandered away with a lit candle. Maurice had served his purpose. If they could have heard they would have shaken their sorry skulls as the madman faded away with his flickering orange light and

341

strange mixed chatter about "that stupid woman" and "good wind resource" or "clean free and green".

It was some twenty-seven hours later that he by chance alone found a way out. A tunnel leading sharply upwards provided a soft unpleasant smelling breeze. He emerged with much scrabbling and swearing through a badger's set that had conveniently penetrated the collapsed rear entrance of the cave system. He thought that whatever creature lived there smelt bad and attracted some unpleasant mosquito-like things. If they could have, the mosquito-like things would have commented on just how bad *he* smelt.

Casey stood looking around him. He gnawed a bit more off the beeswax candle he had been carrying and declared to the welcoming bracken "What's up doc?" and wandered off. In his other hand he clutched the Reivers map, possibly the most important Scottish historical find of the century.

It was Billy Tolk who spotted him from afar when he was checking his sheep in the upper Ashburn valley. He lent on his stick and watched the odd man wander about in a strange way. He stopped by a burn and washed his face, drank and then carried on up the valley towards Billy. As he got closer Billy saw that he was dressed in an army uniform. Picking up a bit of grass and chewing it between his yellow teeth, Billy waited until the man came to him. He wasn't overly impressed if there was a military exercise going on that he didn't know about. He didn't want his sheep disturbed or people poking about on his patch of hills.

Billy's eyes grew large and he cursed beneath his breath when the strange figure eventually reached him. The grass fell from between his thin lips and his jaw dropped. There before him stood an army officer in uniform complete with medals, brass buttons and all. He looked like he had just stepped off the Somme battlefield in that uniform, covered in blood and mud.

Billy didn't know what to do and stammered "Err... hello... can I help you?" Officer Casey seemed suddenly to notice him and stood up straight, saluted Billy and said, "Yes sir! Just as you say sir. Mission accomplished." Then after receiving no response from the bemused Billy, "Bloody peasant."

"Okay... may I ask where the rest of your unit is?"

"Nineteen effing forty-seven man! Don't you even know your maiden name?"

Realising he was dealing with a complete nutter Billy decided to play along. As he seemed to make no aggressive moves and was armed with nothing more than a large alter candle, he said, "Follow me young man, the General is waiting for you." Officer Pritchard obediently followed and they went back over the hill towards Billy's Landover and he helped him into the passenger seat. Seeing that his nose looked like it had been bitten off by a badger, he thought he would get him back to the farmhouse and call for an ambulance and the police. By the time he had given the man his third cup of tea and another plate full of biscuits, he knew all about wind power and Casey's great aunt Jeana. He was very glad when the emergency services arrived some forty-five minutes later.

Back in the Tower Jenny, the Shepherd and the tall tingly man sat around Penny's bed. Baby Heather was sleeping with one tiny hand grasped tightly around the Shepherd's gnarled forefinger. Heather within Heather lay in bliss, eyes closed listening to *her* father telling the story of *her* birth and how *she* had hung onto his finger for the first time, *her* first smile, first steps...

"Thanks for letting me burn that statement Penny," whispered Jenny.

"That's okay pet," smiled the new mother. "Just remember a few things. While you choose to stay with us you are Michelle, you help us all and you learn to speak French."

Michelle smiled, nodded, picked up a pair of nail scissors off the bedside table and quietly proceeded to cut off the ragged tips of her bright red fingernails.

A month later

Rosie had decided to visit Casey in the secure hospital. She found him sitting in his bedroom slumped forward staring out of the window. The headlines of the newspaper lying next to him read "**Turbine Tax**.... The government has introduced a mechanism to tackle fuel poverty....a new tax designed to transfer funds back from the subsidy suckling developers to those struggling with excessively high electricity bills has been welcomed by the House of Commons..."

Finding Casey unresponsive to her greeting and thinking that he was too hot in that stuffy room, she went to open the window. "Don't do that!" wailed Casey, "I hate the wind. Wind is nothing but trouble." She turned back to him but he had returned to staring blankly through the window. A cherry branch caught in the gentle summer breeze tapped on the window at random intervals. Casey pointed his foreshortened nose at the glass and pretended Rosie didn't exist. Rosie, having seen enough, left the room as a nurse entered. "Hello Casey, how are you today? Any more morsels of Morse code from that tree?"

"Yes," mumbled Casey. "Plenty. Wind turbines are marching from the west but the drones are taking them down."

"That's good news then," said the nurse preparing the syringe. "Now then, let's have your arm; you'll just feel like, you know, a little prick."

Later that summer

I had learnt to milk the cow. One thing I couldn't do was drink black tea. Penny needed the calcium and we had to be resourceful. The day I arrived with the funny little Jersey cow filled us with joy. It was hot and the cow, that became known as "Jenny the Cow", had brought great amusement. I had got her from a rare breed sale as an in calf three year old. Got the paperwork sorted and had her delivered to Billy Tolk's place, from where I walked her the last few miles into the Shepherd's land. Learning to handle her, milk her and keep her great mucky hooves out of the pail was not easy.

Elliot had arrived with the County archaeologist to talk about protecting the hills from inappropriate development and we sat out at a table in the cobbled yard in the warm afternoon sun. The archaeologist sat sipping his coffee enriched by the Jersey milk and exclaimed, "I had absolutely no idea about this place. There is just so much here—why the records are so thin I can't understand."

Baby Heather looked up from Penny's lap and gurgled. The Shepherd smiled to himself. He knew why. He was the one, stifled with grief so many years ago, that misled the surveyors. Now that he had discovered the slab leading to the caves below he was still unsure as to whether to expose all the valley's secrets. Michelle returned from the Tower with a bottle of vintage red. I opened it and we all sat around discussing the

Tower, trees and history. The Shepherd thought about the contents of his third vault, the large padlock and the key hidden in his library. 'One day I will show them, one day.'

Elliot handed the Shepherd a letter from Grimms. He opened it and read it. He put the letter down and chuckled, his brown eyes sparkled and he held his head up and laughed even more. We all watched and waited. When he was ready he looked at us, lent across to baby Heather and brushed her cheeks with his large knuckles. "It seems Casey had faked some documents. All Grimms could find out about this place is that the sale had never been completed, as the deeds were never delivered. Casey had picked up the file and not noticed the faint pencil marks on the cover saying 'pending', then realised a little too late and thinking he could get away with it faked some documents. So it seems I do own this estate and Tower and its crumbling cottages and sheds to do with as I please." Michelle went a bit pink and looked down at the hardening surfaces of her hands; Casey had got her to do all sorts of things like that. We all noticed her shame, but said nothing. They couldn't do without Michelle; she had become a kingpin, keeping the day-to-day domestic life running smoothly and willingly looked after the baby to give Penny a break as often as possible.

Penny looked at the Shepherd and smiled her best smile. "Would you like us to mend a little cottage for you?" He smiled and replied, "Of course, that would be very kind."

I had to ask, "What do you think happened to your brothers and the deeds?" The County archaeologist produced a full size laminated copy of the Reivers map and declared, "Firstly I must tell you that this is an amazing find, a really important bit of Scottish Borders History. It is being conserved and studied by some very excited historians in Edinburgh. It is expected to become a leading museum exhibit." He also extracted from his rucksack a large brown envelope and spread dozens of photographs across the table. "I warn you some of these are quite disturbing." The photographs were selected from Sarah's memory cards and files at work. We looked through them with awe and horror. The corpse, cave interior, Casey's mad face and many landscape shots. "So with your permission we would like to survey your subterranean kingdom. Sarah will be here tomorrow with her new camera equipment and Johnson who is keen to see you all and the caves. He said he would like to wrap this case up once and for all." Michelle went a little pale; Penny patted her leg beneath the table reassuringly.

"There is so much more to learn about this place. There's the boys' treasure map, the carvings everywhere, the engravings on the crooks and loads of other things," commented Elliot with enthusiasm.

"What a relief we are not going to be plagued by turbines," I announced.

"Let's drink to that," the Shepherd declared and we all chinked our glasses.

"I hear there's talk of the Northern Cheviots becoming a National Park."

"About time too!" five voices replied in unison.

"It appears our newly elected benevolent leader has a heart after all."

The late afternoon light sparkled upon the wine. Spirit Heather smiled and nestled back down within the baby. She hardly came out now as it just felt so perfect.

The Golden Tower glowed in the evening warmth and stretched its foundations in the soft fertile earth, like a child's toes wriggling in the sand on a beach. A new millennia to look forward to.

Five miles away Billy Tolk closed the renewable energy brochure. On the cover a bright turbine was set against a perfect blue sky. He looked at it for a moment, drummed his fingers on the image a couple of times, then went to make a cup of tea.

And so the world continues to turn.

The End